Haven of Hope

A Novel

D1741823

TERESA TUTEN

outskirts
press

Outskirts Press, Inc.
http://www.outskirtspress.com

ISBN: 978-1-9772-0762-3

Outskirts Press and the "OP" logo are trademarks belonging to Outskirts Press, Inc.

PRINTED IN THE UNITED STATES OF AMERICA

Every time you smile at someone, it is an action of love, a gift to that person, a beautiful thing.

—*Mother Teresa*

Other books by this author:

Silent Agony A novel
Forever Changed A Novel
Faded Memories A Novel
Apple Peelings of Faith
A Journey to health, healing and weight loss

ACKNOWLEDGMENTS

Many thanks go to those of you that read my books. I put a little piece of my heart and soul into each one. The journey of writing a novel is always a new adventure. And I'm excited to see where the next one leads. Thanks also to my Lord and Savior for the gifts and talents He has given me to share with others. And thank you to my family and friends for their prayers, support, and understanding of why I embark on such a grueling endeavor. May this book bless you, minister to you, give you *hope,* and touch your heart in a special way as you read the words.

ONE

Jewel Conner poured the last cup of coffee of her twelve hour shift, feeling relieved the night was almost over. Her feet were hurting from the worn out soles on her shoes. Raising a child alone had been hard in every way, and she'd sacrificed a lot to keep a roof over their heads and lights on. Jewel had worked at Main Street Diner for over two decades, ever since she turned seventeen, except for a short break while pregnant with her only child, Abby.

Removing her apron, she reached in a pocket to grab tip money. Some days weren't much. Only enough to get gas or grab milk and bread on the way home, but every dollar helped. It seemed to be a way of life, and over the years nothing much had changed. Jewel stuffed a wad of dollar bills in her jeans, hung the apron on a nail, and grabbed her purse from a rusty locker by the back door. Walking out, all she wanted was a hot shower and a good night's rest.

When Jewel arrived home, her daughter was already in bed. She cracked the bedroom door open and peered in. The room was dark, so she eased the door shut and went to shower.

Feeling exhausted, Jewel decided to forego dinner because nestling under the bed covers seemed more important than a growling stomach at eleven-thirty that night.

After drying off and slipping a pair pajamas on, she slid under the covers and switched off the lamp to get some rest. In a mere few minutes she was dead to the world from having worked sixty hours that week. Each week tended to be the same, a frequent group of customers occupied the booths. She knew most by name, even men that took pleasure in flirting and hitting on her as she penned their order. Often times, she was surprised by the ones who offered big tips for an afternoon of entertainment later on. However, Jewel had managed to press on and decline their advances. Raising Abby was her first priority.

Darcy Malone has the reputation of a trouble-maker. Ever since she turned thirteen, she's been in trouble over and over. Being the youngest of six kids, she was forced to stay with her seventy-five year old grandmother, Leona, because her parents kicked her out after posting bail numerous times. Her father realized she was going through a rebellious stage, and it broke his heart to experience such agony. He had always worked hard to provide for his family. They're not well off by any means, but he is a decent-honest man. Last summer he had to spend a portion of his retirement to keep Darcy from serving jail time. If it were not for her uncle pulling a few strings with his position as an attorney, Darcy would've been sent straight to juvenile hall. Since then, she's been forced to live in a six hundred square foot house with no AC, stripped of the comforts a close family once provided. Her grandmother was widowed ten years ago, and lives off funds from her social security check. Having

Darcy around challenges her in many ways, but has also kept Leona from living alone, so she couldn't sit back and allow her to live on the streets. No. There are bad people lurking around nowadays, searching for their next victim, especially men who would promise Darcy the moon and stars, then force her into sex trafficking. Leona knew these things were prevalent in today's world and she prayed she could help Darcy by showing her love during this phase of life because it was the only hope she had left.

Darcy lay on her bed around midnight, talking on the phone. "Oh, come on, Abby. Your mom will never know. You've done this several times. She never bothers you after you go to bed. You know I'm counting on you. Tuck some pillows under your comforter and let's have a little fun, let our hair down. It's summertime. Please..."

Abby hesitated. "I don't know about this, Darcy. I've already been in enough trouble. Mom would literally ground me for life if she found out I left tonight."

"I thought you were my best friend, Abby. I'm so disappointed in you." Darcy pursed her lips, waiting for Abby to change her mind.

Feeling guilty, Abby said, "All right... All right... But we better not get into trouble again."

Darcy laughed. "Oh, girl, you worry too much. I'll be waiting in my usual spot. See you soon."

Abby slipped on blue jeans, a T-shirt and sneakers, grabbed her ID and phone, and raised the bedroom window. After rolling out on the ground, she met Darcy, who was waiting a couple blocks away in her grandma's Buick. After Abby arrived, she got in and they sped off in the night.

"That's my girl," Darcy said, tapping her fingers on the steering wheel. "I knew you'd give in. You like the high as much as I do. Believe me... it's better than doing drugs."

Feeling worried, Abby remained quiet.

Minutes later, Darcy parked and pulled the brim of her hat over to hide her face. "Let's go. This is an old store, not much business after dark. An older man and woman works here. I've observed the action for a while now, the type of people coming and going. It should be an easy target."

Abby put on some dark shades, and grabbed a jacket and a baseball cap off the back seat. "I hope you're right," she said, walking toward the door. Inside, she felt a rush of excitement flowing through her veins, like she'd shifted away from the innocent young girl back in her bedroom. She drew in a breath and they sashayed inside like they owned the place.

Once inside, Darcy cased out the surroundings and decided to slip some snacks in her jacket, so she motioned for Abby to get the cashier's attention while she grabbed the items. Soon, it all backfired. The old woman saw Darcy on a camera in back of the store and walked out to confront her face to face.

"May I help you with something?" she asked.

Darcy was shocked to see her standing in front of her, brow furrowed. "No. I'm just trying to decide what I want," she replied, walking toward the cooler of cold drinks.

Moments later, a police officer walked in.

"She's over there," the woman said, pointing to Darcy by the drink cooler.

The officer walked over to her as Abby stood frozen like a statue. "What do you have in your jacket?" he asked.

"Umm. What do you mean? I don't have anything," Darcy said, shrugging. "I'm still trying to decide what I want to eat and drink."

"Unzip your jacket," he said, hands now rested at his waist.

"But I...I don't have a shirt on under it," she said, feeling embarrassed about exposing her bare nakedness.

"Unzip it or I'll do it for you," he said without one ounce of remorse. He waited, arms now crossed— hoping he wouldn't have to arrest her.

Embarrassed and scared, Darcy unzipped her jacket, revealing her small perky breasts as three packs of crackers fell onto the floor.

He shook his head. "Okay. Put your hands behind your back," the officer said. "You're under arrest." He clicked the cuffs and proceeded to read Darcy her rights.

Abby was standing there, taking in the scenario. *Oh no! I'm dead! Mom is going to kill me this time.*

After handcuffing Darcy, he asked Abby to zip her jacket shut. "Did you have anything to do with this young lady?"

Abby gulped. "No sir. I was only here with a friend. I didn't know. I mean..." Feeling shaken, Abby grew quiet and realized if she said much it could be used against her without an attorney present.

He then rolled his eyes toward the cashier. "Is she telling me the truth?"

"I believe she knew what was going on, but she's been standing right here the whole time."

"Okay. Now, unzip your jacket," the officer told Abby. With hands shaking, she complied.

He drew in a breath and exhaled, puffing his lips like a blowfish. "I'm glad you're clean, but you'll need to come to the station to give a brief statement and account for your actions and whereabouts tonight. This does make you an accessory to larceny. The judge frowns upon things like this at your age."

Abby nodded and frowned. *I knew I should've stayed home. Now I'm doomed. I'll never see daylight.*

Backup arrived, and two officers escorted both girls to the patrol car for transport to the station for a detailed report. It was the end of one officer's shift, so he passed Abby to the next officer. Darcy was taken to a holding cell while Abby sat, waiting for her mom to be notified about what happened.

At one in the morning, Jewel was awakened by the phone. Startled, she reached for it off the nightstand and said, "Hello," unaware Abby had plummeted out the window.

"It's Buck Schuller. I hate to be the bearer of bad news this time of morning." He paused.

Jewel's body grew tense, eyes wide.

"What's happened? What's going on?"

"It's Abby."

"Umm, I don't understand, Buck," she said, yawning. "She's asleep in her room. I checked on her a little while ago."

"No, she's not. I have her here at the police station with me."

"Wait a minute, Buck." Jewel walked over to Abby's room. Sure enough, the window was unlocked, pillows stuffed under the bed covers. Jewel sighed. "Oh no! What's she done now?"

"She was with a friend, Darcy, who got caught shoplifting at a local convenience store earlier tonight."

Jewel bit her bottom lip and rubbed her temples.

The pain in her head seemed to amplify along with the unwelcome news. "I can hardly believe this. She knows if she gets in trouble again she'll be sent away."

"Can you come get her?"

"I should let you keep her in a holding cell overnight. Teach her a good lesson," Jewel said, feeling angry and disappointed.

"If it was anyone else other than Abby," he said and sighed.

"Thanks Buck. I'll be there as soon as I can."

"All right. I'll be here for the remainder of the night. I'm working graveyard shift this week."

Jewel got dressed, pulled her hair in a ponytail, and grabbed her keys to head over to the police station.

Abby was sitting across from Buck's desk with her hands behind her in cuffs. "Is she coming?" Abby asked, wondering what was going to happen to her. "Did she sound angry?"

Buck nodded. "Yep. Not thrilled about you sneaking out again." He leaned against his desk and crossed his arms as he stared at her, trying to figure her out.

Abby shrugged. "Well, she'll have to get over it. I'm not a baby anymore. It's time for me to start living my own life, making my own decisions."

He frowned. "I'd drop the attitude before she gets here if I were you. I've known your mom a long time. And..."

Just then, Jewel walked in and Abby witnessed anger firsthand as her cheeks flushed before she said a mere word. "How could you do this again, Abby? I thought you had learned your lesson. You were supposed to stay away from Darcy because she's nothing but trouble."

For a few minutes Abby remained silent, like she was ignoring every word Jewel said, which only seemed to intensify things between them.

"I'm talking to you, young lady. Don't ignore me. I'm your mother. Answer me!" By this point, Jewel had begun to raise her voice more and more. Her loud words echoed in the room.

Abby shrugged. "I don't know why I did it, Mom. I guess I got bored tonight and Darcy just wanted to have some fun. Gee, stop attacking me. I haven't done anything wrong. I didn't steal a thing."

Jewel reached for her arm and Abby stood. "So, you think shoplifting is fun? Is that it? Well, you're grounded for the entire summer. I'm tired of this crazy behavior of yours. It's going to stop right now."

Feeling reluctant, with mixed emotions, Buck grabbed the key and removed the cuffs from Abby's wrists. "Take her home, Jewel. This whole ordeal doesn't look good. I could be fired if my boss found out I let her go. They don't play games when it comes to larceny." He rubbed his chin. "I'll talk to the store manager about not pressing charges. I frequent the store often. They're good Christian people. I believe they'll understand."

"You don't know how grateful I am," Jewel said, eyes teary. "Thank you!"

"Oh, come on. Why don't you just tell mom you have a thing for her, Buck?" Abby said with sarcasm, rubbing the red lines on her wrists.

Buck blushed, bit his tongue, and tried to refrain from saying what was on his mind. Instead, he grew quiet as his cheeks began to burn.

"Shut up, Abby! You have a lot of explaining to do,"

Jewel said, grabbing her arm, walking with her toward the door.

After they got in the car, Jewel grew silent on the drive back to the house. Her head, feet and body now ached.

When they arrived, Jewel told Abby to get some sleep and they would talk later. Her nerves needed a break. Not to mention the nausea she was feeling from the stress of it all.

"What? I can't believe it. You mean you're not going to interrogate me the rest of the night?" Abby said, waiting for Jewel to drop some choice words on her like a bomb.

Jewel stopped and drew in a breath, trying to keep her composure. "Now's not the time," she said. "Go to bed, Abby. And leave your room door open. Your privacy privileges have been revoked."

Abby huffed, pounced over to her room, and slammed the door shut anyway.

As much as she hated it, Jewel knew what she had to do. She had to swallow her pride and ask for help. After hesitating for what seemed like an eternity, she grabbed her phone and punched in Beatrice Bigelow's number. It was the only hope she had left to save Abby from destroying her life.

"Hello," Beatrice said, groggy.

"It's Jewel Conner. I need your help."

Surprised, she said, "Really? How so?" Beatrice switched on a lamp, trying to become more alert. "What's going on? Are you and Abby okay?"

"I need to send Abby your way for a while. I don't know what else to do. She's been in trouble again and I need a break from this." Her voice quivered, making it evident Jewel was more than shaken by the situation. Abby was all she had—her pride and joy. After Jewel explained all the details to Beatrice, she agreed to purchase Abby a plane ticket right away.

"I know we haven't always seen things eye to eye Bea, but—thank you."

"Of course. Regardless of anything past or present, she's my granddaughter, Jewel. I do love her, you know."

Jewel sighed. "Yeah, I know. And I'm grateful you do because she's at a tough age right now."

"I will do whatever I can to help," Beatrice said.

"Okay. I'll have her at the airport first thing in the morning."

After their conversation ended, Beatrice purchased Abby's ticket and let Jewel know the time of her flight.

In a sense Jewel felt relieved, but she was a little worried about Abby traveling without her. It was hard for Jewel to get much sleep, but she had to do whatever was necessary.

Come daybreak, Jewel told Abby she would be going to visit her grandmother in Texas for the remainder of summer vacation.

Abby was shocked by the news because Jewel never talked about Beatrice much. "Are you sure this is what you really want, Mom?"

"Look! I don't know what else to do. If Buck hadn't have helped you out last night, you'd be in the slammer today along with Darcy."

Abby stared at her a minute. "What's going on between you two, anyway? Did you sleep with him or something? Is he an old boyfriend?"

"Abby, that is none of your business! Let's just say...

we've known each other a long time, and we've been friends since our high school days."

"Well, you don't have to get so defensive about it." Abby gave her an odd look, wanting to hear more about Jewel's high school adventures.

"Clean your room and get your bags packed. I have to take you to the airport soon."

"Can't we talk about this, Mom? I mean—"

"It's a done deal this time, and you're not going to change my mind. Now do as I asked." Jewel turned to walk away, heart breaking as she tried to grasp what was happening. She felt like her daughter was slipping away from her—out of reach.

"But Mom..." She stammered back to her room and threw everything off her floor into the closet. After grabbing some clothes, she packed her bags, hating she'd have to forego lounging by the community pool each day with friends. Now she'd be entering freshman year white as a ghost. And she couldn't fathom why her mom was brushing her off so easy. What was she thinking? Maybe she wanted to have a fling with Buck while she was away. Looking at the clothes she packed, a knot gnawed in Abby's gut. After all, she'd never met Beatrice Bigelow—her father's mother, and she hated the idea of staying at a smelly ranch in Texas. It was beyond cruel punishment, for sure.

Setting her bags on the floor, Abby ran her hands over the bed, smoothing wrinkles out of her comforter. She loved her bed, and spent most weekends playing games on her cell phone, texting, and watching YouTube videos.

"Are you about packed and ready to go?" Jewel asked, poking her head in the door.

Abby frowned. "Yeah, I guess so."

"Okay. Then let's get you to the airport. Your grandma said your flight leaves in two hours."

Abby grabbed her things and glanced over her shoulder, trying to absorb the reality it would be a while before she laid eyes on her bedroom. She was not happy about this crazy arrangement one bit.

"Come on. You're going to be late," her mom yelled. "You know traffic is always heavy in Atlanta."

"Okay, Mom! I'm coming. Chill out."

"Watch your mouth, Tinkerbell!"

"Uh...Don't call me that. In case you haven't noticed, I'm not five anymore." She raised her hands in the air, revealing several chips in her black nail polish.

Jewel rolled her eyes as she locked the front door and put Abby's things in the trunk. It was hard for her to discern what was going on inside Abby's teenage mind.

With a pouty lip, Abby realized it had to be the last straw with her behavior for Jewel to take such drastic measures with her discipline.

Driving, Jewel hoped time away would help Abby get back on track, or she'd have to spend her high school years home-schooled. Something Abby nor Jewel never intended to happen.

Riding along, Abby remained quiet while gazing out the window. Many thoughts reeled in her mind. One being: how she wished she could change her fate. After getting in trouble over the past couple months, she wondered why she'd been so stupid in the first place and listened to Darcy. Was it only a rebellious stage she was going through at thirteen? Or was something much deeper involved?

For years, Abby had dealt with the rejection and disappointment of not having a father in her life. Emptiness enveloped her, which magnified the feeling no one cared. Did a place exist in this world where she felt like she belonged? She longed to understand something better, much deeper, while searching for the true meaning of her existence.

Twenty minutes later, her mom pulled over and parked beside a curb. "We're here," she said. "I guess this is it." She clenched the steering wheel tight and drew in a breath, dreading what was still to come.

"Oh, how great! I can hardly wait for my grand summer adventure to start," Abby said, unbuckling her seat belt.

Jewel got out and grabbed Abby's things from the trunk. "Come on. Let's hurry. You can't miss your flight."

Abby got out and followed Jewel inside. Then they took the tram to get off at section C to obtain her ticket. At the counter, she handed the attendant her ID and retrieved the ticket Beatrice bought. Afterwards, Abby's suitcase was weighed and checked in for flight 2112 to Dallas with no layovers.

Fear of losing Abby made Jewel's muscles grow tense. Feeling another headache coming on, she rubbed her temples with her fingertips, trying her best not to dwell on what was about to take place right then. "Well, I guess this is your flight," she said, following Abby to the gate while trying to maintain her composure, but inside she was desperate to scream at the top of her lungs.

Abby grew quiet, trying to act tough, not cry. "Yeah, I guess so," she said, voice shaky as they hugged goodbye. Inside, she was terrified of flying without a clue of what to expect.

Jewel held her tight for a few moments and prayed she'd have a safe journey. They'd never been apart for more than a day or two and this decision was more than difficult for her.

Releasing the embrace, Abby walked through the metal detector with her carry-on bag. Afterwards, she handed the attendant her ticket and walked in the corridor to board the plane without bothering to look back once more.

By now, Jewel's heart bled, having to send her daughter far away like that. It would take some time to get used to not having her around, even if they did never get along much. The two of them had stuck together through thick and thin. Good and bad times. All she wanted was for Abby to be able to spread her wings and live her dreams, not struggle the way she had. With teary eyes, Jewel squared her shoulders back and headed outside. At the car, she leaned her head on the steering wheel and questioned if she might've made a mistake. After all, Beatrice had resented that Jewel was pregnant when her son, Billy, married her. They were only married a couple years before Billy left Jewel for his high school sweetheart.

Inside the plane, most seats were occupied as Abby stopped at row 19 seat B. There was an older gentleman already seated by the window. She placed her bag in the overhead compartment, then sat and fastened the seat belt as her stomach churned with butterflies because she'd never flown before.

Minutes later, a flight attendant made an announcement over the intercom. "Close all overhead compartments, silence your cell phones, fasten your seat belts, and prepare for takeoff. Also, please remain seated until the seat belt lights are off. Beverages and snacks will be served soon. Thanks for your cooperation and enjoy your flight to Texas."

Abby drew in a breath, trying to prepare for the worse summer of her life. As the plane entered the runway for takeoff and increased in speed, she felt her pulse surging with great force, like a raging waterfall. She clenched the armrests tight and shut her eyes, hoping she'd be able to sleep during the flight and awaken in Texas. Or better yet—awaken to find summer over and this whole ordeal had been a bad dream.

Back at home, Jewel removed a trunk from the closet and sifted through old tattered letters along with a few of her mother's things. As hard as she'd tried to be a good mom to Abby, she felt like she'd fallen short in so many ways.

Since Billy remarried he only spent time with the son he and Lola had, and Jewel made it a point to never mention anything about them to Abby. She knew Abby had questions, but she couldn't give her the answers she longed for. The reason Billy left and never looked back. Another reason Beatrice and Jewel never got along. Billy had had everything handed to him on a silver platter since birth. He was the only son of a successful ranch owner and businessman, but Jewel Conner was not well off, and had worked long hours as a waitress just to pay the bills. Then Billy met and wooed her one night, soon introducing her to a better way of life. Before long, Jewel was wearing designer clothes, sporting trendy hairstyles, and getting her nails manicured twice a month. It was a whirlwind Cinderella story until she discovered she was pregnant. Billy had married Jewel out of obligation—not because he truly loved her, and the marriage began to sour. Things never improved after Abby was born, and Billy started seeing his ex Lola and worked late as an excuse. When a friend told Jewel they were together in a restaurant, it shattered Jewel's hopes and dreams and broke her heart. She confronted Billy about his actions, and he confessed to cheating on her.

With tear-stained cheeks, Jewel gathered the items and placed them in the trunk, along with a photo of their wedding day. Against her wishes, they'd been married in a barn at his parent's ranch. He wore blue jeans, a white shirt and cowboy boots. Jewel wore a white sundress, white cowgirl boots, and her bouquet was made from wildflowers out of Beatrice's garden. After their wedding day, Jewel never stepped foot on the ranch again. She simply detested the sight and smell of things, from the scent of hayfields, to cows, horses, and smelly hog pens.

With every ounce of strength she had Jewel said, "I hope I've done the right thing." She'd never felt such uncertainty about anything before. Jewel and Abby had been inseparable since Billy left, and to lose Abby now would be more than she could bear.

TWO

A little over two hours later, the plane landed at Dallas Fort-Worth International Airport. Abby exited, anxious to grab her suitcase at baggage claim. The flight had seemed long with a crying baby and its mother sitting right behind her, making it hard to sleep much.

Ten minutes later, her bag appeared on the winding belt. She grabbed it and stood waiting for someone from the ranch to come. To her left a man lifted a poster board that said *Bigelow* in bold black letters. Abby assumed it was her ride and walked toward him. "I'm Abby," she said. "Are you my ride?"

He nodded. "Hi, I'm Niles. It's nice to meet you." He lowered the sign and they shook hands. His palms were dry and calloused, fingernails grimy, but he had a strong grip and squeezed her fingers hard.

"Niles... Like the Nile River in Africa?"

He grinned. "Yeah."

"How interesting," Abby mumbled, walking a few steps behind.

They walked outside and Niles threw her suitcase in back of a rusty Chevy pickup.

Abby stopped and perched her hands on her hips. "Oh no...You're kidding me, right?" *This is a nightmare. I hate you for this, Mom!*

"What do you mean?" he asked, placing his hand over his heart, like he was hurt by the rude insult. "You don't like my truck?"

Abby pursed her lips. "Okay, I get it. The jokes on me, right?" She threw both hands in the air. "Now where's my real ride to the ranch?"

"This is it, kiddo!" he said, opening the door.

"But this old thing has no AC. And it's summertime, hot as Hades out here."

Niles got in the truck and shut the door. "You're right, it doesn't." *You'll have to deal with it.*

"Really? I can't ride in this. I mean..."

He gazed at her through the open window. "Well, it's this or you can walk for fifteen miles. I'll give you precise directions to the farmhouse, so suit yourself." He turned the key in the ignition and the truck's muffler rattled, soon drawing a lot of attention to them.

In disbelief, Abby tilted her head as her mouth dropped open. Then she got in without saying another word. *Oh, this can't be happening. What have you done to me, Mom? I cannot believe this.* She slumped over near the door, placing her hand over her eyes to hide her face and obvious embarrassment.

"Buckle up, buttercup!" Niles said and laughed.

Reaching for the seat belt she said, "I didn't say you could call me that. I don't know you well enough yet. Abby, will do fine for now."

Niles grinned. "Oh, the name fits you well. Believe me." He put the truck in drive and took off. His patience was already wearing thin with Abby's rudeness and cocky attitude. Who was she to be so ungrateful? And she'd insulted his truck in the first five minutes after they met. He gazed toward her. *Seems like you're a spoiled brat to me. I'd put you over my knee, teach you some manners and respect if you were my daughter.* But he kept his thoughts to himself.

The windows and back glass were open as wide and far as they could go. Abby's hair kept blowing against her face. "Oh, I hate this already," she said, brushing hair out her eyes as sweat beaded on her top lip and forehead.

"You might as well get used to it because you'll be around for the next couple months. This is how we roll around here. Ain't a thing fancy going on. Ms. Bea is a frugal-conservative woman. She won't spend a penny for anything that's unnecessary."

Abby stared at Niles a minute and wrinkled her forehead. "You call her Ms. Bea?"

"Yeah, we all call her Bea because she likes it that way."

"Do you do everything she likes or demands of you?" Abby asked, thinking he was a little hen-pecked from the start.

Niles grinned. "Yes, I try my best," he said.

Abby grew quiet, then out of the blue she asked, "Are we related?"

Niles was surprised she had asked such a question. "Nah, we aren't related." *Thank God. You'd never survive with me in your life for too long.*

Abby sighed and messed with a hangnail on her finger for a moment. "So, you're just one of the ranch hands?"

Niles cocked his head to the side and gave her an odd look. "Excuse me? Did you say ranch hand?"

She shrugged. "Yeah, you know, someone who takes care of the smelly animals and cleans poop out the pens and such."

Niles shook his head at the gall of her to say such a thing. "You really don't know anything about ranch life do you?" Niles placed both hands on the steering wheel, clenching it tighter and tighter, even though he felt like slamming on the brakes, and dropping her out beside the road to walk the rest of the way.

She gasped, placing a hand on her chest. He had bit back regarding her behavior. "Oops, did I offend you?" she asked, covering her mouth.

He drew in a breath and exhaled hard. "No, I'll survive," he said and continued to drive as the muffler rattled even louder, like it might fall off anytime.

Feeling impatient, Abby asked, "How much longer before we're there?"

"It's only a few more minutes till I turn off this road." Niles turned the radio dial and cranked the volume loud to one of his favorite country music stations.

Abby shook her head, wondering what in the world she'd gotten herself into. She hated country music, only listened to pop and rap. *I should've behaved and listened to mom and not Darcy. Then I wouldn't be here wasting my summer in this misery.* But it was too late for her to have regrets now. She was stuck for the next few months, whether she liked it or not.

Fifteen minutes later, Niles turned off the main road and passed through a white wooden gate. The road was a mile long, and there were hay fields on each side with cows and horses grazing. The pleasant aroma had blanketed the air, slapping them in the face. Abby wrinkled her nose in disgust. Nearing the end of the road, a woman was standing on the front porch of the house with a watering can in her hand. She saw the truck and set the can next to her arrangements of potted flowers.

Beatrice had only received a few photos of Abby thus far, and so she felt anxious to see and meet her in person for the first time.

Abby got out and stood beside the truck while Niles grabbed her suitcase. When Bea took one look at her she knew without a doubt she was Billy's kid. Her stance and hair and eye color made it apparent.

She walked over to the porch with her things in hand. "Well, I guess you must be my grandma?"

Bea smoothed a couple unruly tendrils back off her forehead. "Yeah, I'm Beatrice, but everyone around here calls me Bea."

Abby didn't know whether to hug her, or just make a quick attempt at shaking her hand.

"Well, come on and give me a hug," Bea said. "Welcome to Texas. We're all huggers around here. Everyone is like family."

Feeling nervous, Abby set her bags on the ground and reached out for Bea. She squeezed her tight, made her feel welcome and accepted. It set Abby's mind at ease because she had no idea what to expect from a complete total stranger.

"Let's go in, and I'll get you something to eat. I know those airlines only give you snacks these days."

Abby agreed. "Yeah, you're right. I am a little hungry."

Bea nodded, walking in the door. "Well, I love to cook," she said, grabbing a dish of chicken casserole from the fridge to warm in the microwave.

Niles stood there, taking it all in. Things felt a little odd with Abby around. He'd worked for Bea a long time, and she'd always been attentive to his needs. He couldn't help feeling a little jealous over the attention

Abby was getting, like she was the only one in the room. He coughed, reminding Bea he was still there too.

"Are you hungry, Niles?" Bea motioned for him to have a seat at the table.

"I sure am," Niles said, pulling a chair out.

Abby noticed the way Niles was looking at Bea with a gleam in his eye, and she wondered if they were more than friends.

Minutes later, Bea set the casserole, a pan of buttermilk biscuits, and a bottle of syrup on the table and sat across from Niles. "Okay. Dig in. If you leave hungry it's your own fault." She grinned.

Niles grabbed a biscuit and dropped it on his plate in a hurry. It was still steaming hot. "Yep, these are hot," he replied, reaching for the syrup.

Abby spooned some casserole onto her plate and took a bite. "This is tasty. You need to give me the recipe so mom can fix this for us at home," she said.

Bea nodded. "Sure. Remind me, and I'll give you a copy before you leave."

When they had finished eating, Niles left and Bea showed Abby to her room. On the way to the second floor, the wooden stairs creaked with each footstep they made. Bea stopped for a brief moment at a room near the bathroom and opened the door. "This used to be your daddy's room." She paused. "I imagine it's probably the place you were conceived."

Surprised, Abby said, "Grandma!"

Bea grinned. "Well, it was either here or out in the barn. They spent a week with me right after they met. I knew then Jewel was not in favor of living on a ranch because she complained of the sight and smell of things from day one."

Amazed, Abby just looked at her. "You do seem pretty confident about it, but I really didn't need that kind of image stuck in my head."

"Oh, child. Isn't it a part of every young couple's life?" She giggled at Abby's obvious embarrassment about her parents being intimate together.

There was a blanket draped across a square metal rack near the window. Bea grabbed it and slung it across the foot of the bed. "I haven't been in this room for quite some time. When I found out you were coming to visit, I cleaned from top to bottom. There's nothing better than a clean set of sheets for a good night's rest."

"Thank you," Abby said, trying to be polite. She'd only been at the ranch a few hours, but Bea had already earned her respect. There was such gentleness about her, and she spoke what was on her mind without mincing her words.

"Well, I know it's been a long day, so I'll let you unpack and get some rest." Bea ran her hands over her apron then clasped them together and rubbed her palms. "If you need anything I'll be downstairs."

"Okay. Thank you."

Abby unpacked her bags and tried to get settled in. So far, her adventure had been quite interesting from the minute she boarded the plane.

Bea cleared away the leftovers and ran a broom over the kitchen floor. As she opened the closet door to grab the dustpan Niles walked in, got close to her and whispered, "You'll have your hands full with Abby here."

She turned to face him. "Hmm...You think so?"

Niles nodded. "Oh, yes. I'd be willing to bet money on it."

Bea smiled. "I guess we'll see what tomorrow has in store. Now, would you like another biscuit and a glass of milk before you go?"

"Sure. How can I refuse?" Niles sat and waited for her to join him at the table.

Bea fixed a hot coffee and they talked about things regarding the ranch, a new Thoroughbred, and how he'd had to fix a broken horseshoe on one of the mares that afternoon.

THREE

Early the next morning, Abby was awakened by some kind of machinery running in a nearby field. She threw the covers back and peered out the window. A guy was on a tractor bush-hogging one of the fields. "Gee, I'll never get to sleep in like this." She got back in bed and buried her head under the pillow to muffle the sound.

Minutes later, there was a knock on the door. "Come in," she said, revealing only her eyes and the top of her head.

"Morning. I hope you slept well," Bea said.

"I think so," Abby replied, glancing at the clock on the nightstand. It was barely seven-thirty.

"I assume you're probably accustomed to sleeping till noon," Bea said, opening the window blinds as a ray of sunshine began to stream in.

Abby nodded. "Yeah, pretty much." She yawned. "Mom either works, or sleeps all the time. So I'm left alone a lot."

"Well, we're all out and about early around here. Breakfast is ready. If you're hungry, get dressed and come in the kitchen to join us."

Abby covered her mouth to hide another yawn. "Okay. I'll be there in a few minutes."

Bea left and closed the door behind her. *Kids these days...*

"I'll be so glad when this summer is over," Abby mumbled, walking toward the closet to get some more clothes.

After she dressed in something more appropriate, she stepped in the bathroom and squirted mousse in her hands to tame her unruly locks.

Niles was seated at the table reading the daily newspaper. When Bea walked in, he lowered it and looked over the top of his reading glasses. "Morning. Something sure does smell delicious. I can always count on you to keep me well fed and hydrated." He grinned with the paper still in hand.

"Morning." Bea smiled, thankful for his kind words. "It's a comfort to know I'm good for something," she teased, setting plates on the table along with a platter of scrambled eggs and crispy bacon.

"You've outdone yourself," Niles said.

"Is Kyle stopping by to join us this morning? I haven't told him about Abby. You know what a reputation he has." Bea grinned. "Of course she thinks she's already grown, but in reality she has a long way to go," Bea said, adding napkins and forks by the plates.

"Oh yes, she's a grown know-it-all in my book." Niles frowned and folded the newspaper in half. Abby hadn't made the best impression on him from day one.

"I take it you two didn't hit it off when you first met?"

Niles nodded. "Well, I wasn't going to say anything, but you're right. She's lacking a lot when it comes to knowing how to use proper manners and respect."

Just then, Abby walked in the kitchen. "You're right about what? Am I slack?" She pointed to her chest. "Were you talking about me, Niles?"

Before Niles responded Bea jumped in, changing the subject so Niles couldn't answer. "There's a lot of work to be done on the ranch today," she said. "The temperature is supposed to be in triple digits the next couple days."

Abby sat at the end of the long farm table. "Wow! You've cooked enough food to feed an army. How many ranch hands do you feed each day?"

Bea paused and looked at her. "I like to refer to them as friends and our hired help, not ranch hands."

Abby shrugged. "Okay. Whatever makes you happy, I guess." Abby scooped some food on her plate as Bea's words seemed to roll right on across the table.

Niles finished his breakfast first and set his empty plate in the sink. Neither he nor Bea had said a word more. On the way out he grabbed his thermos and glanced back over his shoulder. "Thanks for breakfast. It was delicious."

Bea nodded. "Make sure you stay hydrated out there," she said. "It's going to be a scorcher of a day."

He nodded and closed the door behind him.

Abby witnessed a definite connection between them, but didn't dare inquire about it. She'd just arrived, and needed more time to get to know her grandma on a personal level. After all, she and Niles appeared to be around the same age, and she wondered if they'd ever been lovers.

After she ate Abby set her plate in the sink. "Thanks for breakfast, Grandma. You're a fabulous cook. You sure could teach mom a thing or two. At times, she tends to scorch rice and burn eggs."

Bea grinned. "You're welcome. Lunch is at noon, dinner is at six sharp. There are usually not many leftovers after all the guys eat, so I'd be on time if I were you."

Abby walked toward the stairs and Bea stopped her, grabbing hold of her forearm.

"Change into some old clothes. I have a few chores for you to do today," Bea said. "After all, you're not here for a delightful summer vacation."

Abby nodded, darted upstairs, and stomped her feet when she reached the top, making the floors creak loud. "How wonderful!" she shrieked.

Bea washed the breakfast dishes, wiped off the table, and removed her apron while she waited on Abby's return.

Soon, Abby walked in wearing khaki Capri pants, a frilly white shirt, and flip-flops. Things she would choose to wear when going out with friends.

Bea stared at her for a few moments and tried to keep a straight face. "Is this the oldest set of clothes you have with you?" she asked.

Abby gave her an odd look. "Yeah, I like to look good when I go out. These are some of my older clothes though. I've had these for about a year or two, since I've stopped growing so fast."

"Well, I sure hope you don't ruin them today," Bea said.

Abby hadn't a clue of what ranch life entailed, but she was about to find out. Bea walked outside and motioned for Abby to follow. "Come on. You've got to start somewhere." *This child is in for a rude awakening. Oh Lord, help me to teach her something beneficial.*

Unsure of what she meant, Abby followed close behind with caution. Soon, the lingering stench in the breeze was breathtaking, and not in a beautiful sunny-day way. She pinched her nose shut and tried to breathe through her mouth. "Ugh…This is awful."

Bea stopped. "This is a good day because it hasn't rained yet," she said in regards to Abby's disgust of the smelly hog pens. After grabbing a bucket of feed, she opened the metal gate beside a long hog trough. The hogs started making noises while waiting on their food, and they all began to gather closer and closer to Bea. Before long she was surrounded by them.

"Oh my! How can you do this every day?"Abby said, feeling nauseous. "These animals are so filthy and disgusting."

Bea tossed some feed in the trough and grinned. "Where do you think the bacon you ate this morning came from?"

Abby stopped in her tracks, feeling even more nauseous at the thought. "But...But bacon is so good," she stammered. "Although, I don't know if I want to eat pork again after seeing this."

Bea stopped with the bucket in her hand and looked Abby in the eye. "Yeah, it is. Hogs are some of the nastiest animals on the planet. But there are a lot of tasty dishes you can make from their meat. Like bacon, ribs, and barbeque."

Abby frowned and placed her hand on her abdomen, feeling like she might barf right there.

When Bea reached the other side of the pen, she handed Abby the empty bucket. "This is your job tomorrow, so I hope you were paying close attention to everything."

Abby froze and bit her bottom lip, eyes wide. "You're kidding, right?"

Bea wiped sweat from her brow and perched her hands at her waist. "No. I'm not kidding. It's time for you to learn the ends and outs of operating a ranch. Besides, the experience will be good for you."

"But I don't want to do this?" Abby said. "I'll never live on a ranch. I can't stand the sight or smell of things here. So, what's the use? I don't want to waste your time with teaching me something I'll never use."

"Listen, you're here in my territory now, and before you leave you'll be able to do a lot of what I do," Bea said, voice firm. "Who knows? All of this may start to grow on you after a while."

Abby followed Bea to the end of the pen and caught her flip-flop on an extension cord, sending her straight to the ground hard. The bucket flew out her hand and she landed face first in the mud. Realizing what had happened, she reached for Bea to lend her a helping hand. Bea tried to stifle a giggle and helped her to her feet. Abby stood and tried to brush mud off her clothes. And the only thing Bea could see of her face was the whites of her eyes.

"I'm sorry I didn't remind you to watch your step on the way out. I reckon I need to add a bottle of stain remover and bleach to my grocery list."

Abby walked out the gate with mud covering her and her clothes. "Yeah, I guess so," she said, worried she'd ruined her clothes the second day on the ranch.

Soon, they heard a tractor in the distance. One of the guys was out baling hay in a field.

"I guess you're wondering who he is?" Bea said, realizing it all had Abby distracted.

"Let me guess, another one of the ranch hands? Or rather, your hired help?"

Bea replied, "Yep. You'll come in contact will many people during your stay. Just wave, smile, be polite, and everything will be fine. They each have a job to do around here."

Abby set the bucket out by the fence. "Can I go in and change my clothes now?"

Bea reached for the bucket. "Yeah, you probably should shower too," she said and wrinkled her nose. "I can smell you from way over here."

Feeling embarrassed, Abby scurried back to the house to take care of things. Her morning had definitely not gone as planned. So far the best thing about the day had been breakfast.

While Abby was washing and changing her clothes, Niles walked in to get another thermos of water. "How's it going with Abby today?" he asked. "I saw the two of you in the hog pen earlier."

Bea leaned against the kitchen counter and grinned wide. "It's been an eventful morning, I'd say. She knows nothing about ranch life, but I suppose it's not a surprise though. Her mother, Jewel, hated it as well. And Abby's a bon-a-fide city girl. But I'm confident I'll have her familiar with a few things before summer is over and she returns home."

After taking a drink of water, Niles grinned and wiped his mouth on his shirt sleeve. "Well, if anyone can do it, you can."

"You sure have a lot of faith in me," Bea said, folding clean dish towels she'd brought in from the clothesline.

"Anyone who knows you knows the kind of woman you are."

She walked over to Niles. "Oh, yeah. What kind of woman is that, might I ask?"

Niles screwed the top on the thermos and looked into her alluring blue eyes. At fifty-six she was still attractive with sun-kissed skin, and only a few gray hairs shining at the hairline. Most women her age had salt and pepper hair, but hers was still as black as midnight. She seemed to have a way of causing Niles to lower his defenses. She met his gaze, and neither said a word for a few seconds. Then Niles broke the silence and said, "You're a good hard-working woman." Bea grinned and he glanced at his watch. "I guess I better head on back out there. The day seems to be flying by and those two new Thoroughbreds need my attention."

Just as Niles was leaving, Abby walked in the kitchen. "Hello, Niles. It's good to see you again."

Niles reached for the doorknob and tipped his hat. "Ladies..."

Abby had caught Bea off guard when her thoughts were still quite adrift. "He came in for another thermos of water. Been real hot these past couple days. Last thing he needs is dehydration."

Abby nodded, thinking nothing of it, and gazed out the window as a guy without a shirt on parked an old C-tractor next to the barn. He appeared to be young, tan, and had six-pack abs. "Who is he?" Abby asked, wanting to meet him right away.

"Kyle."

"Is he part of the hired help?"

"Yeah, Kyle helps out with the horses and spends his free time here each summer."

"Maybe I'll cross paths with him sometime," Abby said, checking out his chiseled physique. She ran her fingers over her brow, longing to know more about this mysterious good-looking young man.

Bea pursed her lips and didn't say a word. In fact, she hoped Kyle would keep his distance from Abby. She was too young for him, so she planned to do whatever she could to keep them apart. Last thing she needed was for Kyle and Abby to get together because Jewel would never forgive her. And for a brief moment it brought back memories of when her son, Billy, had met and married Jewel. Abby's birth had been the only good thing to come from the marriage. Right then, Bea could tell Abby had ways like Jewel. She seemed to want to live life free as a bird on her own terms, and it concerned Bea regarding Abby's future.

FOUR

Kyle unloaded the last bale of hay and removed his gloves, wiping sweat off his brow. Like Abby, he'd made mistakes and had learned some things the hard way. Being there at the ranch was like a breath of fresh air, time away from the rat race. Life hadn't always been easy though. After his mother died, Kyle left home to follow his dream of becoming a musician. He played in one place after another, struggling to make ends meet. Soon, he decided to pursue other interests and discovered his love for horses. He'd worked for Bea the past two summers, and she'd offered him room and board in back of the barn. Nothing fancy, just a twelve by twenty room with a twin bed, small bathroom, a microwave, fridge and a sofa. But it got him settled in for a few months, and he was grateful to stay there and save some money for later on.

Washing dishes, Bea gazed toward the barn as Kyle led Cocoa out and placed a saddle on her. She was a gentle horse, tame since the day Bea bought her. Kyle placed his foot in the stirrup and jumped on for a ride. Bea's heart grew warm watching them. *No doubt, he's a natural with these animals and really speaks their language.* It made her suspect there was more to Kyle's life story than he'd previously shared. He was a young man, and she couldn't figure out why he'd want to be there in such a remote place. *Maybe he's still trying to find his way, trying to find where he belongs.* She dried her hands and grabbed some tea bags from the cabinet. It was almost lunchtime.

Soon, Niles walked in, removed his boots, and washed his hands and face at the sink. "Something smells good, Bea. What do you have cooking?" He removed his hat and ran his fingers over his graying beard.

Bea placed the tea bags in water and turned toward him. "Pinto beans and ham," she replied.

Niles laid his hand on his chest. "You're a woman after my own heart," he joked. "How long before it's ready?"

"An hour or so," Bea said with a grin.

"Was that Kyle I saw riding off on Cocoa a few minutes ago?"

Bea nodded. "Yep. He has such a way with those horses. No doubt, he's a natural."

Niles sat at the end of the table. "Can I get a glass of iced tea to quench my thirst? This heat is taking it out of me today."

"Of course." Bea grabbed the pitcher out the fridge and reached for a glass out the dish drainer. "Better stay hydrated, for sure. We're in for a hot summer over these next few weeks," she said, pouring the rest of the cold tea for him.

Niles took a swig, and drank the entire glass without as much as taking a break. Then he set the empty glass in front of him. "Man, I was thirsty. Nobody can make iced tea as good as you." His voice sounded a little funny from the sudden brain freeze.

"You don't say?" she said, looking at the empty

glass. "Looks like I better make a couple more pitchers for later on."

One of the guys stormed in the back door with his hat in his hand. "We need help quick! Kyle's in one of the fields with Cocoa and something's happened. She appears to be hurt by the look of things."

Bea's heart sank. "Oh no! What happened?"

Niles stood and grabbed his hat and boots. "Let's go, Bud." They stormed out to saddle two horses and head over to the field. When they arrived Kyle was lying on the ground near Cocoa, trying to comfort her however he could.

"What happened?" the men asked.

Kyle shook his head, eyes teary. "Everything was fine. Then all of a sudden Cocoa went crazy and bucked me off. I believe it must've been a rattler in the grass. She took a hard fall. I think her back leg is injured because she neighs and flinches when I touch it."

Niles sighed. "Man! Bea's going to have a fit over this."

"Let's try to check her out," Bud said. "Maybe things aren't as bad as you think." As Bud ran his hand over her leg, she flinched and let out a neigh. "We need to get her to the vet. Only thing is...closest place is forty miles away."

"Oh, I cannot believe this is happening. Everything I touch seems to crumble or disappear," Kyle said, standing and running his hands through his hair, feeling distraught. Shaking his head he said, "Ms. Bea will never forgive me for this. Never." Kyle began to cower, worried that he would be fired.

"Now's not a good time to play the blame game," Bud said. "It's not your fault. It could've happened with any one of us out in the field."

Niles rubbed his chin and seemed to be in deep thought. "Wait a minute. How about Maggie Davidson? Her place is only ten miles away. She's an excellent vet."

Bud frowned. "But she's not a vet anymore. Remember, her license was taken away after she allowed one of Mayor Beaufort's horses to die. Then Beau was later found dead."

"Well, it's a good choice in my opinion," Niles said. "Everyone threw Maggie under the bus because of one incident. I know for a fact she did all she could. The horse was too old to save. She had to euthanize her. Beaufort's had it in for her ever since Beau died."

Kyle chimed in. "Yes. Let's get Cocoa over there now before the muscles become stiff. Maybe Maggie can do something to help her."

"Okay. But I don't like this," Bud said. "It's sketchy having to move her around like this."

Niles rode back to the house to grab the truck and a horse trailer. Bea was standing on the porch anxious for details of what was going on. She knew by the look on Niles' face it was bad. "She hit the ground hard. We're taking Cocoa over to Maggie's," he said without even asking permission. He knew when it came to the horses Bea would agree he knew what was best.

Bea hung her head. "Do whatever you can, Niles. I trust you." With eyes teary, she turned to walk back inside. *Lord, please help my girl.*

"Bea?"

She stopped. "Yeah."

"I promise you this: I'll do everything I can for Cocoa to be okay. But your continued prayers for her are appreciated."

Bea nodded as the screen door shut behind her.

Abby walked in to see what was going on. "What's all the commotion about around here?" she asked. Seeing Bea's tears, told her something was bad wrong.

Bea wiped her eyes. "One of the horses is hurt, bucked Kyle off in the field. In fact, she's my favorite girl. Cocoa."

"Oh no! Are you okay, Grandma? Can I do anything to help?" Abby said.

"Nah. We'll have to be patient and wait and see what happens. Just pray Cocoa will be okay."

Abby placed her hands on top of Bea's shoulders to offer solace. "I'm so sorry," she said. "I can see how much she means to you."

After making a splint, the guys harnessed Cocoa and used a winch pulley system to load her onto the trailer. Kyle stayed close and kneeled beside her, offering comfort. He felt terrible about what had happened to Bea's favorite girl, and he'd grown rather fond of her as well.

When they arrived, Maggie was outside in her flower garden and met Niles near the picket fence. "Hello Niles. What brings you over this way today?"

"We need your help, Maggie."

She saw the horse trailer hitched behind the truck. "Really? What's wrong?"

"It's Cocoa. She had a fall this morning. I think she may have sprained or broken a leg."

Maggie frowned. "Oh, Niles. You know I'm not licensed to practice as a vet anymore."

Niles' eyes met hers. "Please Maggie. I'm begging you. This horse means the world to Bea. She's her pride and joy." Niles had such a look of desperation. It was hard for Maggie to refuse such a request.

Maggie sighed. "Okay. But you've got to keep this between us. If Mayor Beaufort finds out, he'll make my life a living hell around here, not that he already hasn't."

Niles nodded. "My lips are sealed, and so are Bud's and Kyle's." He looked at them. "Ain't that right boys?"

They both agreed.

Maggie grabbed her doctor's bag from the house and prepared a sedative to calm Cocoa, so she could give her a thorough examination. Then she grabbed a stethoscope and a pair of disposable gloves.

The guys paced back and forth in the gravel driveway, waiting for news from the exam.

After completing a checkup and drawing some blood, Maggie gave them the news. "Well guys, it's like this, Cocoa's leg is sprained and a tendon may be torn. There's a lot of swelling right now." She removed her gloves and tucked her hair behind her ears. "But that's only half of it." She paused and sighed. "She's also pregnant. Without proper equipment I can't diagnose her situation for certain. She needs to have an x-ray, but I have seen an injury like this before, so we'll treat it as best we can."

"What?" Niles said in disbelief. "I thought she was fixed when Bea purchased her. I mean...I didn't think she could get pregnant." He removed his cap and wiped sweat with his handkerchief.

Maggie grinned. "Well, most male horses are gelded before three years of age, but if she's been in close contact with Hershey..." She furrowed her brow. "However it happened, Cocoa will be having a colt or a filly before long."

"What can we do to save her leg, Maggie?" Bud asked.

"No route we choose is going to be an easy one." Maggie pondered on a few things before making a final decision. "You'll have to give her urgent care every day. Years ago they used to shoot a horse with a similar injury like this. But nowadays we have a better way to help with things."

"What is the worst case scenario?" Kyle asked.

"The options are few. We can give the leg a chance to heal, or I can send her to another vet to have the leg amputated below the joint. But if you're willing to go the distance, we can get her stable and see what happens over the next few weeks. I'll need to speak with Bea concerning all of this first though," Maggie said.

Niles chimed in. "I'll stand good for anything you need to do. Bea trusts me with all the horses. I've trained several for her over the years, including Cocoa."

Maggie hovered over Cocoa a few minutes, stroking her mane. "Okay. Let's get her back to Bea's place and we'll go from there."

Niles placed his hand on Maggie's shoulder. "Thanks Maggie. I know Bea will appreciate everything you're doing to help Cocoa. And I do too."

"No problem. Just because I'm not allowed to work with equine doesn't mean I care any less about them." Maggie frowned.

Back at the house, Niles gave Bea a quick update on Cocoa after she was settled in the barn. Bea felt grateful and relieved Maggie had agreed to help her. Right now, she didn't know if she could handle another loss.

"Thanks for all you and the guys have done today," Bea said. "I have a great group of men working with me here on the ranch."

Niles grabbed his cap and grinned. "You're welcome.

It was our pleasure. We all know how much Cocoa means to you."

Bea nodded. "Yes, indeed. I'd be lost without her."

"Kyle feels awful about what happened. Said he believes Cocoa came upon a rattler in the grass and got spooked."

"Oh, it's not his fault. It could've happened to anyone this time of year. Those rattlers are all over the fields in search of aestivation or mating."

"Yeah, I told him the same thing, not to blame himself for what happened. He's a good kid."

Feeling grateful Bea said, "I'll talk to him first chance I get. He does a great job with the horses."

Niles agreed. "I know he'd appreciate your forgiveness."

"Of course. Kyle is a real asset here at the ranch. Sometimes accidents happen. No matter how careful we try to be."

Later on, Bea fixed the guys a plate of ham and beans and let them know how grateful she was for all their help. However, Kyle stayed at the barn because it broke his heart to see Bea hurting like that. And he'd never forgive himself if she were to lose Cocoa.

FIVE

The next day, Maggie stopped by the barn to check on Cocoa. She'd been more than generous by offering her services, even though the mayor would have her arrested if he got wind of it.

When she walked in Kyle was in the stall spreading out some fresh hay. Cocoa was still resting and Maggie said she'd be better off that way for a few weeks. It would keep her calm, and protect the pregnancy. An IV had been placed to keep her comfortable and Kyle made sure she had help eating, even if he had to hand feed her. It seemed like a lot to do for a pregnant horse, but Bea loved her and everyone was willing to go the distance with whatever it entailed to save her.

While Maggie was assessing Cocoa, Bea walked in to check on her. "Hello Maggie. How's she doing?"

Maggie was on her knees listening to the heartbeat, and placed the stethoscope around her neck and stood. "She's stable for now and I pray things continue on the same path."

Bea nodded. "Me too. Thank you for everything, Maggie. I know the Good Lord will bless you for doing all this."

"You're welcome. I wouldn't have it any other way. Cocoa is a special horse. I'm sorry I can't treat her at my place to keep a closer watch on her." Maggie frowned. "Niles did tell you she's pregnant, didn't he?"

Bea's eyes grew wide. "No. I guess he forgot to tell me with all the commotion going on."

"Well, she's doing okay for now, but her leg needs to heal before she labors with a colt or filly."

Kyle finished with the hay and leaned the rake against the gate post. "This should last a day or two," he said, trying to break into their conversation.

Bea and Maggie were so distracted they paid him no mind, so Kyle politely excused himself, but felt relieved to hear Cocoa had a good chance to recover from her injuries.

After being there a few days, Abby realized things were not as boring as she'd once thought. There was a lot involved in operating a ranch, which was all new to her, and believe it or not, the sight and smell of the place was beginning to grow on her a little. In a weird way, something made her feel like she belonged there. However, things were quite different than being in the city. There were no ranch hands with nose rings, tats, I-phones, or pants sagging at the waistline. These guys were hard-working men who worked from sunup to sundown. Once in a while see witnessed a man spitting out a mouthful of tobacco or snuff. And then there was Kyle. Something about him had her intrigued, making her wonder what his life story is. He seemed to work as hard as the other guys, pouring his heart and soul into his work. It seemed everyone there had a good work ethic as well.

Since arriving, Abby hadn't thought much about missing out on summer vacation with friends. Inside she was feeling a calm serenity—something she hadn't felt since she was at a young age.

Just then, her phone rang and she glanced at caller ID before answering. "Hi Mom."

"Hey baby. How are you adjusting to life on the ranch?"

"Oh, it's much different here than in the city."

"Yes. I can imagine."

"Yeah, it's kind of hard to explain though. I mean..."

Jewel could hear something different in Abby's voice. A change in her tone, and she hoped being there would help open Abby's eyes and get her back on track. Help her make right choices. "How's Bea treating you?"

"Fine."

"Really? Just fine?"

"Yeah."

Jewel knew there was no use in pushing for more information. Abby was hard-headed and would only say what she wanted her to know. In fact, she was a lot like Billy when it came to certain things.

Abby saw Bea walking toward the door with her hands full. "I've got to go, Mom. I'll talk with you later."

"Abby..." Jewel's phone went silent as Abby ended the call.

Jewel sighed and shook her head. *I guess that's all for now. Oh, how I hope this trip is doing her some good.*

Abby opened the door and grabbed a bag from Bea's hand. "How's Cocoa?" she said, setting the bag and phone on the kitchen table.

Bea set her keys and a couple bags on the counter. "I reckon she's doing as well as she can be right now.

Maggie's keeping her sedated for a little while, so the injury can have time to heal without her moving too much."

"But why? Won't that make her body stiff and hard to move later on?"

"She said the less she moves over the next few weeks, the better off she'll be. And she also told me Cocoa's pregnant."

"Oh my! How's the baby doing?"

"Doing fine. Has a strong heartbeat so far. I'm thankful for that because things could've been a lot worse. Now, if Cocoa can only get through the birth."

Abby frowned. "I'm sorry, Grandma."

"Oh, I believe she'll pull through. Maggie's doing all she can to see to it and I trust her. She's gifted at what she does. I've never met a better veterinarian."

"Where is Niles today?"

Bea furrowed her brow. "Gone into town to get a few items but he'll be back soon."

"You really like him, don't you?"

Surprised, Bea said, "What? Don't be silly. We've been friends a long time. He's one of the hardest working men here on the ranch, and I don't know what I'd do without him."

"Has he ever been married?"

Bea crossed her arms. "What's with all the questions today?"

"No reason. Just curious, I guess. It's good to ask questions. It's how you learn things."

Bea laughed. "Yes, you're right, missy."

Abby pointed at her chest, eyes wide. "Missy?"

"Yeah, it's something we say all the time around here."

Abby grinned. "Well, I'll try to get used to it. Kind of reminds me of a dog I had years ago."

"Oh, I've been meaning to ask you. Have you talked with your mom yet?"

"Yeah, she called earlier."

"Okay. That's good. I don't want her to think I'm trying to prevent you from talking with her."

Abby rubbed her chin. "Hmm. What's the deal with you and mom anyway? I don't see any reason why you two couldn't get along."

Bea pursed her lips. "I won't go into the past because Jewel and I have made peace over things." She paused. "Both she and Billy have moved on in life. So I won't say anything more about it."

"Fair enough. I guess."

Bea gathered a few items she needed from the fridge and tied an apron around her waist. "I've got to get things ready for lunch. Niles and the guys will be starving, come noon."

Abby said nothing more, but knew Bea cared a lot about Niles, whether she admitted it or not.

Bea scurried around the kitchen, dropping chicken legs in a fryer. Niles loved her fried chicken, it was a favorite of his. He'd been good to her, and she didn't know what she'd do without him around there when she needed a man's help. Ever since he lost his wife, Bea felt like she needed to see Niles was taken care of. She'd promised her friend, Mary, she'd look after him. They were best friends for years, and she couldn't break a promise to someone who had meant so much to her.

At noon, Niles parked the truck near the barn with a load of supplies. He'd always been a man of his word and Bea respected him for it. He shut off the engine and unloaded several bags of feed. When finished, he closed the old truck windows and made his way over to the house for lunch. When he walked in, Bea was plating the last few pieces of chicken and turned to face him. "Have a seat. Lunch is almost ready," she said.

Niles walked in a small washroom and left the door open. "Something smells mighty good. I've been starving ever since I missed breakfast this morning."

Bea grinned and set a platter of chicken on the table, along with mixed vegetables and a small bowl of leftover pinto beans and ham. "Dig in," she said. "I knew you'd be famished by noon."

Soon, Abby came in from feeding the hogs and slipped her rubber boots off by the door. "Man, something smells good," she said. "It's making me hungry."

"Have a seat. You're just in time for lunch," Bea said.

Abby washed her hands and arms and sat by Niles at the table. "So, how's it going?"

"Well, I just got back from town with a load of feed. How are things with you? Are you catching on? Getting used to how things are done around here?"

Abby grabbed a chicken leg. "I'm not fond of feeding the hogs. They are such nasty-smelly animals. But I'll feel much better after I eat some of this chicken." She laughed.

"No problems in the hog pen today?" Bea asked with a grin.

Abby already had her mouth full of chicken and wiped it with a napkin. "Not today. I watched where I stepped this time. That extension cord is nothing but a deathtrap."

Bea grinned.

Niles was amazed how Abby was devouring the food. "Bea makes the best fried chicken around." He grabbed two legs for his plate. "I say all the time she should've opened a restaurant instead of operating a ranch."

Bea blushed. "Oh hush, Niles. You're just starving, that's all. I believe you'd eat anything I cooked if you were hungry enough."

Abby saw Bea's face come aglow as she bit into another piece of chicken. Niles always knew how to make her smile. It was like he saw a side of Bea no one else knew. They always joked and talked like they'd known each other for years. Without a doubt, Abby knew they were hiding a few secrets of their own.

The phone rang and Bea went to answer. But caller ID showed it wasn't someone she cared to talk with, and her expression grew sullen as she listened to the caller's words. After the conversation ended, she knew the mayor had gotten wind of Maggie treating Cocoa, and she knew he had enough power to have Cocoa euthanized. The situation had her worried because someone had to tip him off about it. It was one more problem she'd have to face head-on. And Bea didn't know what she'd do if Maggie were arrested because she didn't have extra money right now to bail her out.

After they ate, Abby left to finish her chores and Bea cleared away the dirty dishes. She said nary word, but didn't have to tell Niles who had called because he suspected as much by her silence. Beaufort was a sore subject with Bea. Niles placed his hands on top of her shoulders, hating to see her so withdrawn. "Thanks for the meal," he whispered. "And don't worry so much. Everything will be okay. Cocoa's going to be fine and so is Maggie. God will take care of them."

She managed an uh-hum, trying to keep her emotions in check because she could have cried an ocean of tears. "Make sure you stay hydrated this afternoon," she said.

Niles nodded, and grabbed his thermos of water. "I'm going to take Hershey for a ride later. Would you like to join me with Caramel?"

Bea shook her head. "No. But maybe another time," she replied.

After Niles left she dried her hands and walked to the study. There was a photo of her and William Jake hanging on the wall above the fireplace. It was taken the day they bought their first horse together. Midnight had been as black as a lump of coal. A lot of things had happened since then. Some good. Some bad. But nothing would ever change the way she felt about her beloved horses. From the day she bought the first Thoroughbred...she knew it was meant to be.

SIX

While sleeping, Jewel had a nightmare about the past. It broke her heart having to be away from Abby because her greatest fear was not being a good mom.

With a cold sweat covering her body, Jewel recalled a little girl standing in the doorway, watching her mother drive away in an old car. Grief enveloped her with a burning reality her mother abandoned her. What had caused her to leave? Had she been too bad? Jewel was left with no one to see after her, and later placed in foster care to be bounced from one home to another. Tears streamed as she remembered the cold wintry day her life changed forever.

Sitting on the side of the bed, a lump formed in Jewel's throat as she recalled the smirk on her mother's face. Feeling stressed, like she might hyperventilate, Jewel screamed as loud as she could. It had been years since that day, and she wondered if Jazz was still alive. "Oh God. What kind of mother would do this to a child?" She ran the sleeve of her pajamas across her cheek. "I'll never put you through such an ordeal, Abby. No one deserves to be treated like they don't even matter."

There were many things Jewel needed to tell Abby about her childhood, but she had to deal with them as her heart would allow. Like the fact her grandmother, Jasmine, had been a prostitute, moving Jewel from place to place the first five years of life, and then abandoned her. Before Abby was born Jewel promised herself and God she'd never leave Abby to figure life out on her own. Regardless of the rebellious spirit Abby had, she still loved her and would do anything to protect her.

It had been a long time since Jewel had a nightmare about the day she was abandoned. Not something she liked to recall. She'd managed to bury some emotions deep, and figured being distraught over Abby being away had her feeling alone with those thoughts roaming in her subconscious mind. She drew in a breath and went to the kitchen for a drink of water. After turning on a light she gazed at the calendar and realized Abby would be away a few more weeks, time for Jewel to ponder on a lot of things and her past mistakes.

Unable to sleep, Abby pulled the curtain back and peered out the window. There was a light on in the barn. She hadn't ventured there yet, but looked forward to meeting Kyle whenever he was around. Bea had bragged of how he handled the dire situation with Cocoa and Abby wondered why he chose to help out there, and if he had a family or maybe a girlfriend.

Minutes later, Abby saw Kyle step outside in his boxers and her eyes grew wide. With heart racing, she stepped away from the window and got into bed. Seeing him stirred something inside her. She was certain he reminded her of someone. There was something familiar about him—the way he moved, carried himself. Even though she was young she believed in *true love*—the kind that weathered storms and made you stronger from them. Making her wish she'd been able to live with her dad and mom and witness *true love* between them.

After grabbing something out of the truck, Kyle hurried back to the barn. He knew Bea would scold him good if she caught him. He'd heard about Abby being there, and Bea wouldn't like him walking around indecent anytime day or night. She kept a tight rein on everyone at the ranch. It was her rules and they all respected Bea. After summer he'd be back on the road, so he figured it wasn't long to settle in one place then move on, which seemed to help keep things in perspective. He grabbed his pocket knife and began to shave off bark from a small tree limb. Something he enjoyed doing on nights he couldn't sleep.

After a few days, Jewel received a call from Buck Schuller. "Hi Buck."

"Did you give Abby a good send off the other day?"

"Yeah. She's at Bigelow Ranch. I hated to do it, but she left me no other choice."

"You can't take the blame, Jewel. You know Billy is the one who caused all of this. If he hadn't of walked out..."

"He left when she was two. She doesn't have any memories of him being around. The absence has left a void in her life. A void I cannot fill alone, no matter how hard I try."

"I know. I've always said he was a fool for turning his back on you two."

Jewel smiled. "You're too kind."

"I meant what I said. You're a great mom. Don't ever let anyone tell you otherwise."

"Thanks." Jewel grew quiet.

Buck heard the silence. Like he was there in the room with her. "You okay?"

"Yeah, I miss Abby. I still catch myself going in her room to say goodnight when I get home late. We've never been apart much."

"Oh, I'm sure you do," Buck said. "But keep the faith, Jewel. Things will work out the way they're supposed to."

Feeling hesitant, she said, "I don't know. You seem confident not to have kids of your own."

"I am. You're not the only who cares about Abby. Give her some time. Allow God and Bea to show her some things, help her change for the better."

Surprised, she said, "Gee. Thanks. I never knew you were such a man of faith."

Buck grinned. "Well, she's not my biological child, but I do care about her. I know she's harboring a lot of hurt and disappointment inside. Hurting people hurt others. My parents have both gone on to be with the Lord, but they divorced when I was eighteen. Even though I was a young man, it still hurt to witness how it tore us apart as a family. Things were never the same. There was always tension at family gatherings. Dad used to get drunk and beat mom a lot until she found enough strength to leave. I guess it's what made me want to go into law enforcement. I got tired of watching the abuse and wanted to do something about it. Years later they both come to know the Lord and I'm grateful of that."

Touched by his words, Jewel said, "Thanks for calling to check on us and sharing your heart with me." She was amazed how Buck could relate so well to her, even if she hadn't expressed her feelings regarding the abandonment.

"You're welcome. Besides, what are friends for? I've known you a long time, Jewel."

Jewel said goodnight and wondered if Buck might have another motive in mind. In high school they'd talked a few times, but nothing clicked between them. Now years later, Jewel believed he still carried a torch for her. Why else would he be so concerned about her and Abby? Unless he knew more about Billy than he'd let on. *This is crazy. I need to stop trying to analyze his motive and be glad someone cares,* she mumbled. However, Buck was not the type of man she needed right now. And she wasn't sure any man would suffice until Abby was out of school and she could focus on her own life for a change. Jewel had sacrificed a lot for her daughter, and she intended to finish the job—see to it Abby got a four year college education and a good start at adulthood. Something she never had the opportunity to obtain herself.

SEVEN

Come daybreak, Maggie grabbed her bag to head over to Bea's to check on Cocoa. She knew the situation was risky but she didn't want to worry Bea. Cocoa had a lot of healing to do and being pregnant would not help her get back on her feet—meaning it would make her labor and delivery more difficult—if the colt or filly survived during birth. Now Maggie worried there may be an early labor due to pain and suffering Cocoa was enduring from the injury. On the way out she heard a vehicle pull in the yard and hid her bag just in the nick of time. A short-plump bald man got out and walked toward the house. "Morning Maggie," he said.

"Morning. What brings you out this way, Beaufort?"

He rubbed his hands together. "You should already know the answer," he replied.

Maggie shrugged. "I'm sorry. Why don't you enlighten me?" She leaned against the picket fence and crossed her arms.

"I hear you've been treating Bea's Thoroughbred over at the barn because she took a pretty hard fall."

Maggie tried to keep her cool as heat rose in her cheeks. "You don't have proof of anything. And besides, I don't have a license to practice with equine anymore. Remember?"

Beaufort paused. "Well, you know you could be

fined and arrested if you're practicing without a legal license in this state."

Maggie grew angry. "I have you and your assistant Lance to thank for losing my license," she said. "You used him to trick me and you know it! Then you paid off the crooked judge on duty at the hearing."

Beaufort narrowed his eyes in the bright sunlight. "What? I'd never do such a thing, Maggie. How could I? After all, you were supposed to be my future daughter-in-law."

Maggie clenched her hands into fists by her sides. Everything in her wanted to punch him straight in the face and watch him roll like a ball on the sloped driveway.

He frowned. "Beau loved you, Maggie. From the first day you met, you could do no wrong in his eyes."

"Hmm. Love had nothing to do with it. Beau wanted a cook, a maidservant, and a woman he could control. Not a wife. And he's dead now from a drug overdose and self neglect. "

"Watch your mouth, Maggie! He didn't commit suicide. Beau would never do that. It was only a simple mix of alcohol with his medication. He was so distraught over losing you."

"Believe whatever you want to believe, Beaufort. You're oblivious to the truth because death certificates don't lie."

Beaufort's eyes welled. "You broke his heart, Maggie. You pushed him into a dark pit toward his own death. He was never the same after you left."

"I couldn't stay with him for another night. There's a lot you don't know about what I had to endure in that relationship. Things I've never shared with anyone."

"Like what?" he asked with sarcasm.

"You wouldn't believe me if I told you," Maggie said, trembling. "Beau wasn't the perfect son you had put on a pedestal. He had a lot of flaws."

He walked closer and raised his hand toward her cheek. Maggie's reflexes kicked in and she grabbed his wrist, gripping it tight. "Don't do this. Not now. Let it go and get on out of here. I mean it. Or else..."

"You know, you're such a beautiful woman. Maybe there is a way we can work something out," he said, eyes roaming over her from head to toe.

Feeling creeped out, Maggie loosened the grip on his wrist. "Never in a million years. I'm happy the way I am, and I'd rather die first than have to be with the likes of you."

His eyes widened and he stepped away from the sting of rejection. "Those horses can't keep you warm at night like a real man can."

"I think you need to go," Maggie said, voice stern. His gaze caught hers in a way he knew she was serious.

He turned to walk away. "I'm going to keep an eye on you, and if you're doing anything illegal I'll catch you. Then you'll be sorry when I do."

"Is that a promise?" Maggie said mad as a hornet.

"Well, aren't you a feisty one?" Beaufort laughed. "I can see why Beau was so crazy about you. You're pretty, a little crazy, and smart too."

"Listen, I didn't kill your son. The things he got involved in all contributed to his demise. I had nothing to do with it."

Beaufort opened the car door and ignored Maggie's last few words. On the way out the driveway he squealed the tires, leaving a cloud of dust lingering behind. She leaned her head against the car door, wondering how she could continue to give Cocoa the care she deserved. If Beaufort could make her life miserable, he'd find a way to do it. *Oh, Lord. What am I going to do now?* She grabbed the bag out of the bushes and drove off toward Bea's. Maggie loved Bea and there was no way she was going to turn her back on her—even if it meant she might go to jail all for the sake of helping Cocoa.

When she arrived, Bea was in the barn observing Cocoa's every breath. Maggie walked over and placed her hand on Bea's shoulder. "She's still in some pain, but it will become less and less as she heals." Maggie reached for her stethoscope to listen to Cocoa's heartbeat.

With tears in her eyes, Bea nodded. "Do you think she'll be able to tolerate foaling at the time of birth?"

"I hope so. She's a strong-willed horse. A lot like you, I'd say." Maggie grinned and grabbed a hold of Bea's hand. "We'll keep praying and wait and see what happens."

"Thanks Maggie. You're the best veterinarian. You have such a heart of gold. I know these animals can sense how much you love them."

Maggie was touched by her words. "Well, remind Beaufort I am. All he wants to do is run me out of town and ruin my life. He still blames me for Beau's death after all this time."

"Is he still bothering you?"

"Yes, he stopped by the house unannounced earlier today. Right before I drove over here."

"Did he threaten you in any way?"

"Oh, yes. He tried to lay the guilt trip on me, and throw his weight around, but I wouldn't go for it. I'm sure I could start treating horses again, if I decided to take notice of his awkward advances toward me."

Bea furrowed her brow. "Really? Did he?"

Maggie knew where her mind was headed and frowned. "Oh, yes, he tried. But I shot him clean out the water. I'd rather leave Texas forever than have to be with a man like him. Sad thing is: Beau was just like him. It didn't take me but a year to realize it—thank God!"

"One day Beaufort's going to get what's coming to him. The Good Book says God don't love ugly."

"Ms. Bea, you're right. And I hope I'm around to witness when it happens." Maggie laughed.

Bea shook her head. "Me too."

Niles walked in the barn with a lasso in his hand and the rest of the rope draped over his forearm. "How's Cocoa doing?" he asked, hanging the rope on a hook beside one of the stalls.

Bea's somber expression revealed things weren't too great. "I can't talk about it right now but Maggie can fill you in," she said, and brushed past Niles on her way out the barn. Seeing Niles made Bea realize how vulnerable she's been feeling the past few days.

He stood there dumbfounded. "What's going on, Maggie? I thought... Did I say something wrong?"

Maggie placed her hands on her hips. "The truth is: we may lose Cocoa when she foals. The pain may be too much along with her injury, and if the baby is not in the right position things could..."

"What? You're kidding, right?"Niles could hardly fathom what he was hearing.

"Oh, Niles. I wish I was. But I made a promise to Bea that I'll give Cocoa the absolute best care I can."

She sighed and looked away. "Do you believe in miracles, Niles?"

Niles nodded. "You bet I do."

"Then pray hard. They need all the prayers they can get. Cocoa's weak right now, and it'll take a miracle for her and the little one to pull through this unharmed. And I'm limited with what I can do here without proper equipment."

Niles stood with his arms folded as Maggie grabbed her bag and walked out to the car. *Dear God, Bea can't afford to lose anything else because it would kill her. Please help them make it through this ordeal.* Niles leaned against the gate for a few minutes, observing Cocoa. It broke his heart at the thought Bea may lose her. Over the years, he'd witnessed Bea deal with more pain than any woman should ever have to endure, and he'd made a decision to stay on at the ranch after the love of his life passed because he knew Bea needed him—someone she could trust and count on to help out with things around there.

Back at the office, Beaufort mulled over the words Maggie had said. He knew he'd always blame her for the death of his son. And as long as he lived he would try to make things difficult for her. Beau was dead and he couldn't bring him back, and because he was feeling guilty and miserable, his goal was to make Maggie's life miserable. No matter the cost and who he hurt along the way. He knew Beau had developed an addiction to drugs, but he never attempted to do anything about it. His refusal to acknowledge Beau had a problem had cost him his life. And no matter how much Beaufort wanted to change the outcome, he couldn't.

EIGHT

Since Beaufort's visit, Maggie hadn't been able to get Beau off her mind. They'd met at a horse show and he'd caught her eye. He knew a lot about horses, and Maggie had never met anyone as passionate about them before. They hit it off right away and soon became an item. He respected the type of work she did, and had often gone out with her on a call during the middle of the night, or on weekends when he was off work. He'd worked as an EMT for ten years and loved his job. Throughout his career he'd saved many lives, but couldn't save his own. Beau and Maggie had a few months together before he began using drugs and acting out of sorts. One night after Maggie came in from a midnight call, Beau was waiting for her, punched her in the face, and accused her of cheating with an ex boyfriend. Over the next several months, Beau became more and more jealous and insecure, and when Maggie had had enough, she ended the relationship. A couple months later, Beau was found dead lying on his kitchen floor. His dad, Beaufort, had since had a hard time comprehending the death was from an actual drug overdose. After hearing the news, Maggie doubted if it had been accidental. Her thoughts leaned more toward suicide. But only Beau and God know the truth of what happened that night. However, Beaufort won't allow her to forget and throws a guilt trip on her every chance he gets.

Maggie wiped sweat off her brow as her heart raced, causing a thumping sound in both ears. She took deep breaths and exhaled to calm her nerves. "I've got to get this off my mind. It wasn't my fault, and I'm tired of Beaufort making me think it was," she said. "I'm tired of playing his mind games." The muscles in her neck were now tense, her skin achy to the touch, and she realized she also felt a little feverish. Right now, all she needed was to get sick with so much already going on.

Before Maggie lost her license, she'd managed to save enough money to tie her over a few years. After the nest egg was gone, she had no idea what she'd do next. Not a place she wanted to be, but she had no other choice. Without a license, she couldn't practice anywhere else either. If she hired a good attorney she could try to fight what Beaufort did to her, but spending thousands of dollars was not an option right now, making things even more complicated nowadays.

After taking some medicine Maggie decided to take a nap, hoping she'd feel better later on. After she closed her eyes there was a knock on the door. When she answered, it was Niles. Surprised she asked, "What brings you over?"

"Hello Maggie. I was hoping we could talk about Bea and Cocoa in private. Can I come in for a few minutes?" he asked, removing his hat.

Maggie stepped back for Niles to step inside. "Of course you can. Have a seat," she said, motioning toward the sofa.

"I'm sorry to drop by unannounced, but I'm real worried about my two favorite ladies."

"I understand," Maggie said, witnessing deep concern and compassion in Niles' eyes.

"Is there anything else we can do to save Cocoa and the baby?" He laid his hat over his knee. "If Bea loses her, she'll be devastated. I don't know if she can handle it. She's loss so much already."

Maggie sat across from him. "I'm doing everything I can, Niles. Honest, I am. Now it's in the Good Lord's hands. I know Bea is attached to Cocoa, but this is a risky situation, especially when she foals then delivers the colt or filly."

Niles hung his head. "Well, whatever happens good or bad, I'll stand beside Bea. She's been good to me since Mary died, and I don't know what I'd do without her. You know they were best friends for years. We all were."

Maggie nodded. "I understand. And I'm truly sorry I can't do anything more. If Beaufort was not such a..."

"Oh, yes, he enjoys trying to make your life miserable. He's blamed everyone for Beau's death but himself. I found out they had a heated argument the night before Beau died about something. I assume the drugs. Afterwards, he found Beau dead the next morning."

"Hmm. I find those facts interesting." Maggie rubbed her chin, appearing to be in deep thought over something.

Niles shook his head. "Really? How so?"

"Beau visited me the day before he died around six o'clock. I was trying to get the horses fed after I had finished cleaning out the stalls. He walked in and stood there staring, watching me. His pupils were dilated, eyes cold as ice. He didn't say a word though. It made me feel uncomfortable, but then it wasn't all that unusual for him at times. I guess it was the last time he saw me before he died. Maybe he came to say goodbye and couldn't find the right words. I've wondered about that visit a lot since then."

"Do you think Beau was high on something or depressed during that visit?"

"Maybe, I know he was taking pain meds for a problem with his shoulder. When we were together there weren't many nights he didn't have a few drinks. You know mixing pain meds and alcohol can be lethal. Every pharmaceutical leaflet warns against it."

"Do you think there could've been more going on with him and Beaufort than we knew about? Did they seem to argue often?"

Maggie thought a moment and bit her bottom lip. "Meaning?"

Niles slid to the edge of the sofa. "Seems to me Beaufort was always controlling and demanding of him. He had to keep his dad happy all the time."

Maggie sort of laughed. "Of course, he was. Beau always wanted to please him—even by marrying me."

"So, he did propose?"

Maggie stood and turned away. "Yes. And I said no the first time."

"I assume he didn't handle rejection well?"

"No, he didn't. Afterwards, he lied to Beaufort by saying we were engaged. Then he told me not to say anything about the fact we weren't getting married."

"That's crazy. Nothing makes sense."

Maggie spun around and paused. "Hey, I thought you stopped by to talk about Bea and Cocoa? Beau is dead, we can't bring him back. And I'd really like to one day forget I ever knew him."

"Of course, I'm sorry. I didn't mean to drag on about such things." He grabbed his hat and stood.

"It's okay. Thanks for stopping by," she said, walking with Niles to the door.

He looked back on the way out. "Have a good afternoon."

"You do the same, Niles. And keep the prayers coming."

"You know I will."

Niles left and Maggie leaned back against the door. *Sometimes, God, I feel so helpless.* A tear rolled onto her cheek. It had been a bad day all around, and she thought of getting into bed now. Maybe then she'd feel much better in the morning, and be able to see things in a new light.

When Niles returned, he went over to the barn to check on Cocoa. She was sleeping and he realized she was in pain by her labored breathing. It broke his heart to witness such a sight, and he feared they may lose her. He removed his hat, kneeled by her stall and prayed. With a lump in his throat he said, "God, I know I don't talk with you everyday like I should, and Lord knows I don't deserve any favors, but Bea does. She's a good woman, and she can't lose Cocoa. You see, well, she's been hurt a lot before. Please God, work a miracle here in this barn like when your Son, Jesus, was born. Make this place special too. Let your light flow in. I trust you, Lord. Thank you, in Jesus' name. Amen."

A few seconds later, Niles heard someone clapping. "Bravo. What a beautiful prayer indeed," Kyle said, leaning a shovel against the wall.

Stunned and feeling a little embarrassed, Niles asked, "How long have you been around here?"

Kyle grinned. "Long enough. The prayer was right on point and I know God heard you. Ms. Bea is blessed to have a man like you in her life."

Niles blushed. "Oh, I just do what any man would do in my shoes. Bea is a special lady and Cocoa is a special horse."

"I know you do your best," Kyle said, wiping sweat off his face with a handkerchief.

Niles stood and brushed hay off his pants. "Well, I guess I better head over to the main house now."

"Yeah, she looks for you at suppertime. I've still got to finish cleaning out one last stall." Kyle put on a pair of gloves and reached for the shovel.

"Okay. And Kyle..."

"Yeah?"

"Please keep what you witnessed in here between us. I don't want Bea to worry about things."

"Sure. No problem. You have my word."

Niles left, and walked in about the time Bea set a pan of biscuits and some sawmill gravy on the table. "There you are. You disappeared earlier. I reckon the aroma of supper must've sent you in."

Niles laughed. "Always, Bea. You know I can't stay away from your cooking. You're the best." He washed his hands at the sink and reached for a paper towel.

Bea grinned and set a bowl of mashed potatoes beside the biscuits. "Thanks for the boost of confidence. It helps when you cook as much as I do."

"This looks mighty good," Niles said, sitting at the table anxious to dig in.

Bea sat next to Niles and Abby joined them a few minutes later.

"Are you becoming more familiar with things around here?" Niles asked Abby.

Abby sighed. "I think so. Ranch life is really not my cup of tea, but it'll do until I go back home."

Niles took a bite of potatoes and grew quiet, as he seemed to stare into space. Bea could sense something more was weighing on his mind.

"More potatoes?" she asked, holding the bowl in her hand.

Niles rolled his eyes toward her. "No, thank you. I believe I've had enough already." He patted his belly.

Surprised, Bea set the bowl between their plates. "Okay," she said, wondering if he was feeling bad.

Abby ate in a hurry, ready to shower, and get the smell of the animals and feed off her.

Niles had a lot on his mind and excused himself right after supper. There'd been silence between him and Bea until after they'd finished eating. And she wondered what may be going on she wasn't aware of. Niles had always been talkative during meals, even if he only talked about training the horses. Then she thought of Cocoa and wondered if the incident had Niles feeling as stirred on the inside as she'd been. After all, he'd also spent a lot of time with Cocoa from the beginning.

After supper, Bea walked to the study and grabbed her Bible off a bookshelf. When she had a lot on her mind, reading God's Word always gave her peace when nothing else could. She opened it and began reading from the book of Job, one of her favorite passages of scripture. A few minutes later, she closed her eyes and prayed about things regarding Cocoa, and for whatever was weighing heavy on Niles. Some days it was hard being a Christian because she didn't have all the answers, but with faith she knew the one who did—God.

Later on, while Kyle was playing his guitar, he thought of the simple heartfelt prayer Niles had prayed in the barn. He knew how much Bea meant to Niles, and hoped one day he'd find a young woman just as special to share his life adventures with.

NINE

Lying in bed, Abby recalled times she'd been arrested for shoplifting. It reeled like a movie in her mind, like something she had an addiction to.

"Come on, Abby. You're taking too long. We have to get out of here."

"I'm coming, Darcy. Give me a minute. On the way out the door a man yelled, "Freeze! I'm calling the police," he said with phone in hand.

Abby and Darcy stopped in their tracks. "I told you to hurry," Darcy said. "Now look at us. We got caught." She sighed, perching her hands on her hips. "I knew I should've done this alone."

"Come in here and sit," the store owner said. "The cops will be here any minute. Now give me the scarves you stuffed under your shirts."

Reluctant, the girls handed him the scarves.

"It's a good thing I had surveillance cameras installed, or I'd be robbed blind by you bunch of delinquent kids around here."

Soon, two police officers walked in with their guns already drawn.

Afraid, Darcy remained quiet, realizing they would be calling her grandmother, Leona, again. And she hoped her uncle James would be willing to pull some strings and bail her out once more.

"What in the world are you doing in here, Abby?" an officer said.

"Hey Buck," Abby said and hung her head.

He placed his gun in the holster and saw the scarves in the store owner's hand. "This ain't good. I had hoped you girls both learned your lesson last time."

Abby didn't make eye contact, feeling mad and embarrassed. "I'm sorry, Buck." She shrugged. "I guess I enjoy the adrenaline rush of all this."

"Well, *the rush* is going to get you handcuffed and transported over to the police station. Now turn around and place your hands behind your back." He read Abby her rights and clicked the cuffs around her wrists.

Walking out, he said, "I don't know if you can get out of this another time."

"I feel like a criminal," Abby said, trying to wiggle her wrists side to side.

"Well, shoplifting is a crime punishable in all fifty states." Buck was angry, and hated to call Jewel again. He knew it was hard enough trying to raise a kid alone as a single mom.

Another officer followed behind with Darcy in cuffs as well. She remained silent without nary explanation, or one ounce of reasoning for what they'd done.

"What were you two thinking?" Buck asked as they were escorted to the squad car. "You could face a heavy fine and serve jail time over this."

"I want my attorney present," Darcy blurted. "I know if I say anything you can and will use it against me."

By then, Buck had put the car in reverse, and glanced back at them. "We're not here to hurt you, nor are we out to get you. But the law is the law! You have to abide by it, no matter the prestigious position of your uncle, Darcy."

Darcy dropped a pouty lip, figuring she was in deep trouble this time. Her uncle could only do so much. She rolled her eyes toward Abby. "I'm sorry I got you into this," she said. "I just wanted to have some fun. Do something risky and daring, get our adrenaline flowing."

Buck chimed in. "Well, you should've bought a lottery ticket or something. At least it wouldn't put you in jail or juvenile hall."

"It'll be okay, Darcy. You didn't make me do anything. I came with you of my own free will. I thought it would be fun too, but I had no idea you were about to shoplift again. I still don't understand why you want to because you have money. You're not poor like me," Abby said.

Darcy frowned.

The other officer looked at Buck and shook his head. "Kids these days... They think they can do anything and get away with it. Things sure have changed since I was a kid."

"Yeah, I think we need stiffer laws when it comes to some of this. You never used to hear about this mess happening as often," Buck said.

When they arrived at the station, the girls were each placed in separate holding rooms while their guardians were informed of their behavior.

Buck stood beside the square window and watched Darcy wringing her hands. She was a nervous wreck, even though she'd tried to act cool in front of him. Officer Carter stepped next to Buck. "I'm done here for the night. You think you can handle things until morning?" His voice sounded a bit strained as Abby tried to eavesdrop through the open door.

Buck nodded. "Yep, I've got this. Have you already notified Darcy's grandmother about the episode?"

"Yeah, she sounded upset, but agreed to be here soon."

"Okay. That's good. Have a good night, buddy. Feel better and get some rest." Buck lightly punched him on the arm.

He coughed and reached for a hankie out his shirt pocket. "You too. Try not to let these kids drive you crazy."

Buck gestured with his hand, "Later Carter. Get on out of here."

"Later." He grabbed his hat and jacket and left.

Minutes later, Darcy's grandmother walked in with bail for her release. "I don't know why you want to keep doing this," she said, grabbing Darcy by the arm. "Your uncle is tired of having to get you out of trouble. It makes no sense. Mark my words, one day he's going to leave you in here to rot. Someone needs to teach you a lesson."

Buck heard anger in her voice and felt bad for the old woman, as she signed Darcy's release papers. Afterwards, Buck removed the cuffs. "Go home. I don't want to see you in here again young lady. You understand?"

Darcy refrained from making eye contact and said, "Yes, sir. I understand."

Just as Abby recalled the look on Jewel's face when she arrived at the police station that night she heard a knock on her door, bringing her back to reality. "Come in."

"You seemed to be in a hurry earlier," Bea said. "Are you feeling okay?"

Abby pulled her hair back with a rubber band off her wrist and sat on the side of the bed. "Yeah, I just wanted to shower. The smell of the animals gets to me, and I believe I'm feeling a little homesick."

Bea sat and placed her hand on Abby's knee. "Well, things will get better the longer you're here. Do you care for a snack before bed? I have a few packs of cheese and crackers."

"Nah, I'm okay. Thanks anyway, though."

Bea stood and rested her hands at her sides. "Then I'll be in my room if you need anything."

Abby smiled. "Okay. Thanks, Grandma."

Bea nodded, left the room, and whispered, "Billy, she reminds me so much of you. You've always been stubborn as a bull and she is too." Entering her room, Bea chuckled a little and closed the door to keep the room cool.

Feeling restless, Kyle decided to check on the horses. He was upset about Cocoa, and knowing it was his fault she got hurt seemed to amplify his guilt. He'd had no way of knowing a rattler would spook her where she'd buck him off, resulting in a hard fall to the ground. After he made sure all the gates were latched he sat and leaned against Cocoa's gate. He knew he couldn't do anything to save her or the colt or filly, but being there seemed to help him feel a little better, ease his guilt. He could hear every labored breath, and before long he drifted off with his head against the gate. He'd never dealt with anything like this before, but knew there was something extra special about Cocoa. In fact, he'd suffice to say she'd make a great race horse. She was faster than most Thoroughbred horses he'd ever ridden, and she followed orders well. She tended to have a gentle spirit most of the time but could buck you off if need be.

Since Kyle was a young boy, it seemed he'd been born with the ability to identify to a horses' language, like it was in his DNA. He had used his gift more and more over the past couple years, and had earned money to travel while pursuing his dream of becoming a musician. He'd played in several states with some of the lesser known musicians, and had also helped to train a few of their horses as well.

The next morning, Bea walked in the barn to check on Cocoa and found Kyle sound asleep beside the gate. She smiled, realizing she's not the only one who cares about her survival.

Kyle heard her footsteps and opened his eyes. Getting his bearings he said, "Morning Ms. Bea. I guess I must've dozed off late last night."

Bea smiled. "Yeah, I guess so," she said. She reached out a hand to help Kyle to his feet.

He grabbed her hand and stood. "Thanks. My back does feel a bit stiff the morning."

"Oh, I can imagine. How do you think Cocoa is doing?"

Kyle turned, facing the stall. "Hey. Look," he said, voice now magnified with excitement. "Cocoa's eyes are open."

Bea walked over a little closer. "Yeah, you're right, and those brown eyes sure are a beautiful sight." Amazed, she raised a hand to her mouth. Then reached for Kyle's hand and squeezed it in hers. "She might make it through this ordeal after all. God may have just given us our miracle."

"Maybe you should call Maggie and share the good news," Kyle said, grinning.

Releasing his hand, she said, "I think I will." Then she darted back toward the house.

When she arrived, Abby was sitting at the kitchen table playing with her cell phone. "Is everything all right?" Bea asked.

Abby nodded. "I think so. I've been trying to get in touch with my friend, Darcy, but she's not answering her phone."

Bea couldn't contain her excitement any longer and her eyes grew wide. "Guess what?"

Abby shrugged. "I don't know. What?"

"Cocoa has opened her eyes."

Abby grinned. "Oh, that's great, Grandma. Are you going to call Maggie?"

"You bet. She'll be so relieved to know Cocoa is alert now."

"Wait a minute. Didn't Maggie have her kind of out of it, to keep her from moving around too much?"

"Yeah, but Cocoa is a tough horse. It's hard to explain. I only know I saw something in her eyes. It was like she showed me she had the will to live."

"I'm happy for you, Grandma. I know Cocoa means the absolute world to you."

Bea paused, locking eyes with Abby. "Yes, she sure does. I've had a connection with her from the beginning, something I've never had with any other horse I've owned. She's been special since the day I first bought her."

Abby smiled, realizing what a big heart her grand-mother had. It made her wonder even more why Bea and Jewel had never gotten along. The ranch would've never been the place Abby chose to spend her summer, but being punished hadn't been too bad so far. It gave her a chance to get to know her grandmother, and she was beginning to love Niles more every day. Being away from Darcy and Jewel was making Abby think about a lot of things these days—like how she wanted a real chance at a good future.

TEN

M aggie was in the kitchen folding laundry when the phone rang. "Hello."

"It's Bea. Cocoa is awake, even made eye contact with me. It was the most beautiful thing to see those colossal brown eyes." Bea was talking fast and couldn't contain her excitement, even still a little short-winded from darting over to the house.

"Wow, I'm elated to hear this, but she's not out of the woods yet. There's a lot more healing that needs to take place. It could take weeks to get past the injury."

"Oh, I know. But I believe a prayer has been answered, Maggie." Bea was grinning from ear to ear. Maggie could hear the rush of excitement in her voice.

"I hope she'll continue to show improvement every day. I'll stop by later to check on her, and I'll bring my fetal Doppler. Maybe we can tell if she's having a colt or a filly. But I'll warn you ahead of time though; she may not be far enough along yet."

"Thank you, Maggie. I'm looking forward to it. At this point, I don't care as long as they're both healthy and Cocoa is doing much better before she foals."

Maggie smiled, feeling a little excited herself. "I know what you mean, Bea. That's what we're hoping and praying for. Right now that stall is Cocoa's *haven of hope*."

"Yes, it is. I'll see you this afternoon."

"Okay, Bea. Bye." Maggie hurried to put the laundry in its proper place, and finished with a few things at home before heading over to the Bea's.

Bea decided to walk back out to check on Cocoa again. When standing at the gate, she realized Cocoa appeared to be breathing a lot easier, which meant her pain had lessened some. It gave Bea hope she'd pull through the whole ordeal. She stood there, watching her sleep. *It's going to be okay, I promise. You're a strong girl and I know God is on your side.*

Niles was standing on the front porch, waiting for Bea's return when she headed out toward the house. "How's she doing?" he asked, walking over to meet her.

Bea stopped near the porch and looked at him. "I believe she's going to make it through this."

Niles smiled. Feeling relieved things had begun to improve. "Those words are like sweet music to my ears," he said, as Bea brushed by him to go inside.

Bea grinned. "You're so right," she said. "Now it's one day at a time. Maggie's coming over later to see if she can tell if Cocoa's having a colt or a filly."

"Which do you prefer?" Niles asked.

Bea grabbed a couple coffee mugs and fixed them a hot coffee. "I don't have a preference. All I want is for Cocoa to get well and have a safe delivery. I know the Good Lord is on her side." She handed him the mug.

He slurped a sip and said, "Yes, ma'am, indeed." Niles set his mug on the table and slid his boots off. "I've been working with that new Thoroughbred for hours. She's a stubborn one, but I'm not going to let her wear me out. I will get a saddle on her soon." He stretched his legs and reached over to rub his aching feet.

Bea grinned. "Maybe you need to take a break. Looks like it's time for some new boots too."

Niles sighed and nodded. "Yep, you're right as usual," he said, taking another sip of coffee. "I can always tell when my heels start hurting."

Abby awoke later than usual and wondered if something was wrong. The house was quiet with only the aroma of coffee coming from the kitchen. She threw the covers back and got dressed. All the while, she worried something might've happened with Cocoa last night, but when she walked in the kitchen Niles and Bea were sitting at the table chatting. "Is everything all right, Grandma?"

Bea glanced over at her, brow furrowed. "Yeah, everything is fine. Why do you ask, child?"

Abby shrugged. "Well, you didn't wake me this morning and the house is awful quiet. I usually hear some of the guys talking when they come in for breakfast."

Bea grinned. "Yeah, I know. I decided to skip cooking breakfast for a change, so I spent some time over at the barn. I gave the men some sausage and egg biscuits from the freezer earlier."

"How is Cocoa doing?" Abby asked. "Is she going to be okay now that's she pregnant?"

"I believe so. Maggie will be here later on with the Doppler to see if she can tell if she's having a colt or a filly," Bea said.

Niles finished off the last drop of coffee. "I've got to get back to work. I have a lot to accomplish today, and time seems to be flying by," he said, glancing at his pocket watch before slipping his boots on.

"You need to start working at a slower pace, Niles. We aren't as young as we used to be," Bea said.

He stood, gave her a grin, and headed toward the back door. "I'll keep that in mind," he replied. "You ladies have a good day." He tipped his hat and closed the door behind him.

"You too, Niles," they both said.

"What's on the agenda for today?" Abby asked. Sitting and resting her arms on the table.

"I have some vegetable soup cooking in the crock pot, and I'm going to work on a patchwork quilt I started last winter."

"So, you like to sew?" Abby's eyes grew wide.

"Yeah, I do when I have the time. My friend, Mary, used to quilt with me a lot. We made quite a few quilts over the years."

Abby nodded. "Do you still get together to sew sometime?"

Bea frowned. "No. I'm afraid not. She passed away from a rare form of cancer, but I miss her and think of her often. We were friends for a long time." Her eyes welled.

Abby placed her hand on Bea's arm. "I'm sorry, Grandma. I can see you two were close. I didn't mean to upset you."

"We sure were. Had a lot of good times together. In fact, Mary was married to Niles. When William Jake was alive we used to do a lot of things together."

Out of the blue Abby asked, "Why does Kyle sleep in the barn?"

Bea pursed her lips. "You don't worry about Kyle.

He's nothing but trouble when it comes to the ladies." She slid the chair back and rinsed out the dirty coffee mugs at the sink.

Hmm. I wonder what his story is, Abby thought. But she said nary word more about it.

"Have you talked with your mom lately?"

Abby leaned against the counter. "Yeah, she called not too long ago. We only talked for a couple minutes. She seems to be doing okay, but still working a lot."

"Do you think you need to give her a call with an update on everything here?"

"I don't know. Somehow we tend to argue when we talk longer than a few minutes. I think she's sick of me being around, or she wouldn't have sent me here to get rid of me for the summer."

Bea dried her hands, squared her shoulders back, and turned to face Abby eye to eye. "She sent you here because you kept getting into trouble and she didn't know what else to do with you. She told me about the shoplifting and how you kept sneaking out at night. Now you've been arrested and have a police record for life. For a girl about to turn fourteen that's not a good thing, and I'm certain it is nothing to brag about either."

"Gee. You sound like mom riding my back all the time. That broken record has already been played to death in my life."

"Well, you're here with me now, and things will begin to change for the better. I won't stand for any bad behavior, and people taking things they haven't worked for. It just ain't right. Period."

Abby frowned. "Well, I guess I better go feed the hogs and start cleaning some of the horse stalls, so I can earn my keep around here."

"Yes. Go ahead and get started. The day is already half over. Before we know it, it'll be dusk out."

Abby slipped her feet into a pair rubber boots and went out the back door. Inside, she was angry with Bea for being so rough on her. It made her feel like no one understood her pain, or the need for the attention she craved.

Oh Billy, Abby sure could've used a father in her life. Too bad you and Jewel couldn't get along and stay together when she was younger. Bea grabbed her sewing kit and the patchwork quilt to settle in for a time of sewing. Seldom had she taken a break from cooking three meals a day. Everything going on with Cocoa had her feeling out of sorts, and sewing was an easy way to get her mind off her troubles.

Around three o'clock, Maggie stopped by to check on Cocoa and gave her some meds to relax her, then prepared an area for the Doppler. "Okay. Let's see if we can tell what the sex is," Maggie said. Bea stood frozen, watching as Maggie ran the Doppler over the baby bump. A funny look covered her face when she realized Cocoa was much further along than she'd previously thought. "Oh my," she said, while viewing the placenta.

"What is it?" Bea asked. "Is everything okay?"

Maggie nodded as she moved the Doppler around and listened to the heartbeat. "Look at this," she said, stopping the Doppler for a brief moment.

Bea walked closer and looked at the photo on the small screen. "Hmm. How far along is she?"

"The average time is usually 335 to 342 days. A solid eleven months. But I believe she's about two or more months further along than I suspected."

"Meaning?"

"She could have her filly by the beginning of fall or a little earlier."

"So, it's a girl?" Bea clasped her hands together with excited anticipation.

Maggie nodded. "Yeah, looks like a healthy one too. I'm happy to see that everything looks the way it should."

"Oh, I'm so glad to hear it. Cocoa is a fighter, such a strong girl." It was hard for Bea to put a lid on her excitement.

"Now all we have to worry about is a possible preterm delivery."

"Do you think her leg will be healed by the time of the birth?"

Maggie sighed. "I sure hope so. If not I might have to do a C-section. It would put them both at a greater risk though. If that happens, there's a slim chance she or the filly could possibly die, and there's a risk of infection. These are not the best of conditions to have to perform surgery in."

Bea raised her hand to her mouth. "Oh, I pray not," she said. "The Good Lord has brought her this far, now I pray she'll make it through the birth and they'll both be healthy and strong."

Maggie then stood a few feet away to assess Cocoa's breathing. "Her breaths are more controlled now, so I believe she is on the mend. It also helps when an animal knows it is adored. They can sense that love connection with their owner."

"Can I touch her?" Bea asked.

"Of course. But be gentle. You don't want to startle her. These IV meds will wear off in six to eight hours."

Bea entered the stall and gently stroked Cocoa on her mane. It felt good to connect with her, and she knew without a doubt Cocoa recognized her touch. It gave Bea a sense of peace, like things were going to work out the way they were supposed to. "Hang in there, my girl. I know in my heart you and your filly will pull through this," she said. "I can't allow myself to believe anything else."

Cocoa cracked her eyes open for a few seconds, like she understood what Bea had said.

Maggie's eyes welled as she witnessed the love and special bond between them. And with all her heart she hoped Bea was right—everything would work out and they'd both survive the birth.

ELEVEN

After Abby had finished with chores, she grabbed a pen and paper to start a diary of her adventure. She'd never been far away from home, but she'd been thinking of majoring in journalism when she went to college in a few years. She'd watched Jewel work hard as a single mom to provide for them, not the kind of life she wanted for herself. Abby loved her mom, but they hadn't agreed on much for months. She figured it may have been one of the reasons she'd been so rebellious, along with the fact she missed having a father around at her age. Someone to fill in the gaps Jewel couldn't.

Before going over to the house, Abby saw Kyle riding in on one of the horses. For a split second, she thought of what Bea had said, but those thoughts vanished as she strode toward the barn. When she walked in Kyle was unsaddling the horse.

"Hi. You must be Abby?"

She nodded. "Yeah, you're right. That's me."

"How are things going since you've been here?"

Abby frowned. "Okay, I guess. But I wouldn't have chosen to spend my entire summer here."

Surprised Kyle said, "Why? I love it here. I come here every summer to help out. It gives me time off the road. Besides, there's no other place like it."

Abby was at a loss for words. "Well, okay," she said. "What else do you do on the road?" Before he could answer they heard footsteps coming closer.

Bea walked in and caught them talking. "Get on back to the house, Abby. You have more work to do this afternoon," she said.

"I was just--"

Bea gave her a stern look, like she meant business, so she decided to listen.

"Later Kyle."

Kyle nodded and said nothing more.

"Stay away from her, Kyle. She's Billy's daughter."

Kyle hung the saddle in its rightful place and said, "Okay, Ms. Bea. I didn't do anything wrong. I promise. She just came in here after I brought Hershey in a few minutes ago."

"I know. And you won't do anything to get involved with her because you'll be leaving before long, and she'll be going home."

Kyle grabbed a dandy brush and began brushing the horse's mane. "Yes ma'am, I understand. She's off limits. I get it, and I assure you there's no need to worry."

"Good! Make sure things stay that way. Abby can be stubborn like her dad, and she's been used to doing things her own way for a long time."

Kyle grew quiet as Bea turned to walk off. Then he said, "Ms. Bea, I'm truly sorry about Cocoa. I mean... I love her as much as you do. I enjoy coming here every summer because these horses are like family to me. We can relate to one another."

Bea glanced back at him and grinned. "I know. Hershey adores you. Cocoa does too. If it hadn't of been for a rattler in the meadow, she wouldn't have bucked you off. I know it wasn't your fault and I don't blame you, Kyle. Thank you for wanting to take such good care of my babies."

"Thank you for understanding. I'd never do anything intentional to hurt any of these horses," he said, brushing Hershey's mane.

"I know or you'd already be gone by now. I do appreciate your honesty, though. It shows me you're a responsible-trustworthy young man."

Kyle nodded, hoping she'd leave things alone and not ask about his family. He didn't like talking about family. So when she decided to walk on off, he felt relieved their conversation had ended on a good note.

When Bea got back to the house Abby was in her room, fuming over how Bea had treated her like a little child. It was bad enough when Jewel did this, but now Bea too. It bothered Abby that no one seemed to realize she was almost fourteen, not a baby anymore.

Figuring she was pouting, Bea decided to give Abby some space. The last thing she wanted was for her to inquire anything more about Kyle. She enjoyed him being around to help out, but there was no way she'd allow Abby to get in trouble while she was there. Bea had promised Jewel she'd look after her, and she intended to make good on her promise.

Later on, Kyle was lying in the hayloft after cleaning out the stalls. It was a nasty job, but he loved doing it, along with working outdoors with the horses. Feeling hot, he switched on the metal ceiling fan above. Even at night it was still warm in the barn until the wee morning hours. He usually slept in boxers and kept a flannel blanket within arm's reach. His heart's desire was to find a place he loved and settle down when the time was right. Placing his hands under his head, he soon drifted off while watching the fan blades turn.

Abby didn't join anyone later for supper. Bea realized she could be a lot like Billy by taking things to heart, so she left her alone to get over it. And if she wasn't in the kitchen for breakfast, then she'd go in to check on her. After washing the supper dishes, Bea decided to work on her quilt an hour or so before bed. During stressful times she enjoyed a quiet place to pray and relax.

Around midnight, Bea folded the quilt in half and checked to make sure all the doors were locked. Gazing out the window, she saw a light on in the barn. *I don't know how Kyle stays awake so long and rises so early. I reckon being a young man must help.* She put her sewing kit away and walked to a room in back of the house. A room she used to spend a lot of time in when William Jake was alive. Draping the quilt across his recliner, she looked around the room, wishing he was there, reading the newspaper like he always did after supper. *No matter how old I live to be, I'll never forget the times we spent here in this room.* Feeling tired and emotional, Bea switched the light off and headed toward the stairs to go to bed.

While Kyle was lying in the hayloft he was awakened by someone making a *psst sound.* Then a couple pieces of hay were tossed toward him followed by another *psst sound.* He opened his eyes and lifted his head to find Abby standing right there in front of him. Feeling embarrassed, he grabbed the blanket and threw it over his boxers. "What are you doing here? Ms. Bea will kill us both if she catches you and me here like this."

Abby grinned. "Well, she doesn't know I'm here. So

don't worry about her. Besides, she's probably in bed sound asleep."

Kyle stood and slipped his pants on. "Oh, you don't know her like I do," he said, nervous as could be.

Abby laughed. "Oh, come on. You act like you're afraid of her. She's a grandma for goodness sake. What can she do to either of us?"

Kyle furrowed his brow. "She can kick us both off the ranch tonight. I've witnessed her do it before with one of the other ranch hands," he said, feeling jittery.

Abby walked over and ran her fingers across his bare chest, outlining the curves of his toned muscles. "Man, you're as buff as they come. I bet you have plenty of girls waiting in line to fall all over you."

Kyle shook his head and grabbed her wrist. "This is not right, Abby. How old are you? Let me guess. Sixteen...? Maybe seventeen...?"

"I can be as old as you want me to be," she said. Abby appeared to be a lot more mature than she actually was, especially in size.

"Tell me. How old are you?" he said, loosening the grip on her wrist.

"I'm almost fourteen, old enough to know when I see a fine looking man in front of me."

"Oh my! You've got to get on out of here. Bea would tar and feather me for this, for you even being here. No matter how innocent this does or doesn't look."

"Oh, come on. Don't you want to have a little fun?" She placed both arms around his neck. "You need to relax. I promise no one will ever know I've been here. I won't tell a soul."

"Abby! You're a child! I'm nineteen. Way too old for you."

She ran her fingers through his hair near the occipital bone. "Don't be such a drag, Kyle. I just want to have a little fun. Do you have any booze, maybe even a joint or two?"

He grabbed her wrist again—except tighter this time and reared his head back. "Look! You've got to go now. And no, I don't have any booze or drugs. I don't drink or do drugs. I haven't in a long time. Not since I was sixteen."

Disgusted, Abby took a few steps back. "Well, you've got a nice looking body, but you sure don't know how to have any fun with a girl."

Kyle drew in a breath and turned his back to her, trying to control his mounting frustration. "Look! You don't know anything about me. And it's probably best if you don't. Now get on out of here before you get us both into trouble. You're just an unruly kid who needs to be disciplined."

"I'm not a kid!" she shouted, and then started unbuttoning her blouse, to reveal her breast cleavage.

Kyle tilted his head and tried to look away, finding it hard to believe this was happening. "Don't make me tote you over to the house. Now, please button your blouse and get out of here."

Abby slung her hair back and felt appalled by Kyle's reaction to her mature body. Most guys had said her eyes and breasts were her best features. She said nothing more and stepped off the ladder, feeling humiliated by the way Kyle had acted toward her.

After his nerves calmed a bit, Kyle put the ceiling fan on low and tried to get some sleep. He had taken notice of her cleavage, the dimension of her bosom, the shape and curves of her body. Indeed, she was a beautiful young woman. But he was several years older than Abby. And somehow he knew getting involved with her, even for the summer, would be more than dangerous, if not lethal. It would put him at definite risk of losing his job at the ranch, and he wasn't willing to risk it.

Restless, Bea thought she heard someone moving around upstairs. She switched on the lamp, reached for her robe and checked on Abby, who appeared to be asleep in her bed, and so she sloughed it off as Abby making a quick trip to the bathroom. Little did she know, Abby had snuck out the window and gone over to the barn, to later climb the porch post to come back inside. Abby lay there under the covers with her clothes and shoes still on. She'd heard Bea open her bedroom door and had jumped into bed, pretending to be asleep.

Bea stood there looking at her for a few moments before closing the door. Then she left.

Whew! That was close. I thought she was already asleep this time of night. I've got to be more careful next time. Abby kicked her shoes off by the bed and remained still because she didn't want Bea coming back in there again.

Before going back to bed Bea gazed out the window toward the barn. The light was out, but something felt a little off to her. And she hoped her gut instincts were not right about it. Lying in bed, she wondered what Abby had been doing since she'd caught her in the barn earlier. She'd already warned Kyle to stay away from her, and if they were to get together, it would be bad for everyone involved. Plus Jewel would never forgive her. *Dear Lord. I pray I'm not right about this.* Figuring she was being silly and probably worrying about nothing, Bea switched off the lamp and tried to get some sleep.

TWELVE

Jewel felt like Abby had been gone for months already. She debated about giving her a call, but whether she wanted to admit it or not, she knew Abby was in good hands. Beatrice Bigelow was a good woman. That much she was sure of. Just because things hadn't worked out with her and Billy wasn't any reason to have harsh feelings toward Billy's mom. As Jewel was getting ready for work there was a knock on the door. She answered, surprised to find a certain man standing there. "Buck... What brings you over?"

"I was on my way to work and thought of Abby and wondered how she was doing."

"Oh, that was thoughtful of you. The last time I talked with her, she seemed to be doing okay." Jewel paused. "I miss her a lot though."

"I know. Does she like being at the ranch with her grandma?"

"I guess so. We've only chatted for a few minutes so far." She shrugged. "I figured some space would be good for us both."

Buck was staring at her. Lost in his thoughts, he didn't respond right away.

"Buck?"

"Yeah?"

She laughed. "Do I have something in my teeth or on my face?"

He realized he'd zoned out on her. "Umm. No, you look beautiful as always. Pink is your color."

Jewel glanced down at her shirt. "Thanks."

"Well, I guess I better get on over to the office. It's been crazy around there this week. And graveyard shift is even worse this time of year."

Jewel held the door open. "Thanks for stopping by. By the way, how are things going with Darcy?"

He stopped. "Things don't look good for her right now. Her Uncle James is fed up with her behavior and it's possible she'll be sent to juvenile hall soon."

"I'm sorry to hear it. I had hoped something would open her eyes before it came to that."

"Me too." He frowned and turned to walk away.

"Buck?"

"Yeah?"

"Thanks for everything you've done to help Abby. I know you didn't have to stick your neck out, but you did. I also realize you could've been fired for it."

"Oh, shucks. It's nothing." He blushed. "I would've done the same thing for any thirteen year old girl."

"But we both know Abby is not just anyone. She's a Bigelow." Jewel squared her shoulders back.

Buck nodded as he stepped on the ground. "Have a good night," he said.

"You too," Jewel replied.

After Buck left, Jewel thought about the real reason for his visit. He could've called to ask about Abby, and it made her wonder why he was so concerned. *I hope he doesn't think I owe him anything because he helped Abby.* She thought for a minute. *Nah, he's not really my type, although he is a good-noble man. That's more than I can say about Billy.* Jewel sighed and finished getting ready for work.

On the way out Jewel reminisced of when she and Billy first met and times were good. She hadn't been able to buy a two-hundred dollar dress since their divorce. She'd managed to take care of Abby with minimal help from Billy. During the divorce hearing, he had obtained favor with the woman judge, and was not made to pay alimony. It made her wonder if he'd paid her off, but she had no way of proving it. There were so many things Jewel had her doubts about. Looking back, she now saw things she'd been too cloudy-headed to see before. After all, there'd been a time when she thought Billy could do no wrong, not even when a friend told her Billy was cheating with Lola. At first Jewel didn't want to believe it, but late nights away from home till one and two in the morning should've been all she needed to raise a red flag. She imagined she was just young and in love with a man who'd swept her off her feet, offering her the type of lifestyle she could only dream of. Oftentimes, Jewel wondered where they'd be today if Billy hadn't left. Maybe Abby would have an adequate college fund set aside, whenever she needed it. And who knows? Maybe they would've had another child together.

At work, Jewel's mind kept wandering to the past and back to where she is today in life. There'd been a lot of hard times for her and Abby, but she had managed to survive—not something she wanted Abby to face in life. No. Abby deserved more, more than Jewel could ever afford to give her. The thought made her sad, and often she felt like a failure. Clearing away dirty dishes, she gazed out the window, wondering if this was all her life would ever be. She'd be waitressing and pouring grumpy old men refills of coffee for a long time to earn tips to buy gas for her car. The thought of it made her depressed. And she hoped with every ounce of her being, Abby would not have to walk the same path she had. No. There had to be something better for her.

Just after midnight, Bea had put on her robe and slippers and decided to grab a breath of fresh air. She carried a cup of hot Chamomile tea in hand. As she sat in a rocking chair on the front porch, Niles was leaning against the wooden fence where Cocoa trotted around. She sat, realizing Niles loved the horses as much as she did. A few minutes later, he turned around, saw her and walked over to join her. She smiled and motioned for him to come have a seat.

"I suppose you couldn't sleep either," she said, taking a sip of tea.

Niles nodded. "You're right. I guess I must have too much on my mind tonight."

"Hmm. Is it something you care to share with me?"

"It's been another year," he replied, clasping his hands together. "I had hoped it would get easier as time goes by."

Bea reached for his hand, rubbing it with hers. She said nothing, but offered a listening ear as Niles began to talk about his beloved Mary.

"I don't know how I would've gotten through these past few years without you, Bea. I mean..."

"It's been hard on both of us."

"Yeah, I know."

Bea set her cup of tea on a small table between them.

"She was more like a sister to me. You know how close we were. We did everything together." A tear welled in eye. "No one could ever replace her in my heart." She let go of Niles' hand. "And you loss the love of your life. It's not something you can get over in a day or two. Sometimes it takes years for the pain to lessen, if it ever does."

"True." Niles grew quiet.

"You okay?"

Niles' eyes met hers, as he searched for the right words to share his feelings without offending Bea. "I just... Well..." He stuttered around with his words. "I feel so alone, sometimes."

Bea frowned. "I know you do. I miss her also."

"There's nothing like a wife lying beside you at night. I could move my leg over and touch her as she slept. Something simple as that gave me such peace and comfort. But when she got sick, it all changed. The closeness we used to share. I mean, it was like she turned into a different person, someone I didn't know anymore." He lifted his hat and rubbed his forehead, feeling distraught.

Bea's heart ached, listening to him. And she wanted to tell him how he made her feel, but she refrained from doing so. Because the last thing she wanted was to use his vulnerability against him. Knowing Niles like she did, Bea knew he wouldn't appreciate it. They'd shared some close moments before, and it seemed to be happening more often, like they were growing even closer. Last thing she wanted was to push or scare Niles away. No other woman knew him better than her now. His wife was gone, but Bea had promised to always honor her memory, by doing anything she could to help Niles get through such a terrible loss, so she remained quiet, and continued to listen and reached for her cup of tea.

"You're quiet tonight," he said.

She took a sip. "Not really. I'm just finishing my tea before it gets cold, that's all."

"I'm sorry about rambling on so long," he said.

"Oh, it's okay. Sitting out here gives me time to clear my head and enjoy the night air too."

Niles stood and stretched. "Well, I reckon I better try and get some sleep. Goodnight, Bea."

"Goodnight."

Bea watched Niles walk across the yard then went inside and set her cup in the sink. Tea would usually help her relax, but not tonight. It seemed to be having the opposite effect, and listening to Niles talk about Mary had her feeling blue.

THIRTEEN

At daybreak, Maggie loaded some flowers in back of her truck and headed to the cemetery. It wasn't something she did often, but Beaufort's visit had stirred something inside her, and she wondered if Beau would still be alive if she'd married him. Since the news of his death, Maggie had had mixed feelings, and couldn't help wondering if Beau had been ill or depressed. She'd pretty much accepted the fact he'd overdosed on a mixture of pain meds and alcohol. After dating a while, Maggie thought she knew him better than that, but realized he must've been at his lowest point in life to have committed suicide—intentional or not.

Arriving, Maggie shut off the engine and grabbed a small shovel and two flower pots of yellow mums. It felt peaceful out with a gentle breeze blowing. At his gravesite, she got on her knees and dug out a shallow two inch deep hole to set the pots in, then compounded dirt around the bottoms of the pots to keep the wind from blowing them over.

Beaufort had managed to keep Beau's gravesite well maintained. He'd even put in a load of gravel and granite coping to block off the area.

After getting the flowers in place, Maggie brushed off her pants and sat on a wire metal bench beside the tombstone. "I don't understand what happened to you,

Beau. I truly loved you with all my heart, but the mood swings and problems with your temper kept coming between us. It got to the point I couldn't trust you anymore, and without trust, there's not a true relationship as far as I'm concerned." Maggie sat, reminiscing of times she'd spent with Beau, times when they were happy without all the confusion and strife his addiction had caused.

Minutes later, an old jeep downshifted and turned in the entrance gate. It wasn't someone Maggie knew, but she decided to go ahead and leave anyway. They pulled over and parked just as Maggie drove out the exit gate.

Watching her, a man then reached for his phone. "She's gone now. Left in a hurry, soon as I drove in and stopped."

"Good. Keep an eye on her, but don't let her become aware that you're watching. Stay a good distance away."

"Okay."

"I trust you'll do a good job with this."

"Of course. I'll try my best. She should be out of town by the end of the month."

"Good. That's what I want to hear."

"By the way, when do I get compensated for doing this?"

"In due time, try to be patient. We can't rush things like this. If word got out it could ruin my reputation."

"Okay, boss. I understand."

"Later."

Their conversation ended and the guy sat gazing around the graveyard. "She's gone, so I better see if I can locate her whereabouts next." He shifted the noisy jeep into drive and exited the gate.

Back at the house, Maggie couldn't seem to shake her uneasiness. She hated the feeling because it usually meant something was about to happen in life. From past experience, it hadn't been a good thing. And she hoped Beaufort wouldn't pay Bea a surprise visit, trying to cause problems regarding the treatment of Cocoa.

Kyle was working in the barn and kept thinking of how Abby had acted last night. He knew she was from the city and appeared to be a little on the wild side, something Kyle wasn't used to. He'd helped out several small communities in past years doing some summer mission work. It seemed to keep him out of trouble and away from certain tempting things. Abby was a beautiful young lady, but part of the problem was her age, and also the fact she was Bea's granddaughter. He knew Bea simply wouldn't allow it. She'd already asked him to stay away from Abby, but he was a good-looking guy, and he couldn't say what might happen, if she kept coming to see him each night. But he already knew if anything were to happen between them, Bea would see to it he'd never be able to help out at Bigelow Ranch again. He loved being there, and he wasn't sure if he wanted to jeopardize that for a short-term fling with Abby.

Abby was still feeling bruised by Kyle's rejection as she took care of her chores. It seemed her life had been plagued by one rejection after another. First, Billy. Then school boys. Now Kyle. It made her wonder if something was wrong with her. Was she worthy of ever being loved by a man? Soon to be approaching the eve of fourteen, it made it hard for Abby to understand some things. Not to mention the surge of hormones circulating through her body like a cyclone. A tear rolled onto her cheek as she tried to block out what had happened. Being at the ranch hadn't been so bad, but she didn't know what was next. Life wouldn't always consist of feeding hogs and scooping poop out of horse stalls. Soon, school would start back and life would return to the way it's always been, living with a single mom, trying to make ends meet without a supportive father figure around. Most of her friends had homes with loving parents to care for them. At times, Abby felt robbed in many ways. It was hard not to be envious of others. Even though she had some friends at school, it hadn't filled the gap in her life—the feeling something greater was missing—something greater than she'd ever experienced thus far.

After talking with Niles, Bea lay awake a while, finally drifting off during the wee hours of morning. She'd been a good friend to Mary and Niles. When Mary became terminally ill and passed away, Bea tried to push her emotions aside and be strong for Niles' sake. He and Mary had once been inseparable. Some days were still harder than others for Bea because she'd also been widowed when her husband William Jake died suddenly. Since then she'd sworn off love again, and had remained true to him. However, she now had mixed feelings for Niles. They'd been friends for years, just as she and Mary had been friends since high school. In a way Bea felt like she'd betray Mary by loving Niles, even though she'd promised to see after him. But how much longer could she continue to deny what she was feeling? And she was almost certain he felt the same way about her. Bea sighed, trying to clear her mind of such things. There was so much to worry about con-cerning the ranch and Cocoa right now, and she real-ized her pity party would have to take second place for the time being. In her heart, she secretly hoped she and Niles would get around to talking about such things when the time was right, and she looked forward to the day it happened.

Later on, Maggie stopped by the library, searching for anything to help her get her vet's license back. She'd spent years studying, working, and training for the job. Maggie loved animals and they loved her. She'd had a special way with animals since she was a child, and had planned to become a vet since she was ten years old. But Beaufort had control in the town where she lived and usually got his way—even if he had to pay the judge off to have it. For a couple years Maggie accepted the fact Beaufort had won, but not anymore. Treating Cocoa sparked something inside her, rekindled a fire, helping her put things into perspective to discover her true purpose here on earth. Now she was ready to give Beaufort the fight of his life. He was angry because he lost his son, and since then he'd blamed Maggie. Now she was tired of carrying the guilt of what happened. Things needed to change.

After watering her flowers that afternoon, Maggie settled in to do some reading, and became so enthralled with things she forgot to eat, taking one page of notes after another from the stack of books she'd chosen from the library.

Later, she glanced at the clock and realized it was getting late. She'd buried herself in those books, grasp-ing at straws regarding the law and rules and regulations of veterinarians. Feeling tired, she scooted the chair back a little, resting her head on her arm. One afternoon would not be enough time to find the answers she needed. No. She had just scratched the surface.

FOURTEEN

E ven though Bea felt sleep deprived she was dressed and in the kitchen. So many things had been reeling in her mind. Mary's birthday was soon approaching and she planned to fix one of her favorite things, no matter if she wasn't there to enjoy it. And she figured the gesture would be much appreciated by Niles.

Minutes later, Niles walked in and slipped his boots off beside the door. The weather forecast had called for thunderstorms most of the day. He was also feeling tired in body, but didn't complain to Bea. "Do you have a cup or two of hot coffee left?" he asked.

Bea wiped her hands on her apron and reached for a mug. "Sure thing…"

Niles sat, crossed his arms, and rested them on the table.

Bea noticed how quiet he was, like he had a lot weighing on his mind. "How are things going out there this morning?" she asked, setting a mug of coffee in front of him.

"Well, it's hard to get anything bush-hogged right now because of the rain," he said, slurping a sip of coffee.

Bea nodded and stirred the syrup she had melting in a pot on the stove.

Niles leaned back in his chair. "What are you making?" he asked. "It smells sweet, yet oddly familiar."

"I'm working on some peppermint candies like Mary used to make." She walked over to the table with a spoon in her hand. "She has a birthday coming around real soon."

Niles nodded. "Yep, she sure does," he said, slurping another sip of coffee.

"I like to do something in remembrance of her every year." Bea paused. "I'll never forget her as long as I live."

"I think it's a fine thing to do," Niles said. "I know Mary would be well pleased by your loyalty."

About that time, Abby made her way into the kitchen and left her shoes next to Niles' muddy boots. "Something smells good, Grandma. I'm hungry."

"I suppose you are," Bea said, and reached for a box of cereal and grabbed some milk out the fridge.

Abby sat across from Niles. "How's it going?" she said.

Niles finished off the last few swallows of coffee. "As good as it can go today. This rain has put a halt to doing much in the fields. I can't take a chance on bogging my equipment in the lower ends where there's no drainage in that area."

Abby poured some cereal and milk in a bowl and spooned it to her mouth, crunching loud with her mouth half-open.

"Goodness child. Close your mouth when you chew, you're at the table," Bea said.

Abby grinned. "Sorry, I told you I was hungry."

"Well, if you'd have joined us for supper last night you wouldn't be so hungry."

Abby felt her body grow tense, wondering if Bea knew about her sneaking to the barn to see Kyle. Then she stuffed another spoonful of cereal in her mouth and said nary word.

Niles set his empty mug in the sink and slipped his boots back on. "Thanks for the coffee, Bea. It sure did help my achy bones in this dreary weather."

Bea rolled her eyes away from the stove a quick minute. "Oh, you're welcome."

Abby noticed a bit of tension between them and wondered what had happened she didn't know about. At times she wished Niles would go ahead and kiss Bea and get it over with. After she finished eating, she rinsed out her bowl and set it in the sink. Bea remained quiet and kept stirring the ingredients for the candy.

"You feeling okay, Grandma?"

Bea rubbed her lips together and laid the spoon on a napkin beside the pot. "Yeah, why do you ask?"

"No reason. You just seem quieter than usual this morning."

"No worries, child. I'm fine. Got a lot on my mind, that's all."

Abby nodded. "Care to talk about any of it?"

Bea was surprised she had asked, but thought it sweet she was concerned. "Nah, I'm okay. I didn't sleep well last night, and today is so dreary with all this rain. It's all got me feeling a little out of sorts."

"You're right. I could've stayed in bed half the day myself. At least till noon." Abby laughed.

"Well, there's work to be done around here," Bea said, reaching for a canister of granulated sugar.

Abby walked over to the stove and gazed in the pot. "Will you teach me how, Grandma?"

"Absolutely. This is something I make each year to honor the memory of a dear friend who's gone on to be with the Lord," she said, adding a scoop of sugar to the hot peppermint mixture.

Abby smiled. "I see. It looks and smells yummy to me."

Bea grabbed Abby an apron and another few sheets of parchment paper to place the hot candy on. After the sweet mixture was ready, she spooned some from the pot and said, "This is how I've always done it. My dear friend, Mary, taught me how to make it. I miss her a lot."

Abby frowned. "I sort of know how you feel."

Bea furrowed her brow. "You do?"

"Yeah, it's the same way I miss dad not being a part of my life except he is alive."

Bea felt a hard tug at her heart hearing Abby's words. And she wished there was a way she could make Billy understand how much Abby needed him. He'd said his time with Jewel was a mistake and later realized he was on rebound from Lola, the true love of his life. He'd been angry and had ventured into where Jewel worked, and she'd been struggling, seeking a better way of life when they met. For a brief time she filled the gaps in Billy's life, but then everything changed.

After Bea and Abby spooned the candy onto parchment paper, Bea gathered the dirty dishes and ran some soapy dish water.

"I'll get them for you," Abby said. "Thanks for showing me how to do this. Maybe I'll make some for mom when I go back home."

Bea grinned. "It was a pleasure, Abby. I believe one day you'll make a fine cook and baker. You have a gift. I can tell."

Abby laughed. "I don't know about that. But thanks for the confidence you have in me."

As they cleaned the kitchen, Bea couldn't get Abby's words about Billy off her mind. It broke her heart Billy had turned his back on Abby and Jewel. It didn't seem fair for them to have to suffer that way. And the longer Abby was at the ranch Bea discovered even more of herself in her. She'd missed out on a lot with Abby thus far. Those early years of her life were over, but Bea vowed to be a part of Abby's life from now on because they'd already lost enough time. She loved Abby and would do whatever she could to be a part of her life, even if it meant getting along with Jewel Conner.

Maggie awoke and brewed a pot of coffee. Her neck felt stiff where she'd fallen asleep with her head resting on her arm. She'd spent several hours taking notes, praying she'd find a loophole to exploit what Mayor Beaufort had done to ruin her career. And she still had a lot of digging yet to do. Her gut was telling her something was off about Beau's death, so she felt Beaufort must be hiding something.

While Maggie was stirring her coffee a call came in listed as an unknown caller. It seemed odd she'd receive a call like that. Not many folks knew her cell number, just a handful of people she'd given it to. She grabbed the phone and hit mute. If it was regarding something important, they'd leave a voicemail for her to call back.

Yawning, Maggie sipped her coffee and settled in to search through another law book. She knew she needed to hire an attorney, but funds were low right now. The only person who might be able to help was Bea Bigelow. It was a lot to ask, but Maggie had agreed to treat Cocoa, and the money would give her a chance to get even with Mayor Beaufort, by exposing what he was hiding.

Minutes later, there was a knock on Maggie's door. Knowing she looked a hot mess, she debated about even answering it. Hesitant, she ran her fingers through her hair and walked toward the door. A middle-aged man dressed in khaki pants and a red shirt stood in front of her. "Hello. May I help you?"

He squared his shoulders back. "Are you Maggie Davidson, the popular equine vet around this area?"

Taken aback, Maggie thought a few moments before answering. "I used to be, but not anymore. I'm sorry. I can't help you with your horse. Closest vet is now forty miles away."

"What?" The man looked distraught and rubbed his chin. "I was told you were the best at treating equine around these parts. I have a sick Thoroughbred I paid a lot of money for."

Maggie smiled. Being cautious she said, "Well, I don't know who told you such a thing because I haven't been able to practice for a few years now."

"Hmm. I'm sorry to hear this." He shook his head. "You were recommended by an old friend of mine from Houston Texas."

Reaching for the door she said, "Gee, I'm sorry you wasted your time coming here. Now, is there anything else I can help you with?"

He thought for a minute and shifted his feet back and forth in the sand. "Nah, I don't believe so. But thanks, anyway."

Maggie stared at him, wondering what the true purpose of his visit was all about. "By the way, what's your name? I don't think I caught it in your introduction."

"Oh, it doesn't matter. I'm new in this area. And I apologize, I should've never bothered you today."

Amused, Maggie furrowed her brow. "Okay. Well, have a good day," she said, shutting the door with the man still standing there.

Going back to his car, he made a call. "Hey, it's me. She wouldn't take the bait. I tried though."

"Well, keep trying," a man said. "We'll get her out of town one way or another."

"Okay, boss." The man got in his car and left.

As he drove off, Maggie peeked out the kitchen window to see which direction he went. She figured he was lying when he refused to reveal his identity, and she wouldn't be surprised to find out Beaufort sent him to get her to agree to practice without a license. But Maggie was no fool, she knew how to be cautious because Beaufort would stop at nothing to make her life miserable.

FIFTEEN

Kyle got a slow start to his day and still felt terrible over Cocoa being hurt. He showered, dressed, and walked over to her stall. She was sleeping and seemed peaceful, and so he tried not to wake her. There were three more horse stalls close by, but none of the other horses touched his soul quite like Cocoa. She was gentle inside and out. It was like her dark colossal eyes could pierce straight to his soul. She had a way of speaking, even if she couldn't say a word, and he knew she was fighting to get better because of her little one. A tear welled in his eye, watching her lying there so still. He hoped she wasn't in much pain now because Maggie had tried her best to keep her comfortable.

Just then, one of the other horses let Kyle know he wanted some love and attention. He grabbed an apple from the croker sack and walked over to another stall. "What's going on, Hershey? Are you hungry, boy?" Kyle fed Hershey the apple and the crunch echoed throughout the stables. Then he grabbed a pitch fork and sifted some cured hay for him. "There you go. Now I'll only need to shovel out the poop later on." While Kyle was putting the pitch fork away someone touched him on the shoulder. Startled, he turned around. "What are you doing here?" he asked.

"I wanted to offer you an apology for the way I act-ed," Abby said. "I shouldn't have done that."

Kyle raised both eyebrows and smiled. "Okay, apol-ogy accepted." He reached out his hand for a shake.

Abby shook his hand and grinned. "Things are a lot different in the city, Kyle. It's like guys there expect so much more from girls."

He paused. "You mean girls are easy, right?"

Abby lowered her head. "Yeah, you could say they are. Every guy I've dated so far has had certain expecta-tions of me."

"Well, I believe it's worth waiting for the right kind of person to come along."

Abby was surprised to hear him say such a thing. "Well, what kind of girl are you looking for?"

Kyle grinned and gazed off in the distance. "You wouldn't understand if I told you," he replied.

"Hmm. I bet I would. Why don't you give it a try?"

"Does your grandma know you're here in the barn with me?"

"Umm. No, actually, she doesn't."

"Well, you better get going before we both get into trouble. She was adamant about me leaving you alone."

"Why would you get into trouble for talking with me? We aren't doing anything wrong. I enjoy being around you, Kyle. There's just something about you I adore."

The last girl to tell Kyle those sweet words had since hurt him beyond repair. "It's dangerous, Abby. I'm a young man and you're a young lady. We all have wants, needs, and desires." His eyes locked on her low cut blouse, revealing her cleavage. "I would've never guessed you were only thirteen. You're so... I mean..." He was stuttering, trying to find the right words.

"Oh, I get it. I appear to be more mature than I actually am, and you like the way my body looks."

Kyle broke his stare. "Yeah, you could say it's something along those lines."

Abby laughed, walked closer to him, and whispered in his ear. "Well, it's good to know you do find me attractive. I was worried that something was wrong with me."

Kyle felt a lump form in his throat and he gazed into her eyes. "Duh. Of course you're an attractive girl. You'll make some lucky guy happy one day."

Abby just stared back for a few minutes, trying to deal with the surge of hormones rushing through her body right then.

Breaking his gaze he asked, "What?"

"Oh, nothing," she said.

He grinned. "I guess you better go before you get caught out here with me."

Abby turned to leave. "Kyle?"

He stopped and then faced her. "Yeah?"

"Please keep wearing the same cologne you have on. It suits your body chemistry well."

Kyle shook his head and said nothing as Abby left the barn. Inside, he was burning hot and couldn't believe a girl so young could have that kind of effect on him. There was something special about Abby. An innocence beyond her tough facade, but he knew not to tell her because Bea would not allow them to ever get together. Abby was a Bigelow. And he'd never fit the mold of what Bea wanted for Abby.

Back at the house, Bea inquired about Abby's whereabouts earlier. "I took a walk and peeked in on Cocoa for a few minutes. She seemed to be peaceful as she lay there sleeping."

"I see," Bea said. "I'm glad to hear some good news. The poor thing has been through so much already."

"Do you think she'll be able to have the baby without any problems, Grandma?"

Bea sighed. "I sure hope so. I pray she's healed enough by then because I'd hate to lose either of them."

The love Bea had for her horses was clearly evident, and Abby hoped she was right about Cocoa being on the mend. Now only time would tell if things would work out for their good.

"After the candy cools and sets would you like to help me wrap it and put it away?" Bea asked.

"Sure." Abby slipped on an apron and waited to help out, still recalling the conversation she'd had with Kyle. She wanted to inquire more about him, but she was afraid Bea would get suspicious and try to keep her away from him.

They wrapped the candies in pieces of parchment paper, tied ribbons at the ends, and put it in small zippered storage bags. "There. This is the last bag," Bea said. "Thanks for your help, Abby. When you leave to go home you'll have learned a little something from me." She grinned.

Abby paused. "Grandma?"

"Yeah?"

"Would it be okay if I spent every summer here on the ranch with you for the next few years? You know, just till I graduate and go off to college."

Bea grinned. "I think it would be fine, child. I'd love to have you around and I know Niles would too."

They finished with things in the kitchen and Bea made Niles a ham and cheese sandwich for lunch. Making homemade candy had been a lengthy process, and so she'd skipped cooking breakfast and lunch that day.

Bea walked outside with a paper plate and Mason jar of sweet tea in her hands. Niles was in the fence smoothing out wet soil from the recent downpour. He saw her and walked on over. "I brought you some lunch," she said, as he removed his work gloves.

"Much obliged," he said, grabbing the plate and jar. And for a moment he could've sworn he saw an image of Mary standing there in front of him. His heart leaped in his chest from excitement.

"I'll have something much better for supper. The candy making has kept me busy today," Bea explained.

Niles bit into the sandwich. "Oh, this is fine. I appreciate you taking time to think of me. I could've survived on a pack of crackers and a soda."

"Well, I couldn't leave you out here all day without some proper nourishment," she said, teasing him.

Abby was looking for Bea and walked out the door and heard them laughing. "What's so funny?" she asked, wondering what was going on with them now.

Niles handed Bea the empty plate and grinned. But neither of them said a word, a quick smile was sufficient enough.

"I brought Niles some lunch, Abby. What are you doing?" Bea said.

Abby grabbed a metal bucket from by the fence. "I guess I'll feed the hogs and gather eggs from the chicken pens."

Bea nodded. "Great. I would appreciate it. The weather forecast is calling for more rain over the next couple of days. The more we get done now, the easier it'll be later on. Those pens can get nasty real fast."

Abby hung her head. "I know, Grandma. I know." Then she darted off toward the shed to grab a pair of rubber boots.

"You're teaching her something she can take back home with her. I'm glad to see this," Niles said.

Bea giggled. "I don't know. But I'm doing what I can to keep her occupied and out of trouble. There's so much more she can get involved in living near Atlanta. Kids aren't like they used to be when we were coming of age. Times have changed a whole lot."

"Yeah, you're right. But you're setting a good example for her. Something she's probably not getting much of back home."

"Well, I know Jewel has tried her best while working two jobs to make ends meet. I do admire her for it, even though we haven't always agreed on things much."

"What happened between her and Billy anyway? Mary never liked to hear you talk about it."

"Billy was on the rebound when he met Jewel. I guess he figured it would be a good way to get back at Lola for cheating on him. However, it all changed when Jewel got pregnant with Abby."

"Do you think he ever loved Jewel?"

"No, I don't think he did. I believe he felt sorry for her more than anything. And she was there to fill the gaps and meet his needs at the time."

"I've seen a few photos of her. You know how Mary enjoyed taking family photos. She's a beautiful lady."

"Yeah, she is. I reckon they met and one thing led to another. Billy only brought her to the ranch once before they were married. I think it's probably where she conceived Abby."

Surprised, Niles said, "Bea, you shouldn't talk about those types of things, especially not around Abby."

"Why not? It's true. I counted the days of Jewel's pregnancy." She sighed and furrowed her brow. "We aren't living in the stone age now, Niles. Things happen."

Niles leaned against the fence. "Yeah, I guess we're not," he said. "But sometimes I wish we were. Life seemed much simpler back then."

Bea glanced at her wrist watch. "I have to get back to the kitchen."

"Okay. I'll get things finished over here. Maybe the rain will hold off for a little while."

Bea took off toward the house with the empty plate and jar. It was well past noon, and she had intentions of making another batch of candy before starting supper.

After Abby had fed the hogs and gathered eggs from the chickens, she debated about sneaking back over to the barn to spy on Kyle. If she got caught, she could always use Cocoa as an excuse. But what she really wanted was time to get to know Kyle. In less than two months, summer vacation would be over and she didn't want to look back and have regrets.

SIXTEEN

Bea kept Abby busy most of the day doing one thing after another. Every time she thought she might break away, Bea found something else for her to do. It was like she sensed Abby was hiding something, making Abby feel like she stayed at her heels. By the time Bea started cooking supper Abby was ready to call it quits. It made her wonder how Bea had energy to do the same old things day in and day out, and she even questioned if she ever got bored with life. Bea was the kind of woman who always did for everyone else. She cooked, cleaned, sewed, fed the animals, brushed the horse's manes, and still found time to sit and read her Bible after supper. Just thinking of Bea's daily routine made Abby exhausted.

At six o'clock, Bea set a pan of biscuits on the table along with some plates, forks and napkins. Brushing her sleeve over her face, she swept a fallen tendril of hair off her cheek. "There. Now all we need is another pitcher of tea," she said.

Abby watched in amazement and wondered if this was how Bea's life had always been. Doing this and doing that—always *serving* others. It was evident she had a servant's heart and lived by what she believed. But Bea never mentioned her late husband William Jake. Abby figured some things were still too painful to talk about right now.

After everything was ready, Bea stepped out on the porch to motion for Niles and a couple other guys to come in. Most men went home at a decent hour because the ranch was nothing more than a day job. But to a few men, Bea and the ranch was all they had. Bigelow Ranch and Bea were like family to them.

When they'd all made it inside and washed their hands, Bea said grace and they passed the dishes of food back and forth across the table to fill their plates.

Abby noticed Kyle was not in the group seated around the table and wondered if he was ever invited. Bea had said he only helped out over the summer, but he had as much right to a hot meal as any man. The room grew quiet as they ate, except for the clatter of silverware when a plate was almost empty.

Niles was the last man to clear away his dirty dishes. "You've outdone yourself again, Bea," he said, setting his plate and fork in the sink.

Bea smiled. "I'm glad you enjoyed it," she replied.

Abby said nary word as they chatted back and forth, feeling there had to be something more between them. After Niles left, Abby decided to be inquisitive, but realized she had to be careful how she approached such a serious subject. "Grandma?"

"Yeah?"

"Will you tell me more about my family?"

"Sure. What do you want to know?"

"What made you decide to move here, buy the ranch, and settle in Texas? You could've lived anywhere in the world."

Bea sighed and ran her hands over her apron. "I was afraid you might ask me this one day," she said.

"Is something wrong?" Abby asked.

"No. It's not something I enjoy talking about much." Bea grabbed a hold of Abby's hand. "All of this won't be pretty," she said. "But I'll share with you what I know."

Abby sat closer, ready to hear what Bea had to say. Inside, she was a little worried about it.

"When I was visiting my Aunt Helene in Georgia I met your grandpa. He had the bluest eyes I'd ever seen. We had gone to get a new set of tires on my aunt's car, and there he was, standing behind a sales counter at an automotive store. It was love at first sight for me. Every time he smiled his lip curved a little, leaving a slight dimple in his cheek. There was something bigger than life about him. This was in the late eighties and we were both in our twenties back then. Before I left I gave him my phone number. He called me later that week and we started dating. Never would I have thought I'd find my soulmate so easy."

Abby grinned. "What happened next? How long did you date?"

"Oh, I guess it was six months or so before my parents found out."

"I take it they weren't too happy about it."

"Yeah, daddy didn't like guys that didn't have money and prestige. He was such a prejudged person."

"Did he want you to end the relationship with him?"

"Oh yes...but I wouldn't do it. A couple months later William Jake proposed and we eloped. It was one of the best decisions I ever made in life."

"What did your parents say when they found out?"

"They were upset of course. But I was twenty-three by then, of legal age."

"Why were they upset if you were in your twenties?"

Bea let go of her hand, stood, and paced back and forth, trying to gain complete control over her emotions.

Abby could see how nervous she was. "You okay, Grandma?"

Bea nodded. "Yeah. It's hard for me to talk about some things."

"It's okay. You don't have to," Abby said. "I don't want to upset you."

Bea turned to face her. "I'll tell you what...tomorrow I'm going to take you to meet someone in the family."

"Really? Who?"

"Your Great-grandma. She's my stepmother. She can tell you about a lot of things I can't."

"How old is she? I don't think mom has ever mentioned her before."

"She's ninety-one. And that's because she's never met Mimi as far as I know."

"I don't think mom knew a lot about the Bigelow side of the family. It seems that she didn't get along with many people back then."

Bea nodded. "Yeah, sad to say, but seems to be so. But the past is the past, and it's time you found out more about your family."

"Maybe they'll want to be in my life more than dad ever wanted to. He deserted me, but mom has never told me the reasons why he left. And I've often wondered if it was because he didn't want any kids."

"Oh, it ain't so, Abby. He had mixed-up emotions when he and your mom met. I believe it was bad timing on his part."

"But why would he just throw me away like I didn't even exist? Like I was a piece of trash."

"Oh Abby, I really wish I could answer that question for you, but I can't."

Bea removed her apron and decided it was time to get out of the kitchen. "Come on. Let's go in the living room. I need to read the next few chapters in my Bible."

Abby followed her and sat on the sofa, as Bea grabbed her black leather bound Bible. Jewel had never taught Abby about going to church or reading the Bible. She'd heard about *Jesus* from time to time, but that was as far as it went.

It was obvious Abby was feeling a little uncomfortable. "Do you have a Bible?" Bea asked. "It's the most important book you'll ever read."

"No, not since I was a young girl. I believe I once had a little red New Testament Bible. I think someone gave it to me for my fifth or sixth birthday."

"Well, I'll get you one tomorrow. Every young woman needs her own Bible."

Abby smiled, unsure of what to expect, and she hoped Bea wasn't about to go all religious on her.

There was a home and garden magazine lying on the coffee table. To cover her obvious embarrassment Abby grabbed it, and started flipping through the pages. Bea said nothing more as she focused on her Bible reading.

Later on, Abby lay in bed wondering what Bea was hiding from her. She'd never heard Jewel make mention of her Great-grandmother, but for some reason she was anxious to meet her. There was more to the brief story Bea had shared with her about meeting William Jake and she wanted to hear it. Maybe by some slim chance it would reveal why Billy left her and Jewel and never looked back. Was there a pattern of behavior between the two men? Was there something in the family *bloodline* Abby didn't know about? Or did her dad not want either of them?

After Kyle had finished cleaning out the stables and fed the horses, he got settled in a small room in back of the barn that Bea converted for him to sleep, eat, and bathe. It wasn't the best of conditions, but he had the place all to himself. He had five weeks left before he'd be moving on. He hadn't told Bea he'd be leaving a little early because the opportunity had not presented itself yet. And after this summer, Kyle didn't know if he'd return, no matter how much he loved it there. Becoming a famous musician was his dream, and he planned to pursue it however he could—even if he had to move to Nashville and sleep in his car. After showering, Kyle grabbed his guitar and began working on the music to a new song, the perfect way to end his day.

SEVENTEEN

The next morning, Bea got dressed and knocked on Abby's bedroom door. She'd thought off and on all night about Abby meeting Mimi Satterfield.

Abby opened her eyes and said, "Come in."

"You need to get yourself together so we can ride over to your Great-grandma's house," Bea said, hands perched at her waist.

"How come you haven't told me about her before now?" Abby asked, feeling curious to find out more. "I've been here a while."

"These things take time. And besides I wanted to be certain you weren't going to come here and get in trouble again."

"Oh, I see. I had to earn your trust first." Abby grinned.

Bea cocked her head to the side. "Yeah, I guess you could say so," she said, turning to walk away.

"Wait. Is she a nice person, Grandma?"

Bea chuckled. "Nice enough. You'll see. Now get dressed." Bea left and Abby made her bed and got herself presentable before going to meet Mimi.

When Abby walked in the living room, Bea was knitting. "What are you making?" she asked.

"Another blanket for my bed," she said. "It gets pretty cold during wintertime." After setting the yarn and blanket on the coffee table, Bea grabbed her keys. "You ready?"

Abby nodded. "As ready as I'm ever going to be."

"I'm sure this feels odd to you since you don't have much family back home."

"Yeah, it is. I hope she likes me."

Bea walked out the door. "I'm sure she will. She always thought the sun rose and set in Billy."

Bea got in the old rusty truck Niles had driven to the airport and Abby frowned. At least it was early morning and the temperature was not 100 degrees yet. She opened the door, got in without saying a word, rolled the window down, and placed her hand on the back of her head to keep her hair in place, hoping it wouldn't be a mess by the time they reached their destination. "How far do we have to travel?"

"We'll be there in about fifteen minutes. I gave her a call earlier this morning, so she's expecting us."

"Okay."

Abby braced herself for what was to come. She had no idea how Mimi would react to meeting her, and her greatest fear was not being accepted.

When they arrived, Bea parked in front of an old house made from fat-lighter wood. The cement steps leading to the porch were cracked in several places and the smell of smoke lingered in the air.

They walked on the porch and Bea knocked on the door. A few minutes later, a short-petite lady stood in front of them. "Well, come on in," she said.

Bea walked in with Abby close behind. The house smelt like a mixture of coffee and cigarettes. "You two care for a cup of coffee?" Mimi asked.

"Sure," Bea said. "I don't mind if I do."

Abby stood still, watching Mimi in the kitchen.

"Have a seat, child. I promise I won't bite you," Mimi said, grinning.

Abby sat and waited for Bea and Mimi to join her. She was surprised Mimi was so tiny and short.

Mimi sat in a rocking chair, cup in her hand. "Well, look at you. You do favor Billy a lot. This is the first time I've ever laid eyes on you." Mimi started rocking back and forth. The old oak floor beneath her feet creaked like it was going to break into pieces.

Abby was feeling nervous. Mimi appeared to be nice, but she'd bet she could raise a roof if need be. You know, one of those little but loud women.

"How long have you lived here?" Abby asked.

Mimi stopped rocking and locked eyes with her. "I reckon about all my life, ever since I married back in 1950. We had a good life till Arthur died. If he'd lived six more months we would've been married 65 years. I believe dementia is a disease from the ol' devil. He's been gone eight years now."

"I'm sorry. I mean..." Abby hung her head.

"It's okay, Abby. I know what you meant."

Bea changed the subject to try and lighten the mood. "Are you making some progress with your quilt?"

Mimi stood, set her cup on table, walked to the bedroom, and grabbed the quilt to show them. "I still have a little hemming work to do, but I'm satisfied with the overall design."

"Oh, it's so beautiful, Mimi," Abby said. "Could you make one for my bed?"

"I'd be delighted to," Mimi replied. "What size do you need?"

"I have a queen size bed," Abby replied. "I've

wanted to learn how to quilt since I was ten years old. Could you teach me a few skills to take back home with me?"

She nodded. "If you stop by a couple afternoons I can get you started with the simple basics."

Abby glanced in Bea's direction with a gleam of excitement in her eyes. "Can I, Grandma?"

Bea nodded. "Sure, but only after you've finished with all your chores at the ranch."

Abby stood and hugged Bea tight. "Thanks."

Mimi grabbed an empty cup off the table to refill with coffee. "I drink coffee all day long. I know it's a bad habit, but Arthur got me started years ago." She laughed. "I guess between black coffee and cigarettes, something is bound to kill me sooner or later."

Bea didn't say anything. Mimi had survived so far, and at her age she figured she'd earned the right to do whatever she pleased.

"Well, Abby, how do you like staying at the ranch?" Mimi sat and crossed her legs.

"At first I wasn't happy about being there. It's quite different than living only minutes from the city. And I didn't want to forego spending my summer vacation with friends."

"I see. But you stayed in trouble back there, didn't you?"

Abby frowned and rolled her eyes toward Bea before answering. "Yes, ma'am, I did."

"Then being at the ranch has been good for you. Wouldn't you say?"

Abby nodded. "Yes ma'am, it has. I've learned a lot about how to take care of the animals."

Bea chimed in. "Abby's been doing whatever I've

asked of her thus far. It's been a pleasure having her with us for the summer."

Mimi grinned. "How's Niles doing?"

She caught Bea off guard. "He's doing okay," Bea said. "He stays busy like William Jake used to."

Mimi started rocking again. "Yes, I miss William Jake. He was a good man, loved God and you."

A tear welled in Bea's eye. "Yes, he sure was. I miss him every single day."

There was a tattered Bible lying on the table by Mimi's saucer. Abby glanced at it, wondering if being a Christian was really all that important. Mimi realized it caught her eye and she grabbed it. "This is the Bible me and Arthur laid our hands upon when we said our vows. We never had one of those fancy church weddings because we were poor back then and couldn't afford too much. But I believe our love for each other supplemented what we didn't have. Since Bea's mother and brother died years ago in childbirth, Arthur told me he promised God he'd never be without His word nearby. We've kept this ol' Bible even after all these years." Mimi flipped it open to reveal coffee stains and small tears in the delicate, now yellowed pages.

"Yeah, Mimi, I believe this Bible would be considered an antique," Bea said and grinned.

On the inside, Abby felt herself pull away from the ol' book, but then something about it had her yearning to learn more, like something was tugging at her heart. Being religious was not something Abby was accustomed to. During her childhood, Jewel had only taken her to church on Easter and Christmas. However, she had always told Abby to say her prayers before bed. So she figured Jewel must love God in her own kind of way.

Bea could sense Abby was feeling a little uncomfortable. "You about ready to head back?" she asked. "I need to get something cooking."

Abby stood. "Sure."

Mimi stood. "Give me a hug," she told Abby, reaching out her thin wrinkly arms.

Abby gave her a hug, feeling enlightened by the visit. Things had gone better than she'd expected, and now she wanted to visit again and learn how to make a quilt. "Can I come over next week?" Abby asked.

Mimi loosened their embrace. "Of course you can. I'll even bake some chocolate chip cookies to go with our black coffee."

"That sounds good," Abby said, walking toward the door. "I'll see you soon."

Bea and Abby left with Mimi following them on the porch to offer a wave as they drove off.

Going back to the ranch, Abby began to understand why living there meant so much to Bea. It was a different way of life, less complicated. She knew it was hard to keep things going at the ranch, but Bea had a great group of men that would do anything for her. In fact, Bea treated them like part of her family. And Abby was beginning to see what the true meaning of family was—even if they weren't blood kin. It made her realize anyone could be considered family if you wanted them to be.

EIGHTEEN

B ea and Abby returned to the ranch before noon. Fourth of July weekend was fast approaching, and a lot needed to be done if they were going to have the annual get-together. The outer wall of the barn needed to be painted, and Niles planned to make two long tables to seat everyone. The annual event usual consisted of cooking a hog with all the fixings. Some local church musicians got together to play a few songs as well. Bluegrass music was popular around that part of Texas. William Jake had played the harmonica prior to his death. Since then, no man had attempted to fill his shoes. It seemed appropriate being William Jake and Bea had first founded the event years ago. Everyone tried to keep his memory alive, and Bea placed a photo of him close by. Bea couldn't be angry because he'd died doing what he loved. Each year she replaced the tattered American flag out front. It was now faded from the sun. She thought about taking Abby by the cemetery, but not today. There were too many other things to do, and she didn't have time to get all sappy.

While Bea was in the kitchen, a few teenage girls arrived at the ranch. She hadn't bothered to tell Abby about the summer program of *hope* she offered to wayward kids. Their behavior had all but caused them to be sent to juvenile hall. Already in alternative schools, it was sad to witness what not having a supportive role model had caused. Their ages ranged from thirteen to seventeen. Some had already had an abortion, and others had allowed their newborns to be adopted. Without a job and a secure home, there was not much *hope* for a child born into poverty. Bea had a desire to help these girls get on the right path, maybe because she never had a daughter of her own. They usually spent two weeks under her supervision while she taught them about respect, how to take care of a household, and how to deal with bad situations. And most of all, she told them about her Lord and Savior. Everything in Bea's life centered from her beliefs, and she always gives credit where credit is due.

After William Jake died, Bea thought she might lose her mind, but she found new purpose by getting involved with others not as fortunate. It gave her peace, helped her to do something to serve others, by helping the least of these. And if he were there she knew he'd be supportive of her. A smile covered her face when she greeted the group of girls. "Come in," she said. "Welcome to my home: Bigelow Ranch. I'm glad you've come to spend this short time with me."

Abby heard the commotion and walked in the foyer to see what was going on. Surprised, she asked, "What's going on, Grandma?"

Bea motioned for the girls to sit. "This is my summer group of girls," she told Abby. "Each summer I have a few girls come stay with me. They've been in trouble and don't have a summer job."

Abby shook her head. "But Grandma, I don't understand. How can you help *them*?"

"Well, I start by welcoming them in and showing

them love. Sometimes a person needs to be nurtured and cared for. They need to know they're important to someone, that their lives matter. God has a purpose and a plan for each of us."

"Really?" Abby sighed and placed her hands on her hips, feeling a little overwhelmed by having to share Bea with the girls.

One of the girls looked at Abby with disgust. "Looks like you've had everything handed to you on a silver platter," she said, "with your name brand this and that."

Appalled, Abby frowned and reached for Bea's hand. "Can I have a word with you, Grandma?"

"I'll handle this," Bea said. She made eye contact with the one girl. "What's your name?"

"April."

Bea frowned. "Well, April, we don't disrespect each other here. Let me introduce you to Abby. She's my granddaughter and she's spending the summer with me. I expect you girls to be respectful to others while you're here."

April huffed. "Respectful? What's that?"

"It's simple. Treating others the way you'd like to be treated," Bea told her.

April nodded and hung her head. "I'll try Ms. Bea. But I'm not making any promises."

"That's better. I trust you will try to work with this program, not against it."

"May I be excused?" Abby asked.

Bea could tell Abby was upset over the girls being there. "Okay. I'll let you know when supper is ready."

Abby said nary word, turned and left the room. On the inside, she wondered what Bea was thinking by allowing them to come. So far she'd had a peaceful stay, and now Bea had to go and spoil it, by allowing a bunch of troubled brats to come in. Abby hates being in crowds, the reason she only has a couple close friends back home. And she had no plan to befriend any of the girls. Truth be told, she was a little jealous. Bea had made her feel like she belonged for the first time and Abby didn't want to lose that connection now. She lay across the bed, lips pouty, like a blowfish. Her home and Jewel were hours away, but she wasn't prepared to leave just yet. Besides, she'd promised Mimi she would visit her soon to work on quilting.

Bea showed the girls to their rooms, and told them to get settled in while she finished making a chicken casserole for supper.

Abby heard doors opening and closing, and soon realized she'd have to share a bathroom with the girls. The more she thought about it, the madder she got. They were invading her territory and she detested every minute of it.

After the noise settled, Abby walked in the bathroom and removed her toiletries. There was no way she'd share her things with complete strangers. She didn't know if they had diseases or STD's, and she wasn't willing to chance getting anything.

On the way out April passed Abby in the hall. "I know you hate we're here, but you don't know what life has been like for me or any of us for that matter."

Abby sighed. "No, I don't know. And I don't want to know. I'll be leaving to go home soon, so you can keep your problems all to yourself."

April froze. "Well, Abby, I can see you're a snob without an ounce of compassion or consideration for anyone but yourself."

HAVEN OF HOPE

Abby stopped and looked her in the eye. "You don't know anything about me or my life. So don't judge me by something you think you might know."

"Well, aren't you being defensive?" April furrowed her brow and stood there staring at her.

Just then, Bea stepped on the top stair and the girls went their separate ways. She could feel tension already brewing between Abby and April and didn't like it at all. Bea had strived to keep peace in her home and she intended to keep it that way. So she planned to talk with Abby later on after supper.

At dusk, Niles came in and washed his hands at the kitchen sink then he removed his cap and boots and sat at the table. "I hear your new group of girls arrived this afternoon."

Bea nodded. "Yep, they sure did."

"How did Abby take their arrival?" he asked.

"Not good," Bea replied. "I'm going to talk with her about it after supper."

"Yeah, I think it would be a good idea. I imagine she may feel a little threatened by them."

Bea turned to face him. "What? Not you too, Niles." She shook her head in disbelief.

"What?" Niles grinned.

"I don't think anyone is happy to see the girls other than myself. You have to give them a chance, get to know them."

Niles rubbed his hand over his gray beard. "I reckon you're right, Bea. Besides, I don't know of any other woman willing to help complete strangers like you do."

"That's what I'm here for."

Niles stared at her a minute. "Yeah, and you have a big heart Beatrice Bigelow." He grinned.

Bea grabbed an oven mitt and set a casserole dish on the table along with some yeast rolls from the oven. "Supper's ready. Now I only hope I've cooked enough to feed these girls."

"Is Abby coming in to eat with us?" Niles asked.

"I hope so. She seemed pretty upset earlier, and I witnessed some friction between her and April when I went upstairs. You know how I am about keeping peace around here."

"Yes ma'am. I know it's a must. And I admire you for it," Niles said.

"I want to take Abby to church this Sunday."

"Really? Do you think it's a good idea?"

"Of course. Just because she hasn't been raised to go doesn't mean she can't learn about the Lord now." Bea grew quiet.

"I guess you're right. How about the other girls? Are you taking them too?"

"Not yet. I want them to settle in and feel comfortable with things around here first."

Bea fixed Niles' plate and then called the girls for supper. Everyone came to the table except Abby. Right then, she knew without a doubt, Abby hated the girls being there. And Abby had since hidden in her own cocoon away from everyone.

As they ate, there was a vacant chair next to Bea—Abby's. The girls were quiet for the most part and Bea cleared away dirty dishes as soon as everyone had finished. After wiping off the table, she gave the girls a list of rules regarding their stay then knocked on Abby's door, but there was no answer. Figuring Abby was asleep Bea went to her room and thought nothing of it. *Well, I guess I'll talk with her tomorrow.*

She grabbed the book she'd been reading and settled in for the afternoon, figuring she'd better enjoy some quiet time while she could. Before long she'd be more involved with the girls after supper.

NINETEEN

Past midnight, Abby wandered around using the flashlight from her phone. She'd grown accustomed to sneaking out. Doing something daring made her feel important in a weird sort of way. And if she got caught she'd receive the attention she longed for. All her life she'd wondered if her father had really wanted her; which made her feel like a mistake. It was hard for Abby to carry the burden of guilt, and at times, she felt overwhelmed by it.

Niles had already led the horses to their spots in the stables, so Abby didn't have to worry about spooking them. She could take her time, enjoy the night sky, and maybe even wish upon a star. Ever since she was a little girl she'd had the same birthday wish—that Billy would come home and the three of them would be a real family. She'd been to friends' birthday parties and imagined how it would be to live in a home with a loving mom and dad. No doubt, Abby knew something was missing—something greater—more fulfilling. She hadn't tried to do bad things, it just seemed to happen. She couldn't control her actions, and she liked the adrenaline rush it gave her. There were a lot of things Abby had done by age thirteen, things Jewel would not be pleased with. Sneaking out at night, shoplifting, meeting boys, drinking, smoking weed, and lying about her age to get a fake ID.

Outside, Abby walked near the barn and saw a light in the window where Kyle stayed. He'd already told her to stay away, but something in her longed to do the opposite. Even though she was young, she knew he was attracted to her. Going to see him this time of night would be like playing with fire—the kind that could burn her in the worst way. She stopped, turned off the light, gazed at the night sky, and decided to walk in. The only light was a slight glimmer from the nearby security light. She slid the door open and walked easy as to not rouse the horses. To her surprise, Kyle was in the stall with Cocoa. His head was leaning against the wall where he'd fallen asleep. It was a beautiful sight. Cocoa had her head near Kyle's hand as if he'd just fed her. Abby smiled as she stood watching them both sleep.

A couple minutes later, Hershey flinched, let a neigh out and startled Kyle. When he opened his eyes and got his bearings he asked, "What are you doing here, Abby?"

"I couldn't sleep. Grandma has a group of girls staying over, so I thought I'd take a walk to clear my head. The stars are beautiful tonight."

"This time of night?" Kyle said and stood.

"Yeah. What's wrong with taking a walk? I'm not hurting anything or anyone."

Kyle brushed fresh hay off his pants. "You'd better go back to the house. If Bea catches you here..."

She shrugged. "What if she does? Why are you so scared of her?"

Abby had caught Kyle off guard, but waited for his answer.

He shrugged. "I don't know what you're talking about. I'm not afraid of her. Besides, I know she keeps a tight rein on things around here, and she won't stand for me having girls over."

"Oh, I see. So she's caught you with a girl before?" Abby moved further away from him.

Kyle fumbled for his words. "Umm. Yeah, I guess you could say she has." He was beginning to feel exasperated the more she nosed around about his past.

"You strike me as the type of guy who could have a different girl here every weekend," Abby said.

"You don't know much about me, then. I'm not like that at all." He laughed.

Abby walked closer and caught a whiff of the cologne he was wearing. "You smell good," she said.

Kyle laughed. "I'm probably harboring the scent of fresh hay mixed with horses at this late hour."

"No, remember? I told you it went well with your body chemistry."

Kyle grinned and now looked a little confused. "What?"

"Your cologne, silly."

"Oh, right. I had forgotten about that. Look, it's late, so you need to head back to the house before Ms. Bea realizes you're gone."

Abby turned to walk away and paused. "You're such a party pooper, Kyle. I'd say a handsome face is the only thing you have going for you." She slung her hair back and took a few steps forward.

Kyle stood there dumbfounded by what she'd said. A few minutes ago she'd complimented him, seconds later, she'd insulted him. After she left, Kyle got ready for bed, wondering what her life story was. Why was she there? What had she done for her mother to send her to Texas? Did she need some kind of rehab or something?

After being around her more Kyle figured Abby was a party girl, and he'd bet she could handle a few shots of alcohol and a joint or two.

Lying on his back, Kyle placed his hands under his head and closed his eyes. There were several things he needed to do later in the day, and it was already past two, and so he tried to calm his racing mind to get some sleep.

Abby made her way back to the house—except this time—Bea was sitting in a rocker on the front porch. "Where have you been?" Bea asked, catching Abby off guard. Abby squared her shoulders back. "I couldn't sleep, so I thought I'd take a walk and check on Cocoa."

Bea gave her an odd look. "Are you certain you're telling me the truth?"

"Of course, Grandma. Why would I lie? I have nothing to hide." She smiled. "Aren't the stars just beautiful tonight?"

"Yes, they sure are." Bea stood and motioned for Abby to go inside. "We both have an early morning, so you need to get to bed now."

"How early?"

"Six o'clock."

Abby stopped. "Why so early?"

"You'll see later on," Bea replied.

Abby walked on ahead of her inside, and the floor creaked when she stepped off the last stair.

Bea watched her go in her room and doubted if she'd stay for long. Jewel had already informed her about Abby sneaking out at night. Now she had to keep more of an eye on her, and she figured she'd soon be asking Niles to help out also. He could do some things in certain ways Bea couldn't. And on top of things, Bea had other girls to worry about as well. She slipped off her robe and got into bed. It had been a long night and she was feeling beyond exhausted.

While sleeping, Bea dreamed of when she was married and how much she had wanted to have another child. She loved Billy, and it broke her heart when William Jake died. For a while, she didn't know if she'd be able to go on without him. It was hard to fathom he'd never again be nestled there in bed beside her, and the realization made her feel so empty.

Just before sunrise, Bea awakened and wished she could talk with Niles right then. There was so much she wanted to share with him—if her heart would allow it. She dressed in her everyday clothes and tried to pull herself together in spite of flagging fatigue because she had girls coming to the kitchen for a hearty breakfast.

When she walked in the kitchen Niles opened the back door. "Morning, Bea."

She grinned. "Good morning, Niles. Have a seat. I'll have some coffee going in a few minutes."

It was like Niles had sensed she needed to see him right away. There was no way it was only a mere coincidence.

Niles sat and remained quite—like something was weighing heavy on his mind.

Fifteen minutes later, Bea set a platter of scrambled eggs on the table and poured them a hot coffee. "Something on your mind this morning, Niles? Anything you care to talk about?"

Niles took a sip of coffee and set his cup on the saucer. "I didn't sleep well last night. My mind kept roaming from one thought to another."

"Hmm. You've been thinking about Mary again?"

Bea made eye contact with him. He nodded. "Yeah, I had a vivid dream about her. She was holding a blue-eyed baby girl, singing her a beautiful lullaby."

Bea walked closer and rubbed Niles on the shoulders. "I know how much you two wanted kids. I'm sorry you never had any."

A tear welled in Niles' eye. "Yeah, me too. I think we would've been good parents."

Right then, the group of girls came in the kitchen. The silence was short-lived, and so was the tender heart-felt moment between Niles and Bea.

"Have a seat. Breakfast will be ready soon," Bea said, as the girls filled the chairs around the table.

Niles remained quiet and wondered what having a daughter of his own might've been like. However, there was no chance of it now. Mary was gone, and he was certain he'd never love another woman the way he loved her.

TWENTY

After breakfast, Bea cleared away the dishes as Abby and the girls sat around the table. Abby had no idea what was in store. Bea had been helping other girls for the past few years. Something Abby had not been made aware of.

"So, what's on the agenda for today?" Abby asked, wondering what was going on.

Bea dried her hands and removed her apron. "I want you girls to go in the living room and have a seat and I'll be there in a few minutes."

The girls said nary word and did as Bea had asked. By the serious look on her face, they all knew something was about to happen, whether they liked it or not.

Abby sat in Bea's chair and gazed around the room. She detested the other girls being there because she craved attention. Not happy about the situation, she wondered what Bea was about to say and do.

A few minutes later, Bea came in with some books, notepads and pens in her hand, and proceeded to pass them out. "I figured this is a good place for us to start," she said.

The girls grabbed the books and pens and frowned when they saw what one of the books were—a Holy Bible.

Bea didn't like it, but bit her bottom lip, trying to

refrain from speaking her mind. "I know you may not have ever read this book, but now is the time. It'll help you get back on track and lead you on a new path away from sin."

One girl rolled her eyes at Bea, making it obvious of her disgust regarding the subject.

"I think we'll start with you, Megan. God wouldn't be pleased with your actions." Bea opened the Bible and her notepad.

Megan frowned. Well aware Bea was not pleased with her attitude. "Yes, ma'am."

"Now, we are going to start with John 3:16. It's my favorite verse of Scripture in the Bible."

"Ms. Bea?"

"What is it, Megan?"

"I'm not a Christian. I don't believe in the Bible or God. This is just a book of history like all the others. It has no relevance whatsoever in my life. So, why force me to do this?"

"Well, we all need God to survive in this world. In order to do that, we need His guidance every day," Bea said. "Our instructions of how to live daily are in this book." She held her Bible up.

Megan just stared at Bea. *But I don't need him.* Inside, she felt angry with God, like He'd never cared anything about her. Out of respect for Bea, she flipped through the pages to find the Bible verse and placed her finger there.

"Okay. If everyone has found the Scripture we'll get started." She glanced at Megan and held her stare. "You ready, Megan?"

Megan nodded, dreading that she had to read something she didn't even understand. *For God so loved the world, that he gave his only begotten Son, that whosoever believeth in him shall not perish, but have everlasting life.* Those words made no sense to her. None. At all.

After she read the verse there was silence in the room. And Bea knew it would be much harder than she had anticipated to offer *hope* to these girls. "Do you understand what these words mean?" Bea asked.

The girls just looked at her for a few minutes. Then Abby chimed in. "It means if we know the Lord Jesus as our Savior we can eternal life with Him when we die."

Bea smiled. "That's right, Abby. This is the promise we have by knowing Christ and having a personal relationship with Him daily."

Megan sighed. "Do I really have to sit here and listen to this? I've already told you, I'm not a believer. Why are you trying to make me one?"

Her behavior caught Bea off guard and she furrowed her brow, trying to maintain her composure. "Yes, you do, Megan! It's a part of the program I have here. I teach you about the Bible, and how knowing Jesus can change your life."

About that time, Niles walked in. "I'm sorry to interrupt ladies, but Maggie's here to check on Cocoa. I thought you'd like to know, Bea."

"Thanks, Niles. You're right. I believe I could use a little break about now," Bea said, closing her Bible. "You girls think about what you're thankful for, and we'll continue with our conversation later." Bea got up and left the room.

Niles was waiting for her on the porch. "Seems you have a hard-headed group of girls this time," he said, shaking his head.

"Oh, you don't know the half of it," Bea said with a little sarcasm while walking over to the barn.

"How much longer are you planning to do it?" Niles asked, as they walked side by side.

"I don't know. I guess until I know God is done with me reaching out to help lost, abused, neglected, needy girls."

Niles smiled. "You would've been a wonderful mother to a daughter," he said.

As they walked in the barn Bea said, "Thanks. You always seem to know how to make me smile and bring some light into my life."

Inside, Maggie was already in the stall with Cocoa checking her vital signs.

"How are things going?" Bea asked.

Maggie removed the stethoscope from Cocoa and stood. "She's actually doing pretty well from what I can tell. I'm most worried about the baby, though. I'm going to do an ultrasound now."

"Oh, this is so exciting," Bea said, reaching for Niles' hand.

Niles grinned, grabbed her hand, and waited with anticipation also.

After a few minutes, Maggie gave them the news. "Everything looks good from what I can tell. Now we only need to keep her still a while longer. Afterwards, she'll definitely need to be walked on a daily basis to strengthen her muscles again. It'll take Cocoa a few months to get over this."

"What are you thinking about naming the filly?" Niles asked Bea.

"I've been thinking, and if you don't mind, I'd like to name her Mary after our beloved Mary."

TERESA TUTEN

He squeezed her hand. "I think it would be fine. Mary would love it if she were here. I know she'd want to witness the birth firsthand." Niles let go of her hand and they hugged.

Maggie finished examining Cocoa and placed her things back in her bag. "I admit I've had my doubts about Cocoa surviving this. She's really something special. And I believe she realizes how much she's loved." Maggie grinned.

"Oh, yes. That she is," Bea said with a grin.

Kyle heard voices and walked in to see who was in the barn. "Morning," he said. "How's she doing?"

"She's healing day by day and doing rather well," Maggie said.

Kyle said, "That's great! I knew she'd pull through." A tear welled in his eye at such good news. Since it was his fault Cocoa got hurt in the first place, he felt relieved to know she was going to be okay.

"I really need to head on back," Maggie said. "I'll stop by to check on her next week. Call me if you need anything."

Bea walked with Maggie back to her truck. "Have you heard anymore from Beaufort?" Bea asked.

Maggie opened the door and set her bag on the seat. "Oh, yes. He came by the house and threatened me. He blames me for Beau's death, but I didn't kill him—a drug overdose did. I ended the relationship because of his attitude, control issues, drinking and temper. However, Beaufort doesn't believe me. I guess he'll blame me till he's lying cold in his grave."

"He shouldn't be able to keep you from practicing with equine, Maggie. It wasn't your fault. You're a great veterinarian. God has given you a gift. Have you thought about hiring an attorney to fight this thing?"

"Yes. But attorneys don't work for free, and I cannot afford one. I'm barely getting by right now as it is."

"I'm sorry to hear that, Maggie. I really appreciate you taking a risk over here to help with Cocoa."

Maggie got in the truck. "I've got to run, Bea. It was good seeing you. Like I said, if you need anything or notice a change in Cocoa, don't hesitate to call me before next week."

"I will." Bea stepped out of the way and threw her a wave as she drove off.

As clouds began to hover above, Niles walked over to Bea. "Guess I'll get back to work. Looks like we might get some rain this afternoon."

"Yeah, I believe so," Bea replied. "I reckon I need to check on the girls. I have much to accomplish with this group."

Niles nodded. "I agree," he said. "Guess I'll see you at dinner..."

"Sounds good," Bea said, as she started walking toward the house.

And for a split second, Niles could've sworn he saw Mary standing on the porch, waiting on Bea's return.

TWENTY-ONE

When Bea walked in, to her surprise, the girls were still sitting with their Bibles open. "Well, have you thought about what you're thankful for?" she asked.

Megan gave her a cold stare. It was as if Bea could see straight into her calloused heart. Something awful had happened to her, Bea was sure of it because she had a chip on her shoulder the size of Texas. Abby was the only girl to answer. "Yeah, Grandma. I'm thankful mom didn't abort me when she found out she was pregnant out of wedlock. Those things used to be frowned upon years ago. From what I've read, most parents sent their daughters away until after they had the baby to save disgrace on the family."

Bea was taken aback. "What on earth made you say that?"

Abby shrugged. "Well, my parents never would've married if mom hadn't of been pregnant. So I guess I was a disgrace to both families."

Bea sighed. "I see. But you need to realize it wasn't your fault they divorced. They were never right together." She reached for Abby's hand. "You're not a mistake, Abby. God does not make mistakes. You're the best thing that came from that marriage. Even then, God had a plan. And you're here now because of it."

"Still..." Abby said and shrugged.

"How about you, Lori? Bea asked. "How'd you wind up here?"

"Mom said it was the last option or I'd be going to jail."

"What did you do?"

"I got in a couple fights at school."

"How so?"

"Well, I got tired of snooty preps making fun of me all the time. I've been overweight most of my life. I eat healthy, but mom said obesity runs in the family. It got to the place where I couldn't take name calling anymore, and I punched one girl so hard I broke her nose. She just happened to be captain of the cheerleading team."

Bea frowned. "How about you, Megan? Why are you here?"

Megan stared at Bea for a brief few moments.

Bea reached for her hand. "It's okay. I'm not here to judge you. I'm here to help you work through some things. You can trust me, okay?"

Megan drew in a breath, feeling nervous on the inside. She hadn't trusted anyone in such a long time. "I tried to commit suicide, but failed, twice."

Bea's heart sank as she felt deep concern for Megan. "What caused you to want to take your own life?" Bea asked.

Megan's eyes welled with tears. "I've been bullied since first grade. We never had much money and mom worked two jobs just to keep the lights on. I never had expensive clothes or shoes to wear, and everyone made fun of what little I had. I never seemed to fit in the mold everyone tried to put me in. I was always an oddball it seemed, an outcast in the group."

Bea gave her hand a gentle squeeze. "I'm sorry," she said. "Kids can be so cruel. It makes me wonder what kind of parents they must have to do such awful things."

Megan wiped tears with her shirt sleeve. "I really wish I had succeeded," she said. "And sometimes it's not the parents fault. They don't even know what's going on at school with their kids. Most parents work and there's not much time left at the end of the day to talk about things. Besides, some kids are just pushed aside, ignored."

"No! Don't even speak those words. You're a beautiful person, and you deserve to live a good fruitful-blessed life," Bea said. "So, you never told your parents about the bullying?"

Megan smirked. "Of, course not. They were always more interested in my baby brother. It's not like they would've listened to me anyway."

"I'm sure they would've listened had you told them how you were feeling," Bea said, feeling worried Megan may still be suicidal.

"Not when you feel like you're always the one invisible thing in the room," Megan said.

Bea let go of her hand. "Things are a lot different nowadays, for sure. We did our homework and had chores to do every day when I was coming of age. There wasn't time for much else."

The room grew silent as Bea sought direction from the Holy Spirit. "Okay. I'm going to give you girls some Scripture verses to read and we'll talk about it tomorrow." Bea grabbed a pen and jotted a few things on a notepad. The she told them the list of Bible verses.

Cora sat quietly, hoping Bea wouldn't ask her any questions.

Bea handed them each a piece of paper. "Tomorrow we'll hear what Cora has to say." Cora said nary word and took the paper from Bea's hand. She seemed to be withdrawn, an introvert, and Bea wondered if she'd been abused or bullied. Teenage years seemed to be tough for these girls, a time of discovery—a time when their self esteem either soared or was non-existent. Bea remembered when she was that age, things were quite opposite back then. There wasn't as much peer pressure, and girls weren't pressured to drink, have sex, and do other things at such a young innocent age. Most kids road the school bus because few kids had their own car to drive. After school kids had chores to do and some helped their parents work the crops in the fields, and tend to animals on the farm. And the older kids would help care for their younger siblings when need be.

After the girls left the room, Bea grabbed her apron and got busy in the kitchen. While flouring some beef stew to braise, she couldn't get Cora off her mind. She'd seen girls like her before and it bothered her Cora hadn't talked about why she was there. She had a way of finding out without Cora knowing, but she decided to give her adequate time to feel comfortable enough to talk about things. And she'd bet Cora came from a home with a long history of abuse.

Abby finished with the chores she needed to do. She'd been on schedule with feeding the animals and gathering eggs from the henhouse. Bea had given her a new pair of rubber boots and Abby was careful not to trip over extension cords lying near the hog pens. Falling face-first in the mud had caused her to be extra cautious with such things.

Shutting the gate to the pen, she glanced toward the barn to see if Kyle was around. She was tempted to walk on over, but changed her mind when she saw Niles walking out. He saw her and headed in her direction. "How's it going, Abby?"

"Okay. I'm almost done here," she said, fastening the latch to the gate.

"Looks like the hogs are happy," he said, watching them eat.

Abby laughed. "Yeah, I hope so. Grandma treats these animals like they're her babies."

"Indeed, they are," Niles said. "She'd have it no other way." He laughed.

"Can I ask you a question?"

"Sure, Abby."

"How long has it been since you shaved your beard?"

Niles pulled on the longest center part of his beard. There was more hair on his face than on his head. "Hmm. I believe it's been about a year. Why do you ask?"

"I just figured you're probably hot with all that hair on your face," she said. "After all, this is Texas during the summer." She grinned.

Niles laughed. "Well, I guess I've gotten used to it. I'd probably feel a little naked if I shaved it off now."

Abby grinned. "By all means, please keep it then."

Minutes later, Kyle came out the barn riding Hershey and headed toward one of the fields. Abby stopped mid-sentence and watched them as far as her eyes would allow.

"Kyle has been a real blessing around here during the summer. Sure has taken a lot of work off me," Niles said. "Has a special way with these horses. It's a gift."

Abby looked over at him. "I'm sorry. What'd you say?"

"Oh, nothing important. I'm heading to the house to get a thermos of iced tea. I'll catch you later."

"Okay. See you later," Abby said, wondering if Niles had noticed how distracted she was when she saw Kyle out on the horse.

Bea was sitting at the table waiting for the timer to go off when Niles came in. "I'll tell you, Bea, if Kyle and Abby ever got together we'd be in trouble."

Bea gave him an odd look. "What do you mean, Niles? Have they?"

After filling his thermos with tea, he turned to face her. "I'm not sure. But she was very distracted as soon as he came out the barn with Hershey."

"Really?"

Niles nodded. "Yeah."

"Well, keep a closer eye on Kyle. We can't chance the two of them getting together. I've already talked with him concerning things. He knows I don't want Abby to get hurt."

"Will do!"

"Thanks, Niles. I really don't know what I'd do without you." She gave him a pleasant smile.

Niles walked over and kissed her on the cheek. "Thanks, Bea, for all you do for me. You're a fine example of a Christian woman, indeed."

Bea grinned. "Thanks. That's good to know."

Niles threw a hand in the air as he walked out the door. "See you at suppertime."

Bea sat at the table, pondering on what to do next. She didn't want to ask Abby anything because she'd have questions Bea wouldn't know how to answer.

Just then, Abby walked in. "Hey, Grandma. What are you cooking? It's smells delish."

"I'm baking some chicken to make a pot pie, and I braised some beef also," she replied, really debating on whether to ask Abby if she'd had more face to face contact with Kyle, but she refrained.

Abby pulled out a chair and sat. "Why didn't you tell me you had a Christian summer program here for troubled teens? I thought I'd be the only one staying here for the summer."

Bea stood and ran her hands over her apron before answering. "Would you have still agreed to come if I had?"

"I never agreed to come." She shrugged. "Mom made me do it. She said I didn't have a choice in the matter."

"Are you glad you're here now?" Bea asked.

"I guess so... Give me a few more weeks and I'll let you know." Abby laughed.

"Get yourself changed and wash your hands. I'll show you how to make a crust for the pot pie."

"Do I have to?" Abby frowned.

"Yes, you do," Bea said. She handed Abby an apron. "Get ready and put this on. You don't want flour all over your clothes."

Walking off to change, she grabbed the apron. "So I guess you're going to teach me how to cook too?"

"Of course. You could stand to gain a few pounds. How much do you weigh, anyway?"

Abby stopped. "One hundred pounds. I like being thin."

Bea laughed. "That's what I thought. Now hurry on back. I'll be waiting." She grabbed a bowl, some flour, lard, a rolling pin, and dusted a cutting board with some flour. After ten minutes Abby returned.

"Now let's get started," Bea said.

Abby looked on as Bea went through the dough making process. Inside, she was glad she was teaching her some skills. It gave Abby a sense of peace, like she'd found a place she belonged.

TWENTY-TWO

Maggie continued her search to find something she could throw at Beaufort for what he'd done to ruin her career as a vet. With the information she'd read so far, she knew she'd have to hire an attorney to help put things in motion. And somehow she also needed to prove Beau's death was from an overdose—something Beaufort was trying to hide, but she didn't know why. When they were together, Maggie had suspected a problem with substance abuse and alcohol. However, she'd never followed through on her suspicions. Sitting at her computer desk, she searched Google for any information she could find on Beaufort. Just because he was Mayor didn't mean he'd never been in trouble, had speeding tickets, or charged with DUI or a misdemeanor before. Something wasn't right because one night when Beau had too much to drink, he told Maggie about Beaufort's shady past, but there was no record of anything as far as Beaufort was concerned. No arrests, no jail time, no bail. Nothing. The only thing she discovered was Beaufort had a reputation clean as a whistle. Maggie sighed and grabbed the coffeepot for another cup of coffee. The stress of it all was beginning to get to her, making her wonder if she was grasping at straws. Maybe it was possible Beau had actually died of natural causes. Maybe he hadn't realized what he was doing. But something in her gut had Maggie still thinking otherwise, although she had no way of proving it. And she knew there was no way she could request his body be re-examined by another coroner out of state, someone Beaufort couldn't pay to keep his mouth shut, prevent the real truth from being exposed. All of this made Maggie question if Beaufort had something to do with Beau's death. After all, he was quick to nail his demise on her. If Beaufort was involved and knew what caused Beau's death, Maggie knew he was capable of doing anything. He'd never struck her as the type of man who believed *blood* was thicker than water.

A few minutes later, a small piece of paper was slid under Maggie's door. She returned the coffeepot and walked with caution over to the door. Peeking out, there was no one in plain sight. She reached for the paper and opened it. A message was written in bold black letters. *"You need to stop this now before someone gets hurt! Heed this as fair warning."*

Maggie gasped. "Oh, no! Now I know my instincts were right," she said. "I have to find out the truth! I can't stop until I do. And I pray it doesn't cost me my life."

Minutes later, her phone rang. Hesitantly, she answered, "Hello." There was only silence on the line. "Hello," she said again. "Who is this? What do you want?" Maggie's heart raced as the line went dead. She held the phone, trying to calm herself. "If Beaufort is doing this... He's gonna pay..."

Later on, Maggie couldn't sleep. Her mind kept drifting back to the summer she and Beau talked about getting engaged. She felt certain he was the man for her. She'd only dated a handful of men, but none had treated her as special as Beau had. He had a love for horses and respected the fact her job was time consuming, as she could be called out any time of night for emergencies. It was back around Fourth of July and Beau had brought over a picnic basket and a blanket. He had a way of getting Maggie to take a break, it was as if he knew when she needed to stop and relax. There were so many things Maggie admired about him. He was handsome, polite, loved animals, and treated her better than any other man had. One afternoon Maggie was able to get off work a little early and decided to surprise Beau. When she arrived at his house, he was glassy-eyed, high as a kite. It was then she discovered the seriousness of his substance abuse. He'd managed to hide it from her for a year. Inside, Maggie was scared and devastated because she didn't know what to do to help him. Beau was not the type of man to admit weakness, and he never asked for help from anyone. He promised her he'd kick the habit before they were engaged, but as time passed Maggie realized Beau was getting worse, not better. She'd tried her best to get him to check into a facility and get clean. A few months later Maggie had met with Beaufort about Beau's addiction, and Beaufort had blamed her from that moment on. After that day things began to change for the worse.

Maggie walked to the kitchen and switched on a light to get a drink of water and a muscle relaxer. Sometimes too much caffeine tended to have an opposite effect on her body. She hated when she couldn't sleep, and it had been a long time since thoughts of Beau crossed her mind so vivid. For some reason, she kept thinking of how loving and kind he'd been prior to his addiction and control issues. Standing at the sink, Maggie gazed out the window and wondered if she and Beau would've had a couple kids by now. It was something she'd always wanted—a home and family, the patter of little feet running around, and kids crawling in bed with them during a thunderstorm. She sighed, wondering why life had to be so complicated at times.

Re-examining the note that was slid under her door, she studied the letters and felt sure it was written by a *lefty*, and so she tried to think of who it might possibly be.

Maggie put on her robe, turned the porch light on, and walked over to the barn to check on her horses. She'd kept Beau's horse. They'd purchased their horses the same day, naming them Bonnie and Clyde. Beau had said they would breed their Clydesdales', but it never happened before his demise. Maggie stood by the stall and stroked Bonnie's mane. She let out a neigh and gently moved her head against Maggie's hand. "There girl, I know you're enjoying this. I imagine you're wondering why I'm out here this time of evening." Bonnie moved her head as if to nod an agreeable yes. Maggie grinned. "You're such a smart girl." She heard a whiney noise coming from Clyde, letting her know he expected some attention as well. She walked over to the gate and stroked him on the ears—something he always enjoyed. "You're smart too, boy. I've got to get you two together before long." Clyde looked into her eyes like he comprehended every word. "I'm sure you will enjoy some alone time with Bonnie." Clyde brayed as she continued to talk in a calm soothing voice.

An hour later, Maggie walked back to the house and tried to get some sleep. Spending time with her beloved horses always helped to calm her, it gave her a sense of peace and touched her heart in a way nothing else ever had. Those horses were her pride and joy. And it broke her heart to think she might never be able to legally practice with equine again.

After supper, Abby lay in bed thinking about the time she'd spent there at the ranch. Never had she thought she'd enjoy it as much. The first day Niles gave her a ride in the old truck she felt certain she'd hate having to stay. But as time passed, she was settling in. She hadn't liked the fact there were other girls there because she'd never found it easy to make new friends. Trust was a definite issue. During the years of elementary school, Abby had been teased and made fun of because she didn't have a father at important school events. And on occasion she was also bullied by a classmate. It made her go into her own shell in fear of being hurt. It was bad enough Billy left when she was two, something that had caused her to carry guilt at a young age.

While there, Abby hoped Bea would contact Billy and he'd take initiative to come visit her. He had only sent a gift on her birthday and Christmas, but it wasn't like him being there to show he cared, and she'd never had any man tell her they were proud of her. Things any child needed to hear from their parents. Jewel had done the best she could to raise Abby, trying to be a father and mother to her. However, Abby still had an empty space inside, something she hadn't been able to fill.

She took a deep breath and rolled over on her side. Thinking, she wondered if she'd be able to be a good wife and mom one day. After all, she hadn't a clue of what a stable-loving home felt like. There was a photo of her grandfather William Jake sitting on the bureau. He had dark hair, blue eyes, and looked rather handsome with his square jaw line and neat side part of his hair, making him sort of distinguished looking. "I wish I could've met you, Grandpa," Abby whispered. "I believe I would've liked you." A smile covered her face as she closed her eyes.

Later that night, the house was finally quiet. All the girls were in their rooms and Bea sat in her easy chair to relax a few minutes, reminiscing of times when William Jake used to brew them a pot of coffee and sit beside her to read the daily newspaper. Nothing fancy, just the comfort of knowing they were side by side—together. At times, she really missed him and often felt his presence there with her. "Oh, William Jake, I miss you so much. No man will ever captivate my heart like you did. You left me way too soon."

Moments later, there was a knock on the door. Bea set her things on the coffee table and went to answer. It was Niles. And immediately she worried if something was wrong because he never came in at such an hour. "Is anything wrong?" she asked.

Niles stepped inside. "Well, I can't sleep. Thoughts of Mary keep clouding my mind tonight. It's been another year today. You know, since..."

Bea reached for his hand and they walked over to the sofa. "I'm sorry, Niles. And I understand your pain. Next month will be the anniversary of William Jake's death."

Niles sat and nodded. "I know, Bea. I guess your pain is still as great as mine." He looked Bea in the eye.

"I—I miss her, Bea. I miss her so much sometimes it's hard to breathe."

"I know. I've been sitting here thinking about William Jake. When it happens—my thoughts are always consumed for a while."

Niles nodded. He was too emotional right then to say anything. But he didn't have to because if anyone understood him, it was Bea. "Thanks for being such a good friend. I couldn't have gotten through the loss of Mary without you, Bea."

"We both have a strong connection to her, so it does help make things a little easier," Bea said.

"There's something I've never told you," Niles said.

Bea leaned forward and furrowed her brow in curiosity. "Really?"

"Yeah." Niles drew in a breath and paused. "Right after Mary and I were married we lost a baby. A son. We tried a few times after that, but Mary never made it past six weeks after the first pregnancy ended. She'd always miscarry. And before long we stopped trying. It was too painful for us both."

"Oh, Niles. I'm sorry, and surprised to hear this. Mary never told me about any of it."

"I know. She wouldn't tell anyone or allow me to tell anyone. It wasn't something she talked about—as if she'd just swept what happened under the rug and kept on living. But I know different now. The losses took a lot out of her. She never liked to cry around me, but one night I awoke and found her sitting on the front porch in tears."

"Did you go out and talk with her?"

"No. But I've wished a thousand times I had. I believe she was sick back then and didn't want to tell me because she didn't want to be a burden to me."

"You mean with the cancer?"

"Yeah."

Bea thought for a minute. "Well, it was her choice not to say anything. And it wasn't your fault it happened."

"Maybe I could've done more to help her, Bea. It's something I'll live with for the rest of my life. Not knowing..."

For a minute, Bea was unsure of what to say. Niles had lost the love of his life and nothing could bring her back. And now was not the time to second guess his actions. "I'll put on a pot of coffee. Would you like a blueberry scone?" she asked.

Niles nodded. "Sure."

At midnight, Bea and Niles sat around the table eating, chatting, and sipping a hot coffee. It wasn't something Bea did often, but she knew Niles needed a listening ear—a friend. Someone he could trust. And she understood how it felt to go through dark times ever since William Jake's death.

Out of nowhere, she lifted her cup for a toast. "To Mary and William Jake," she said, grinning through her tears.

Niles lifted his cup and they made a toast. "Yes, to Mary and William Jake," he said. Then he grinned from ear to ear. Being there with Bea was what his heart needed that night, and he was grateful for their special friendship—a friendship that had weathered many storms over time.

TWENTY-THREE

After Niles left, Bea decided to review over the files of the girls staying there. She already knew coming to the ranch had been their last chance to get on the straight and narrow and do right. When William Jake was alive he'd talked from time to time about helping troubled teens. Being the oldest of nine children, he'd understood how easy it was to get on the wrong path. His father was in the military, but had never spent much free time with them. William Jake had cared for his younger siblings like they were his own. On occasion he'd shared things about his life as a kid. It seemed some days were especially hard for Bea without him there to help her, but reaching out to offer *hope* to others made Bea feel as if she were honoring him and his *dream*. And she saw their home as a *haven of hope* for troubled teens.

Flipping through the files, Bea wondered if they'd had any kind of upbringing at all. It was sad to see the things they'd been through. One of the first kids to stay with her over the summer was Kyle. He'd been wandering around on the streets for months, surviving however he could. When she counseled him and showed him love, things began to turn around for Kyle. Afterwards, he never failed to help out there during the summer. Helping kids made Bea feel like she was doing God's work. And she knew William Jake would be happy about all the good she had done.

Glancing at the clock, Bea realized she needed to get some sleep. She put the files away, knowing it wouldn't be an easy task to help any of the girls. But the most important thing was to show them the *love* of God from the beginning. It would help pave the path to a new way of life.

Around three in the morning, Bea was awakened by a loud noise. She threw on her robe and walked in the hall to witness a fight between two of the girls. "Okay, that's enough. Stop it," she said, walking closer to them.

Abby heard the commotion and opened her door. "What's going on?" she asked. Then she saw Bea with the other girls and rushed on over. "You okay, Grandma?"

"Go back to your rooms. We'll talk about this after breakfast," Bea told the girls, raising her voice.

Abby placed her hand on Bea's shoulder. "I can't believe they were fighting here in the house like that."

Bea reached for Abby. "I know. But they'll have a chance to duke it out later."

Confused Abby said, "What do you mean?"

"Well, the only way they'll move ahead is to get rid of the anger they're carrying inside."

"How are they going to do that? I'm confused," Abby said.

"I might take them outside so they can fight it out. You see, anger is like a disease, eating away at their flesh."

Abby's jaw about hit the floor. "What? I thought you were supposed to help them, not let them kill each other."

Bea paused and looked eye to eye with Abby. "Trust me. I promise I know what I'm doing. And if it goes too far, I'll have some men step in and put a halt to it."

Abby grinned. "I believe these girls could hold their own with any man, so I hope you're right, Grandma."

"Now, go on back to bed. I'll see you at breakfast in a few hours."

"Night."

"Night, Abby."

They all went back to their rooms and the only noise heard was creaking of the floorboards.

Bea lie in bed, heart racing. She knew it was only a matter of time before a kid got angry enough to hit her. "Oh, William Jake, it is times like this I really need you here to intercede with such things."

At breakfast, Bea was yawning when Niles came in. "Looks like you must've had a late night," he said, teasing.

Bea turned to face him, grabbed a trivet, and set an iron frying pan of scrambled eggs on the table. "It was quite an emotional night," she said, brow furrowed.

"Hmm. How so?" Niles asked, wondering what was going on now.

"After I went to bed I was awakened by two of the girls fighting."

"Dag on it, Bea. I told you not to let things like that happen. One day you're going to get hurt in the crossfire. This is crazy."

Abby was standing in the doorway and nodded. "I agree, Niles." She frowned and sat next to him.

"I think I handled the situation all right," Bea said with confidence, squaring her shoulders back.

"Next time don't hesitate a minute to give me a call.

I'll come over even during the middle of the night. And I mean it," Niles said with a look of concern.

"Where are the girls now?" Abby asked.

"After thinking things over last night, I called a taxi early this morning and sent Cora and April home. Their problems are much greater than I had anticipated."

"From the sound of things, it was probably for the best," Niles said.

"I really hate to not help someone, but I witnessed rage in their eyes last night. And I was afraid of what they might try next. I believe they come from a long family line of abuse."

"Grandma! Why didn't you tell me this?" Abby asked.

Bea shrugged. "I figured I could handle things myself. There was no need to worry you."

Niles scooped some eggs on his plate. "I'm glad you're okay, Bea. You had me worried there for a minute."

About then, Megan and Lori came in the kitchen. "Have a seat, girls. I'll fix you a plate of breakfast," Bea said.

Niles and Abby said nary word. They just observed the girls behavior. It was all Niles could do to bite his tongue, refrain from speaking his mind. Because he couldn't sit around and allow Bea to be disrespected in her own home.

"When you're finished with breakfast, you've got chores to do," Bea told the girls.

"But I'm not here to do chores," Lori chimed in.

That was it. Niles couldn't help breaking in. "Well, you'll do whatever Bea asks you to do," he said. "She's a fine woman and you'll treat her with respect while you're here. Understood?"

Bea was shocked by his words. "Umm...Thank you, Niles. But I can take care of things from here on out." She smiled and placed her hand on top of his shoulder to calm him a bit.

Niles reached for her hand, grew quiet, and finished his breakfast, then left to work with one of the new horses.

After breakfast, Bea gave Lori and Megan a list of things to do and cleared away the dirty dishes. "When you're done with everything head back over here this afternoon."

Abby was taking it all in, and was glad Bea had given chores to someone other than her for a change.

Bea removed her apron. "You have dish duty for a while," she told Abby. "And make sure you wipe the table and stovetop off." She handed Abby a clean dish rag and turned to leave the room.

"Grandma?"

Bea stopped. "Yeah?"

"Is everything okay? You're acting a little strange today. Like something's off."

"I'm just a little tried this morning, that's all."

Abby nodded and ran some water in the sink to wash dishes. It was the first time Bea had left her alone in the kitchen, so Abby knew something more had to be troubling her. Usually, Bea hung around to inspect everything when Abby was done.

While Niles was loading hay bales on back of a flatbed truck, he noticed a tire was almost flat. "This is not a good place to have a flat," he said. "Now I've got to walk a mile back to the house to get some tools and a tire. Things like this hadn't happened often, but

Niles always hated when it did. He hadn't seen Kyle out and about yet, so he grabbed his thermos of water and started back toward the house. *Where are you when I need you, Kyle? I'm getting too old for this.*

About halfway he spotted Kyle out on Hershey and threw him a wave. Kyle saw him and took off toward him. "What's going on?" he asked.

"I was loading hay and noticed the truck had a flat. Can you help me out?"

"Sure. Climb on up. I'll give you a ride."

Niles joined Kyle and they made their way back to the barn, making a quick stop by the tool shed. "Can you take me back over with the tire and tools?" Niles asked.

"You bet." Kyle unsaddled Hershey, tied him out, went to get a truck, and pulled beside the shed to load everything for Niles.

"Thanks, Kyle. I'm glad you were around this morning."

Kyle grinned. "No problem. I'll help you get it changed. Get in."

After everything was loaded they took off toward the field. On the way, they saw a white car pull on the dirt road and head toward the house. Neither Kyle nor Niles recognized the vehicle. "That's kind of odd this time of day," Niles said. "Bea never receives any orders except late in the afternoon. Then it's usually by Federal Express."

Kyle slowed the truck to try and take a closer look at the driver. "I can't make out who it is," he said. "The windows are tinted. Do you think we need to go back to the house?"

Niles thought a minute and sighed. "I'm not sure,

so let's hurry with changing this tire out. I'll come back and get everything else later."

Kyle sped along and they got the tire changed. On the way back the car passed them again going out the driveway.

"There is something off about this," Niles said. "I have a weird feeling deep in my gut. It's making me nervous."

Kyle could sense that Niles was right. Something did seem out of the ordinary.

They pulled in front of the house. Bea was on the porch with her purse and keys in hand.

Niles got out. "What is it? What's happened? he asked, realizing Bea had been crying.

"It's Mimi. She's..."

Niles reached out for her. "Oh, no! Is she gone?"

"I don't know. She had a heart attack this morning, so I'm on my way to the hospital."

"I'll take you," Niles said. "Can you take over things here for a while, Kyle?"

"Yes. Go ahead. I'll be praying for Mimi," Kyle said, giving Bea a quick side hug.

"Thanks! I'll update you when we know more," Bea said. "Please let Abby know what's going on when you see her."

Kyle paused. "I will. Don't worry."

Once again, Abby heard commotion and came out to see what was going on. Kyle was standing on the porch. "What are you doing here?" Abby asked as they drove off. "I thought the house was off limits to you with us girls here?"

Kyle turned to face her. "Mimi had a heart attack and Niles left to drive Bea over to the hospital."

Abby walked closer and wrapped her arms around Kyle trying to seek comfort. "Gee. I only met her once, Kyle. And I really liked her. I hope she doesn't die. Grandma would be devastated."

Kyle wrapped his arms around her and his heart began racing in his chest. He knew he shouldn't be there with her. It was dangerous being around her. On the outside she was beautiful and mature, but the fact she was so young worried him. And he knew with everything in him, he had to fight what his *heart* was feeling right then. "I have to get back to work," he said, loosening the embrace with the scent of her damp hair lingering on him. By now his mind was racing as well. And he knew if he didn't walk away, he may make a mistake he'd regret later on.

Abby didn't want to loosen the grip she had on him. He smelt and felt good, like the outdoors, rugged and strong, fresh as morning dew. She didn't know if it was his cologne or a mix of his body chemistry with hers. Whatever it was, she liked it. "Do you really have to go," she asked, holding on to his forearm tight.

Kyle tried to pry her hand away from him, but she kept him close. He looked in her eyes with a gleam and desire and clenched his jaw. "Don't do this, Abby. Please, I have to go. Niles is depending on me to help out today."

"Do you really have to? Grandma is not here. You could come inside for a while and we could hang out."

He stared at her for a moment. "And do what? Bea would literally kill me if she caught me with you. Niles is the only man she allows in her home and I assume in her bed."

Abby released him. "It's really not like that between

them, Kyle. I know they care about each other, but grandma is a Christian woman. She doesn't go for any hanky-panky. She has a reputation to uphold around here."

Kyle grinned. "You sure about that? We all get lonely," he said. "I've watched the way they look at each other. So I just figured..."

"Well, you figured wrong. She's still in love with my grandfather."

"But he's dead. What can he do here now?"

"You're right. But her heart still belongs to him. I can tell by the way she talks about him. There's a photo of him on the bureau in my room. You want to see it? He was such a handsome man."

"No, I'll pass. There is no reason for me to go in your room, whatsoever."

"You're such a gentleman, Kyle. We don't have guys like you where I come from. Most guys are jerks, and they have no respect for themselves or any woman."

Kyle's eyes met hers. All he could think about was the fact she was much younger than him. If she was sixteen or seventeen he'd take her in his arms and never let her go. There was something special about her. He could see it in her eyes. She liked to pretend with such a tough exterior, but he knew she was lonely, had a compassionate heart, and as much as he stood there fighting it, he knew he wanted her, this child living in a mature woman's body.

Abby could read something in his eyes by how he was looking at her. "What is it? You can tell me," she said, reaching for his hand. "You can tell me anything."

"Oh, it's nothing. But I do have to say this. You have beautiful alluring eyes for a girl your age."

Abby grinned. "Thank you."

Kyle released her hand and turned to walk away, then glanced over his shoulder. "See ya."

Abby stood there with her heart being held captive by him. "See ya later," she said. *One day you'll be mine, Kyle Davies. We were meant to be together. That much I do know. It's just a matter of time before you realize it.*

TWENTY-FOUR

When they arrived at the hospital, Niles opened the truck door for Bea and walked in with her to check on Mimi. He could tell she was upset because she'd cried off and on during the trip. Inside, Niles felt like something more was troubling Bea, but he knew not to press for answers right now.

They walked to the nurse's desk to inquire about Mimi. "She's in ICU at the moment. You can go in for a few minutes at a time," a nurse said.

"Thank you," Bea said. "How is she?"

"As good as expected at her age," another nurse chimed in. "The man upstairs must've been on her side this morning or she'd be a goner, for sure."

Bea and Niles walked in Mimi's room. She had all sorts of IV lines everywhere, it seemed. Bea placed her hand over her mouth to not gulp at the sight. "Poor Mimi," she said. "She's a tough one. I hate to see her lying here so lifeless though," she whispered. "Oh, Niles. This makes me feel so helpless. I just want to cry a river."

Niles walked over and placed his hands on her shoulders. "I know, Bea. I wish there was something more I could do," he said. "I hate to see you having to go through this."

Bea grabbed his hands. "You're here with me," she said. "I'm so glad you came. Thanks for the support."

A few minutes later, a nurse walked in. "It's time to go now. She needs a lot of rest. It might be a day or two before she's able to interact with anyone."

Bea reached out to touch Mimi's hand. It was cool to the touch, as if life was almost gone, blood had left her body. "Hang in there, okay. I don't want to lose you," she whispered. A tear dropped onto Bea's blouse.

"Come on," Niles said, leading her away from the bed.

At the door, Bea stopped and wiped her cheek with the back of her hand. "I don't know what I'll do if she dies."

Niles' heart was breaking for Bea because she'd already lost a lot. "We'll keep praying that she'll pull through. I know the Good Lord hears our prayers," he assured her.

In the hallway, Bea stopped and looked at Niles. "Sometimes it's hard to hold on to my faith. I know God hears my prayers, but he's allowed me to lose William Jake and my father in such a short time." Tears were streaming now, and Bea felt such anxiety over the situation. "I know God says He won't allow more on us than we can stand, but I think I'm at my limit right now."

Niles said nary word and wrapped his arms around her offering comfort. Bea laid her head on his shoulder and wept. "It's okay, Bea. Everything is going to be okay. I'm here with you and I won't ever let you be alone." Inside, Niles felt as if his heart might burst. Bea had a way of making him emotional at times and today was one of those days. He closed his eyes and held her in silence there in the hallway.

Back at the ranch, Kyle gathered the hay and took the truck back to the yard. It wasn't something in his job description, but he thought the world of Niles and Bea and would do about anything to help them. While he was unloading hay bales, Abby brought out a ham sandwich and a glass of iced tea. Kyle skipped lunch a lot on busy days, so the treat was much welcomed today.

"I thought you might like something to eat and drink," Abby said. "It gets mighty hot out here this time of day."

"Yeah, it does. Thanks." He removed his gloves and took the plate and glass out her hand. "Thanks for thinking of me," he said. "I'm trying to help Niles out with a few things while they're away. You know, take a load off of him."

Abby smiled from ear to ear. "You're welcome. It's the least I could do. And I know Niles will appreciate the help."

"I don't think the other guys need to see us together too much though. If word got back to Bea, I'd be in big trouble," Kyle said.

"Hmm. Why's that?" Abby asked, crossing her arms. "You haven't done anything wrong. I only brought you some lunch. So there's no harm done."

"Well...it's...it's complicated," he said.

"How so?"

"You're under age for one thing," Kyle replied.

"There you go with that age thing again. It really doesn't matter," she said, placing her hands on her hips. "It's just a stupid number. Get over it."

Kyle shook his head. "Yeah, it does. It matters a lot." Kyle took another bite of the sandwich and his cell phone rang. "Hello."

"We're on the way back to the ranch," Niles said.

"Mimi's not doing too well and we could only stay in a few minutes with her."

"Okay. I'm sorry to hear that. I've taken care of a few things for you," Kyle said. "And I'm fixing to distribute fresh hay to the horses in a few minutes."

"Sounds good. I'll see you soon. Thanks for helping out today. You've been a real blessing."

"Of course. No problem."

After Niles ended the call Kyle looked at Abby. "They're on the way back, so you need to get away from here, okay. But thanks again for lunch. It was sweet of you and it meant a lot."

Abby frowned. "Maybe I don't want to leave just yet," she said. "Why don't you join us for dinner tonight? You can sit beside Niles at the table."

Kyle was getting more nervous by the minute. "I can't," he said.

"Why not?"

"I'm hired help, remember?"

"So is Niles, but he eats with grandma all the time."

"It's different with the two of them, Abby."

Abby shrugged. "Okay, suit yourself then." She took the empty plate and glass and took off toward the house.

Kyle grabbed the pitch fork and watched her walk away. He didn't know how he was going to just let her leave after summer vacation. His feelings for her were growing stronger and stronger. Abby was a little sassy, rough around the edges, but her beauty compensated for what her personality lacked. Besides, no one else had ever taken the time to bring him lunch. *Abby, you are something else girl!* Kyle struggled to get his mind off her as he unloaded the last bales and spread out some hay. And he tried to push away thoughts of what he'd like to do with her in the hay.

When Niles and Bea returned, Bea kissed Niles on the cheek and thanked him for being with her. "I couldn't have handled things as well without you today," she said.

"It was my pleasure," Niles said. "If you need anything don't hesitate to call."

They walked in and she set her purse on the table. "I will," she replied.

"I guess I'll get to work for a few hours then," Niles said, grabbing his hat off the rack beside the door.

Bea nodded. "Sure. I'll see you later this afternoon." Then she stepped over to look out the kitchen window and noticed a dirty plate and glass in the sink. *Hmm. Looks like someone got hungry while I was out today.*

Abby was in her room when Bea and Niles returned. She'd honored Kyle's wishes by leaving him alone. And the only people who could snitch on her were a couple of men working in the fields. Lori and Megan had been upstairs ironing for Bea, so she hoped she and Kyle would both be in the clear for now.

Bea had planned another session with the girls later on, but after Mimi had taken ill, she decided to wait a few days because her frame of mind was not clear as it should be. And she knew these girls were not going to be easy on her in regards to anything, so she had to have her game on, able to answer any questions they threw her way.

An hour later, Abby walked in the living room. Bea was sitting on the sofa reading her King James Bible.

"How's Mimi doing?" Abby asked.

"As well as expected at her age," she said.

Abby sat and crossed her legs. And realized Jewel hadn't made any effort to read a Bible in front of her that she could remember.

Bea lifted her head. "I found an empty plate and glass in the sink. Were they yours?" she asked.

Abby refrained from looking her in the eye. "Yeah, they're mine. I got a little hungry between meals today. I hope you don't mind."

"Nah, it's fine." Bea continued to read a few more Bible verses. It helped her mind and body relax, and some days she could sit and read for hours on end. At times, the emptiness she felt since William Jake died was almost unbearable. Spending time in the Word tended to give her strength to continue on with tasks ahead of her. The house was quiet, something unusual that time of day. She had vegetable beef soup cooking in the crock pot for supper and it felt good to be out of the kitchen a little while.

Abby sat with her about thirty minutes, and left because she didn't want Bea to get preachy. She didn't know if she was ready to jump into learning more about the God stuff quite yet.

Lying on her bed, Abby thought about the few minutes she'd spent with Kyle. They seemed to click on so many levels—it was as if he understood her without her uttering a word about herself. She figured he'd probably met his fair share of girls by now though, and she wondered why he wasn't engaged, or at least in a relationship with someone. He seemed like the ideal guy, but some things didn't make sense to her. Why would he want to stop with his everyday life to come there for the short duration of summer? There was something intriguing about Kyle, and she figured he was hiding

something. For all she knew, he could be some distant kin to the Bigelow family. It would explain why he
was so worried about Bea becoming upset with him.
The more Abby thought about it, the more she wanted to press Bea or Kyle to get the answers she needed.
Jewel had never spoken of Niles or Kyle before, and
she didn't know if it was intentional, or if there was
something Jewel was hiding as well. Like some dirty
little secret they didn't want her to know. Either way,
it made Abby want to dig her heels in and explore the
past where Niles, Kyle, and Bea were concerned. She
knew there was something more, some kind of connection, and she intended to find out what it was before
she left the ranch.

TWENTY-FIVE

S ince Abby left, Jewel Conner had been staying busy to keep her mind off things. Abby had been getting in trouble off and on for a while, and Jewel had once overheard Abby say she blamed herself for her parent's divorce. When Jewel and Billy met things moved along fast and Jewel got pregnant. Marrying Billy was a much better way of life for herself and the baby. The pregnancy was easy and Billy was ecstatic when Abby was born—or so Jewel thought. Soon afterwards, things started to change between Billy and Jewel though. Abby suffered from colic and cried a lot, and so Billy found reasons to stay at the office late. Jewel was awakened several times a night to feed and rock their baby. Before long, Billy would only come in to shower and change his clothes the next morning. Later on, Jewel realized another woman had to be involved because Billy never had time for her. It was a hard blow to take. Then her picture-perfect life started to fall apart, unravel at the seams. Finding out Billy had checked out of their relationship for his high school sweetheart, Lola, made the pain even worse. The wounds cut Jewel deep and have never healed after all these years.

Sitting on Abby's bed, Jewel gazed around the room at posters and other things Abby had taped on her wall. There was a photo of the *three* of them when Abby was one, but Abby had taken a Sharpie pen and blackened Billy's face out. Jewel knew Abby was angry and felt rejected by her own father. And Billy never even cared to see her nowadays, not even on her birthday and Christmas.

Abby had always been a good student and applied herself in class, but over the past couple years, she'd been hanging out with kids who were the opposite of her, and Jewel wondered if Abby was trying to find something or someone to fill the void of Billy not being there.

Jewel stood and sighed. *Of course she is.* Tears welled in Jewel's eyes. *Oh Lord, I've failed as a mother. I was so worried about providing for us, making ends meet.* She wiped her eyes with her fingers and stood in the empty room, alone. Then there was a knock at the door. Surprised, she went to answer it and tucked her hair behind her ears, realizing she looked a hot mess. "Hello," she said. "What brings you over?"

"Hi Jewel," he said. "I was in the neighborhood and thought I'd stop by to check on you."

"That was thoughtful of you. Please, come in, Buck."

Buck walked past her and they sat on the sofa. "Are you okay?" he asked. "I see you've been crying." He gave her a sympathetic look, gazing into her eyes.

Jewel sighed. "I probably look a sight," she said. "I was just in Abby's room. I miss her so much."

Buck leaned back. "Of course you miss her. She's all you have."

"Gee, thanks for reminding me," Jewel said with sarcasm and frowned.

"No. No. I didn't mean it like that. I meant to say..." He bit his bottom lip in search of the right words.

Jewel stretched her arm toward him and stood. "It's okay. Just let it go, Buck. You don't have to remind me of what a failure I am."

Buck hung his head. He'd been there five minutes and had already upset her. It was no wonder he didn't have a wife and family. His track record with women had never been the best. "I'm truly sorry," he said. "I was..."

"It's okay. Can I get you a glass of water or something?" Jewel asked.

He nodded. "Sure. Water is fine. Thanks."

Jewel grabbed them both a glass of water and remained quiet, wondering about the real motive for his unexpected visit.

Buck sipped on the water and began to fidget.

"What's the real reason for your visit?" Jewel asked. "You're too nervous for this to be just a casual drop-in."

Buck frowned. "Yeah, you know me too well," he said without making eye contact.

"Well, what's going on? You're acting real strange. Are you sick or something?"

"My boss found out about me taking the initiative to call you to come get Abby from the station."

Jewel was shocked. "Really? How did that happen?"

"Evidently, he had installed some new surveillance cameras a while ago without bothering to tell me, so he saw and heard our whole conversation that night when he reviewed the footage."

"Oh, no! Please don't tell me he fired you?"

"Not yet. But I may be put on leave without pay while he goes over more of the recorded footage. I'm holding my breath on this one. It could go either way."

"How long has the cameras been there?"

Buck stood and paced around the room. "I'm not sure." He turned to face her. "Bad thing is: I may lose my job over it, Jewel. Even after all the years I've worked there."

Jewel gave him a hug. "I'm so sorry," she whispered. "I never meant for any of this to happen to you. You've been a good friend to us."

Buck was feeling a little vulnerable and held onto Jewel for a few minutes. He closed his eyes, savoring the moment.

Jewel released the embrace and reached for his hands which were around her waist and looked into his eyes. "I want you to know I'm here if you need someone to talk to."

Buck smiled. "Thank you. You've always been a sweet woman and friend. I knew I could count on your friendship and support."

Jewel nodded. "Of course. What are friends for?" However, she knew Buck wanted more than simple friendship between them because he'd had a crush on her for years.

After confiding in Jewel, Buck drank the last few swallows of water and handed the glass to her. "Thank you for listening," he said. "It really means a lot." He walked to the door and gave Jewel a quick hug and kiss on the cheek.

"Anytime," she replied. He left and she closed the door, feeling guilty about getting Buck into trouble. If Abby had not of been an accessory to shoplifting, Buck wouldn't have had her at the station in the first place. Jewel leaned her head against the door, debating on whether or not she ought to fly out to Texas to see for herself how things were going.

Later that afternoon, Buck cleaned out his desk and packed some personal items in a box. While going through his things he came across a Ziploc bag of photos tucked in back of a drawer. He'd forgotten about them. He opened the bag and flipped through each one. About halfway through he paused and stared at a man for a few moments. He remembered well the time he had trained under this man's supervision, during the early years of his career.

"Officer Bigelow, I'll never forget the time I spent with you. You were the best of the best. All officers should strive to be like you. A man of excellence and integrity." Buck had never told Jewel about the three months he lived in Texas training under William Jake just months before he quit the force to work at the ranch full time. She married Billy right after, and so he figured there was no use in mentioning it. But Buck knew he had acquired his quick response and CPR skills from William Jake. And when he heard the news of his tragic accidental death it floored Buck. After all, William Jake had taught him about safety and how to take the precautions necessary when approaching an armed criminal. However, one accident had caused William Jake to sever an artery and bleed out before Niles found him later in the field. It was a tragic way to die. Tears welled in Buck's eyes as he raised his hand to salute and honor William Jake. "You'll always be a hero in my eyes," he said, slipping the photos of them in the box.

Later on, Jewel counted the money she had left over after paying bills. Thankfully, with what she'd managed to save over the past couple years, she would have enough for a flight to Texas. Now she only needed to be certain if it was something she wanted to do. Being there would bring back both good and bad memories. Even though many years had passed, it only seemed like yesterday when Abby was conceived. Billy had taken her there to meet his family and introduced her to ranch life—something she still detested to this day.

From then on Jewel's life had not been easy. From her unexpected pregnancy, to their whirlwind romance, and marriage ending in divorce. She was thankful for a handful of customers who still tipped well, helping to ease the financial burden.

There were times she loathed Billy, and then there were times she wondered how their lives might've been today had he not left. After showering, she towel dried her hair as many thoughts filled her mind. Some good. Some bad. But one thing she was certain of, she had never once regretted having Abby. In fact, she didn't know what she would do without her. Marrying Billy may have been the worst decision of her life, but striving to raise her daughter was not a mistake.

After Jewel slipped on her clothes, she again debated about going to Texas. She hadn't been there in fourteen years, but something seemed to be drawing her there now. And it wasn't because she hoped to run into Billy or Bea. No, it was something much greater—something she didn't quite understand. If nothing else, maybe it would be a way for her to make peace with the past. That is, if she could find enough courage to go.

TWENTY-SIX

B ea lay awake worrying about Mimi. She'd been so supportive when William Jake died, and Bea had never met another woman as strong as her.

Billy never visited his grandmother for whatever reason. He'd often said a mother shouldn't out live her child. And she had loved William Jake like a son.

Hopes and dreams he and Bea once shared were buried right along with him. And Bea figured Billy had dealt with loss the best way he could, just as she had. After all, they had no idea he wouldn't return the last day he went out in the fields. There'd been a problem with a tractor disk, but William Jake was a stubborn man. He didn't like to bother other hired help much, and the slip of a wrench and a disk in the soft dirt proved to be fatal. When Niles later found him, he applied pressure to the wound, but it was impossible to save him. William Jake was already blue and in shock from losing too much blood.

Teardrops fell onto Bea's pillowcase as thoughts of that horrific day plagued her mind. Things she'd pushed away and hadn't recollected for years. She figured her nerves were a mess because Mimi was sick, and it was one of those nights she wished with all her being William Jake was there to comfort her, by reassuring her everything would be okay. But he wasn't there and he never would be again. As loneliness enveloped her, Bea felt nauseous, like she might be sick. She walked to the bathroom, turned on the faucet, and splashed some water on her face. Drying off with a towel, she was certain it was going to be a long night, and made her way back to bed, finally drifting off right before daylight.

Early in the morning, Bea was awake and dressed. There were several things she needed to do, but her mind was still stuck in another place. It was one of those days she'd have to push herself along the path a little at a time as she cooked breakfast.

After breakfast, Bea made the girls a list of chores to do and some Bible verses to read before she and Niles left to visit Mimi at the hospital. She needed to spend more time with them, but under the circumstances she trusted God would lend a helping hand with His word. It was all she could manage to accomplish right now.

Walking down the hospital hallway to ICU, Bea began to feel nauseous again. Niles reached for her arm when she almost stumbled over her own two feet. "Are you okay?" he asked, feeling concerned. He'd never seen her in such a state because Bea managed to hide her emotions most of the time. She stopped and leaned her head against his shoulder, hoping the nausea would pass quickly.

"I think so," she said. "I don't know what's been going on with me the past few days."

Niles pulled her close and held her. "It's going to be okay, Bea. I promise." He loosened the embrace and planted a gentle kiss on her forehead. "I'm here for you. You're not alone," he said and sighed.

Bea smiled. "I don't know what I'd do without you,

Niles. You're such a gentle caring man. It's no wonder Mary loved you so," she said, eyes teary.

His eyes met hers. "You ready?"

Bea drew in a breath. "Yeah, ready as I'm ever going to be." She reached for Niles' hand and they walked in to see Mimi.

Mimi was lying on her back, and still hooked up to a heart monitor. IV tubes were now in both arms and her complexion appeared pale, even a little ashy.

Bea walked over to the bed and touched her hand. "Mimi? Can you hear me?" She stroked the top of her hand, praying for a response. A couple minutes later Mimi opened her eyes and then shut them. "It's okay," Bea whispered. "I'm here with you. Stay strong. You're a fighter, always have been." Bea stretched toward Mimi and kissed her cheek. "I love you, Mimi. You've always been like a mom to me. Now get well soon because I'm not ready for you to leave me yet."

Niles was standing beside Bea, touched by the genuine love she had for Mimi. It made him admire her even more. He knew Bea was beautiful inside and out, but it was hard for him to think about loving another woman after he lost Mary. He and Bea had lost their soul mates, and both had remained unmarried ever since. He figured as much time as they'd spent together, they understood each other's pain, and oftentimes no words were needed.

Bea leaned in closer. "I'll check on you tomorrow, Mimi. I love you," she said then turned to face Niles. "I pray she can overcome this. She's a fighter, and has weathered a lot of storms in life."

"Knowing Mimi like I do, I'd say she would quote one of her favorite Scriptures. You know... the one that says we overcome the devil by the blood of the Lamb and the word of our testimony."

"Thanks for the words of encouragement," Bea replied. "Yeah, she's always loved you and Mary like her own children."

Niles nodded. "She sure has. And we loved her. Heck, I still do. There's nothing I wouldn't do for her to get better and walk out of here."

"I know or you wouldn't be here with me like this. I know this is hard for you. It has to bring back sad memories."

"Well, I'd never allow you to deal with this all alone," he admitted. "Mary would never forgive me if she were still alive. And I know she'd be by your side also."

Bea smiled. "Let's go," she whispered.

They left and said nary word while walking down the hall. Once outside, they stopped on the sidewalk before getting in the truck. "Can we drop by the cemetery on the way back?" Bea asked, feeling vulnerable.

Niles shook his head. "Okay. It's been a while since I've stopped by," he admitted. "Just don't seem right, Mary's body lying in a cold dark grave." His heart ached at the thought.

"I know what you mean. But remember this, her *soul* is not there."

"I tell myself that all the time, but it doesn't make me miss her any less, Bea. I just..." He ran his hand over his face, feeling distraught.

Bea rolled her eyes toward him. "I understand. If it's any consolation I'm right there with you."

It was like a bad dream they both wanted to awaken from. Tears welled and Bea reached for Niles' hand. It didn't lessen the pain, but offered a touch of comfort in a way.

"You know, I can't understand why bad things happen to good people. Mary was a beautiful person. She loved God and her friends and family with all her heart." A lump formed in his throat, he paused to let it clear.

Bea was at a loss for words because she knew Niles was hurting, and she wanted to take his pain away, but she couldn't. All she could do was be sympathetic and pray for him, and she hoped in time he would find love again. She knew it would take a special woman to take Mary's place, just as it would take a special man to replace William Jake.

Stopping at the cemetery, Niles parked and unbuckled the seat belt. "I'm not sure I'm ready for this today, so forgive me if I get a little too emotional," he said.

Bea nodded and said nothing.

As they walked to the back row of tombstones, Mary and William Jake's burial spots were situated right across from each other. Niles drew in a breath and stooped to straighten the vase of flowers on Mary's grave. He remained silent as Bea brushed the sand off William Jake's flowers with her hand. She remained quiet as well. It was calm there with a gentle breeze blowing. The cemetery was a little ways off the main road and the only noise they heard was the clang of wind chimes close by. Niles and Bea wanted to say a lot, but today was not the day for it. They were both feeling emotional and their actions were beginning to speak louder than words ever could.

Fifteen minutes later, they left the cemetery. Driving back to the ranch, Niles asked Bea about the girls staying there. "Do you think you're going to be able to make headway with some of them?" he asked.

Bea shrugged. "I sure hope so. But I don't know for certain. It's been bad timing for me this summer, but I have to forget about myself and reach out to them. The ranch is their *haven of hope*." She shrugged. "I mean, there's one girl, Megan, she had a baby at fifteen and has been in and out of trouble several times. And then there's Lori. She's similar to Abby—sneaking out at night, shoplifting, smoking weed, and hanging out with the wrong crowd."

"I don't know how you do it," Niles said. "I think my patience would run out after the first few days." He grinned.

"I believe it's the reason my gray hair has doubled over the past couple years," Bea replied, brushing a wavy tendril off her cheek.

"What? You still look beautiful for your age. Besides, I haven't noticed any gray hair on your head."

"You're such a sweet talker, Niles. But thanks for the compliment." Bea grinned.

When they arrived, Kyle was out front in the fence with a new Clydesdale. Niles was usually the one to tame and break the horses in, but he could already see Kyle had the ability also. He parked the truck and sat, watching Kyle in action. The horse was bucking and trying to pull away, but after a few minutes Kyle had him calm and then stroked his mane.

"Look at that, Bea. Kyle has a special way with these horses."

"Yeah, I guess he has a way with them like he does with the ladies," Bea chimed in.

"Yeah, I reckon you might be right," Niles said, getting out the truck.

Kyle saw them, tied the rope to a post and stepped out the gate. "How's Mimi doing?" he asked.

"About the same," Bea replied. "Thanks for keeping a watch over things while we were gone."

"You bet." Kyle raised his gloved hand and wiped sweat off his brow.

Abby walked out on the porch. "There you are, Grandma. I wondered where you and Uncle Niles disappeared to this morning."

"Uncle Niles?" Bea said and grinned.

"I hope you don't mind. He's always around and I feel like he's my uncle." Abby laughed.

Surprised, Niles grinned. "No, Abby. I don't mind at all."

As they walked inside, Bea was surprised by the liking Abby had taken to Niles. It made her wish Abby had met William Jake before he died. She knew Abby would've loved him the way she loved Niles because they were alike in so many ways.

Later that afternoon, Bea gathered the items she needed to have a Bible study with the girls. She knew reaching out to show them they needed *Jesus* wouldn't be easy, but she knew she had *God* and the help of the *Holy Spirit* to guide her along the way.

TWENTY-SEVEN

The passage of Scripture was from first Corinthians chapter thirteen and Galatians chapter five. It talked about patience, kindness and love—something these girls needed a lot more of. The Holy Bible lay open in Bea's lap. She drew in a breath and read verses four through seven of chapter thirteen.

The girls seemed attentive to her words except for Megan, the atheist in the room. This caused a heaviness to blanket the area where they were sitting. Megan sat with her arms folded, smug look on her face. Several guys had told her how much they loved her as a ploy to get what they wanted. Inside, she felt dirty, unworthy of love. Abuse had started when she was twelve by her own stepfather. Her mom worked second shift, the perfect opportunity for him to obtain sexual favors. He'd threatened to hurt her if she told anyone. It wasn't bad enough she had to listen to them making out late at night. Her mom, certain her beloved was a wonderful man, had no idea what was happening while she was away. Things like this happened on a consistent basis, more often on Friday and Saturday nights. Sitting there, Bea's words tended to go in one ear and out the other as Megan recalled the things she'd endured at such a tender young age. Afraid to tell her mother, she'd told no one about it. With the pain she'd already suffered, Megan was certain God couldn't be real, or he would've saved her from such terrible things, like giving birth to her stepfather's baby. And she couldn't understand why God would allow her to be hurt in such an awful way. Trying to shift her thoughts, she closed her eyes, wishing to halt the tears, as a lump formed in her throat.

After Bea read a few Bible verses, she paused as a strong compassion swept over her like a tidal wave. She placed her hands on the Bible and closed her eyes. "I know in my heart, without a doubt, God wants each of you to know how much He loves you. You are His beautiful creation, a result of His handiwork, and you deserve to be cherished for who you are. A child of the Most High God."

Silence hovered, except for striking hands of an old grandfather clock. Bea sat still, waiting for the Holy Spirit to give her clear direction. Things like this hadn't happened often, but Bea had learned how to listen when it did. She'd been sensitive to the Holy Spirit ever since she'd given her heart to the Lord. She said a silent prayer. *Your will be done precious Lord. Your will be done.*

By now, the atmosphere in the room was too much for Megan to handle, and tears had begun to stream like a river. Right then, it was as if she felt God wrap His loving arms around her, embracing her tight. Tears continued as she felt the guilt and condemnation of her past mistakes being cleansed away. The warmth, peace, and love of God touched her heart and soul. She didn't understand what was happening, but she knew whatever it was, it made her feel complete to her innermost being. Worthy. Accepted. Loved.

A few minutes later Bea lifted her head and said, "You've experienced the unfailing, unchanging, love of God." Her hands were now clammy, heart racing, as she received confirmation God was at work.

Abby and Lori sat there with their eyes closed, unaware of what was really happening. However, they knew they needed to respect what Bea was saying.

As thoughts of her mistakes clouded Abby's mind, she whispered, "Forgive me, Father. Please, forgive me. I want to know you, Lord. I know I need you in my life." She clenched her hands into fists beside her, longing to experience this great love from God.

Lori knew something Spiritual was going on, but she had no idea of the full extent. Her emotions were an open book as well, and she recalled the real reason she was at the ranch—to change her life and get on a better path before it's too late.

Bea shifted in her chair and continued to read the rest of the Scripture passage on love. When finished she said, "God is love. And you will never find a greater love than God's love. This world can offer you temporary things, trick you into believing there is something greater, but don't be deceived. Satan has nothing better to offer you. He is only here to steal and kill and destroy your life. He wants to rob you of what God has for you—hope and a great future."

By this time, Bea had the attention of all three girls. They had experienced something like never before: Love, peace, and compassion from Almighty God.

There was a lot more Bea could say, but she knew the Holy Spirit had done the work that needed to be accomplished there in the room. "Do you have any questions?" Bea asked.

Abby nodded. "I seem to recall feeling this way when I was a small girl," she said, "when I went to church with a friend a few times."

"Really?" Bea was surprised.

"Yeah, it was as if I knew someone was praying for me. Of course, I didn't know who though. Mom has never been a religious person, so I haven't been to church much."

Bea grinned. "When we found out Billy was going to be a father, me and William Jake prayed each night for the baby. Even though he's gone I still continue to pray for you, Abby. We all need prayer, you know. Prayer opens the windows to heaven."

Abby was in awe of what Bea had shared with them during the Bible study. It was like something had changed on the inside of her. The anger she'd felt toward Billy was not as much as before, and she felt more peaceful and happier.

Megan dried her cheeks with her shirttail, unknowing of what to say, but there was one thing she was now certain of. God loved her. "Over the years I've been angry at God for allowing me to be hurt in the worst kind of way. I never thought He loved me. My life has been so dysfunctional for so long. Can you help me, Ms. Bea? I want to get better, get past this," Megan said.

Bea stood, reached out her arms, and they embraced. "I know a Man who can help you," Bea said. "His name is Jesus and He loves you so much. Lean on Him and give your hurts, fears and burdens to Him. You can overcome with the Lord's help and have a better life." She stroked Megan's hair and kissed her on the cheek. "And I love you, too," Bea said, nurturing her like a mother would. "Everything's going to be okay, and I'll help you however I can."

Megan closed her eyes and just wept. For the first time in years, she felt safe, valued and loved. Free of the abuse, fear and pain, that had paralyzed her entire being.

Niles had walked inside and heard them as Bea was praying. He stood silent with his hat in his hand in reverence to God. *"Lord, bless these women,"* he whispered. *"Help Bea with these young girls. They need you, Lord."*

Before Bea said a closing prayer, she looked at each girl eye to eye. "Remember this always. There is nothing going on in your life too big for God to handle. Just take it to Him and trust Him for the answer," she said, holding the Bible in her hand.

Megan chimed in. "Is it really that easy?" she asked.

Bea set the Bible in her lap. "Yes, it is! God loves you and He knows everything about you. The good. The bad. The ugly. Your mistakes. Your failures. Even your fears. And it's through the blood of Jesus that we can overcome."

After the Bible study was over, Bea walked away feeling enlightened and overjoyed at the same time. She'd been of the Christian faith for many years, but she realized God still has a way of surprising her with the little things He does.

Niles stepped into the kitchen while Bea was running a drink of water from the faucet. He walked up behind her and whispered, "You really are something special Beatrice Bigelow."

Bea spun around to face him with the glass in her hand. "How much did you overhear?" she asked.

"Enough to know a godly woman when I see one," he said, giving her a tender kiss on the cheek.

She smiled. "God's been good to me, Niles. So I try my best to help these girls. For some, being here is their only *chance*."

"And you do a great job. You've always been a good example for them to follow," he said. "You really do walk the walk and talk the talk. I don't believe there is a fake bone in your body," he said, feeling confident of his words.

Bea raised her brow. "Well, I appreciate the kind words, but don't go putting me on a pedestal. I'm just a middle-aged woman who happens to enjoy working for her Lord and Savior."

Niles stood in awe then shook his head and grinned. "What time will the food be ready?"

"Six or so," she replied. "I'm running a little behind."

"Sounds good. I'll finish working with a few of the horses and see you a little after six."

Bea nodded and threw him a wave as he walked out the back door.

After the girls finished with their chores, they sat and talked in the living room. It was a beautiful sight, another prayer answered. It warmed Bea's heart in a special way nothing else could. And she so wished William Jake was there to witness such a beautiful thing. *Oh honey, you'd be so proud of these girls.* She gazed out the window as a beautiful butterfly landed on the lantana bush and fluttered its wings. It was times like these she missed William Jake most.

TWENTY-EIGHT

Jewel tossed some laundry on the bed to be folded. There weren't as many dirty towels since Abby had been away. She missed her daughter, but hoped being at the ranch would help Abby in more ways than one. They hadn't talked much, just a brief few minutes. However, she knew Bea would call if need be. She could only assume all was well. Jewel had been busy, and tried not to worry every waking hour. And she'd since decided not to spend her extra funds on a plane ticket to Texas. There were just too many memories she didn't care to recollect. Commitments scared Jewel in many ways, and she didn't know if she'd ever get past how Billy Bigelow hurt her and Abby. The life Jewel had dreamed of was shattered when Billy walked out, and she didn't know if she'd ever find someone and fall in love again.

Since Abby left, Buck had called or stopped by to check on Jewel. She felt thankful he cared about her. In fact, she even volunteered to make dinner a couple times, but there were also times when he grabbed Chinese takeout before coming over. If it weren't for Buck, Abby would be awaiting a court hearing along with Darcy. And if anything, Jewel felt indebted to him for taking a risk to help her.

After Jewel had folded the laundry and put it away,

the doorbell rang. She wondered who it was because she and Buck had no plans that afternoon. Walking to the door, she fluffed her hair with her fingers, and rubbed her lips together certain she looked a mess without giving herself the once over. When she opened the door she was taken aback. "What are you doing here?" she asked.

"Can I come in?" a man asked.

Jewel stood with the door half open, jaw about on the floor. "What do you want?"

"Look, I know you're still angry with me. But please, can you hear me out? It's important. I promise."

Stunned, Jewel stepped back for him to enter.

"Thank you," he said, brushing on by her.

She closed the door and stood in silence, arms folded. *This better be good.*

"I know you're wondering why I'm here," he said, "especially after all this time."

She nodded and furrowed her brow. "Yeah, you could say that."*I'm waiting.*

"I need to ask a favor of you. And I know you don't owe me anything. But please, just give me a minute to explain the situation."

She furrowed her brow once more. "I don't follow you. What's going on? Is Abby okay?" She rested her hands at her sides, feeling perturbed.

He sighed and avoided making direct eye contact.

"Just spit it out, Billy! What do you want? Why are you really here? You and Lola having marital problems or something? Don't tell me you're on the rebound again."*You're trying my patience.*

He paced and started wringing his hands. "I need to see if you'll allow me to have Abby's bone marrow tested."

Jewel froze, not feeling amused by his words. "Excuse me...What are you talking about?"

"My son, Bill, needs a transplant and Abby could be a match. He's at stage three with the horrible disease now."

"I see. What about you and Lola? Have you both already been tested?"

"Lola is not a match. Neither am I."

Jewel rubbed her chin as anger began to well inside. She bit her bottom lip and drew in a breath, trying not to lose her cool before speaking. "So you want to use our daughter as a guinea pig? Is that it?"

Billy threw both hands in the air. "No, it's not like that. I mean... And now is not the time for you to be difficult, Jewel."

"Then how is it, Billy?" There was fury in Jewel's eyes, and she fought hard to refrain from punching him in the face for all the grief he'd caused her and Abby.

Billy stopped, faced her, and said nary word.

"Why are you staring at me?" Jewel asked.

"You are still so beautiful when you're angry. Sexy too." He grinned. "I remember the day I first met you. You were angry with a man who made a pass at you, so you served his glass of water to his crotch. Then you offered him a polite, but fake apology."

Jewel huffed and made an ugly face. "My apology was genuine," she said.

Billy laughed. "Not the way I witnessed it."

Jewel turned away from him. He still had a way of messing with her head, like he could read her thoughts before she could, and she hated it.

He walked over to her. "Jewel?"

Oh Billy, how I remember your touch and how

good we used to be together. But I can't do this. She felt angry and bitter, and had to guard her defenses around him. But she was lonely and recalled good times when they were married. "Give me a few minutes," she said. He looked as handsome as ever, only older. Her heart was racing and there was a knot in the pit of her stomach. *God, help me.* She placed her hand on her stomach, trying to get it together. There was no way she was going to give Billy the satisfaction of knowing he still got to her even after all these years. But she'd never loved another man the same since they were together.

"Are you okay?" he asked, wondering what was going on with her.

"I think so," she said, turning to face him.

He walked closer and ran his fingers across her cheek, the way he had many times before. "Well, can you help me or not?" he asked, gazing into her eyes.

For a moment, she only wanted him to hold her, take her back to years ago, to the place when they were happy. She closed her eyes in search of reality; then found herself seething because he still had a way of captivating her without an effort of even trying.

Billy reached for her hands. "Please help me, Jewels. I wouldn't ask, but it's my child. He could die."

"Your child?" Jewel said. "How about our child? The one you walked away from when she was only two. You never even looked back, Billy. How were you able to do that to her? You have no conscience or an ounce of remorse."

"I know you'll never forgive me, Jewels. I'm sorry. Really, I am. But I haven't come here to argue with you. I'd do it for Abby in a heartbeat, if need be."

"You've done nothing for her. She doesn't even

know who you are because you never bothered to be a part of her life. Why should me or Abby agree to help you?"

Billy looked in her eyes and said nothing. It was like he could see deep within her soul, see the hurt he had caused her. And he knew she was a woman scorned. "You're a fair woman, a woman who once loved me. But I was stupid enough to throw it all away. From the beginning, I didn't deserve you or Abby."

Jewel stared at him for a moment unsure of what to say. His unexpected visit had caught her off guard, sent a ton of emotions rushing through her like a raging waterfall. One part of her wanted to tell him to get lost—but the other part wanted to help him. She still wanted the kind of life when everything was great between them. But in a split second, Jewel realized it wasn't possible now. "Give me some time to think about it. Abby is in Texas with Bea right now."

"I don't understand. Why is she there with mom? I thought the two of you didn't get along."

"She kept getting into trouble, and so I figured it was time she met her grandmother."

Billy shrugged. "Okay. Makes sense, I guess."

"That's really all you have to say about her? I mean, you don't even know anything about Abby."

Billy stepped back and Jewel could feel tension building between them. Her mind was telling her one thing, but her heart was on a different path, like she was going back to years ago. She turned away. "No! I can't do this, Billy. Not again."

Billy stood there, feeling confused. "What are you talking about, Jewels?"

She spun around and sighed. "Don't call me Jewels,

okay?" Jewel covered her face with her hands. "I don't know about any of this. I mean..."

"I understand. Again, you don't owe me anything, but I'm asking for my son."

"As I said before, Abby won't be home till the end of the summer. You'll have to talk with her face to face concerning this. And she may not agree to it."

"Can I fly out to Texas and get her to have the test done there? I really need to see if she's a match." Billy asked with a look of desperation.

"What is it?" Jewel asked. "There's something more going on here. I can feel it. What are you not telling me?"

Billy locked eyes with her. "You always could read me like a book from day one."

"—And?"

"Things are not so good with Lola and me. In fact, right before we found out Bill was sick she had threatened to pack her things and leave."

Jewel rubbed her lips together. "Oh, I see," she said. "What happened? After all you walked out on me and Abby, said you were sorry and our relationship wouldn't survive because of you being on the rebound. Maybe this is payback for you."

Billy ran his hands over his hair, feeling angry at her remark and sighed. "I'm sorry. That's all I can say. I'm a man and I made a mistake. No one is perfect."

"Yeah, you did. And for the record, Abby and I were not two of your mistakes. We're real human beings with feelings. Whether you want to admit it or not, you have a beautiful teenage daughter. She is so much like you, headstrong, stubborn. It drives me crazy. "

"I'll book a flight to Dallas-Fort Worth first thing in the morning."

Jewel said nary word more and walked to the door.

"I guess that's my cue to leave," Billy said.

Jewel held the door open; refraining from speaking what was on her mind.

Billy left and Jewel shut the door and leaned against it. Her nerves were shot, emotions all over the place, a knot still in the pit of her stomach. She hated how Billy made her feel when he was around. Many memories reeled over and over in her mind. She drew in a breath and rubbed her forehead. *I've got to get a grip on this now. I've come too far to let the past haunt me again.*

TWENTY-NINE

Maggie Davidson had spent hours in search of anything to help get her veterinarian's license reinstated. She'd worked hard to earn the degree and adored working with large animals. At times, she wished she'd never met Beau though. They'd met at the local feed and seed store one Saturday morning. He was good looking, buff, and had a way with words. In fact, she'd once said he could talk syrup right out of a bottle. When they started getting to know one another, Beau was great at supporting her and her endeavors, and he seemed to have a love for animals as well, all qualities Maggie was looking for in a man. But after a few months in the relationship, Beau's behavior had spanned between loving and controlling if he didn't get his way. Maggie tried not to look at his faults and loved Beau for the person he was. Looking back on things, especially the way he died at such a young age made Maggie sad. But she was thankful she'd broken things off before they got any worse.

Beaufort was a powerful man around that area. He'd earned respect from most folks, and Maggie knew it wouldn't be easy to step out and accuse Beaufort of punishing her because of his own guilt and pain. She believed the root cause was because he wasn't around when Beau needed him most. Maggie being a vet had nothing to do with the grudge he had against her. No, it was much deeper than that. And he wanted to hurt her however he could. Watching her suffer seemed to make Beaufort happy. If he couldn't be at peace over Beau's death, he wasn't going to let her either, even if his demise was not her fault.

Bea left around nine o'clock to check on Mimi. She hadn't received any news from the hospital, and so she prayed no news was good news. Niles met her at the truck to go into town. Not that she couldn't drive herself, but Niles liked to help and she enjoyed his company. Being with Niles tended to make her feel closer to William Jake. It was comforting to them both, she believed.

"Hopefully, we'll get some good news on Mimi this morning," Niles said, sensing Bea had a lot on her mind, as he'd also remembered the eve of William Jake's death was fast approaching.

Bea glanced over at him. "I sure hope so."

Niles patted her on the hand. "We'll keep the faith like we always do," he said and grinned.

"That was an interesting Bible study with the girls."

"Yeah? What happened?"

"Well, I found out Megan was an atheist."

"Oh, I see. Was?"

"Yes. I believe God touched her in a special way though. She began to weep as the sweet presence of *Jesus* joined us there in the room."

"Oh, I know. I walked in to get some water and removed my hat. It sent chills throughout me. I'm glad to see you and the Lord making a difference in their lives."

"I try. But God knows what He's doing. The Holy Spirit is what makes the difference. He can remove those walls around a heart when nothing else can."

"That's so true. The healing Power of God is such an awesome thing. I've witnessed it in action myself."

"Yes, indeed. It is."

"Did you leave the girls a list of chores?"

"Of course. I have to admit I'm getting used to having extra help around here." Bea laughed. "It's making me a little lazy these days."

Niles grinned. "Well, you deserve it. And I've never seen you lazy, not even once in all the years I've known you. Sometimes you do need to stop and smell the roses. You know, do something that makes you happy."

Spoken like a true-caring man. Sweet Mary loved you so..."

Minutes later, Niles parked in the hospital parking garage and they made their way inside to check on Mimi. After stepping off the elevator, they stopped at the nurse's desk. "How's Mimi doing this morning?" Bea asked. One of the nurses walked over to her. "Come with me this way," she said. "You can see for yourself."

When they walked into a different room they realized Mimi had been upgraded from ICU. All her vital signs were now stable and to everyone's amazement, she appeared to be on the mend. "You have some visitor's," the nurse said, pulling a curtain back between two beds. Mimi's face glowed when she saw Bea and Niles standing at the foot of her bed.

"Come here. I'm so glad to see you two," Mimi said. They walked over and gave Mimi a hug.

"You're doing quite well from what the nurse said," Bea told her, feeling in awe over things.

Mimi grinned. "Yeah, the Good Lord has spared me once again. Guess it's not my time yet." Mimi threw her hands in the air to offer the Lord some praise.

Bea grabbed hold of her hand and ran her fingers around hers. "Well, I'm glad you'll be around a while longer. Yes, praise the Lord! God is so good!"

Niles watched the two of them interact. It was a special bond, for sure. Mimi and Bea were a lot alike, especially when it came to their faith in God.

"I'm glad to see you're going to pull through this," Niles said. "I'll admit, you've had me a little worried this time."

Mimi reached for his hand. "You're a good man, Niles. I know you were praying for me, so don't worry. I'm not going anywhere just yet." She pulled him toward her and then kissed him on the cheek.

Niles nodded. "I hope you're out of here real soon," he said.

Mimi yawned and closed her eyes, so they decided to let her get some rest. At her age it would be much harder to bounce back from any sickness.

Walking out, Bea felt relieved Mimi was doing so well. And she was thankful God had touched her once again. Another prayer answered.

After Maggie found a stopping place with her research, she decided to ride over to the ranch to check on Cocoa. She loaded the things she needed in her bag and locked the door. On the way down the steps a car slowed and someone appeared to be taking photos of her. She froze with the bag by her side. *What are you up to now, Beaufort? Why can't you just leave me alone?* Feeling sarcastic and disgusted, Maggie threw the guy a wave. When he realized she'd caught him snapping photos he sped off. Then she got in the car and headed toward the ranch. If Beaufort were to come by trying to harass her, she'd file a complaint against him and get a restraining order to put a stop to it.

When she arrived, Kyle was in the barn cleaning out the stalls. "Hi Maggie." He leaned the shovel against the gate and reached for a bottle of water out a small cooler. "I've been spending as much time as I can with Cocoa. She seems to be doing much better every day."

Maggie stepped inside the stall with Cocoa. "Looks like you're doing a great job, Kyle. I know Bea is glad you're over here looking after her."

"Of course. I wouldn't have it any other way." Kyle lowered his head and watched as Maggie worked.

Maggie listened to the heartbeat then used a special instrument to check out the little filly. Placing the stethoscope around her neck she said, "Your tender-loving-care has helped Cocoa a lot, Kyle. Keep doing whatever you've been doing because it's working. Both heartbeats sound normal and strong. I believe Cocoa seems to be getting better each day too."

Kyle shoved his gloved hands in his overall pockets and grinned. "I'm glad to hear it," he said. "Ms. Bea will be so happy about this."

"By the way, where is Bea?" Maggie asked. "Is she around?"

"I don't think so. I saw her and Niles leave in the truck earlier this morning. Mimi had a heart attack a few days ago, so I figured they might've went to visit her at the hospital."

"Oh my. I hope Mimi is doing better real soon.

Please tell Bea I stopped by and I'll check on Cocoa later in the week."

"Sure thing. Thanks Maggie."

Maggie grabbed her bag and opened the gate. Just then, a car was driving up the road near the house. Maggie saw it and thought she recognized the vehicle. Feeling tense she asked, "Can I hide out in here a few minutes?"

Kyle realized something was wrong by her facial expression. "Yeah, follow me." He led her to the room where he stayed. There was a plain door that blended in with the wooden walls. Unless you knew it was there you wouldn't be looking for it. "Stay in here and be quiet. I'll get rid of whoever it is," he whispered.

"Thanks," Maggie whispered and prayed Beaufort hadn't come to cause her anymore grief.

Kyle walked out front and watched as the car parked in front of the house. Then he debated about walking on over to see who it was. A man dressed in a navy blue suit got out and went to the door, but there was no answer after a few knocks. Soon after, he got in the car and drove toward the main road.

After he left, Kyle went back to get Maggie. "He's gone. Are you okay?" He stared at her a few seconds. "Gee, you look white as a ghost. I'll get you some water before you leave?"

Maggie drew in a breath and exhaled. "I think so. I guess I'm being a bit cautious these days. Without a legal license to practice, I could be in big trouble if the right person caught me over here. Beaufort would do anything to ruin my life."

"I understand. I'm glad I could help out. I know you're taking a risk every time you're here," he said.

Maggie breathed a sigh of relief. "Yeah, you're right, Kyle. But thanks for hiding me." She grinned, trying to lighten the mood as he handed her a bottle of water.

After Maggie left, Kyle wondered what else had her so unraveled. He knew she was taking a chance being there, but he felt like there was more to this thing with Beaufort. Something didn't feel quite right. And he wondered if he should mention it to Bea in hopes she could shed some light on it.

THIRTY

Riding home, Bea felt relieved Mimi's condition had improved. She rolled the window down and enjoyed the air blowing through her hair. There weren't many days she did things like that, but it was a way she let go of troubling things. Niles said nary word. He adored Bea, but held back from sharing many things. Even though Mary was gone, he still felt like he had an obligation to her. And there was no way he'd cross the friendship line with Bea unless they both felt the same way and were willing to step out and love again.

Bea gazed over at him. "You appear to have a lot on your mind," she said. "Anything you care to talk about?"

"Nah, just enjoying the drive back," he replied, adjusting his cap.

Bea nodded, understanding what he meant. At times it seemed they could read each other's minds. No words were necessary. She grew quiet and closed her eyes as hair blew over her face. Even at her age she was still a kid at heart.

When they arrived Kyle met them at the truck and tried to stifle a giggle. "Looks like you had a good trip back," he said, noticing Bea's windblown hair.

Bea opened the door and stepped out. "What's going on? Is Cocoa okay?" She ran her hands over the tangled locks, realizing by Kyle's little grin she must look a mess.

"Yeah, she's fine. Maggie stopped by to check on her and soon afterwards a car pulled in front of the house and parked. She seemed alarmed, so I hid her in my room. Then a man got out and knocked on your door."

Bea frowned. "Did you get a good look at him?"

"No. Maggie said she thought it may have been a man Beaufort sent over to check up on her."

Bea placed her hands on her hips. "I agree, Kyle. It's like he's wanted vengeance on her ever since Beau died. I don't know why he can't leave her alone."

"Weren't they engaged?" Kyle asked.

Bea nodded. "Maybe, I'm not sure. But I know Maggie got enough of his bad behavior real quick."

"I had only talked with him a couple times when I went into town to purchase nails to repair the fence. He seemed like a nice guy though."

"Well, looks can be deceiving." Bea turned the key in the door to go inside. "Thanks for telling me about this. I'll be on the lookout for anyone lurking around. If you see anything or anyone suspicious on the grounds let me know."

"I will," Kyle said.

Niles walked in behind Bea and closed the door. "What do you think Beaufort is trying to do now? He needs to give up before things get bad. Maggie's been hurt enough."

Bea turned to face him. "I don't know, but if I catch anyone else around here I'll go into town and pay Beaufort a visit. He needs to mind his own business, stay off my property, and leave Maggie alone."

"I agree," Niles said. "Poor Maggie. I'm sure she

feels like she can't go anywhere without looking over her shoulder these days."

"Yeah, and it just ain't right. Maggie has a big heart and I know she loved Beau, but..."

Niles nodded. "I agree. Please let me know if you need anything."

"I will. Thanks for going with me to see Mimi."

"Of course. I'm so happy she's doing better."

"Me too."

Back at her place, Maggie unloaded her things and found a note in her door. She opened it. *I know what you're doing and I'm going to prove it.* She grabbed it and ripped it into pieces. "Beaufort, you are fixing to cross the line," she said, dropping the paper on the ground. "I don't know how much more of this nonsense I can take. Enough is enough!"

"I agree," a man said, standing behind her.

Stunned, Maggie turned around to find an old friend. "What are you doing here?" she asked.

"Aren't you glad to see me?"

Maggie sighed. "No, not really. I thought I left you and all the bad memories back in El Paso."

"How long has it been? Five or six years ago?"

"I don't know. I've tried to forget I ever lived there. I've moved on now, set roots deep here on my own property."

"I can see that. But I've never forgotten about you, Maggie. We had some good times back then."

"Yes! Back then. It was years ago when I was young, naïve and foolish."

He walked closer and stroked her cheek with his thumb. "Still smooth as silk," he said, "just like I remember."

Maggie reached out and moved his hand off her face. "Please stop this," she said. "Nothing has changed since the day I left."

"Oh, come on, Maggie. I know you once loved me and I believe you could again."

"Stop Marlon! This isn't amusing. You being here unannounced. Clear out of the blue like this."

Marlon stared at her a few minutes. "Hmm, something has caused you to grow even colder toward me. What's happened to you since you left?"

Aggravated, Maggie perched her hands at her waist. "Life has happened," she replied, reaching for the pieces of paper. "Did you leave this at my door?"

Marlon glanced at the pieces of paper in her hand. "Nope, sorry darling... It wasn't me."

Maggie sighed and put both hands over her face. "This day can't get much worse. Really, it can't!"

Marlon reached over and started massaging her shoulders. "Man you're tense," he said. "What has got you all worked up? Remember how you always loved for me to massage your back and shoulders?"

For a brief moment, Maggie closed her eyes welcoming the massage. Then she said, "Please stop, Marlon. I can't do this. Not now. What's the real reason you're here? Are you in some kind of trouble?"

He stopped and removed his hands. "No. I'm ready for a change. You know, a new season." He shrugged. "I want you back in my life. I've missed you, Maggie. I miss what we used to have together."

Maggie furrowed her brow. "Well, you should've thought about that before you cheated on me with every woman you could," she said, voice loud.

"Oh, come on. It was only one time with a gal from

the local pub. We'd had a fight and I had too much to drink. I was drunk and feeling rejected. I admit it was a bad mistake, okay. Gee. I'm not perfect."

"This is so typical of you, Marlon. But it's not okay. Not then. Not now. Not ever. Nothing has changed with you. You're still the same self-absorbed person you always were."

Marlon stuck out a pouty lip. "Oh, I see. I reckon you'll hold my mistakes against me till I'm dead."

Maggie nodded. "Yes, I will. You should've never cheated on me. I was good to you."

"I'm sorry I hurt you. I was stupid back then. You're a beautiful woman and you deserve so much better from a man."

"Yes, I agree."

"But I need you to do me a favor, Maggie."

"Figures." She rolled her eyes. "I knew there was a reason you'd come all this way."

"I need a place to stay for a couple weeks."

"What? Why would you think I'd even consider helping you out after all these years?"

Marlon reached for her hand and looked in her eyes. "Because you're a fair woman and I know you still have some kind of feelings toward me."

Maggie looked at the pieces of paper again. "I don't have feelings for you, Marlon. Not like that. I don't hate you, but I don't trust you either. What we had is over and done with. It ended the night you slept with someone else—a woman you didn't even know."

"Please, look at me, Maggie."

Maggie drew in a breath and looked him in the eye. "There's nothing more you can say to change my mind. We're not getting back together. Period."

"Can you rent me a room for a little while? Just until I find a job and a place to stay. I could help out around here to earn my food and keep. Please, Maggie. I'm desperate because I have nowhere else to go. I'm homeless."

Maggie thought for a few minutes and rubbed her chin. The idea of watching Marlon shovel horse poop almost brought her to laughter. "I tell you what... I'll rent you a room for two weeks. After that you need to be on your way—understood?"

Marlon stuck his hand out for a handshake. "Understood! I promise you won't be sorry. Thanks."

With reluctance, Maggie shook his hand and prayed she hadn't made a mistake by allowing him to move in because it would be like history repeating itself again.

"I parked my truck a mile or so away. Can you give me a ride to get it?" he asked.

Maggie thought how odd it was but agreed. "Okay," she said, grabbing her keys to take him to get his vehicle.

When they arrived, she shut off the engine. "I'm curious. What made you park so far away from the house?"

"I wasn't sure if this was where you lived. I asked about you at the diner in town and a waitress gave me this address."

Marlon got out and retrieved his keys from his pocket then followed behind Maggie to the house.

Inside, Maggie showed Marlon to his room. "This will be your room and bathroom," she said, leading the way. My side of the house is off limits to you." She stretched out her leg and drew an imaginary line with her foot.

Marlon nodded, walked in the bedroom, and slung his bag on the bed. "Okay. I hear you loud and clear."

Maggie turned to walk off and Marlon reached for her arm. "Thanks, I know you don't owe me anything. You're such a kind woman," he said. "I was a fool to ever let you go. Maybe someday you'll be able to forgive me for being such an idiot."

Maggie frowned, removed his hand and walked out the room, trying to ignore him.

Now in the living room, she put two fingers on her wrist to feel her pulse. Her heart was racing. "Oh, my goodness. What am I doing? He shouldn't get to me after all these years. Help me, Lord, or I'll be in big trouble."

Marlon unpacked his bag and lay across the bed. "Well, I finally found you, Maggie," he whispered. "But this time I won't let you go. I'll do whatever it takes to get you back in my life for good."

Soon, Marlon's cell phone buzzed. He answered. "Hello."

"Are you in yet?" a man asked.

"Oh, yeah. For two weeks. I guess she still cares a little bit about me."

"Will it be long enough to take care of things?"

"I believe so. She has no clue of why I'm really here. I believe she's feeling sorry for me right now because I said I was homeless. That was a genius move on my part." Marlon grinned.

"Good. Be careful and keep things that way."

"Of course. You know you can trust me. I haven't disappointed you so far with things."

"Okay. Later."

"Yes. I'll call you later when she's not around."

In one aspect Marlon was happy to see Maggie again, although he wasn't there looking for a job like he said. He already had one—one that paid well. Now he just needed to keep things on a cordial basis and focus on the job he was getting paid to do. And if Maggie grew soft toward him, it would just be like icing on his cake.

THIRTY-ONE

J ewel paced back and forth in her apartment. She'd
been doing a few things out of the ordinary, going
out with Buck Schuller for one. She didn't know if it
was because she was feeling vulnerable since Abby was
away, or just longing to have a man in her life. She'd
previously said she'd never get involved with another
man until after Abby left for college. However, she'd
been enjoying Buck's company. Now years later, he
seemed like such a nice-sweet guy. And it made her
wonder if the man she'd been searching for had been
right under her nose.

Jewel had never found herself attracted to him, but
there was something different about him nowadays.
He seemed to be more caring, attentive to her needs.
Making her wonder if he was feeling sorry for her. After
all, she was a single mom suffering from emotional
distress these days. She didn't like to see herself as a
weakling at her age, but some things simply couldn't
be helped. It'd been years since she'd been able to stop
and take a breath because she'd always made Abby
her priority in life. Not having her around had been an
adjustment.

Buck was supposed to stop by after work to take
her out to dinner. In a way, she felt guilty, like she was
taking advantage of his good-heartedness. Then on the

other hand, she was delighted to have him around to fill the gap of Abby not being there.

Minutes later, the doorbell rang. Jewel drew in a breath and answered. Buck was standing there with a bouquet of mixed flowers in his hand. She smiled. "Oh, how thoughtful of you," she said, grabbing them.

Buck grinned. "I'm glad you like them," he said, admiring her. "You—you look beautiful."

Jewel had on a little black skirt and a white blouse with matching flat shoes. After she put the flowers in a vase of water they left for dinner. While driving to the restaurant Buck reached for her hand. Jewel felt a little hesitant, but said nothing and obliged, as memories of when she and Billy were together seemed to cloud her mind. A time before life had become so complicated.

On the road Buck kept on talking and gazed over at her. "You haven't heard a word I said. Is there anything you care to talk about?" he asked. "I know something has you preoccupied."

Jewel smiled. "Nah, I'm fine. Just pondering on what I want for dinner."

He nodded. "I see."

"I'm sorry. I didn't mean to ignore you."

"Well, we're almost here," he said, pulling in the parking lot at the restaurant.

Soon, they got out and made their way inside. It was around six o'clock, but the place was already busy. Three rows of square tables filled the center of the room with booths tucked against the surrounding walls. "Have you been here before?" Buck asked.

Jewel shook her head. "No. But I hope the food is as tasty as it smells." Her stomach rumbled as she pressed her hand against her waistline.

A long buffet table was sitting in a corner of the room, and had everything from spaghetti and meatballs, to mashed potatoes and gravy and pasta salad.

"Hmm. This is a diverse group of foods," she said, fixing her plate. "Now I understand why they call this place: All American Foods."

Buck laughed as he scooped some veggies on his plate. "Yeah, it makes sense I guess."

At the table Jewel gazed through the crowd and soon realized a lot of people were there with their children. It seemed to be a family oriented restaurant. While married to Billy, they never ate at restaurants like this other than the diner she'd worked at. He had preferred a fancier place with linen table cloths, so she figured Bea must've instilled those things in him during his upbringing.

"This is a pretty decent restaurant," Buck said, lifting a fork to his mouth.

"Yeah, it is. Thanks for bringing me here. I like the atmosphere. It seems real family oriented. "

"You're welcome. I think this might be one of my favorite new places."

Jewel nodded with her mouth full and drank some water. "I agree. The food is so delicious."

"Yeah, this place is a little diamond in the rough, for sure." Buck grinned.

Jewel grew quiet without responding to Buck's last comment.

"So, what's your next move?" Buck asked.

Jewel's eyes grew wide. "I'm sorry. I guess I zoned out for a few minutes. What'd you say?"

Buck reached for her hand and gazed in her eyes with a gleam. "What's your next move?" He grew quiet. *What is our next move?* he thought.

She shook her head. "Umm, forgive me. I don't follow you."

"Regarding Abby? After she returns home and everyday life gets back to normal."

Jewel set her fork beside the plate and wiped her mouth with a napkin. "I'm not sure yet, but I pray Bea has been able to reach her in ways I've failed. I know she can't continue on the same path with those bad friends of hers. Something has to change."

"I know you miss her. But know this: you've done all you can to keep Abby on the right track. It's been tough with you being a single mom and all. And I respect and commend you for it."

"Well, it has been hard trying to play the role of a mother and father. She was so young when Billy walked out on us. It hurt her in a lot of ways and she never talks about her feelings." Jewel grew tense and pulled her hand away.

"What is it?" Buck asked with concern in his voice. "You know you can tell me anything."

Jewel hesitated a few moments. "Billy came to visit me the other day."

Buck leaned back in his chair and felt his cheeks flush. "Why now? I don't understand. What did he want?"

"He wants Abby to have her bone marrow tested. His son is sick, and he thinks she can help him recover."

Buck shook his head in disbelief. "Oh, Jewel. What'd you say?"

Jewel drew in a breath and exhaled. "What could I say? It's his child, Buck." She looked away without making eye contact. "He wants to go to the ranch and talk with Abby about getting tested soon."

Buck frowned. "I'm sorry. I know this wasn't an easy decision for you. So, you agreed to it?"

Jewel laid her napkin on the table. "I'm leaving the decision to Abby. If she says no, then it's finished. I'm not going to pressure her to help someone she knows nothing about, and it still doesn't change the fact that Billy deserted her without an ounce of remorse."

"So, you're stepping aside and leaving the decision in her hands? Wow! I don't know if I could do it. You're such a strong woman."*You should've told Billy to take a hike.*

"If nothing else, he can have Bea tested to see if she's a match as well."

"Wait a minute. Billy wasn't a match?"

"No."

"Then there's a good chance Bea and Abby won't be either. How about his wife?"

"Nope, she's not a match. And I'm not sure if Abby will have anything to do with Billy. She's angry and I don't blame her. She's felt rejected and abandoned ever since she's been old enough to understand the reason that he left us."

Buck blinked and gazed in her eyes. "One day Billy Bigelow will realize what a fool he was for ever leaving you both."

Jewel grinned. "You're too sweet, Buck. But I don't think he cares anymore. He made a choice back then and we both lead different lives now."

"I'm only speaking the truth. And believe me, he cares, although he may never admit it to your face."

A few minutes later the restaurant was filled with chatter as a birthday party got in full swing with a table full of young kids.

"You ready to get on out of here?" Buck asked.

"Yeah, we better go before we get caught in the middle of this party and playing games." Jewel laughed.

Buck paid the bill and held the door open for her to exit. "After you," he said.

On the road, Jewel felt nervous and said nary word. *What am I doing here with him like this? Oh, I pray I'm not leading him on. He'll never forgive me if I hurt him. He deserves so much better than the mess I'm dealing with right now.*

They arrived at Jewel's place, and she thanked Buck for dinner without inviting him in and placed her hand on the car door. "I have a headache. If you don't mind I'd like to get some extra sleep," she said. "It's been a long day, so I think I'll take some medicine and go straight to bed. I do hope you understand."

Buck shrugged. "Okay. Sure. I hope you'll be feeling better in the morning," he said.

Jewel opened the door and got out. "Thanks again," she said before closing the door.

Buck nodded. "No problem. We'll talk later." He sat watching as Jewel walked away. The night had not gone like he had hoped, but he knew she was going through a hard time right now, and had hoped taking her to dinner would take her mind off Abby. It aggravated him to know Billy still got to Jewel the way he did. And he'd give anything to have that kind of effect on her.

Buck decided to stop by the office on the way home. There were some new developments in one of the theft cases he'd been working on. It was around eight o'clock, so he decided to take a few minutes to review over things. Little did he know he'd find something he hadn't bargained for. A friend of Abby's had been involved in a home invasion where several firearms were stolen. Now he wondered if he needed to ask Jewel to search through Abby's room. The more he uncovered things, the more he worried about Abby's past behavior and what all she had done. If she had been an accessory to a crime, he had protected her. Not something his boss would be happy with. He paused, rubbing his chin. *Oh, Abby. I pray not. Your mom would never forgive me if I had to arrest you now.*

Around nine, Buck decided to call it a night. The information he'd read had him feeling more and more troubled. He and Jewel had renewed an old friendship, and it seemed he may have more than his career on the line this time. After all these years it didn't seem fair that things like this had to happen to him. *Oh, Lord. I can't seem to catch a break.* He closed the manila folder, logged off his computer and turned the light off. *Now all I can do is stand strong and see what happens. Anything can happen as a result of this.*

Driving home, all Buck could think about was the fact he always tried to be the nice guy, but this time a lot was at stake. Everything he cared about, including his career.

THIRTY-TWO

L ate in the afternoon, Kyle was in the stable spreading fresh hay in the stalls. Ever since he'd hidden Maggie in the barn he kept thinking of her. She was an excellent vet and she'd been attentive by helping care for Cocoa. But something hadn't felt quite right about her sudden nervousness, making him question what Maggie was hiding. Like everyone else, he knew she had a past, but realized there had to be more to it. And he wondered why anyone would want to cause problems for a veterinarian.

After brushing Hershey's mane Kyle checked off the last item on his to do list and went to take a shower. He undressed and threw a towel on the bed, just outside the bathroom. He figured no one would be around, so he never worried about privacy. While showering, there was a knock on the door. When there was no answer, a woman opened the door and stepped inside. Soon, she realized Kyle was in the shower. *Oh my. Maybe I need to go.* But she saw the towel lying on the bed and walked toward the bathroom with the towel in hand. The room was filled with steam, and so she stood beside the door waiting for Kyle.

When he turned off the water and pushed the shower curtain back, Abby was standing there and handed him the towel with her eyes closed. Kyle grabbed it and wrapped it around his waist. "Really, Abby! What brings you over?" he asked, feeling embarrassed. "Can't a guy at least have some privacy around here?"

"I wanted to see you," Abby replied, walking behind him out the bathroom.

Kyle slipped his pants on under the towel then let it drop to the floor and ran his hands through his wet hair. "I already told you, you're too young for me."

"I see the way you look at me, Kyle. If I was eighteen things would be a lot different. I know they would."

Kyle sighed. "But you're not. That's the point! And you'll be flying home in a few weeks to start your freshman year of high school. Then I'll be back on the road until next summer. We won't see each other."

Abby made a pouty lip. "But you're so handsome and hardworking. Any girl would be crazy to not want to be with you."

He sighed. "I appreciate the compliment but..."

Abby walked over and placed both hands on his damp bare chest. "You're so buff," she whispered. "I can just imagine you holding me in your arms."

Kyle reached for her hands, grabbing hold of her wrists. "This cannot happen," he said, looking into her eyes. For a moment, he wanted to forget about her age. But knew he couldn't.

"See. I know you're feeling the same way," Abby said. "You can't deny it. I know by the way you're looking at me."

Kyle let go and turned away to clear his head. She had a way of gripping his heart—stirring emotions he hadn't felt in a long time. It was like she could see straight into his heart. He drew in a breath, trying to calm his racing pulse. "You're beautiful, Abby. But you're so young, and you have your whole life still ahead of you. I'm not what you want or need right now, I promise. You'll meet several guys before you find your soul mate."

"But you're all I think about. Dream about. All I want," she admitted, touching and kissing his back.

Kyle shook his head, not wanting to hear those words. "Okay. It's like this. You're infatuated with me. That's all. After you get back home, you'll forget all about me."

Abby huffed and placed her hands on her hips. "Well, you're not that much older than me," she said.

Kyle turned to face her. "But it's enough to matter right now. Look at me. I'm all over the place during the year. Wherever I can find a job and still play guitar. It's not a stable lifestyle for anyone."

Abby walked even closer. "Okay. Then do this for me and I'll leave you alone—walk away forever."

Kyle furrowed his brow. "Okay. What is it?" he asked. "What will get you to leave me alone?"

Abby looked in his eyes. "I want you to take me in your arms, close your eyes, and kiss me."

He studied her for a few moments. "You're serious about this, aren't you?"

"As a heart attack," she said.

Feeling annoyed, he reluctantly agreed. "Okay, but just this one time. If it makes you come to your senses and stops all this nonsense."

Abby stood facing him, looking into his eyes. She could feel the air from his nostrils, and realized he was nervous and uncomfortable by his breathing. Then she took a step closer and grabbed his hands, resting them at her waist. "Now hold me and kiss me," she said. "Like I know you want to."

Kyle said nary word as he closed his eyes and kissed her. In his mind he wanted the kiss to be short and sweet, something to pacify Abby's teenage desires. But when their lips met, he felt like his heart had found its home. The tender kiss seemed to linger and he didn't want to open his eyes to such a young girl. So they kissed once more before he stopped. Then he held her close as his heart raced like a galloping horse. What had happened he didn't know, but he'd never felt anything like it before. He opened his eyes without saying a word. She had ignited a passion in him with her mere innocence, but he knew there was no possible way they could be together, even though he wanted it to be.

Abby tilted her head and said nothing. Her expression was showing what he had feared. She'd felt the same way about their kiss. It had touched something in her, making her wonder if a girl her age would know what *real love* feels like. After a few moments she said, "Thank you. I know you understand what I've been trying to tell you now," she said, reaching for his hands.

He nodded. "Yes. You're so mature for your age. But a young girl still. I only wish..."

"I know I look older and you wish I was older too. Maybe I should've never told you my age. Would things be different between us if I had said I was eighteen or twenty?"

Kyle was fighting a raging battle inside. A part of him wanted to kiss her again and again and never let her go—but he understood he couldn't follow his heart. He had to think straight, be logical. "I will tell you this," he said. "You stirred something inside me, Abby. It was like we had a real connection when we kissed. And that hasn't happened with someone before."

Abby grinned. "I know, Kyle. I think I'm falling in love with you."

He turned away. "No! This cannot happen. Not now, anyway..."

"Kyle Davies, you now hold my heart in the palm of your hand," she said, standing on the tips of her sneakers like she was a ballerina.

Kyle shook his head. "No. No. Don't say things like that. I mean—it's not right."

Abby ran her hands across his shoulders and over his arms. "It's okay, really. I asked you to kiss me and you did. But I don't think either of us had anticipated what would happen next."

Feeling frustrated, Kyle hung his head and covered his face with his hands. "You need to go now," he said. "You've got to go before this progresses any further, so I won't be tempted to kiss you again."

"Is that it?" Abby said, beginning to feel perturbed. "You're going to forget about me and what you're feeling." Her eyes welled.

"I think you're beautiful and you'll make some lucky man happy one day. And yes, if you were older we might have a fighting chance. So do this. Finish school, stay out of trouble, and make plans for your life. Set some goals for the future."

Abby hung her head. "I see. I guess I should be going then." Feeling disappointed, she turned to walk away as a tear rolled onto her cheek.

"Abby..."

She stopped and looked back at him. "Yeah?"

"Thank you."

She wiped her cheek. "For what?"

"For being you," Kyle said and grinned.

Abby nodded and walked out the door. Inside, her heart was pounding and she felt vulnerable. All Kyle would've had to do was ask her to stay because she wasn't concerned about anyone else or what they may or may not think. She had tasted the passion of *first love* and it had her longing for more.

Kyle lay on the bed, playing what happened with Abby over and over in his mind. He knew she was an aggressive girl from day one, but he had no idea how getting close with her would affect him. Their kisses made him want to cross the line and forget Abby was there to get her life back on track to finish school. In a way, he wished he'd never asked her age. Putting his hands behind his head, he gazed at the night sky through a window, wanting to wish upon a star and have his wish come true that night.

THIRTY-THREE

After supper, Abby snuck in and went to her room. She didn't care if Bea or any of the other girls came looking for her either. Her head was still in the clouds and she'd lie and say she had a headache, end of story. Seconds later, there was a knock on the door. "Come in," Abby said.

Bea walked in and shut the door behind her. "Where were you this afternoon? You missed supper."

"I went out for a walk to clear my head. I've had a headache all day."

"I'm sorry. Can I get you anything?" Bea asked, feeling like there was more to Abby's story.

"Nah, I'm okay. I believe I'll turn in a little early. Where are the other girls? It's awful quiet upstairs?"

"I sent them to clean Mimi's house. She'll be coming home before long."

"That's great news. I can tell she's a wise ol' woman. I can hardly wait for her to teach me how to quilt."

Bea grinned. "Yeah, she's a special lady, for sure."

Seconds later, Bea heard Niles calling her name downstairs. "Oh, my. I'd better see what's going on, so I'll check on you later."

"Okay, Grandma. Thanks."

Bea hurried along and Niles saw her walking toward the living room. "There's something I need to tell you," he said.

"What's happened?"

"I think you need to sit for this news."

Bea gave Niles a strange look. "Is it that bad?"

"Yeah. Well, almost."

"Okay." Bea sat and leaned against the sofa, preparing for the worst.

"I saw Abby coming from the barn earlier this afternoon."

"Yeah, she likes to check on Cocoa sometime. I think it's sweet of her to care so much. She's grown rather fond of all the horses."

Niles frowned. "I saw her coming from the back near Kyle's room." He removed his hat and set it on his knee. "I don't know what to make of it."

Bea looked amused. "Really? Are you sure it was her, Niles? You know how he is with the ladies."

Niles nodded. "Oh yes, it was her."

"Okay. So you think they may have something going on between them?"

"I'm not sure, but I know Abby is straightforward when it comes to getting something she wants."

"Oh my. And so is Kyle."

"Well, I guess we can keep closer tabs on their whereabouts to see if it happens again."

Bea agreed. "We must be careful though. If Abby finds out we're snooping she'll be upset."

"Yeah, you're right. I'd never hear the end of it."

"I just checked on Abby. She said she'd taken a walk to clear her head because she'd had a headache all day."

"Well, maybe they bumped into each other at the barn by accident."

Bea sighed. "Let's hope, that's all. Thanks for telling me. I'll keep an eye on her for a little while. After a few more weeks they'll both be leaving and going their separate ways."

"Sure. No problem." Niles grabbed his hat.

"Go have a seat at the table and I'll warm you something to eat and fix us a hot coffee."

"Thanks, Bea."

She grinned. "Of course."

While Niles waited, all sorts of thoughts reeled in his mind. Thoughts of Mary and how they'd never had kids, then thoughts of Bea, and how Billy never came to visit her.

Bea sat beside Niles while sipping a hot coffee. "You seem to be in deep thought this afternoon," she said, handing him a homemade cookie.

Niles took a bite and wiped his mouth. "Just thinking of what I need to do this week on the ranch," he replied.

Soon, there was a knock on the door. And to their surprise Billy walked in with a suitcase in tow, dressed in faded jeans and a T-shirt.

Bea stood, walked over, and gave him a hug. "This is quite a surprise," she said, grinning. "You didn't tell me you were coming for a visit."

Billy laughed. "I know, Mom. Sometimes I like to surprise you," he said, kissing her cheek while gazing over at Niles. "I see you're still letting him hang around."

"How's it going, Billy?" Niles said.

"Well, I figured it had been too long since I've visited. So, here I am." He shrugged.

Niles sat observing Billy's behavior, and realized he hadn't come for a quick visit. In fact, he figured Billy must want something from Bea because it was the only time his feet touched Texas soil. It made him angry the way Billy treated her, but he managed to keep his mouth shut. After all, Billy was her only son, and seeing him made her happy.

Bea grabbed a plate from the cabinet. "Have a seat and I'll fix you something to eat," she said.

Niles scooted his chair back. "You can have my place," he said, looking eye to eye with Billy. "I have a few more things to do before bed."

Billy sat as Niles exited the room.

"Well, what brings you here this time?" Bea asked.

Billy was taken aback by her tone. "Gee. What do you mean, Mom? Can't I come see you without having an ulterior motive? "

Bea set a plate of food in front of him. "It's been a while since you've come," she said, "so I figured there has to be a reason."

Billy gave her an odd look. "Really? I can't visit you whenever I want to?"

Bea sat next to him. "I suppose so. But usually there is something wrong, like you need to borrow some money, or you need a new vehicle."

Billy dug in and wiped his mouth on his shirt sleeve. A habit he'd acquired since childhood. "Yeah, I guess you're right, Mom. I admit I haven't come as often as I should. And I reckon there's no excuse for it." *Geesh, give me a break.*

Surprised, Bea wondered what was going on. "Is everything okay?" she asked. "You know, with you and your family?"

Billy paused. "Well, I may need Abby's help this time."

Feeling concerned, Bea asked, "Really? How so?"

"It's Bill. He—Well, he is..."

"It's okay, son. You can tell me." Bea reached for his arm, moving her fingers back and forth.

"He's real sick and I need to see if Abby can help out with his medical treatment."

"Cancer?"

"Yeah. A type of..." He paused.

"I'm so sorry, Billy. What can I do to help?"

"Just pray, Momma. I'm not sure if Abby will even talk to me. I went to see Jewel right before I flew here and she told me Abby was staying with you over summer break. I'm sorry about showing up here like this."

"So, let me guess. You need Abby to give blood or something?"

"Not really. I need to see if she is a bone marrow match for Bill. I'm not. Neither is Lola."

Bea frowned and leaned back. "Oh, I see. Things are serious at this point."

"Do you think if I stay here tonight Abby will talk with me in the morning?"

"I believe so. She turned in early because she wasn't feeling well, so I wouldn't dream of disturbing her with this kind of news right now."

Billy nodded. "I understand. How's Abby doing? I know Jewel hates me for leaving them, but I couldn't live a lie any longer. And I knew I'd never love her the way I love Lola. I know what I did wasn't fair to her or Abby, but I can't change the past."

"Well, I wouldn't mention Lola if I were you. When you talk with Abby ask about how she's doing and let her know you care before you mention the real reason you're here."

"I know I've been a lousy father to her, but Jewel

made life rough when Abby was little. I could never do anything right. It was like she wanted to get back at me every chance she got, and I know it caused more distance between us."

Bea cleared away the dishes and listened as Billy talked. "Brace yourself when you see Abby. That child has a lot of hurt, anger, and disappointment buried on the inside, and I don't know if she'll agree to help you."

"I know. But it might be the only chance Bill has to ever be well again."

Niles had eased in the front door and sat on a bench to slip off his boots. While untying them, he overheard Bea and Billy talking. It wasn't like he was trying to eavesdrop, he just happened to catch the tail end of their conversation, and it made him wonder what was going on. He wanted to walk in and ask Bea, but figured now was not the right time. However, he could tell by her tone something had her emotional. He hated seeing her that way and hoped she'd volunteer to tell him about things. He sat a few minutes and bowed his head because the only thing he could do right now was pray. *God, I know I don't pray as often as I should, but I'm asking you to help Bea with whatever is going on. In Jesus' name. Amen.*

Just then, Bea walked in the room. "Niles... How long have you been sitting here?"

"Just long enough to take my boots off," he replied, not letting on he overheard their conversation. "I think I'm finally finished for the day."

"How about another hot coffee?" she suggested.

"Sounds good." Niles followed Bea and stopped in the living room, hoping she'd join him for a few minutes, but she kept walking straight to the kitchen. That let him know she didn't care to talk about things. And he figured whatever Billy had said to her would take some time to sink in. Hoping she'd soon be willing to talk, Niles sat without saying a word, waiting for her to take the lead.

THIRTY-FOUR

The next morning, Abby dressed and went in the kitchen early. Bea was standing in front of the stove scrambling eggs. She'd gathered a dozen or so from the henhouse just after sunrise—something she did most every day.

"Good morning, Grandma. Something smells good," Abby said, walking over beside her.

"Morning. I hope you're feeling better today."

"Yeah, I needed a good night's rest to sleep that headache off. I get those things once a month, if you know what I mean."

Bea smiled. "Have a seat," she said with a spatula in her hand. "I have something important to share with you in a few minutes."

Abby sat, wondering if Bea had gotten wind of her being over at Kyle's room. And she hoped none of the other guys had been tattle-tales.

Bea scooped eggs onto an oval platter and set it on the table. "You care for a hot coffee?" she asked.

"Sure. Thanks." Something felt way off because Bea was acting a little strange so early in the morning, and the anticipation was killing Abby.

Bea set a plate of bacon on the table, sat across from Abby, and clasped her hands together. "I really don't know how to tell you this..."

Abby furrowed her brow. "What's wrong? Has something happened?"

Bea drew in a breath and laid her hands on the table, as if to lay her cards out on the table. "Billy came over last night."

Abby thought for a minute. "Billy?"

"Yes. I'm talking about your dad."

Abby said nothing, trying to absorb her words, allow the shock to sink in. "But why? What did he want? He never visits you. You said so yourself."

"He wants to see you." Bea reached for Abby's hand. "I think you need to talk with him about the reason he's here."

Abby sighed. "Really? Why should I?" She slid the chair back and stood, pacing back and forth in front of Bea.

"Look, I know you're upset, and you have a right to be, but just hear him out, okay?"

Abby looked at Bea with a significant amount of disgust. "I want nothing to do with him. He left me and mom, turned his back on us, like we never even existed. Why would I ever want to see him again?"

Bea remained silent and listened to Abby vent her frustrations, unsure if it was a good idea for Billy to be there. She spooned some eggs onto her plate and began to eat. "It's a decision you have to make, Abby. I can't make it for you," she said.

"Good! You won't have to. I can't believe he had the nerve to come here, not now. Not after all these years, after all I've been through."

About that time, Niles walked in the back door for breakfast. He could see how upset Abby was. "Good morning. Is everything all right, Bea?"

Bea shook her head as Niles sat at the table.

"Go ahead and tell him," Abby said. "Tell him about the lowlife snake I have for a father."

Niles frowned and cleared his throat as Bea poured another cup of coffee. She said nothing and handed the cup to him. "Thanks," Niles said.

Abby froze and watched them both remain quiet. "I'm not hungry anymore. May I please be excused?"

Bea nodded. "Sure. I'll fix you a plate for later on."

"Thanks." Abby walked toward the stairs and was out of site in a matter of seconds.

"I guess she wasn't too happy about Billy coming here unannounced?"

"Yeah, you're right. And I don't know what to do to fix things. After all, Billy hasn't been a good father, so I really can't blame her for how she feels. She has a right to be angry."

Niles agreed as he ate his eggs. All the while, his mind reeled with thoughts of when he and Mary were married. She'd never been much for eating breakfast, but Niles always enjoyed a hot meal first thing in the morning. He was grateful William Jake had enjoyed breakfast as well, and there weren't many times they hadn't shared breakfast before starting with work on the ranch. Many times since, Niles caught himself mid-sentence about to say Mary's name. He knew it was Bea there in the kitchen, but memories of Mary seemed to be fresh as a morning's sunrise. It was like she'd visited while he slept. Other times, he could walk in their home where the scent of her perfume seemed to still linger. He couldn't see or touch Mary, but in his heart, he knew she was there, and it brought peace and comfort to Niles. He ate the last bite of breakfast and set his plate and fork in the sink. "Thank you for break-fast, Bea. Thank you for all you do for me every day," he said. "I know I don't thank you often enough. But I do appreciate everything."

Bea grinned. "You're welcome. Besides, somebody has to look after you and feed you," she teased.

"And you do a fine job of it," he said, slipping his boots back on.

Bea filled his thermos with ice water and handed it to him. "Stay hydrated," she said.

Niles grabbed the thermos. "Thanks. I'll try my best," he said, walking toward the door. "I have to get that new Thoroughbred in the fence today, so I'll need it for the extra energy."

After he left, Bea leaned against the door and wondered how things would go when Billy talked with Abby. *Oh, Lord. Please intercede in this. Abby's been hurt enough already. Calm this storm raging inside her and bring peace. Thank you, Lord. Amen.*

Later that morning, Billy planned to talk with Abby. She'd been sulking in her room, wondering how she was going to see him without punching him straight in the face. A lot of anger had been brewing inside for a long time. She had so many unanswered questions, but figured it wouldn't make any difference because she was older now, not two anymore. And she didn't know if she'd ever forgive Billy for walking out on her and Jewel.

Instead of barging in the room, Billy knocked on the door. He had no way of knowing where Abby was at. And the fact he hadn't seen her for quite some time, made him beyond nervous. A couple minutes later, Bea said, "Come on in. Have a seat and I'll let Abby know you're here."

Billy reached for Bea's hand. "Momma, wait!"

Bea stopped and stared at him, witnessing fear in his eyes. "She's not happy about you being here."

Billy squeezed her hand. "I'm not surprised. I guess I need to prepare myself for what is to come, if that's even possible."

"I'd say so," Bea replied. "Anything could happen today. Good or bad. Expect the unexpected."

Billy waited for Abby to walk in the room. Five minutes passed. Then ten. Then fifteen. It seemed like an eternity of waiting to him.

Finally, Bea returned with a worried look on her face. "She doesn't want to see you. I'm sorry, Billy. But I tried." She shrugged and frowned. "I was worried this might happen."

Billy paced back and forth, unknowing of what to do next. "I need to see if she can help Bill. It's possible she may be a match, and I can't leave here unless I have the answer I came for. She has to see me, if only for a few minutes."

Soon, Abby entered the room. "Really? You monster! How about the answers I've needed all these years? I was the mistake you made and then decided to walk away from. Pretty easy for you to leave and not look back, I'd say. You never cared if I lived or died all these years."

Billy was taken aback by Abby's blunt words. "Look, I know you're angry with me, but I never meant to hurt either of you. I did love you both. But that wasn't enough to make a lasting relationship with your mother. We were too different, came from opposite backgrounds. After a while it just didn't work anymore."

"Liar! You can't lie to me like you did to her to get what you want. All you wanted was to get in her pants; afterwards you walked away, never giving an ounce of thought to the consequences regarding me or mom. That's beyond selfish of any human being."

Billy hung his head. Abby was a little fireball like Jewel, for sure. And he knew her words spoke nothing but truth. He drew in a breath. "I really need your help, Abby. It's a matter of life and death."

"Oh, really? For who? You or your precious Lola?"

"No, Abby. It's for my son, Bill. He's very sick and his body requires a certain type of medical treatment to have any chance of survival."

"So, let me guess, he has some form of cancer?" She rested her hands on her hips, eyes teary.

With a look of desperation, Billy looked her straight in the eye. "Yes, he does. He needs a bone marrow transplant or he could possibly die soon. He's at stage three now."

"What do you want from me?"

"I would like to see if you're a match, Abby, if you'll agree to it."

Abby stared at Billy for a moment. "You're serious about this, aren't you?"

Billy nodded. "Yes, I am. Will you please consider helping Bill? He's your step-brother."

Abby rubbed her forehead, trying to take it all in. "I—I don't know. I don't even know my own little brother because we've never met. Yet you want me to help him." She shrugged. "Well, at least you got the son you wanted."

"Don't do this, Abby. It's not about the two of you or the reason why I left. Bill could die in a few months.

It's about him getting the medical treatment he needs. Nothing more. Nothing less."

Bea walked over and touched Billy's forearm. "Why don't you give Abby a day or two to think things over. This reunion is all of a sudden, you know."

Billy agreed and nodded. "Yeah, you're right, Momma. I really hate I had to come here under these kind of circumstances."

Abby stood there staring at him. A part of her wanted to ask why he left and deserted her and Jewel. But her heartbreak outweighed it, and the fact she always felt like it was her fault. She felt hurt, rejected, and confused at the same time.

Billy walked closer to Abby. "Thank you for thinking about things, Tinkerbell. I do appreciate it."

"Don't call me that!" she said. "Only mom calls me Tinkerbell."

Billy turned to walk out and Bea followed close behind. "Give her some time to let things sink in. She really is a sweet child. She's just hurt and confused right now," she whispered.

"Okay. I'll give you a call in a couple days," he said, giving Bea a hug. "Thanks for everything, Momma. I'm sorry I've been away so long. I promise I'll try and do better. I love you." A tear rolled onto Billy's cheek.

Bea squeezed him tight. "I know, baby. You're always welcome here, and you know I love you no matter what."

After Billy left, Bea decided to give Abby some space. She had planned to have another Bible study with the girls later on, but the phone rang, and the news caused her to change her mind.

THIRTY-FIVE

Later, Bea lay on the bed singing lyrics to one of Mimi's favorite songs. *Bless the Lord, Oh my soul...* It had been an emotional day, and the phone call was more news regarding Mimi. "She's had a stroke and now there's a good chance she'll be paralyzed on one side. We're not sure about her speech yet," the doctor had said.

Those words were not what Bea expected to hear. Mimi had always been a strong woman and Bea admired her. She was the one person Bea could go to for anything. There'd been several times since William Jake's death when Mimi had offered a shoulder for Bea to cry on. She was Bea's rock along with Niles. While feeling emotional, there was a knock on her door. She swung her legs off the side of the bed and stood. "Come in," she said, trying to regain her composure. To her surprise it was Niles.

"I'm sorry to hear about Mimi. Is there anything I can do?" He stepped closer.

"How'd you know?"

"I called the hospital to check on her and they told me what had happened?"

"I think it's bad," Bea said. "But they don't know for certain yet, not until the test results are in."

Niles nodded and reached out to her. "It's going to

be okay, Bea. No matter what happens I won't leave you alone to get through this," he said. "You've always got me to lean on."

Bea wept and laid her head against his shoulder. It felt wonderful to have a man make her feel safe. Someone she could trust, let her defenses down with. She was scared, feeling alone, and distraught. Niles had a way of providing what she needed right then. "I don't know what I'd do without you," Bea said. "You've been here for me ever since William Jake died."

"Shhh. It's okay. I'll be here for however long you need me to be," he replied.

Bea drew in a breath, trying to calm a rush of emotions inside. She lifted her head and wiped her eyes with her fingertips. "I probably look a mess," she said, feeling a little embarrassed.

Niles grinned. "You look beautiful as ever," he said. "There's nothing wrong with a woman being a little emotional from time to time."

"Oh, you're just saying that," she said. "You're trying so hard to help me feel better."

"Well, is it working?" he asked with a grin.

"Of course it is," Bea said. "You always know how to make me feel better."

Niles realized how vulnerable she is and it melted his heart when she was like that. At times, she was so much like Mary. He had to be careful though, because he wanted to hold her and never let her go. Once again, he refrained from telling her how he was feeling. There were so many things he wanted to say and do to prove his love, but he was afraid of losing her. So he was willing to be however she would accept him, simply because he couldn't imagine living without her.

"What is it, Niles? What's on your mind? You've been so distant lately."

Niles gave her a half-grin. "I know. I'm sorry. I don't mean to be. It's just…" He released the embrace.

Bea looked in his eyes. "It's just what? What is it? You know you can tell me anything."

"I guess I've been feeling a little blue. You know, down in the dumps, that's all."

"I see. Is it because you've been thinking of Mary so much?"

Niles gazed at the floor and tried to swallow the lump in his throat. He nodded. "Yeah, you could say that."

Bea reached over and wrapped her arms around him. "It's all right, Niles. I understand," she whispered. "I know how you're feeling. And I want you to know I'm here for you also. I believe we have a bond between us that cannot be broken."

"Really? How so?" For a minute Niles was feeling a little optimistic.

"Well, we both loss the love of our lives, and we know what it feels like to experience that kind of heartbreak."

"Yeah, you're right," he said, hoping she would've said something a tad bit different. And it made him wonder if she would ever get past losing William Jake. But he couldn't compete with William Jake's memory or even take his place for that matter. Niles wanted Bea to love him for the man he is, not compare him to what she and William Jake once shared. With those thoughts, he felt an ounce of discouragement and wondered if he'd ever find true love again.

"The visit with Billy did not go well this afternoon," Bea said, turning her back, changing the subject. "Abby was awfully hard on him."

"I figured as much," Niles said. "He hasn't been there for her during those important younger years."

"He has a son that needs a bone marrow transplant."

"Oh, I'm so sorry."

"Yeah, I am, too. And I'm worried that Abby may not agree to see if she's a match for Bill."

"Wow," Niles said, rubbing his hand over his beard. "I guess Billy is in a tough spot right now."

"Of course he is. His daughter doesn't want to talk to him, and his son may die if he doesn't get the medical treatment he needs."

"Where is Abby?"

"In her room, I believe. I decided to give her some space this afternoon. I haven't told her about Mimi yet. She really took a liking to Mimi and I know the news will upset her even more."

"It seems Abby has had such a hard life so far."

"Yeah, she has. I wish I would've had the opportunity to get to know her way before now."

"You can't go back and change the past, Bea. But you can keep moving forward. It's not your fault Jewel wouldn't agree to let you be part of her life."

"Yeah, I know." Bea turned to face him. "Thanks for checking on me," she said.

"No problem."

Bea walked to the door and Niles followed. "Have a good night," she said, holding the door open.

"You too."

After Niles left, Bea decided she'd go to the hospital first thing in the morning, but she didn't ask him to come along this time. It seemed odd he hadn't offered, but she felt like there was more on Niles' mind than he'd let on. When he embraced her, she had felt warmth and love like she hadn't since before William Jake died. It scared her in a way, but she would never share such intimate thoughts with anyone other than Niles. He understood her and how they both lived with the devastation of losing a significant other. But she wasn't sure if anything could ever fill the hole William Jake had left in her heart.

Niles went out to prepare a space for another day of horse training. Bea liked to purchase a new Thoroughbred a couple times a year, so Niles had to keep things ready. Cocoa was getting closer to her due date with the filly, and there was no time to waste. During the last thirty minutes of work, Niles couldn't get Bea off his mind. He'd witnessed a different side of her earlier. A vulnerable side, where, for a brief few minutes, she let down her defenses and let him in.

After Niles had finished with things outside, he decided to go over to the small carriage house he and Mary used to share. During training season it had been easier for them to stay there a few days a week rather than having to travel back and forth from the city each day. Turning the key in the lock, Niles drew in a breath and walked inside. Everything appeared how they had left it the day Mary went to the hospital to never return. She'd made Niles promise that he wouldn't allow her to die in the bed they slept in. Niles stood in the doorway and gazed around the room. It was as if his mind were traveling back in time. Every room of the carriage house reminded him of times they'd spent there—even the night she'd sat beside him on the sofa and announced she had terminal cancer. Again, his eyes welled at the thought and he felt as if he'd aged a lot since then. It had been the night he wanted time to stand still, time to have another night with her by his side.

"Oh, Mary, we made so many memories here. I know this house was only temporary while I was working, but it seems as if you should walk through the door any minute." Niles grabbed a hanky from his pocket and wiped his eyes. "I miss you so much. Sometimes I wish I could hear you laugh or fuss at me for not removing my boots by the door. What I would give to hear your sweet voice again, my darling."

Niles slipped his boots off and sat on the sofa. Their bedroom was situated across the hall, but he couldn't find the courage to go in there. All of Mary's things were still lying on the bed from the night he last took her to the hospital. And if he left them there, he knew he could still fool himself into believing she'd one day come back to him. Those thoughts seemed to ease his pain a little, give his heart a snippet of hope. Even though he'd never live there again.

Later on, Kyle was out for a walk and saw lights on at the carriage house. He knew it seemed odd because no one went over there anymore. Bea had been adamant about it after Mary died. Feeling curious, he decided to take a chance and see who was there, so he walked over and knocked on the door. Hoping that it was Bea, Niles answered, but was surprised to see Kyle standing there. "Hello, Kyle."

"Can I come in?"

Niles swung the door open and stepped back. "What has you over this way?"

"I was out for a walk and saw the lights on. I know Ms. Bea had said no one could stay here, so I thought

I'd check things out. You know, make sure nothing was wrong."

"I'm sure she appreciates the fact you care enough to keep an eye on things," Niles said. "But you've got to be careful coming around unannounced like this. By the way, what is going on between you and Abby?"

Kyle thought for a minute. "What do you mean?" he asked, holding his breath.

"I saw her coming from the barn not long ago. You aren't trying to get involved with her are you? That would not be smart on your part."

Kyle shook his head. "No, I'm not. She's a beautiful girl, looks much older than she is, but I'll be leaving soon to get back on the road, and she'll be heading back home to go to school."

"Does she know who you are?"

"Meaning?"

"Does she know our connection?"

Kyle sighed. "No, she doesn't. She thinks I'm a drifter who comes here to help out every summer. In fact, I haven't told her much about my life."

"Good. Make sure you keep it that way."

"Of course. I'd never do anything to hurt Ms. Bea or you."

"Have you written any new songs this summer?"

"No, not since I've been here. This is hard work, and I'm so drained at night I have nothing left. It's hard to concentrate." Kyle laughed.

"Well, I can attest to that," Niles said.

"Niles?"

"Yeah?"

"Are you ever going to tell Bea about what happened the night I was conceived?"

Niles lifted his cap and scratched his head. "I don't know, Kyle. Maybe one day. If the time is ever right and the opportunity arises."

"Okay. Well, I guess I better get back and check on Cocoa before I call it quits for the day. She's been a little restless on and off today."

"When did Maggie say she's coming back to check on her again?"

"In a couple days," she said.

"Okay." Niles walked toward the back of the house. "Let's take you out the back door. I don't know if any workers are out this afternoon, but the last person we need to run into is Abby."

"You're right. She'd have questions right away." Kyle grinned. "That girl has an inquisitive mind."

Niles gazed out the window to make sure the coast was clear before Kyle left. "If anyone asks why you're over this way, tell them you went out for a walk."

"Don't worry. I don't think anyone saw me. But I'll take the back way around just to be sure."

"Okay. I'll see you later. Goodnight."

"Nite."

After Kyle was out of sight, Niles turned off a light, locked the doors and left.

Walking back to the barn he heard a rustle in the leaves, and caught a glimpse of a doe and fawn grazing in a patch of woods near the carriage house. The little fawn still had its spots. Seeing such a beautiful thing brought a smile to Niles' face as he remembered how he used to watch Mary feed them acorns from the palm of her hand.

THIRTY-SIX

Abby was struggling with mixed emotions ever since Billy left. It wasn't like he'd known she was there with Bea or had cared how she was doing. Matter of fact, he had no idea about what was going on unless Bea or Jewel had taken an initiative to inform him. No, his main purpose was what Abby could do for Bill. She knew nothing in regards to being tested for such a thing. And why would she even care if Bill died? If he did, it would serve Billy right for the way he'd treated her. Thinking along those lines made Abby feel a little guilty though. Bill and Abby had never met, but she knew it wasn't his fault he was sick. Regardless of her feelings, Bill was her brother. Moments later there was a knock on the door. "Come in," Abby said.

Bea walked in. "How are you doing?" she asked. "I know Billy coming here unannounced was hard on you." Bea sat beside her.

Abby nodded. "Yeah, you're right, Grandma. He never had anything to do with me when I needed him, but now he decides to come and ask for my help."

Bea swept Abby's hair off her cheek so she could see her eyes. "I know. Life hasn't been easy for you. I wish I had insisted that Jewel bring you here when you were younger, regardless of our differences. I've missed out on so much time with you."

"I've enjoyed being here. I will admit, when I first met Niles, I wasn't too sure though." She laughed.

"Really?" Bea frowned. "What do you mean?"

"Well, Niles is an older man, and I had to ride in an old truck without AC. Not to mention the culture shock. Besides, mom talked like you had plenty of money and lived in an exquisite mansion. You know, like you were snooty and a snob. What else was I supposed to think?"

Bea laughed. "Yeah, Jewel hasn't a clue of what life is like on a ranch. She was only here for a brief time, long enough to get herself pregnant."

"Grandma!"

"Well, it's the truth. I've often felt like she got pregnant on purpose, too!"

"Gee. Why would you accuse her of that!?"

"I know she's your mother, Abby, but we never got along from the beginning. However, you're the best thing that came out of the marriage bond."

"Do you really think so?" Abby asked. "After all, I'm here because I kept getting into trouble. I'm sure you never asked for any of this, having to deal with a teenage girl."

"Oh, quite the contrary. I wanted to see you, but Jewel wanted nothing to do with me or Billy after he left the two of you. I know she was burnt and bitter, but she had a right to be."

Abby frowned. "This Lola woman, I'd like to meet her, and thank her for ruining my life. She stole my future. Robbed me of any chance I had at a good life."

Bea sighed. "No baby. You have your whole life ahead of you. Don't let anyone tell you otherwise. Choose to do what is right, even if it hurts, and you won't be sorry in the long run. I promise."

Abby bit her lip. "Hmm. Now you're beginning to sound like mom."

"I'm going to the hospital to see Mimi in the morning. She's had a stroke. I'm not sure she's going to be able to come home, might even have paralysis on one side."

"Oh, no! I was looking forward to seeing her again soon. She promised to teach me some skills I could take back home."

"She's been a part of my life for a long time. Mom died when I was a little girl and daddy remarried a couple years later. She's the only mom I can remember much about."

"Grandma?"

"Yeah?"

"Why does awful stuff happen to good people?"

"Well, Abby, the Good Book says there are no good people, that Christ Jesus was the only perfect person, the one who never sinned."

"I don't understand the Bible. It doesn't make sense to me. If God loved me so much, why did he let me be hurt and deserted by my own father? After all, I never asked to be born."

Bea rubbed Abby on top of her leg. "Oh child, it's not God allowing you to be hurt. Sometimes things happen in our lives. There's nothing we've done to deserve it. Think of it this way. Jesus was crucified for our sins so we could have eternal life through knowing Him. He was tried and tempted by the enemy, but He overcame. And we can too."

"How can you say he overcame? He died, Grandma."

"Yes, he did. But he could have stopped his death at any time."

Abby nodded. "If that was the case, why didn't he just ask God to stop things before he died?"

"Because he loved you and me so much he was willing to die for our sins even before we were born."

"I could never fathom a love like that. It seems so unreal, so imaginary."

Bea paused a moment. "What do you think Jesus would do to help Bill if he were still here on this earth?"

Abby hung her head and mumbled, "He would do something to save his life."

Bea smiled. "Yeah, I believe he would."

"Then I guess I need to try and help Bill because it's the right thing to do."

"Yes, it is. But you may not even be a match for him since you have different mothers."

"Are you being tested, Grandma?"

"I don't know yet. Billy hasn't asked me to."

Bea stood and walked toward the door. Then she stopped with her hand on the doorknob. "I'm proud of you, Abby. I'm proud you're my granddaughter," she said. "God has a good plan for your life. That, I am certain of."

Touched, Abby's eyes met hers and welled. "Thanks! I'm happy you're my grandma and I'm glad I came here for the summer."

After Bea left a tear rolled onto Abby's cheek. To hear words of affirmation meant a lot because they weren't words she was accustomed to. Lying on the bed, she thought of Kyle and how she wished she were eighteen and could stay at the ranch after summer was over. She could enroll in college there and they could work on planning a future together.

The next morning, Bea was stirring early to go see Mimi. She had no idea what she'd find when she arrived at the hospital. Thinking of such things had her stomach in knots, and she didn't know how she'd ever get through another loss if Mimi died. Just before she left Abby walked in the kitchen. "Can I go with you today, Grandma?"

"Are you sure you want to see her the way she is? It won't be a pleasant sight."

"Yes ma'am. I can handle it."

"Okay." She stared at Abby's bare feet a moment. "Then grab some shoes and we'll get on our way."

"Is Niles coming with us?" Abby asked.

Bea paused. "No. Not today. I already depend on him too much as it is, and he has a lot to do around here with the horses."

Abby slipped her shoes on and grinned. "I don't think he minds going though."

Bea squared her shoulders back. "Well, it'll be just you and me today."

"What'll happen if he comes in for breakfast and you're not here?"

"Oh, he'll be fine. It's not like I'm his wife, you know." Bea grinned, thinking how ridiculous Abby sounded even worrying about such trivial things.

They walked outside on the porch. "Would you like to be?" Abby asked.

Bea stopped dead in her tracks. Shocked, she asked, "Where did that question come from? We've been friends a long time, but that's it. Nothing more. Nothing less."

Abby smiled. "But you didn't answer me, Grandma."

Bea opened the truck door, still dodging the

question. "Come on, child. Let's go. Half the day will be over before we even get to the hospital and back."

"Why didn't you go to see Mimi right after you got the call she'd had a stroke?"

Bea put the truck in gear. "I prayed about things first, and I believe God wanted me to wait until today."

Abby was taken aback. "But I don't understand. An extra day can make a difference with a stroke patient. Do you think she'll even know us?"

Bea rolled her eyes toward her. "Know this, Abby. Sometimes there are things in life we aren't supposed to understand. That's why it's important to have a personal relationship with Jesus. He can lead us; give us direction in our lives when we need it."

"Have you always been a Christian, Grandma?"

"For as long as I can remember. I gave my heart to the Lord at a young age. However, I wasn't as serious about it back then. Not like I am now."

"What changed?"

"I grew older, more mature, and He's taught me on the path through life. I've made my share of mistakes along the way. That's for sure." Bea chuckled.

"So God doesn't expect us to be perfect all the time?"

"Of, course not! He loves us regardless of our ways. His love is unconditional. His grace is sufficient and is renewed on a daily basis."

"He's not disappointed when we don't do everything He wants us to do?"

"Oh, yes. I'm sure He is. But He still loves us anyway. It's our sin He's not happy with. We are all born into this world with a sinful nature."

Abby said nary word more, trying to let what Bea said sink in. There were so many questions she had about God because Jewel had not been the best at teaching her those things.

Soon, Bea parked in the hospital parking lot and they went in to check on Mimi. Walking along the hallway Bea felt her body grow tense. Knowing she needed to trust God to bring Mimi through this, she tried to shake off her doubtful nature and hold on to hope. At the nurse's desk she inquired about Mimi's condition. "How is she doing?" Bea asked.

The nurse reviewed over Mimi's chart and said, "She's holding her own for now."

"Can we visit a few minutes?"

"Sure Bea. I know she'll be glad to see you." The nurse walked with them to Mimi's room. She was lying on her back sound asleep. "Mimi, you have some visitors." The nurse rubbed her fingers over Mimi's arm to wake her.

Mimi opened her eyes. "My girls," she whispered, trying to grin.

The nurse opened the window blind to let some light in. "I'll check on you in a little while," she said and left.

"So, how are you doing?" Bea asked.

"I could be a little better," Mimi mumbled.

"Well, hang in there. You'll be out of here before long. You're a strong woman and you have the Good Lord on your side." Bea could see the obvious after effects of the stroke on Mimi's sagging jawline.

Mimi nodded. "I hope so. But there's not much feeling in this hand," she told Bea, rubbing it with her fingers.

"Oh, physical therapy can help you get stronger each day," Bea said, trying to offer words of encouragement.

Abby stood, observing Mimi, and worried that

things were not so good. She hated it because they'd
had an instant connection when they met. Abby walked
over and gave Mimi a hug. "I hope you have a speedy
recovery," she said. "You're in my prayers." Bea heard
her and those tender words touched her heart.

"Abby?"

"Yes, Mimi?"

"I want you to know how proud I am of you. I know
God has a good plan for your life. Don't halt it by getting into anymore trouble. Keep your eyes upon the
Lord." She paused to catch a breath. "I really mean
it. You're a special girl," Mimi said, looking her in the
eye.

Abby felt a knot form in her throat and swallowed
hard. Mimi's words had touched her clear to her soul,
causing her eyes to well, even if her words were a little
slurred.

Life there in Texas had been totally different for
Abby, and she hated to think about having to leave
soon. And then there was Kyle, someone she believed
God had sent into her life because she'd never met another guy quite like him.

"Are you ready to go, Abby? Mimi needs to get her
rest."

Abby was staring at nothing, lost in her thoughts.

"Abby?" Bea said and touched her arm.

"Yeah. What'd you say, Grandma?"

"You ready?"

"Sure."

They kissed Mimi on the cheek and left so she could
rest.

"Where were you back there?" Bea asked as they
walked out the room.

"I guess I must've zoned out for a few minutes." Abby grinned.

"I tend to have quite a few of those moments myself these days," Bea admitted.

Abby wanted to ask her how Mimi was really doing but refrained from doing so. It was pretty evident things didn't look all that good."

On the way back, Bea realized Niles may be angry with her for not asking him to tag along. He seemed to enjoy keeping tabs on her, but if all he was ever going to be was a friend, Bea didn't see any reason to keep him informed of her every move. And the thought of anything more was only a mere figment of her imagination.

THIRTY-SEVEN

Arriving at the ranch, Maggie's car was parked in the driveway. Bea shifted the truck in park and said, "Oh no! Something has happened to Cocoa. I have a bad feeling about this." Then she got out and darted straight for the barn. Abby tagged close behind. Inside, Maggie was in the stall with Cocoa administering some pain medicine. Bea saw her and stopped, frozen in her tracks. "Is she? I mean..." Sweat had beaded on Bea's forehead.

"Relax, Bea. She's in labor, that's all. We're going to have a filly soon." Maggie stood and leaned against the stall gate.

Bea sighed. "Is she going to be okay? Isn't it too soon yet?"

"She's foaling right now. It may take some time, so I gave her some medicine to help it along."

"How about her leg? Will it be strong enough to handle the filly's birth?"

"I believe so. Cocoa is a strong-willed horse." Maggie wiped her brow. "All we can do is pray and wait till this process is over."

Abby walked in and stood at a distance, observing the scenario.

"Does everything seem to be moving along okay?" Bea asked.

"Yeah, far as I can tell," Maggie replied. "Either I have the due date wrong or she's making her arrival a little early."

About that time, Kyle walked around the corner carrying a bale of hay on his shoulder, and brushed right by Abby as if she were invisible. "I have another bale of hay," he told Maggie. "What else can I do to help?" He dropped it in the stall and starting spreading it out near where Cocoa lay.

"Thanks Kyle. You've been such a big help today," Maggie said.

Abby was fuming inside because of how Kyle had treated her. She wanted to say something, call his behavior out, but she bit her bottom lip so hard it almost bled, and managed to refrain from speaking her mind. It wasn't the time or place to start an argument. She untied the knot she had in her shirt and played with the shirttail. Kyle gazed in her direction for a split second and their eyes met, then he glanced away. At least she knew then he realized she was in the barn.

A few minutes later, Niles walked in. "Can I have a word with you, Bea?" he asked.

Bea could tell by his tone he was upset about something. "Of course," she replied. So they walked outside the barn to chat.

"Where were you this morning? I went over to the house and you were gone. I tried calling your cell phone several times with no answer. I was worried something had happened during the night," Niles said, concern in his eyes.

Right then, Bea felt bad for causing him to worry so much. "I'm sorry," she said. "I should've told you me and Abby were going to check on Mimi. I didn't mean to worry you. I was in a hurry and forgot and left my phone charging upstairs."

Niles breathed a sigh of relief. "Well, I'm glad you're okay. How is Mimi doing?"

"She's not doing well right now, so we only stayed a few minutes. I guess it's all in God's hands. I pray He shows mercy to her because I would miss Mimi beyond words."

Niles was now feeling compassionate toward Bea, causing his anger to subside. He reached out for her and they embraced. Closing his eyes, he said a silent prayer, thanking God she was okay. She meant the world to him, and he realized how much he cared about her regardless of his loyalty to Mary.

Bea leaned her head against his shoulder and thought how wonderful it felt to have a man hold her that way. She still loved and missed William Jake every day, but her heart had a void that needed to be filled. The embrace lasted a few seconds, but Bea wondered if she could ever see his embraces lasting a lifetime. Then she lifted her head and thought how silly it was to think such a thing. But as much as she tried to deny it, she adored everything about Niles.

Niles then looked in her eyes. "Please don't ever scare me like that again, okay?"

Bea smiled and rubbed his cheek gently with the back of her hand. "I won't, I promise."

"Let's see how Cocoa is doing," Niles said.

Bea nodded. "Yeah, I'm excited to have a new addition to the family soon."

He and Bea walked in together to get an updated progress report from Maggie.

"How's it going?" Niles asked.

"She's doing as good as can be expected at this point. The filly is now in position. It could be a few hours, or it could take until later on tonight. Hard to say when she'll make her appearance."

"Can you stay here with her?" Bea asked. "I'll fix you some supper and provide a place for you to sleep tonight."

Maggie stood. "There's no way I'd ever leave Cocoa now. So don't worry, Bea. I'll be here until the birth and afterbirth is over." She stretched and brushed hay off the legs of her jeans.

Bea hugged Maggie. "Thank you. You're a true gem," she said. "I'm so happy you're here to help guide them through this."

Back at Maggie's place, Marlon was wondering what was going on. Maggie had received a call and left without as much as even saying goodbye. Since he'd been staying with her, some feelings he'd once had were resurfacing. She hadn't a clue of why he was really there, and he knew she'd hate him if she found out the truth. After raiding the fridge for something to eat, he decided to give her a call to see when she'd return. She answered, but he could barely hear a word she said. "Where are you?" he asked.

"I'm helping a friend out. One of her horses is having a filly."

He leaned against the kitchen counter, trying to understand. "Oh, I see. You left in such a hurry this morning. I wondered what was going on."

"Yeah, I was in a hurry to get to her. I'm sorry I didn't stop long enough to say goodbye."

"What time will you be home this afternoon?"

"Maggie paused, looking at Cocoa. "Umm, I really can't say. I might not be back until sometime tomorrow. Depends on how long it takes this filly to make her arrival in the world."

"Oh..." Marlon frowned. "Does everything seem to be going okay?"

"Yeah, things were a little complicated with the pregnancy, so I want to stay and make sure everything is on track like it should be."

Marlon didn't like it, but he accepted it. "Okay. I'll see you whenever you get back then."

Half-listening, Maggie said, "Okay. Sure. I'll talk with you later."

After the conversation ended, Marlon debated about giving the man he was working for a call. When he went to hit speed dial something stopped him, and he didn't know if he could do it. Soon, feelings for Maggie and guilt rushed over him because he knew she was an excellent vet. He sighed and for a few moments Marlon had a conscience.

Walking in a spare bedroom, Marlon saw a stack of books sitting on a desk beside the window. They all appeared to be law books. He thought it was odd Maggie had them, and decided to snoop around while she away. He grabbed a book and flipped through the first couple of pages. A small spiral notebook was tucked inside with notes written in Maggie's handwriting. He read the first few lines and realized why she had obtained the books—she was fighting to get her vet's license back. When he read the next line it left him at a loss for words. No doubt she'd been doing her homework. Right then, he knew she had a slight chance of succeeding. He walked over to the window, peered out and rubbed his chin. *This is not what I expected to happen. I don't know what I'm going to do now.* Seconds later, his phone rang. "Hello."

"Can you talk?" a man asked.

"Yeah."

"Where's Maggie?"

"What do you mean?"

"Is she there with you?"

"No, not right now."

"Do you know where she's at?"

Marlon paused and rolled his tongue over his top lip. "Yeah, she went out to get a few bales of hay for the horses."

"Are you sure?"

"Yes, what are you getting at?"

The man sighed. "Nothing, I just want to be certain she's not doing something she shouldn't, that's all."

"Well, I'm here for a reason," Marlon said. "You know you can trust me."

"Don't make me regret the confidence I have in you," the man said.

"Don't worry. I'll be in touch. And don't call me. I'll call you because I never know when Maggie is going to be around."

"Understood…" The man ended the call.

Marlon gazed out the window, thinking he'd gotten in over his head this time. He really needed the money the man was paying him, but he also realized he had a conscience when it came to Maggie. And he didn't know if he could continue with the job. Much less see it to completion.

The foaling continued in the barn, and Maggie

tried everything she could to help manage Cocoa's pain without compromising the filly. Bea prepared a delicious meal that afternoon and took a plate of supper over to the barn.

"I thought you could use a break," Bea said, walking in with the plate covered in tin foil.

Maggie stood, brushed hay off her clothes, and threw her disposable gloves in the trash can. "Thanks, Bea. I have to say, you must've read my mind. I was getting rather hungry."

Bea handed her a Mason jar of iced tea and grabbed a metal chair, so Maggie could sit and eat.

"Thanks," Maggie said. "This smells so wonderful."

"How are things progressing now?"

"I believe it will be a long night for Cocoa. The fact she hasn't been as active after her injury is slowing things a bit."

"I see. How about her leg? Again, are you sure there's not going to be added stress because of the birth?"

Maggie paused while chewing her food. "I'm not certain of it, but I pray not. Cocoa is a tough girl. It's a miracle she's healed as much as she has since the accident."

"Well, I trust you, Maggie. If anyone can help her get through this, you can."

Maggie grinned. "Thanks for the confidence you have in me, Bea. It makes me realize how much I miss working with equine."

After Niles had walked two of the horses he latched the gate and came in to check on Cocoa. "How's it going?" he asked.

"She's coming along. Not at a fast pace though. I believe it's going to be a long night," Maggie said.

Niles nodded. "Is there anything I can do to help out?" he asked.

Maggie handed Bea the empty plate and fork. "Not right now, but I'll let you know if I need an assistant during the delivery."

"Sure thing," Niles agreed. "I've helped out a few times around here. I don't know much about the birthing process, but I'll do whatever I can."

Bea stood watching Cocoa breathing in and out. Some breaths were harder than others, making it evident she was in pain with the contractions, and she wished she could take it away. She sighed. "Well, I guess I'll head over to the house. I need to check on the girls," she said, frowning.

Maggie reached for her arm. "It's going to be okay, Bea. Don't worry. I'll do everything I can to help Cocoa get through this and still protect the filly."

Later on, Bea decided to have one last Bible study with the girls. Their stay would soon be over and they would go their separate ways. And she prayed she'd be able to reach them on a deeper spiritual level. She wanted to let them know God loved them, and He had a good plan for their lives. One to give them hope and a future. Because where they were in life was not where they had to stay.

THIRTY-EIGHT

After supper, the girls gathered together in the living room. Bea had been so busy with things, she hadn't had as much time with them as she'd hoped to. The last time they'd gathered, Megan had experienced the sweet presence of God. However, explaining to a non-believer about God was not the easiest thing to do. Bea drew in a breath and asked the girls to bow their heads for prayer. After the prayer, she gazed over at each girl. "How is life going to be different for you after you return home?"

Abby raised her hand.

"Yes, Abby?"

"I want to be a better daughter and friend to mom. You've been such an inspiration to me, Grandma. You made me realize how I can enjoy life more, even if I did have a crappy childhood without dad around."

Bea leaned back and clasped her hands together. "I'm so proud of you, Abby. You've made a lot of headway since you've been here."

Megan sat still without saying a word.

"How about you, Megan?" Bea asked. "Have I done anything to make your life better since you've been here?"

Megan nodded. "Well, you've taken time to listen to me, and I'm grateful for that. Mom never took time to hear what I had to say when I was younger, so when I got in trouble she couldn't understand why. She didn't know what was wrong with me."

Bea smiled. "Do you understand now that your actions were a cry for attention?"

Megan locked eyes with Bea. Nodding, she said, "Yes, I do now. Before, all I knew was something was missing in life."

"Then you've made progress since you've been here." Bea patted her on the leg. "I'm proud of you also," she said. "Now, let's go back to the book of first Corinthians and talk some more about *love*."

After the Bible study Bea decided to take a walk to clear her head and check on Cocoa again. As it turned dusk out, she noticed a light on in the carriage house, a place she hadn't been in a while. Only she and Niles had a key, so she hoped he was the one over there. But why? That was something she wasn't sure of. The house had been vacated soon after Mary died.

Walking, Bea thought of times she and Mary had spent quilting at the house. Never had she seen anyone make a more beautiful quilt. However, she'd never admit it to Mimi. She'd have to just keep some things to herself as to not hurt her feelings.

Later on, when Bea walked in the barn, Maggie was on her knees wiping the little filly off as Cocoa lay still and quiet. "Are they going to be okay?" Bea asked.

"I was going to send word to you about the birth," Maggie said. "The filly appears to be healthy, but Cocoa had a hard time near the end. She's worn out and it will take a few days to get her strength back after this."

"I understand," Bea said. "Thank you for all you've done for them both."

"It's my pleasure. I love Cocoa. She is a gentle-sweet-spirited horse. I believe she'll do great with her filly. But I'd be sure to have some bottles if you need to help feed her a day or so."

"Of course," Bea replied.

Niles heard them talking and walked in. "How are they doing?" he asked.

Maggie and Bea grinned wide. "We have a new little filly," Bea said. "Isn't she beautiful?"

Niles crossed his arms. "She sure is. And Cocoa? How's she doing?"

"I think she'll be fine, but after a couple days we'll know for sure." Maggie placed the filly next to Cocoa and she searched for the teat to suckle. "That's a good sign," Maggie said. "I'm happy Cocoa didn't reject her straight away."

Bea let out a sigh of relief. "Me too," she said, "our little Mary will be just fine."

Niles grinned and walked over to Bea. "How are things with you and the girls?" he asked.

Bea shook her head. "I'm doing okay. I think I'm making a little headway."

"Glad to hear it," Niles said, giving her a quick nod.

"Could I have a few minutes with you?" Bea asked.

Niles furrowed his brow, wondering what was on her mind. "Sure."

Bea walked outside so they could talk in private while Maggie assessed Cocoa and the filly. "Let's take a walk," she suggested.

"Okay." Niles agreed and followed close by. "What's on your mind?"

"Have you been to the carriage house over the past couple days?"

Niles stopped and looked at her. "Yeah, why do you ask? Is something wrong over there?"

"I noticed a light was left on inside."

As they walked Niles gazed in the direction of the house. "Hmm, I guess you're right. I thought I switched all the lights off before I left. I'm sorry. I'll take care of it."

Bea reached for his hand, feeling like she'd scolded him like a little kid. "It's okay," she said. "I'm just as protective over the house as you are. A lot of special memories are embedded in those walls."

Niles stopped and looked into her eyes. "I don't go in there much, Bea. But some days... Well..."

Bea squeezed his hand. "I know. I miss Mary, too. And I understand."

Niles nodded and said nary word more. He was still feeling vulnerable from reminiscing of his beloved Mary.

Bea stopped and turned around. "Thanks for the chat and walk," she said. "I guess I'll head back to the house now and see what the girls are doing."

"Okay. I'll see you later," Niles said, shoving his hands in his pockets.

Bea darted off and didn't look back—afraid she'd see sweet memories of William Jake or Mary sitting on the porch of the carriage house. Heart pounding, she walked as fast as she could. And she didn't know why she'd allowed her mind to roam to such things all of a sudden. It was one of the reasons she never went over there much—it was just too painful.

Late in the afternoon, Maggie sent word to Bea about Cocoa. Kyle had stayed close by in case she needed help with anything, and had walked over to give Bea the news. When he walked in Bea was surprised to see him. "Is everything okay?" she asked.

Kyle shoved his dirty hands in his pockets. "There's a problem with the filly."

Bea stood and her heart sank. "Oh, no! What's wrong?"

"Umm. You might want to talk with Maggie about things. She's still in the barn."

Bea didn't like the sound of that. "Yeah, I think I will," she said, already walking toward the door. On the way out Kyle followed close behind. "Thanks for coming to get me," she said.

Kyle nodded. "You're welcome."

Bea stopped and glanced over at him. "I appreciate you hanging around to help Maggie with everything," she said.

"Yes ma'am."

When they arrived at the barn Maggie was in with Cocoa, trying to get her and the filly to bond. She walked over to Bea and frowned. "I don't know if Cocoa is going to continue taking care of her, Bea. She's been through a lot and I'm not real sure about things at this point. She was feeding and doing well. But now..." She threw her hands in the air.

"Well, I know Cocoa is a strong-willed horse, even a little stubborn at times. Give her a few hours and see how things go. Maybe she's just worn out from the whole birth ordeal."

"I hope you're right, Bea. You know this filly can't survive for long without its mother. She'll need someone around the clock."

"I'll gather a few bottles from the house, sterilize

them, and bring them over soon," Bea said. "I know she's going to be hungry every few hours."

"Yeah, I'm praying Cocoa will allow her to feed again soon." Maggie removed her dirty gloves and put her things in her bag.

"Thank you again for all you've done for them, Maggie. I could never repay you for everything."

"It's my pleasure," Maggie said. "Beaufort may have had my license to practice revoked, but he can't stop me from helping out a friend in need."

Bea laughed. "Well, sooner or later Beaufort will get what's coming to him because he's not as powerful as he pretends to be."

About that time, Cocoa let out a neigh and then allowed the little filly to feed.

"Look at that," Maggie said. "I guess Cocoa changed her mind. Whew! I was worried about her rejecting the filly from this moment on."

Cocoa let out another neigh as to assure Maggie they were going to be okay.

Maggie rolled her eyes toward Kyle. He was standing by the gate taking it all in. "I couldn't have done as much without Kyle's help. He really has a special way with these horses," she said.

Kyle smiled. "Oh, I try. And Cocoa is a special one, for sure."

Right then, one of the field workers ran in the barn. "Call 911...The carriage house is on fire," he said.

Bea couldn't believe it. "What? I mean..." Stunned, she covered her mouth in disbelief.

Maggie reached for her phone and made the call, rattling off the address to the dispatcher.

Bea stood motionless for a few minutes in complete

shock. "Has anyone seen Niles this afternoon?" she then asked, feeling worried.

The guy understood where she was going with the question. "No, I haven't," he said. "Do you think?"

"Oh no! Get someone over there now!" Bea said, petrified. "Niles could be in real danger." Before she could get all her words out Kyle had already taken off toward the carriage house. On the way he was praying Niles hadn't decided to take another trip down memory lane. "Dear God, please let him be okay. Please...let him be okay."

When Kyle arrived, the house was filled with smoke and he could barely see in the window. The lights were off, so he decided to try the doorknob, but the door was locked. Then he walked around back and peered in through the door and saw Niles lying on the floor. "Niles...Niles...," he said, then looked around for something to break the glass with. After grabbing a stone from the walkway, he threw it through the glass and tried to open the door, but it was stuck, so he stepped back and kicked it as hard as he could. Finally, the door opened. The smoke from the room hit him straight in the face almost taking his breath. "Please be alive... Please be alive..." he said, coughing.

After covering his nose with the neck of his shirt, he stooped over Niles to see if he could feel a pulse then dragged him out to safety. When he was lying on the ground, Kyle heard sirens wailing from the fire truck. He sat and situated Niles' head in his lap to elevate it. Minutes later a fireman walked around back where they were at.

"How long has he been unconscious?" the fireman asked.

Kyle looked at the fireman in shock. "I don't know, but I pulled him out a few minutes ago."

The fireman kneeled and began to assess the situation. "His pulse is weak. We've got to get him on some oxygen now." He reached for his phone and made a call.

Soon, another fireman came around back with portable oxygen gear and a neck brace, and got Niles stable before loading him onto a long narrow board.

"Is he going to be okay?" Kyle asked.

"I'm not certain, but he does have a good chance because you were able to get him out when you did. No doubt, you saved his life."

Kyle stood with soot and ashes now covering his clothes.

"How about you?" the fireman asked. "I think we need to check you out also. It seems you probably inhaled quite a bit of smoke during the rescue."

"Oh, I'm fine," Kyle said, coughing as a fireman took his vital signs.

After the fire was under control and later put out, Bea was allowed to come closer to the house. When she realized Kyle had saved Niles' life she was relieved. "He's alive because of you. I could never thank you enough for saving him," she said. She reached over and gave Kyle a bear hug, not concerned about how dirty he was.

Kyle released the embrace. "I'm so glad I got here in time. And I hope he's going to be okay."

"Me too," Bea said.

A fireman walked over to Bea. "Who's responsible for this man?" he asked, filling out paperwork regarding Niles.

Bea squared her shoulders back. "I am," she said. "He's like a member of my family."

"Okay, then." He handed Bea some papers to sign and asked her to accompany Niles to the hospital in an ambulance.

She signed the papers and asked Kyle to come along with her. "You deserve to be there," she said. "After all, you saved his life. You're a hero."

Kyle agreed, and for the first time in a long time he felt like he belonged, like he had a real family.

Minutes later, Bea left in the ambulance with Niles and Kyle followed suit in the truck. Seeing Niles on oxygen with ashes all over his clothes and face caused a tidal wave of emotions to rush over her. Tears streamed. "I've already lost William Jake. Now I can't lose you too," she whispered, reaching for his hand. Making her heart feel things her mind couldn't begin to explain. It was like William Jake was there watching them. And she wondered if he was trying to give her a *sign* it was okay to open her heart and love again.

THIRTY-NINE

The ambulance arrived at the hospital around nine o'clock and Niles was still unconscious. Bea had sat at his side all during transit. After he was brought into the emergency room, Bea was asked to have a seat in the waiting area. Soon, Kyle walked in to join her. "How is he?" he asked, feeling anxious to hear some good news.

"Still unresponsive. They believe he inhaled quite a bit of smoke." Bea replied, wringing her hands.

Kyle nodded and remained quiet. He had a lot on his mind, it had him feeling overwhelmed. The thought of not finding Niles in time kept reeling again and again, and it made him wonder how often Niles had gone over to the carriage house alone.

An hour later, a doctor walked over to speak with Bea. She stood, praying to hear some good news.

"I'm Dr. Wang," he said, shaking her hand.

"How's he doing?" Bea asked.

"He's a lucky man. If someone had not found him when they did, he wouldn't have made it."

"Is he going to be okay?" Kyle asked.

"It'll take some time to get his strength back. He inhaled quite a bit of smoke. We've got some oxygen going for a while, and I'll request for a CT scan of his lungs in a day or two to see how things look."

"Will there be any permanent damage?" Bea asked.

"It's too soon to tell," the doctor said. "But he's a strong man, seems to be in good health otherwise, so that's a plus at his age."

"Thank you, doctor. May we see him?"

"Yes, ma'am. But only for a few minutes. He hasn't regained consciousness yet."

They followed Dr. Wang to Niles' room. It was dark by that time of night and the room was cool.

Bea felt helpless, watching Niles lying there so still and quiet. If was hard for her to hold back tears as she stood beside the bed and watched his chest cavity rise and fall with every breath. Kyle stepped behind her and placed his hands on her shoulders. "He's going to be okay. I just know it," he whispered. "Try not to worry."

Bea reached for his hands. "Yeah, I hope so," she said. "Thanks for rescuing him and coming with me tonight."

Kyle smiled. "Of course. I'm glad I got there in time. Before..."

"Can you give me a few minutes alone with Niles?" she asked.

Kyle removed his hands. "Sure. I'll be right outside if you need me." He smiled and turned to walk out.

"Okay. Thanks." Bea walked closer to the bed and a tear rolled off her cheek. "I'm so glad Kyle found you in time," she whispered and sniffled.

Niles lay there unresponsive as Bea's emotions were about to consume her. For the first time since William Jake died, she found herself opening her heart to another man—something she figured she'd never be able to do. She leaned in and gently kissed Niles' forehead.

"Keep fighting. I can't lose you too." She wiped her eyes and turned to walk away, but glanced back at him one last time. It was like a peaceful look had spread over his face—like he knew she was there and heard every word. She drew in a breath and pushed the door open. Kyle was anxious for an update. "Any change?" he asked.

Bea was quiet for a minute, trying to get her emotions in check. "No change as of yet," she said.

"Are you okay?" Kyle asked, realizing how hard this was on her.

"Yeah, I'm fine. Just a little tired. It's been a long day."

"Come on, I'll drive you back to the ranch."

"Thanks. But I doubt I sleep much if any tonight."

"Well, they're doing all they can right now. Remember, the doctor said it would take time to tell if Niles would have a full recovery."

Bea nodded. "I know. But I can't understand why Niles went to the carriage house in the first place. Mary is gone. Sometimes I just can't figure him out."

"He's a man, Ms. Bea. Maybe he wanted to reminisce of when he and Mary were married. You know, about good times they once shared."

"True," Bea replied, getting in the truck.

Kyle opened the truck door and they left to head back to the ranch. On the way neither of them said much.

When they arrived, Abby was sitting on the front steps and met them at the truck. "I heard about Niles. How is he? Is he going to be okay?" she asked.

Bea saw such genuine concern in her eyes. "Yeah, they think he'll be okay, but he inhaled a lot of smoke and is on oxygen for a while. Thankfully, Kyle got there and pulled him out before the house was fully engulfed. Niles would've died otherwise."

Abby stared at Kyle for a few minutes. "Wow! You're a hero," she said.

Kyle grinned. "Not really. I would've helped anyone given the circumstances."

"Well, we all know how special a man Niles is. Ain't that right, Grandma?" Abby grinned.

Bea couldn't deny it. "Yeah, he sure is," she replied. "I'm thankful he'll be around a while longer."

Just then, Maggie walked over from the barn. "I think the girls will do fine tonight. Cocoa has taken to the filly. I'm so delighted the situation has worked itself out."

Bea grabbed hold of her hands and looked in her eyes. "I could never thank you enough, Maggie. You're an absolute angel."

"It's my pleasure, Bea. I'm happy they're both doing well. I'll be back in the morning to check on them, but let me know if you need me before then. How is Niles?"

"He's recovering. Should be home in a few days. Go home and get some rest. I know you've got to be exhausted," Bea said.

"Oh, it's all part of the job, and helping Cocoa is worth the hard work. Goodnight."

"Goodnight," they said.

Bea and Abby went inside and Kyle made his way over to the barn. Even though Maggie left, he felt like he needed to check on Cocoa and the filly before taking a shower. Stopping by her stall, they both appeared to be sleeping. It had been a long day, and he was ready for a break, so he decided to call it a day. As he showered he hoped Niles would be released from the hospital in a day or two, and he wouldn't allow his mind to think anything otherwise.

When Maggie arrived home, Marlon was sitting on the sofa watching TV. The house was clean and so were the dirty dishes. She set her purse on the table and glanced around the room. "Gee, you've been busy this afternoon."

"Yeah, I figured you could use the help," Marlon said, standing and kissing her on the cheek.

Maggie grinned, pleased with the way things felt at that moment, something she'd always dreamed of. However, she was afraid to let Marlon get too close, in fear of getting hurt. It had been a while since their last relationship failed; reason enough to make her cautious. "Thanks for all you've done around here," she said.

"You're welcome. I realized after I lost you years ago I could've made things a lot easier on you. I'm sorry I was lazy and took you for granted."

Maggie furrowed her brow. "Really? I never thought I'd hear those words come out of your mouth."

Marlon grinned. "Yeah, you deserve so much better," he said.

"If I didn't know better I'd think you came here with the intent of romancing me," Maggie said with a grin.

Marlon gestured with his hands. "I appreciate you allowing me to stay here when I had nowhere else to go."

"Any luck with the job search or finding your own place yet?"

Marlon shook his head. "Not yet."

"Well, I guess I'm going to get a shower and take care of a few things before I go to bed." She walked toward the bedroom. Marlon wanted to follow her but refrained from doing so. Once again, he remembered how things used to be when they were a couple—before he made a mess out of things. In fact, he was happy Maggie had allowed him to stay there, even if it was only temporary. Then his mind drifted back to the real reason he came. Inside, the guilt was eating at him like pouring salt on a wound. He sat and ran his hands through his hair. *I'm in way over my head this time... But I can't sit back and allow Maggie to be hurt. A few weeks ago it wouldn't have bothered me much. Oh God, Maggie is such a good woman. Help me make things right without her hating me. I've got to tell her the truth.* Marlon ran himself a glass of tap water and tried to calm his raveled nerves, then his cell phone rang. Seeing who it was, he hit decline, silenced the phone, and slipped it in his pants pocket.

Thirty minutes later, Maggie walked out in a pair of shorts and a T-shirt, and had her hair wrapped in a towel. "Was that the phone I heard?" she asked. "You get a call regarding work?"

Marlon caught his breath. "Nah, it was a wrong number," he replied.

"Yeah, I hate those telemarketing calls. Always makes me want to change my number."

Marlon nodded. "Yep. Me too."

Maggie stared at him for a few minutes. He appeared rather nervous, making her question if he was hiding something. In fact, first chance she got, she was going to see what she could find out about him since they had last split. And the more she thought about it, it did seem odd he came there to ask for help rather than going to one of his friends first.

Later, Marlon and Maggie kept their thoughts at bay with small talk, and she did not share any details about Cocoa or Niles. Something felt off and Maggie worried that she might've made a mistake by allowing him to stay there.

FORTY

N ow conscious, Niles lay in bed wiped out from the smoke inhalation. If he hadn't of been trying to burn old documents, the carriage house wouldn't have caught on fire. He felt bad and wondered if Bea would be able to forgive him for destroying something that meant so much to her and William Jake. After all, they had lived there while the farmhouse was being built and later allowed him and Mary to stay there. So many emotions rushed over Niles, it was hard to halt tears his heart wanted to flow. He'd kept a lot hidden from Bea, things he knew would hurt her if she found out. However, he was worried certain things would now be revealed after the fire. Since William Jake died Niles had tried his best to protect Bea, not cause her more pain. But he knew he'd made a mistake this time. He wasn't proud of it, and hoped Bea could somehow find it in her heart to forgive him.

Back when Niles was hired he helped William Jake put in a stone patio at the carriage house. While he and Mary lived there, Niles did all the repairs and kept things well maintained. Being close friends, they always helped each other with whatever needed to be done. Niles and William Jake had a lot in common and William Jake only had a few years before he'd planned to retire and travel with Bea. Reminiscing of times past made Niles sad. He missed William Jake and his beloved Mary. And some things in life just hadn't seemed fair, no matter how hard he'd tried to understand it.

A nurse walked in to check Niles' vitals. "How are you feeling?" she asked. "I'm glad you're awake. You gave everyone quite a scare."

Feeling embarrassed, Niles wouldn't look her in the eye. Oxygen was still on and the nurse reached over and straightened the lead in his nose. "Thank you. I think I may live a little while longer," he whispered with a half-grin.

"Well, I hope so," she said, reaching behind him to fluff his pillow.

Niles noticed the name tag she was wearing. *Mary Wells, RN.* His eyes grew wide, but he said nary word. Realizing it wasn't a mere coincidence, his heart grew warm.

"If you need anything I'll be here all night. So don't hesitate to call."

Niles grinned. "Thank you, Mary."

"It's my pleasure, Mr. Davenport." She set the call button near his hand then left the room.

After she left, Niles drew in a breath and said, "Thanks sweetheart. I know you're still here with me—even if I can't see you." Feelings of warmth and peace overshadowed him and he soon drifted off.

In bed, Bea thanked God Niles was alive. She knew he could've died from smoke inhalation. The thought of losing him made her eyes well. She'd already been through so much when William Jake died in such a tragic way. Their hopes and dreams shattered in an instant. At first, it was hard for Bea to carry on at the ranch without him. If Niles had not been there to help out, she would've probably sold the animals and moved back to her hometown in Maine. A late aunt had left Bea a little cottage nestled near the coast. Not a huge place, just a two bedroom, one bath with a beautiful view. Sometimes she longed to get away—to a place of serenity with no smelly animals, free of responsibilities. However, she hadn't been to Maine without William Jake. And Mimi wouldn't be able to travel now. She still hadn't come home from the hospital, so Bea intended to visit her the next day. With all the commotion at the carriage house, it was more than enough to deal with. She lay trying to sleep, but her mind kept roaming from one thought to another followed by a lot of: what ifs. Making her decide to brew some coffee and work on quilting for a little while. Maybe she could get her mind to unwind a bit.

The other girls left the ranch late that afternoon, and Bea hoped she'd somehow reached Megan and given her hope toward a better future. When she first started reaching out to girls, it was hard to fathom how hard life could be at that age. She'd never been blessed with a daughter of her own, not that she hadn't wanted one, it just never happened. But she'd tell anyone Billy was her pride and joy. He never visited much after William Jake died, and so she figured the memories were too painful. But Bea hoped Abby would have the bone marrow test done to see if she could help Bill. She understood why Abby was angry. She'd missed out on having a father to lead and guide her in life. In a way, she hated Billy and Jewel divorced when Abby was so young. But as much as she wanted to, she couldn't change the past. Abby was a smart-beautiful young woman, and Bea was glad Jewel had sent her there, so she could have a chance to get to know her. It wouldn't replace having Billy in her life, but it would let Abby know she was loved. And Bea had promised to stay in touch with Abby after she returned home.

Feeling restless, Kyle dressed and went over to check on Cocoa and the filly again. He rounded the corner to find them both sound to sleep. Breathing a sigh of relief, he grabbed his wallet and keys from his room and left. The old truck always made a loud noise when cranked, so Kyle put it in neutral and pushed it away from the barn. He hadn't told Bea he planned to go back and visit Niles late that afternoon. It was after visiting hours, but he figured he could throw on some charm with a nurse and sneak a quick visit without Bea there nipping at his heels.

When he arrived, Nurse Mary was watching the news on a TV across from the desk. "May I help you?" she asked.

Kyle leaned against the counter. "Yeah, I really need to speak with Niles Davenport," he said.

Mary furrowed her brow. "I'm sorry. Visiting hours are over," she said.

Kyle thought for a minute. "You have the most beautiful eyes," he said. "They're as blue as the ocean. You should've been a model, not a nurse."

Taken aback, Mary smiled and replied, "Thank you." Then she thought for a minute. "That's the nicest thing I've heard in awhile." She looked him in the eye. "Well, I guess I could let you visit for ten minutes," she said, "as long as you don't tell anyone."

"It's true. You're beautiful. And you have my word. My lips are sealed." He ran his fingers over his mouth and grinned.

Mary felt her cheeks flush. "You do have a way with words, I'll give you that," she said. "Mr. Davenport is in the second room on the right." She pointed across the hall.

Kyle stepped away from the counter. "Thank you, Mary. You don't know how much this means to me."

Nurse Mary paused. "Are you a family member, by chance?" she asked.

Kyle gazed back at her. "Yes, Mary. You could say that I am."

She nodded as Kyle walked off toward the room. *Best looking guy I've seen around here in a long time.* She sat and leaned back in the chair, wondering where Kyle was from and if he might be single.

Walking in, Kyle realized Niles was sound asleep. He stood beside the bed, watching him breathe. There was so much he wanted to say, but he just didn't know how. He'd agreed to come to the ranch and keep his distance like Niles had asked. But the older he got, the harder it was for him to leave after summer. He loved being at the ranch and had a special way with the horses like Niles. But he didn't want to cause any problems for anyone. The truth about Kyle and his life would hurt friendships and loyalty. Often times, Kyle found himself feeling lost in life, trying to discover where he belonged. His love for music and animals seemed to bridge a few gaps. Deciding not to say anything, Kyle turned to walk out and took a few steps.

"Kyle?" Niles had opened his eyes.

Kyle froze, and turned around. "I'm sorry. I didn't mean to wake you."

Niles stretched his arm out toward him. "Come here," he said, "I owe you so much."

Surprised, Kyle walked toward the bed and grabbed Niles' hand. He reached for Kyle and gave him a hug and kiss on the cheek. "Thank you! I wouldn't be alive today if it weren't for you," Niles said, eyes teary.

Kyle was at a loss for words. "You're welcome," he replied. "I'm glad you're going to be okay. You gave us all a scare though."

"I guess you're wondering what I was doing at the carriage house alone?"

He nodded. "Yeah, the thought did cross my mind."

"I had left a light on and Bea asked me about it, but while I was there I decided to burn some old papers and a few photos of a past life and time I don't like to talk about much."

"Hmm. Let me guess." Kyle rubbed his chin. "It was around the time I was born?"

"There are a lot of things Bea doesn't know and I want to keep it that way. And no, Mary and I had prayed to have children. Just not the way you were born."

Kyle grinned. "Well, that's good to know."

"Bea doesn't know all the details about your birth."

"I see. She doesn't know who mom is..."

Niles nodded. "Yes! Exactly."

"Do you think it would really matter after all these years? I mean..."

"I don't know. But I can't take a chance, not now."

"Why not? Mary's gone."

"In my heart, Mary will never be gone."

"But don't you think it's time for you to move on?"

"I don't know about that."

"Why don't you start by telling Ms. Bea how much you love her?" Kyle grinned.

Niles sighed. "I wish I could, but I'm afraid of how she'll react. I don't want to ruin our years of friendship."

"Sometimes you have to follow your heart," Kyle said. "Take a chance. Step out of the box."

About that time, the nurse walked in. "Okay, your ten minutes is up. I'm sorry..."

"Yes, ma'am." Kyle gave Niles a hug then left the room. "Thanks for letting me visit a few minutes," he said, walking beside Mary.

She grinned and said, "Okay. And remember, please keep this little visit between us."

"Sure. No problem. Have a good night."

"Thanks. You too."

On the way out, Kyle mulled back over the conversation he had with Niles. He wanted to go to Bea and tell her what had happened years ago, but he knew Niles would never forgive him if he did. Around midnight, he parked the truck beside the barn, and if Bea asked any questions later, he'd tell her he went out for a drive to clear his head. After all, it had been a stressful day for them all.

FORTY-ONE

Early the next day, Billy came over to hear Abby's decision. He hadn't a clue about what happened to Niles. Driving to the farmhouse, he saw where the carriage house had burned. Knowing Bea the way he did, he knew without a doubt, she was upset over it. After all, she'd said it was the place he was conceived. Bea was sentimental about things. Everything. Always had been. He parked and went inside. "Momma... Momma... Where are you?" he asked, feeling shaken by the apparent damage done to the carriage house.

Bea stuck her head out the kitchen and said, "In here, Billy."

"Are you okay? What happened to the house?" He hugged Bea, feeling grateful to find she was home and safe.

"Niles was over at the house yesterday and there was a fire."

"Oh no! Is he? I mean..."

"He's going to be fine after a few days, I hope. He's in the hospital being treated for smoke inhalation."

Billy ran his hands through his hair. "Did he get hurt or burned by the blaze?"

"No. Thank God, Kyle was around and saw the smoke billowing from the roof. He pulled Niles out just in the nick of time before it collapsed."

"Is Kyle okay? Does he know what happened?"

"Yeah, he's okay. A little shaken over it. I haven't asked Kyle or Niles much about it yet."

"I'm so sorry. I know how special the carriage house was to you," Billy said, frowning.

Bea perched her hands on her hips. "So, I guess you're here to talk with Abby about her decision?"

Billy nodded. "Yeah, Bill is getting worse as each day passes."

"Have a seat. I'll let her know you're here."

"Thanks." Billy sat, waiting for Abby.

A few minutes later, Abby walked in the kitchen. "Hi Dad."

"Hello. How are you?"

"I'll get right to it," she said. "I'll agree to be tested for Bill because he's my brother."

Billy stood. "Oh, thank God! Thank you, Abby. Thank you so much. I was afraid you'd say no."

"Well, I hope Bill would do the same if it were me. Even though I don't know anything about him."

Billy agreed. "Of course, he would. No questions asked. And I'd like to change that in the future. I'd like for you to meet him and you two get to know each other. I know I've made a lot of mistakes." He looked away. "You never deserved the way I treated you or your mom. And I'm sorry for not being there for you and Jewel. I was a coward and walked away from responsibility. That was wrong of me from day one."

Abby shrugged. "Yeah, you're right. But we can't relive the past now. So what do I need to do to help Bill?"

"I will talk with the doctor and let you know when to meet me at the hospital to have the test done."

"Will Lola be there also?"

Billy reached out for Abby and held her for a few moments, stroking her hair. And it made him realize what he'd missed out on all these years. "Yes, she will. I hope you don't mind. She's not a bad person, honey. She just..."

Abby frowned. "I guess it'll be okay. She is Bill's mom, so she has a right to be there, but I'm not looking forward to seeing her."

"I understand. She won't cause you any grief, I promise. I will talk with her beforehand. She will also be grateful to you for doing this."

"Hmm. I think she's already done a good job of causing me grief," Abby said with sarcasm. "I had to live without you in my life."

Billy sighed and looked her in the eye. "I know, honey. If I could change things I would. Thank you again for caring enough to step out and help Bill. It means a lot to me."

Abby pursed her lips. "Well, I know in my heart it's the right thing to do because he deserves a chance to live. He's just an innocent kid. And besides, now I'm a big sister."

Bea chimed in. "She's matured so much this summer. I couldn't be more proud of you, Abby." Bea reached for Abby's hair, pulling it back onto her shoulders. "She's my princess."

Abby grinned. "Thanks, Grandma."

Billy watched the two of them bonding, and realized Abby being at the ranch had been good for them both. "I'm glad to see you two can get along so well," he said. "I believe you're a lot like dad," Billy said, looking at Abby. "I have missed him a lot. And I should have been here to help him with those repairs the day he died. Just maybe he'd..."

Bea reached for his arm. "Stop! You can't change things, Billy. The accident wasn't your fault. You know your dad was stubborn as a mule when it came to asking for much help."

Billy nodded. "I know, Momma."

Abby stared at Niles' place at the table. "I miss Niles, Grandma. He's always in here every morning for breakfast. It doesn't seem right with him not around." Abby wiped a tear off her cheek with her sleeve. Everything had her feeling overwhelmed and emotional.

Bea hugged her. "I know. I miss him too. But he should be home in a few days."

Billy furrowed his brow. "Home? Has Niles moved in, Momma? Is there something you haven't told me about you two?"

Bea was caught off guard and searched for the right words. "Umm. Of course not. She meant to say..."

Abby broke in. "What would be wrong with Niles moving in, Dad? He's here all the time anyway. It's like he's already a part of the family."

Bea clasped her hands together, trying to hide her nervousness. And she wanted to crawl in a hole in the floor. "Are you two ready for breakfast?" she asked, changing the subject. "I'll set another place for you, Billy." She reached in the cupboard for a plate and cup, hoping they'd both let the last question drop.

They sat and grew quiet. Billy realized Bea was feeling a little uncomfortable talking about Niles. She served their plates and then joined them at the table.

"Where is Kyle?" Billy asked. "You said he saved

Niles' life. I'd like to thank him. He doesn't come in for breakfast?"

"He doesn't come over often, but he's such a fine young man, likes to keep to himself and play guitar. I enjoy him helping out with the horses over the summer. Been doing it for a few years now," Bea said with a grin. "I reckon I need to take some time to get to know him a little better. He usually eats at his room near the barn most of the time."

Abby stuffed some scrambled eggs in her mouth and remained quiet. She didn't want Bea to find out she'd sneaked out to see Kyle a few times. As she ate, she daydreamed of what life might be like with Kyle. He was easy on the eyes and knew how to make her heart flip-flop. But then there was the age difference again. Oh, how Abby wished she was older. Things could be a whole lot different then. *I really need to check on Kyle and thank him for saving Niles. It couldn't hurt anything. Besides, I'd have a legitimate reason to see him this time.* Abby finished her breakfast and asked to be excused. She had a plan and hoped nothing would get in the way of her seeing it through. She understood what it felt like to be an outsider, and so she figured that Kyle had a reason for not coming over to the house, but she didn't know what it was.

Feeling tired, Kyle wasn't in a hurry to check on the horses or shovel poop out the stalls. He'd had a late night out visiting with Niles and flirting with Nurse Mary. When he heard a knock on the door he slipped his pants on and went to answer. Surprised he said, "Abby. What are you doing here?"

"Can I come in?" she asked.

Kyle stepped back for her to pass then closed the door. "What brings you over?"

"Aren't you glad to see me?" she asked.

"I thought we got things settled between us on your last visit."

"Well, I just wanted to thank you for saving Niles. You and I both know how much Grandma loves him."

"You're welcome." Kyle played along and listened as Abby talked about this and that.

Abby stepped closer and looked him in the eye. "You can see the chemistry they have between them. You know what I mean, don't you?"

Kyle shrugged. "No. Not really."

"Oh, come on, Kyle. I know you're not that naive."

Kyle turned away. "Why are we even having this conversation?"

"What do you mean?"

"I know you didn't come here to talk about Niles. Why are you really here?" he asked.

Abby shrugged and shoved her hands in her pockets, trying hard not to touch him. "I wanted to say thank you for being a hero, that's all." She turned away, eyes wide.

Kyle walked closer and rested his hand on her shoulder. "Are you sure that's it?"

Abby took a step back. "Uh...Well..."

Kyle now had her backed into a corner. "So, why are you really here? Tell me the truth."

"Do you really want to know?" She gazed at him, narrowing her eyes.

Kyle looked her in the eye and got so close she could feel the warmth of his breath on her skin. "Yeah, I do."

Abby tried to move, but he wouldn't allow her to budge. "What are you doing?"

"What am I doing?" He cocked his head to the side.

"Yes. Don't play games with me."

"I don't play games, Abby."

"Really? You could've fooled me." She tried to move, put some distance between them.

"Am I making you nervous?"

"A little..."

"Good." He leaned over and gently kissed her.

After she caught her breath she asked, "What was that all about? I mean..."

"Isn't it what you came here for?" He gave her a sly grin and furrowed his brows.

She smiled and returned his advance. Then they kissed again and again. Not something Abby had expected to happen. In fact, he'd sent her away the last time. "What's changed?" she asked. "Why the change of heart now?"

He stepped back. "Nothing has changed. I just wanted to live in the moment, for once. I realized how short life can be after Niles almost died."

"What? For once?"

Kyle rubbed his chin. "Yeah."

"I'm sorry. I don't understand."

"For once, I wanted to feel loved and wanted by someone, have a real connection," he replied.

Realizing how vulnerable he is she said, "You are wanted and loved, Kyle. You're a great guy. Any girl would be crazy to not want you in their life."

"What happens when we leave here, Abby?"

"I go to school and you get back on the road to live your dream of becoming a famous musician."

"I'm tired of running, Abby. I want to find the place I belong and settle down, get married, and have a family."

"Oh, how I wish I was eighteen," she said. "I want to be with you, Kyle. You are everything I've always wanted in a guy. Everything I've ever dreamed of."

"You're just saying that," he said, feeling frustrated. "You're still so young. How could you even know what you want right now?"

Abby let go and ran her fingers across the muscles in his toned chest. "I see everything I want, everything I've ever dreamed of, right here in front of me."

Kyle drew in a breath, grabbed her hand, and kissed her in a way she almost lost her breath. Then he pulled her close to his chest. "We have a lot in common," he said. "We're both searching for a place we belong, a place to call home."

Abby closed her eyes lost in the moment—not wanting to leave.

Just then, they heard a door shut. Kyle released her, fearing that Bea had come over looking for her. "Stay here. Don't move," he said. "Keep quiet, and I'll get rid of whoever it is."

When Kyle turned the corner Maggie was standing by Cocoa's stall. He was glad to see it was her and not Bea. "Hi Maggie. How's it going?" he said with relief.

"Good. I thought I'd stop by to check on the girls," she said.

"I believe they're doing well. It's been quiet around here this morning."

Maggie wondered why Kyle was there without a shirt on at mid-morning and his lips seemed to be extra rosy as well. *Hmm. Maybe he has a visitor with him.* She finished checking on Cocoa and the filly and then excused herself. "Tell Bea I'll be back in a couple days," she said with a grin.

"Will do," Kyle replied. "Thanks."

After Maggie drove off Kyle went to check on Abby but she'd left. "Dag on it, Abby, I told you to stay put. Now all I need is for Ms. Bea to find out about this," he mumbled.

Abby snuck in the back door and went to her room. Lying on her bed, she replayed what had happened with Kyle. Never in a million years would she have thought her visit would reap such a reward. But the reality was this: summer was almost over and she and Kyle would be going their separate ways until next year. She closed her eyes, reminiscing of the gentle way he'd held her. No one had ever made her feel the way Kyle had. To her, he was special inside and out. And the thought of having to leave soon made her beyond sad. It was then she knew she'd leave a part of her heart behind at Bigelow Ranch.

FORTY-TWO

Buck had helped persuade Jewel not to go to the ranch, by saying Abby needed some space. In fact, he'd been coming around often. Jewel had been single for a long time, and having Abby gone made things worse. She didn't know if she had romantic feelings for Buck, but he had been good to her over past weeks. He'd really demonstrated how to treat a woman like a lady. In the process, he'd even cooked them a few meals. He was handy with fixing most things and seemed to have a genuine love for God. All qualities Jewel now wanted in a man. As she sprayed over her hair, she wondered where the night would lead. He'd told her to dress fancy because they were going somewhere special. She'd purchased a short red dress and heels to match. Even though she was thirty-something, Jewel was a far cry from ugly. She had a nice figure and when she spent time on herself, she was as beautiful as any woman. It was like she could see her skin glowing again. However, Buck had never married, and she figured he'd been focused more on his career than having a family. Either way, Jewel was enjoying the royal treatment and attention she was getting. After their divorce, Billy had made her feel like she wouldn't be good for anyone. And she'd carried those feelings of baggage around for a long time.

When she opened the door, Buck was standing

there dressed in a suit with a beautiful bouquet of flowers in hand. For a minute, he just stared at her. "You're stunning," he said, handing her the flowers.

Jewel grinned. "Thanks. You look nice as well. The flowers are beautiful," she said, smelling them. "I'll grab a vase."

Buck stood in the doorway, trying to catch the breath she kept taking away. Then he stepped inside and shut the door.

"Okay. I'm ready," Jewel said, grabbing her purse. "Where are we going?"

"It's a surprise," he said, grinning on the way out.

"Okay, I guess surprises are good. You're off to a great start tonight," she giggled.

In the car, Buck reached for her hand and rested his arm on the console. "I hope you'll like what I have planned for us," he said.

"Oh, I'm sure I will."

Arriving at their destination, Buck pulled over and waited for valet parking. He'd taken her to one of the most expensive restaurants in Atlanta.

"Oh goodness," she said, walking inside. "You must've spent a fortune planning this night." Looking around, Jewel realized the only table set was theirs.

"I thought we might have a romantic dinner and a night of dancing," he said.

"You rented the whole dining room tonight, didn't you?"

Buck looked at her with a twinkle in his eye. "Yes, I did. I wanted to do something special for you," he said, grinning.

"Gee. I don't know what to say," she said, eyes teary. "Thank you!"

"It's my pleasure," Buck replied. "Shall we sit and order?"

The waiter handed them menus and set two glasses of water on the table.

Jewel glanced over the menu like she was living a dream. Billy had never even done anything this extreme.

Candles were flickering on the tables in the dim lit room, and cloth napkins housed fancy pieces of silverware. Everything was perfect. Jewel remained quiet while they ate, trying to let it all sink in.

After they had finished a delicious meal, a man walked over with a violin. "Shall we dance?" Buck asked.

Jewel set her napkin on the table and stood. "Where is the Buck Schuller I thought I knew?" she whispered in his ear.

Buck placed his hand on the small of her back and pulled her close. "He's right here," Buck replied. "I've waited for a night like this for a long time."

Jewel looked him in the eye. "Really?"

"Yes. There's nowhere else I'd rather be."

As they slow danced to the violin, Jewel closed her eyes and rested her head on Buck's shoulder. Feeling wonderful, she didn't want the night to end. They swayed back and forth to the music, becoming lost in the moment. She opened her eyes, and without either saying a word, their lips met with a tender kiss. And it was then Jewel knew she was in trouble. She could feel what Buck's heart was saying and it scared her beyond words.

Close to midnight, the dinner date came to a close and they left the restaurant. On the way home, Jewel felt like Cinderella about to lose her glass slipper. "I could never thank you enough for tonight, Buck. It's been so special," she said. "I've never had anyone do something like that for me."

"You're welcome. You deserve many more nights like this," he said.

Inside, Jewel's heart fluttered. It had been a long time since she'd felt so confident about who she is. Buck had no idea what he'd done for her self-esteem. It was like a new beginning was happening, but she didn't know how she'd explain to Abby about her and Buck because Jewel had focused on Abby and her well-being rather than on her own happiness.

When Buck walked her to the door that night he simply leaned over and kissed her goodnight. "Thanks for a wonderful evening," he said.

Jewel caught her breath and said, "You're welcome. And thank you. I enjoyed every minute."

He looked her in the eye and kissed her again. "I'm glad you did," he said. "Goodnight."

"Goodnight." Jewel turned to walk inside and felt as if she were dreaming. She didn't know what was happening between them but she liked it. Kicking her shoes off near the door, she glanced at the clock. It was twenty minutes after midnight.

At home, Buck laid his jacket across the sofa and slipped his shoes off. He felt happy, peaceful on the inside. And he knew without a doubt, he was falling in love with Jewel. They'd known each other a long time. Since high school, but he'd never had the opportunity to get to know her beyond that. And one thing he was a little concerned about was Abby. Walking to the bedroom, he prayed when she returned Jewel would still want to continue with their relationship. He cared for Jewel and Abby, and he was willing to do whatever was needed to make things work for the three of them.

FORTY-THREE

Bea was moving around at sunrise with plans to check on Niles and Mimi at the hospital. She also had a meeting with a home health company to see if they offered therapy regarding Mimi's condition. At her age, Mimi shouldn't have any problem qualifying for help. However, Bea knew all companies were not the same, and some services cost more than others.

At the hospital, she walked in Mimi's room. "Good morning, Mimi." When Mimi didn't answer, Bea felt alarmed and walked closer to the bed. Then her heart sank when she realized she was unconscious. "Mimi! Mimi!" Bea checked for a pulse, praying she was still alive. "Oh, God. No. I can't lose her. Not yet." There was a faint pulse, and so Bea ran to the nurse's desk to get help. "She's not... I mean... She needs help now!"

"Okay, Ms. Bigelow. I'll call the doctor." The nurse hurried and made the call right away.

Bea stood there, shaking in her shoes. "Please be okay, Mimi. I'm here with you," she said, walking back in the room. She stood beside the bed and realized how blue she looked.

Minutes later, a doctor came in the room. Bea moved away so he could do an assessment on Mimi as a nurse gave her some oxygen. Meanwhile, a medical team came in with the cart to shock her heart.

"She has a pulse but it's a faint one," the doctor said. "Blood pressure is real low. We need to move on this fast."

"Is she going to be okay?" Bea asked, covering her mouth in disbelief.

The doctor paused and looked her in the eye. "I don't know," he said. "Time is of the essence."

Bea nodded. "Please take care of her. Do everything you can to save her."

"I'll do my best," he said as they continued to treat Mimi's heart and work toward raising her blood pressure.

"Please have a seat in the waiting room. Someone will speak with you in a few minutes," the nurse said, refusing to tell Bea anything more.

Bea paced back and forth and kept checking her watch. *It's been too long. It's been too long. Where is everyone? What's going on? Why won't they let me see her? Oh, God. Please don't let her pass away.*

A couple of hours later, a doctor walked in the waiting room. "Ms. Bigelow."

Bea stood and walked over to him. "Yes. How is Mimi doing?"

"Come with me to my office," he said, "we can speak in private there."

Bea furrowed her brow, wondering what was going on. "I don't like the sound of this," she replied.

"Please," he said. "We need to talk in private regarding this."

Feeling reluctant, Bea agreed and walked with him. On the way, she felt like she might pass out. "Can I get a drink of water," she asked.

The doctor stopped and turned to face her. "Of

course. My office is over here," he said. "Have a seat and I'll get it for you. You're white as a ghost." They walked in and Bea sat, waiting for the water and his return.

Her hands were clammy, heart racing, and she started taking deep breaths to try and calm her nerves. *Breathe Bea...Breathe. Help me, Lord. Calm my fears. You're in control.*

The doctor gave her a cup of water and had asked a nurse to walk in also for the conference. Then he closed the door and sat at his desk, opening Mimi's patient file.

Bea drew in a breath, hoping for a little bit of good news. *Please Lord...*

"As you know, Mimi has been fighting hard for awhile. However, her heart is tired, worn out at her age. The blood is not pumping as much as it should, and it's working less and less from all the stress. This last episode has left her with more damage to the valve."

Bea raised her eyebrows. "What are you trying to say?" she asked. "Is she going to die?"

"Mimi has been put on life support. She coded twice in an hour. Things don't look real good at this point."

Bea's eyes welled. "Is there anything else you can do? Is she a candidate for surgery to repair the problem?"

The doctor frowned. "I'm afraid not. Her heart is not strong enough, neither is her body. She's weak, so I don't believe she'd survive the surgery."

A tear rolled onto Bea's cheek. She took a deep breath and tried to brace for the worst. "What do I need to do?" she asked, wiping her cheek with the back of her hand.

"Mimi is resting comfortable at the moment. She's

not in any pain, but her breathing is too shallow without a respirator. Her heart could stop at any given time. The respirator is making it easier for her right now, but we can't leave it on for too long."

Bea narrowed her eyes. "And?"

"You'll have to make a decision regarding Mimi soon," he said.

"You mean?"

He nodded. "Yes, I'm afraid so."

Bea tried to hold herself together and placed her hands over her face, then she lost it. Tears began to flow like a mountain stream.

"I'm sorry to have to give you such sad news," the doctor said, placing his hand on her shoulder. "Take some time to think about things and sit with her for a while. Then let me know what you'd like to do."

Bea was so shaken by the news, she couldn't even respond right away. It had her in a shocked daze.

"Stay with her for a few minutes," he told the nurse. "Call anyone she may need to drive her home later."

"Yes, doctor." The nurse tried to console Bea as best she could and handed her some tissues.

After Bea had a few minutes to allow the news to sink in, she thanked the nurse and tried to pull herself together, if for nothing else other than Mimi. "I'm sorry," she said. "I guess I've had too much going on in my life over the past week. I didn't mean to have a meltdown in front of you."

The nurse smiled and offered compassion and a listening ear. "It's okay. I understand," she said. "I've been a nurse for over twenty years and days like these never get any easier."

Bea stood and realized she needed to check on Niles

also. "Tell the doctor I'll get back with him after I've had time to pray and think over things."

"Yes ma'am." They both left the office and Bea got on the elevator to go visit Niles. The events over the past week had her beyond stressed, and she prayed Niles was doing much better now.

When Bea walked in the room, Niles could tell something was wrong by her facial expression. She walked over to the bed and closed her eyes as tears flowed onto her cheeks.

"Oh no! What's happened, Bea? Are you okay?" Niles asked, reaching for her hand. "I hate seeing you upset like this."

She shook her head. "No!" she said. "Everything is wrong."

"Come, sit beside me. Tell me all about it," Niles said. "What can I do to help?"

Bea sat on the side of the bed and wiped her eyes. "It's Mimi," she said. "It's... It's real bad, Niles."

He frowned. "How bad?"

"I found her unconscious in her room earlier."

"Oh, I'm so sorry. Is she going to be okay?"

Bea shook he head, unable to speak for a moment. "It's her heart. It's too weak. Not working like it should."

Niles sighed. "Oh, Bea...I'm so sorry. Can they do anything more to help her?"

Bea shook her head again as tears streamed. "No! I'm afraid not."

Niles leaned forward and held her tight. "It's going to be okay, I promise. I'm here for you and I won't leave you," he said. "We'll get through all this bad stuff together. One day at a time."

"How are you feeling?" Bea asked, sniffling and wiping her nose.

Niles smiled. "I'm getting out of here this afternoon."

"Thank God! At least you're doing better," Bea said. "I've been so worried about you since the fire."

"Please forgive me for destroying the carriage house," he said. "I should've never started going there again. I guess I allowed the memories and my emotions to get the best of me."

Bea sniffled. "Why did you go there in the first place?"

Niles grew quiet. "I guess the memories were something I couldn't let go of. I could feel Mary there with me. I miss her so much sometimes."

"The house had a lot of memories for me also. But I do forgive you, Niles. We've both lost a lot. Now it looks like I'm going to lose Mimi too."

Niles kissed her gently on the cheek. "I know," he said. "But you're a strong woman, Bea. And God will help you get through this."

"I hope so. I don't know how much more I can take." Bea wiped her eyes and leaned her head against Niles' chest. "I'm so glad you're off oxygen and you're feeling okay. I've missed having you around. Abby has also."

Niles ran his fingers through the back of Bea's hair. "Yeah, me too," he said. Inside, Niles was hurting. He had destroyed the one place where he always felt Mary's presence, and he'd also managed to hurt Bea in the process. He closed his eyes and asked God for forgiveness. Tears welled in his eyes, causing them to sting, but he managed to halt the flow in front of Bea. She needed him. It was not the time to show weakness because he had to be strong for her.

A few minutes later, a nurse came in with Niles' release papers. "Fill these out and we'll have you out of here after lunch," she said, setting them on a table by the bed.

"I will," Niles replied. "I'm ready to get out of here."

"I can wait for you," Bea said.

"No. You have things to do back at the ranch. Go on ahead and send someone to give me a lift later on."

Bea leaned closer and kissed Niles on the forehead. "I will," she said. "I'll be glad to have you back at the table for supper tonight."

"I wouldn't miss it for anything," he said. "This hospital food is awful." He laughed.

In the elevator, Bea debated on stopping by to see Mimi again before she left. Praying for strength, she hit the button that led to the ICU floor.

When she walked in, Mimi appeared to be lifeless except for the loud machine making her chest rise and fall. Bea stood by the bed, feeling helpless. Tears streamed and her heart felt as if it might break into. Trying not to make a fool of herself, she gained her composure, and leaned in and kissed Mimi on the cheek. "I love you so much. You mean the world to me. I don't know how I can even consider having to let you go." She bowed her head. "God, please help me do the right thing. Let Mimi feel your love and peace around her." Then she raised her head and walked away. On the drive to the ranch, Bea became lost in her thoughts. So lost, when she parked in front of the house, she couldn't even remember much about the drive home. And she realized it was one of those times when she had let Jesus take the wheel.

FORTY-FOUR

Bea clenched the steering wheel as a rush of emotions overshadowed her. Kyle walked out the barn and saw her, then wondered if something was wrong. It wasn't like her to sit there alone, so he went over to see if she was okay. When he knocked on the window, Bea jumped. "I'm sorry. I didn't mean to startle you," he said. Immediately, he realized she'd been crying when he saw her face. Reaching for the door handle, he opened the door. "Ms. Bea? What's wrong?"

Bea got out and grabbed hold of his hand. "Everything," she said. "This has been an awful morning."

"Is it Niles?" Kyle's heart sunk at the thought.

"No. He's fine. Coming home this afternoon. Thank the Lord."

Kyle breathed a sigh of relief. "That's good."

"It's Mimi. I went by to see her and she was unconscious. Things don't look real good. It's her heart."

Kyle grabbed her other hand. "I'm so sorry. It's no wonder you're upset. Can I do anything for you?"

"Just keep Mimi in your prayers. She's on life support right now, and I have a tough decision to make soon." Noticing the other workers were now onlookers of the scenario, Bea wiped her eyes, put on a brave face and squared her shoulders back. "Keep this between us," she told Kyle, releasing his hands.

"Yes, ma'am. No problem."

"Thanks for checking on me, Kyle. I've often said if I could have had a grandson your age, you'd be it. You're such a thoughtful and caring young man. It means a lot that you care and don't mind showing it."

Kyle grinned. "As long as you're okay, Ms. Bea. That is what is most important here."

Bea walked toward the porch and turned back. "I am. Thanks again," she said, offering a sincere smile.

Kyle smiled and started back toward the barn. Little did he know, Abby was taking it all in from the bedroom window. Wondering what was going on, she hurried in the kitchen to talk with Bea. "You okay, Grandma? I saw you and Kyle talking just now."

Bea grabbed an apron and told Abby to sit. "I have something to tell you," she said, "and I know you're not going to like it."

Abby sat, anxious to hear what she had to say. All the while, hoping she hadn't found out about her sneaking around to see Kyle.

"I found Mimi unconscious this morning and she's now on life support." Bea paused to catch a breath.

Shocked, Abby said, "Why? What happened?"

"The doctor said her heart is not working like it should and there's nothing they can do because of her delicate condition and age." Bea turned away to hide her tears.

Abby couldn't believe it. "But I thought she was doing better now. I mean..."

Bea sighed. "Yeah, me too. But that's not the case. The doctor said her valve is damaged and she's not a candidate for surgery."

"Does Niles know about any of this?"

"Yes. Niles is coming home this afternoon."

Abby's eyes brightened a little. "Good. He'll be here with us for supper tonight."

Bea grinned. "Yeah, he will. Thank the Lord."

"Can I help out with anything?" Abby asked. "Let's fix some of his favorite foods as a homecoming."

"If I didn't know better I'd think you were quite smitten with Niles," Bea said, grinning.

Abby stood. "Grandma he's a great guy. And he's the right one for you. I know it, and you know it."

Bea furrowed her brow. "You really think so?" Bea asked, peeling some red potatoes.

Abby grinned. "For sure."

Inside, Bea was delighted Abby had grown to love Niles in such a short time. And she couldn't blame her because he is a man with a gentle-caring spirit, someone who always thinks of others. The epitome of a man with godly character.

Around two o'clock, a nurse came in to wheel Niles to the front lobby to go home. "It's about time," he said, joking. "I wondered if I was going to have to break out of here," he teased.

"No, Mr. Davenport, you're free to go. But I do have to wheel you to the lobby. It is doctor's orders."

Niles grumbled under his breath and got in the wheelchair. "Okay. Let's go."

The nurse wheeled him near the main entrance door and Bud was waiting just as Bea had promised.

"Hey, Bud. I'm glad you came to get me out of here," Niles said, standing to his feet.

Bud grinned as Niles got in the car. "You're welcome. Ms. Bea is already fixing supper for you. You're such a lucky man. She doesn't treat any of us other workers like she does you."

Niles grinned. "Well, the way I see it, Bea is good to everyone."

Bud nodded and pulled onto the highway for the drive home.

Niles grew silent, feeling anxious to get there. And he also felt thankful to be alive. He'd never had such a close brush with death before. Then he thought of Kyle and how he wanted to do something special to thank him for saving his life.

After they'd finished cooking, Bea removed her apron and went to freshen herself up a bit. Niles was coming back to the ranch—a reason for a celebration. Then she thought of Mimi and hoped having a little joy in the house would help get her mind off the tough decision she had to make.

Niles came in that afternoon and sat where he always did at the table. The meal was delicious and he was touched by such thoughtfulness. Bea and Abby had prepared a meal fit for a king, and it made Niles realize how blessed he is to have them both in his life.

Abby removed Niles' empty plate from the table. "I'm glad you're back where you belong," she said. "Welcome home." Then she patted him on the back. "I've missed you around here."

Niles grinned. "Thanks Abby. It's good to be back." Even though Niles did not live with Bea, being there on the ranch made it feel like he was home.

Later on, Abby snuck over to the barn to check on Cocoa, the filly and Kyle. Bea had retired for the evening, and so she wasn't worried about her coming over unexpected. The horses were quiet and Abby turned the corner to find Kyle lying on a weight bench lifting weights. She walked in. "Hi," she said.

Kyle was lifting a large set of weights. "Hi," he said in-between quick breaths.

"I guess you're wondering why I left the other night..."

Kyle paused. "Yeah. Why did you?" He dropped the weights on the rack and reached for a towel to wipe his sweaty face.

"I had to think about things," Abby said.

Kyle gave her a funny look. "Think? About what?"

"Us."

"And?"

"You're right. We would never work right now."

"Hmm. What changed your mind?" he asked.

She shrugged. "I guess because I still have to finish school and I've decided I want to become a nurse one day."

Kyle walked to her and draped the towel across his shoulder. "That's great, Abby. It's good you have hopes and dreams for the future. You know, that you're figuring things out about life."

"Meeting you has been one of the best things to ever happen to me, Kyle."

Kyle grinned. "Yeah? How so?"

"Well, you know what you want, and you're not afraid to keep working hard toward obtaining it."

Kyle reached out for her and pulled her against his sweaty chest. "I do believe you're growing up," he said.

"I know you'll go far in life. Always remember this: *Never let your dreams die.*"

"You know you're also in my dreams for the future," she said.

Kyle laughed. "I guess I am a little dreamy at times," he joked.

Abby punched him on the upper arm. "You're awful cocky and confident nowadays."

"I'm only teasing," he admitted.

"No, you're not." Abby laughed. "You said that with a serious look on your face."

"I've enjoyed sneaking around with you," he said. "But I know Ms. Bea would have my hide if she ever found out, even though it was innocent in a way."

"The way you treated me the other day, did you realize it would open my eyes and make me think about things?"

Kyle stroked her hair. "Well, I had hoped something would show you how important it is for you to finish school before getting married and starting a family."

"Does that mean you'll never kiss me again?"

Kyle released the embrace. "Not a chance." He looked her in the eye, grinned, and then kissed her a few times.

Abby closed her eyes, trying to savor every minute of their time together. "You know I love you," she said.

Kyle grinned. "I know. I love you, too."

"You do?"

"Of course. What's not to love?"

"Oh, why can't we just be together now?" she said. "Waiting is so hard."

Kyle rubbed her cheek and kissed her again.

"Because it's not the right time yet. Timing is everything. Don't you know that? You have to be patient."

"How can I wait a few more years for you? I'm afraid you might meet someone else and forget all about me."

"If it's meant to be, we'll find our way back to each other in the future," he said.

Abby closed her eyes as Kyle held her against him, and right then she wished time would stand still forever.

"I'll be here next summer," he assured her.

"And I'll be sure to visit grandma also."

"Good. Then we'll see each other in nine months. Time will fly by. You'll see."

"Almost a year is not soon, Kyle. But at least it's not as long as eternity." Abby wrapped her arms around him and they held each other for a long time.

Later in bed, Abby felt more alive inside than she ever had. For the first time, she felt like a man accepted and loved her—something she'd never experienced with her own father as a little girl.

Rolling on her side, she closed her eyes and pretended she was about to turn eighteen. The age when she and Kyle could be together and waiting would be over.

FORTY-FIVE

Marlon lay in bed, thinking about what he'd been hired to do. Guilt was eating at him more and more. He'd been stupid years ago and let Maggie go. However, she'd been nothing but generous and kind. And she was even more beautiful now than before. He had flipped through pages of a book she had regarding law and how to get her vet's license back. He knew what Beaufort had done was wrong, but he'd been in a desperate situation as well. In a way he wished he hadn't of come there. However, he could try his best to do the right thing and make a true mends with Maggie now, even if they were never a couple again.

A little after midnight his phone buzzed. He reached for it off the night stand and realized who it was. He answered, concerned the buzzing sound might wake Maggie. "Hello," he whispered.

"I've been trying to reach you all afternoon," a man said. "Where have you been?"

"I can't talk right now," Marlon replied.

"Why not?"

"I don't want to wake Maggie," he said.

"Since when do you care anything about her? I hired you to do a job not get sentimental on me."

Marlon could tell the man was becoming irate. "I've got to go..." Marlon ended the call and turned the phone's volume off. A few minutes later, he heard Maggie moving around and she stepped into his room.

"Who was that on the phone so late?" she asked.

Shocked, Marlon tried to play it off as no big deal. "Umm, just a wrong number I guess. The guy didn't make much sense. Must've been drunk or something to call at this late hour."

Maggie nodded and yawned. "Okay. I'm getting a drink of water and going back to bed."

Marlon smiled as guilt gnawed deep. *Whew! I don't know how much longer I can hide things from her. And I pray she won't hate me.* Staring at his phone, he tried to clear his mind of what he needed to do to complete the task he'd been paid for.

Back in bed, Maggie seemed to not have a bone in her body that didn't ache. She'd been pushing herself hard over the past couple weeks, trying to look after Cocoa and the filly, and she'd spent many hours searching for how she could build a case to get her license reinstated. And having Marlon come there unexpected had stirred feelings as well. Unable to sleep, her mind reeled of memories when she and Marlon first met and were a couple. It just didn't make sense for him to be back in her life, and he was so nice now. It was like he'd changed compared to back then. But something still felt off. Something she couldn't quite figure out. Gazing at shadows from the trees by the window, Maggie felt her eyelids getting heavy, and she hoped she'd be able to relax and get some sleep.

A ray of sunlight crept in through Bea's bedroom window. It had been a long night. She hadn't slept much because she couldn't stop pondering on how she was going to let Mimi go. Her only hope was that God heard her prayers and Mimi's condition had somehow improved. After all, she'd seen it happen before. And she knew there was nothing God couldn't do—if it were His will.

Minutes later, there was a knock on her door. "Come in," she said.

Abby walked over and sat on the bed at her side. "I have to be tested for Bill," she said, feeling a little uncomfortable and apprehensive about it. "I don't know what will happen if I'm not a match. Dad said he's pretty sick right now."

"When do you have to be at the hospital?" Bea asked.

"In a couple hours," Abby replied then sighed and turned away. "I'm scared, Grandma. From what I've read about the procedure it can be painful. They go into your actual hip bone with a hammer and a chisel to remove marrow."

"I'll be there with you, so try not to worry so much." She rubbed Abby's back. "I have to visit Mimi today— make a decision I don't want to make." Bea's eyes welled at the thought. "I'm not sure if I'm ready yet."

"I know," Abby said. "Sometimes I don't understand why life has to be so difficult."

Bea nodded. "I know what you mean. But the Good Book says God will never put more on us than we're able to handle. And there are times where we have to take up our cross and follow Him. The load can get heavy. But we have to cast our cares upon Jesus because He cares for us regardless of our situation."

"Still... Life is so unfair sometimes."

"I know." Bea hugged her, and Abby laid her head

against Bea's shoulder. "Oh, sweet girl. Everything is going to be okay. We just have to trust in the Lord one day at a time."

Abby closed her eyes feeling loved. "I wish I had known you since the day I was born," she said. "You're such a special lady. Anyone that knows you can see the love of God in your heart and life."

Bea stroked the back of her hair and kissed her cheek. "Me too," she said. "But we have today and the rest of our lives to enjoy together."

"I guess I better get ready for what lies ahead. I'm not looking forward to it. But I know I have to do whatever I can to help."

"I'm proud of you, Abby. No doubt, God has a good plan for your life," Bea said.

"Thanks, Grandma. I've been through a lot already. I'm looking forward to seeing something good come my way. Some beauty for my ashes," Abby said, walking out the door.

Bea nodded. "Yes, indeed."

Kyle was out and about early also. He'd already cleaned two stalls. Staying busy was a way he dealt with troubling things on his mind. Cocoa and the filly were doing well and she'd been able to put some pressure on her leg now. The filly was almost identical to Cocoa in looks. They both had dark eyes and a beautiful silky-brown mane. But she had the same white mark on her neck like Hershey. While Kyle was shoveling poop out the last stall Niles walked in.

"Good morning, Kyle. How's it going?" Niles asked.

Kyle stopped and leaned the shovel against a post. "Good. How are you feeling today?"

Niles walked closer and looked him in the eye. "I'm thankful to be alive. I could never repay you for saving my life."

Kyle shrugged. "It wasn't a big deal. I would've done it for anyone in trouble."

"But we both know I'm not just anyone."

Kyle grinned. "Yeah, you're right. But I'll keep quiet about that. Don't worry."

"I love you, Kyle. And I want you to know I'm proud of you. You've turned out to be a decent young man."

"Awe...Thanks."

"I mean it," Niles said, "I couldn't be more proud of you than I am right now."

"Summer vacation is almost over, so I'll be on the road searching for the right place to help with my music career."

"I'm glad you come here every summer. It gives me time around you, rather than us only talking on the phone."

Kyle grinned. "I don't think you felt that way at first though."

Niles paused. "Yeah, you're right. I admit I was worried Bea might kick you off the ranch because of the girls you brought here a few times."

"You've never told her much about me, have you?"

"No. She thinks you're my nephew."

"How is that? You don't have a sister."

Niles rubbed his chin. "I know. She thinks you're kin to Mary, that her sister had an illegitimate child. I need to tell her the truth. But I don't know how she'll take it."

"You're right. You have way too much to lose in this."

Feeling nervous, Niles stuck his hands in his pockets. "I don't have any regrets though. Mary and I could never have children. So it's a miracle you're here."

"Did you ever tell Mary about me?"

"No. I couldn't hurt her like that. She already felt like a failure because she couldn't carry a baby full term."

Feeling angry, Kyle bit his bottom lip. "Well, did you ever think maybe she would've been happy to know about me?"

Niles grew quiet. "I'm not sure," he said. "Look, I know I haven't always made the best decisions about everything, but I'm only human. I never said I was perfect."

Kyle slipped his glove off and reached for Niles' arm. "I know. And it's okay. I don't know what I would've done if I had been in your shoes back then."

"I don't think Mary would've forgiven me for it," Niles said.

Kyle looked away. "I know I was a mistake. But I'm here, so I guess God must've had a reason for my existence."

"No. I didn't mean it that way. I'm glad you're here. I mean..."

Kyle slipped his glove on and finished cleaning the last stall. "I'm glad you're doing better," he said without looking at Niles because his eyes would've revealed the hurt he was feeling at that moment.

Feeling bad, Niles turned around and walked off. He'd had a heartfelt conversation with someone he loved and he couldn't tell anyone—not even Bea.

Bea saw Niles coming from the barn and walked over to meet him halfway. "How are you doing this morning?" she asked, realizing something was weighing heavy on his mind.

He stopped and looked at her standing beside the car. "I'm sorry, Bea. What'd you say?"

Bea grinned. "How are you feeling?"

"I'm okay," he replied, "just wanted to check in on the horses."

"Well, you don't look okay," she said.

"Oh, I'm fine. Just a little tired."

"Well, don't push yourself too hard and over do it today. Those new horses can wait a week or two to be trained if need be."

Abby opened the front door and walked out to get in the car. "You ready?" she asked.

Bea opened the car door. "Ready as I can be," she replied. Since Niles seemed to not be quite like himself, Bea decided not to mention she was going with Abby and to see Mimi. She felt like he had enough on his mind already. "We'll see you later on," she told him. "We're going into town for a while."

"Okay."

Bea and Abby left for the hospital—both dreading what was lying ahead that morning.

On the way, Bea grabbed Abby's hand and prayed for grace to do whatever they each had to do that day. "God, please be merciful," she said. "We need you today. I know you hold this day in your hands, Lord. And you know the end from the beginning. In Jesus' name. Amen."

Abby said amen and they said nary word more the rest of the trip. Because all they could do was hope for a good outcome.

FORTY-SIX

At the hospital, things still looked grim. Mimi was lying there unresponsive as an awful feeling of doom and gloom seemed to hover in the room. Bea was quiet, trying to hide what her heart already knew. Abby stood afar, watching Mimi's chest rise and fall with every breath. Not only was Abby dealing with Mimi's illness, but she was set to have a test done to see if she was a bone marrow match for Bill. Watching Mimi so still with machines keeping her alive, tended to make things even harder. "What are you going to do, Grandma?"Abby asked, eyes teary.

Bea drew in a breath. "Pray! I'm going to continue to pray. Only God knows the answer to this."

"But didn't the doctor say you had to make a decision soon?"

Bea studied Mimi a minute or two. "Yes, he did. But it won't be today. I need more time. God wants me to tarry."

Abby nodded without saying anything more. She knew Bea was dealing with a lot of things right now. And she admired how she was able to keep her composure through it all.

A few minutes later, the doctor came in. "It's good to see you, Bea. Have you been able to make a decision yet?" He placed his hand on her shoulder, waiting for an answer.

Bea turned to face him. "I would like a few more days if you don't mind. I don't feel like I can rush this decision."

"Sure. I understand. My aunt passed away a couple years ago. She raised me and I loved her like a mother. Take your time and say your goodbyes," he said. "Then you can let me know when you're ready."

Bea nodded. "Thank you," she whispered.

Abby's phone buzzed in her pocket. She looked at it and realized they were ready to do the test. "I've got to go now. Will you be okay, Grandma?"

"Yeah, go ahead and I'll be waiting with Billy in the oncologist waiting room." She gave Abby a quick hug.

After Abby walked out, Bea pulled a chair beside Mimi's bed and started talking to her. "I've always heard a person can hear what you're saying even if they're unconscious," she said. "I don't know what to do, Mimi. You're an important part of my life. I don't know what I would've done without you when William Jake died. Your love, prayers, and words of wisdom kept me going." She paused. "I guess I'm being selfish but I don't want to lose you." Bea reached for her hand. "I'm not ready to let you go yet." A tear rolled onto her cheek and her heart ached like never before. "Oh God, tell me what to do." Then she heard a man's voice behind her.

"I'm not God, but I'm here for you, Momma."

Bea opened her eyes with Billy now standing beside her. "Billy."

"They just took Abby back for the procedure. I pray she's a match for Bill."

Bea nodded. "Me too," she said. "He's way too young to leave this world right now. He has his whole future ahead of him."

"You want to sit in the waiting room with me? Lola decided not to come. She didn't want to upset Abby."

"Sure. I told Abby we'd be waiting in there together when she's done." Bea stood and they left the room.

When they arrived, the waiting room was almost full, and there were small children coloring at a square table in the middle of the room. Some kids had on hats, others bandanas, to cover their bald heads. To look at these kids you'd never know anything was wrong except for a few visible IV's or port lines.

Bea and Billy sat in awe, waiting to hear some news about the test Abby had. Bea kept gazing at the letters on the door across the room: *Oncology Department.* And no matter how hard she tried to forget, those words seemed to stay etched in her mind.

Two hours later, a nurse wheeled Abby to the waiting room. "The procedure went well," the doctor said, walking over in his scrubs.

Billy stood. "How soon will we know the results?"

"A day or two," the doctor said.

"Okay. Thank you," Billy said, shaking the doctor's hand.

Abby was quiet as they talked, still a little groggy from the medicine they'd given her. It made her angry Billy hadn't acknowledged her there in the room. She was in some pain from the procedure and a simple thank you would've been nice to hear.

Bea noticed her discomfort. "Are you ready to go?" she asked. "I'm sure you'll want to take it easy a day or two."

"Yes! I'm ready to get out of here," Abby replied. "I've had enough of this place. I hate being at hospitals."

"Well, I guess I'll head on home to check on Bill,"

Billy said. "Thank you, Abby." He leaned over and gently kissed her on the cheek.

Shocked, Abby replied, "Okay. I hope Bill gets better real soon."

"Me too!" Billy hurried off without hugging Bea or Abby. Bea felt it was selfish of him, but she didn't say anything because he'd been that way since he was a child. He never allowed other kids to play with his toys, and he only had a few close friends.

Bea went to pull the car near the door, so the nurse wheeled Abby out by the curb. "You feeling okay now?" the nurse asked.

Abby shook her head. "No, I'm still a little light-headed. I hope this weird feeling wears off soon."

"It should wear off in a few hours. But you'll need to keep an ice pack on the affected area every four to six hours and take your pain meds for a couple days. If you see any redness, oozing, or swelling come to the ER stat."

"Okay," Abby said.

Bea parked the car and got out. "You ready?"

Abby stood and the nurse helped her get in the car and fastened her seat belt.

"Thank you," Bea said, shutting the door.

"No problem." The nurse rolled the chair out of the way and Bea got in and drove off.

Abby laid her head back against the headrest. "I'm glad you were with me today," she said. "Has there been any change with Mimi?"

Bea clenched the steering wheel tight. "Afraid not," she said and frowned. "I'm still waiting and hoping and praying over the next couple days."

Back at the ranch, Niles was taking things a bit slower than usual. He had two new horses to break in, but getting in the fence right now was not something he was ready for. The last thing he needed was to be kicked by a horse. The smoke from the fire had taken a lot out of him, and the guilt over what had happened also weighed heavy on him as well. He wiped his feet and walked in Bea's kitchen to grab another thermos of water. She was good about seeing that he stayed hydrated, and he missed her being there. In fact, he wondered why she hadn't returned yet. But then, he remembered he forgot to ask where she and Abby were headed in town. *Man, I've got to get myself together.* After grabbing a thermos of water, he decided to go over to the carriage house to check out the remains left from the fire.

About the time Niles was close to the house, Bea's car was spotted traveling on the road that led to the farmhouse. "Oh no, I'll have to wait until later because I know Bea wouldn't approve," he mumbled and darted behind a tree to keep her from seeing him.

She saw Niles, stopped the car, and stuck her head out the window. "What are you doing?" she asked.

Niles thought for a moment. "I'm just taking a walk. You know, trying to get my stamina back." He leaned against the tree, pretending to rest.

Bea stared at him, unsure of whether or not to believe him. "Okay... But don't get too hot out here."

"I won't. I promise." He noticed Abby had her head lying back against the headrest. "Is she okay, Bea?"

"Oh, yes. She had one of those sleepless nights again. Just tired, that's all."

Niles raised his brows and frowned. "Yeah, I know all about those," he replied.

"Come to the house later on for supper," Bea said.

"Sure. I wouldn't miss it. Thanks," he said, breathing a sigh of relief.

Bea parked and helped Abby inside without trying to draw too much attention to them. "You need to rest for a while. I'll check on you in an hour or so," she said, helping Abby upstairs to her room. After getting her settled in, she got busy in the kitchen, and grabbed a potato peeler, some potatoes, carrots and celery. It was as good a day as any to make a pot of potato soup. While peeling potatoes, Bea thought of William Jake and how much he used to love her soup. For a brief moment a gentle breeze filled the room as if he were giving his approval. Then she heard the crystal wind chimes beside the window play a familiar tune. She raised her shoulders as goose bumps covered her arms. *Oh sweetheart, I know you're here. I can feel you right beside me. I miss you so much William Jake.* Trying to hold on to the moment, Bea stood with a half-peeled potato in her hand, wishing she could hit a rewind button and time would stand still.

Around six o'clock, Niles came in and washed his face and hands at the sink. "Something smells mighty good," he said. "You must have a pot of soup simmering."

Bea grabbed a ladle and grinned. "Yeah, you're right. And the soup's almost ready. Have a seat and I'll fix you a glass of iced tea and a bowl of soup."

Niles sat and watched Bea at the stove. She had a certain way she tended to do things, and she never ceased to amaze him with her kind and thoughtful ways. After setting the ladle on a napkin, she set a glass of tea on the table along with the tea pitcher.

Niles lifted the glass to his lips. "Thanks, Bea."

Bea grinned. "You're welcome. Looks like you're beginning to get back to your old self..."

After setting the half-empty glass in front of him he said, "Yeah, I'm trying my best. Just thankful to be alive these days."

"For sure," she said, removing a pan of cornbread from the oven. Then she excused herself and went upstairs to check on Abby.

Abby was asleep when Bea peeked in on her, so she figured the pain medicine had her out like a light. *That sweet child. I'll save her a bowl of soup for later.* Then she eased the door shut and went to eat with Niles.

When she returned with no Abby, Niles was surprised. "Is Abby going to join us?" he asked.

Bea ladled their soup in bowls and set it on the table along with the cornbread. "Nah, she's not feeling well this afternoon. You know, we all have our days."

"Yeah, I guess you're right," Niles replied, taking a bite of cornbread. "This is delicious," he said. "Sure beats the heck out of that nasty hospital food."

Bea just grinned. She was glad to have Niles back at the table with her.

After they finished eating, Bea decided to work on a quilt, hoping it would get her mind off troubling things. She didn't like hiding things from Niles, but she figured right now was not the time to burden him with anything more. No. She'd wait and give him a few more days to recover, and then tell him about the situations regarding Mimi and Bill.

FORTY-SEVEN

After all the years she'd known Buck, Jewel now realized what she'd been searching for was right under her nose. He'd stuck by her and Abby when they needed him. But she refused to open her heart to another man in fear of getting hurt. Buck had saved Abby from more trouble and he'd been attentive to Jewel while she was away. But since summer vacation was almost over, she was uncertain where it would leave things with them. She knew Buck wanted more, but she didn't know if she was willing to risk loving another man. The thought of it caused *fear* to almost consume her.

Buck had worked graveyard shift again. It seemed the longer he worked at the precinct, the more he seemed to get the shift no other officer wanted. He figured it had to do with the fact he was single at his age and didn't have a family to go home to. It wasn't that he didn't want a family—things just hadn't worked out so far. He'd dated a few girls who had used him to get speeding tickets dropped. Afterwards, they had disappeared, never to see him again. Most had been vain with their looks, but he couldn't imagine being married to a high maintenance woman. He was down-to-earth, loved the outdoors, and enjoyed having a few friends over from time to time. The past several weeks had been some of the happiest in his life. He cared a lot for Jewel and Abby, but he didn't want to push Jewel too much and cause her to back away. He was willing to be a good friend, but in reality he wanted more. Jewel had been hurt by Billy, and as much as Buck wanted to heal her wounds he knew he couldn't. However, he could be the kind of man he is and show her how she deserves to be treated, and so far things had become better between them, more intimate. He felt like he was earning her trust one day at a time, and there wasn't anything he wouldn't do for Jewel or Abby. They were not his biological family, but in his heart they were. He'd been single a long time, praying for God to send the right woman in his life. He knew Jewel had scars from past relationships, but he didn't care because he didn't love her for her flaws. Buck loved the beautiful woman underneath all the baggage. He could see into her heart and soul. She'd wanted to go out to Texas to check on Abby's progress, but he'd managed to change her mind and keep her there. In a way he knew it was selfish, but it had given them a chance to grow even closer—which was something he'd wanted even years before she had met and married Billy.

Getting in bed, Buck nestled under the covers and tried to get some rest. It was sunny out, a day he'd have to keep his blackout drapes closed or he'd be unable to sleep. His muscles ached and his eyes stung as thoughts of Jewel reeled in his mind. Everything in him wished she were there to snuggle with him. He glanced at the clock then closed his eyes. *Help my sleep to be sweet, Lord. I have a lot to do this afternoon. And I'm so tired.* Feeling groggy, he soon drifted off.

With only a week left, Jewel decided to give the house a good cleaning before Abby returned. She'd been away for weeks, but it had felt like an eternity. Buck had been around often and he'd managed to keep Jewel's mind off Abby a lot. And she'd witnessed a side of Buck she'd never known before—the caring, loving side. He'd been so sweet and attentive to her needs. Something she hadn't experienced since right after she first met Billy. Their whirlwind romance resulting in Jewel's pregnancy had changed the future she'd once had planned for herself. Billy had money and hadn't been ashamed to flaunt it with Jewel. She'd once had some finer things in life. Expensive clothes, a nice car, and a decent place to live that wasn't rat or roach infested. It really boosted her self-esteem until she discovered Billy had been cheating. She'd struggled a lot as a single mom since then. She could've asked Billy for more financial help, but she was proud and determined to make life work without acting like a beggar. And she'd tried her best to hold on to her dignity.

While hanging clothes in Abby's closet, Jewel found a small photo album tucked in the corner. She opened it to find photos of the three of them when Abby was a baby. She was dressed in a light pink frilly dress, a pink bonnet, and had a stuffed Easter bunny in her little hand. Remembering, Jewel's eyes welled. It seemed like so long ago, a time lost, now gone forever. Something precious she'd never get back. Jewel stood frozen, as her heart ached for what would never be again. She sniffled and shut the album, realizing how hard it was on Abby not having a dad around, and she wondered if having Buck closer would help Abby. But Jewel wasn't sure if she'd allow either of them to be hurt again. Not by a man anyway.

A couple days later, the oncologist called to give Billy the news he'd been waiting for. Seeing the number on caller ID he held his breath and answered. "Hello."

"Mr. Bigelow?"

"Yes, this is Billy."

"We have the results from Abby's test. And I'm sorry to say this… but she's not a match. This doesn't happen often with siblings because there's a thirty percent chance it will be a match."

Billy's heart sank. "You're kidding, right?"

"I wish I was. We see this once in every two hundred cases. Often a sibling is a perfect match for a bone marrow transplant. However, your children don't have the same mother. So I…I can't explain it other than that."

Billy sighed. "What do we do now? What options do we have left?"

"As you know, Billy, your son doesn't have much time without this procedure soon."

Billy blew out a long breath, feeling scared to death. "How long does he have?" he asked, feeling as if he were stuck in the middle of a nightmare he couldn't awaken from.

The doctor grew quiet for a few moments. "Maybe six months, at best. I'm truly sorry. I wish there was something else I could do. There are new strategies being developed everyday over this, but I don't think anything will be approved soon enough for Bill."

"Can we have anyone else tested?" Billy asked.

"You mean another family member?"

"Well, we already know Lola and I weren't a match, and now neither is Abby."

"Take some time to mull over things for a few days and give me a call," the doctor said. "Maybe someone will come to mind."

"What can we do in the meantime?"

"Keep bringing Bill in for blood transfusions. He needs to keep his hemoglobin as high as possible because it's the only hope we have right now."

"Okay. Thank you, doctor," Billy said and ended the call.

Observing Bill in the living room playing a video game, Billy's eyes began to well. Bill was his pride and joy, and there was no way he was going to sit back and allow his child to die. Trying to pull himself together, he walked over, grabbed another game controller and started to play along with him.

"Was that the doctor, Dad?" Bill asked. "Has he found a donor yet?"

Billy gasped. "Not yet. But he's working on it. Everything is going to be okay. I promise," Billy assured him with a smile.

Bill hit the controller button and said, "Boom! I got you. You're dead, Dad." He laughed and leaned his head against Billy's leg.

"Oh, man! I see that. You got me quick. You're getting too good at this." Billy's heart sank at the thought he may lose Bill if things didn't change soon.

A few minutes later, Lola came in from work and knew by Billy's demeanor something was wrong. He laid the controller on the table and stood. She walked over and they held each other without saying a word. At the time, it was the only comfort they had. A tear rolled onto Lola's cheek as she watched Bill playing a video game. Even though things looked bleak, both Billy and Lola tried to remain positive and stay strong for Bill.

FORTY-EIGHT

It was the last week for Abby at the ranch. She'd en-joyed being there and it had added a positive new light on life. At first she'd missed being at home with Jewel, but the more she was around Bea and Niles, the more she could see herself living a different lifestyle. She'd also experienced her first case of puppy love, although she didn't know how she was going to say goodbye to Kyle without her feelings being blatantly obvious. In fact, she'd grown quite fond of everyone, even the other workers. Seeing how Bea worked and lived gave Abby *hope* for the future. She knew she'd been hard on Jewel over the past couple years, and re-alized it was difficult for her being without Billy also. But somehow Jewel had managed to work and take care of them—through good and bad times. And most of all, Abby knew she had to get a new group of friends because the ones she had were leading her on a path to nowhere—that she was sure of.

When she first arrived at the ranch, the sight and smell of things had taken her aback, but the longer she stayed the more it began to grow on her. And listening to Bea minister to other girls in their Bible study group had revealed God in a new light, making Abby real-ize He was the missing link, and how much she really needed Him in her life. Bea had been a prime example of a Christian woman and it made Abby wish Jewel had been there to experience those things right along with her.

Pushing the curtain back, Abby watched Niles in the fence with a new Thoroughbred. He had a way of calming and breaking any horse, and she knew it had to be a gift from God above. Something he'd been born with. Watching, it was like seeing them looking into each other's souls, a real connection. No matter how rowdy the horses were, Niles had a special way of speaking to a horse to reach their level. He'd said it was about respecting each other as well as their boundaries. Abby grinned when Niles slipped the rope around the horse's neck and gently rubbed him on the side. *I've never seen anything like this before. I'm so amazed. He is such an awesome horse whisperer.*

Just then, she saw Kyle walking toward the fence where Niles was standing. Niles looped the end of the rope to the fencepost and paused to talk. Oh, how she would love to overhear their conversation. Niles had a serious look on his face as Kyle stuck his hands in his back overall pockets. "I hope you're not overdoing it out here," Kyle said, look of concern.

Niles grinned and patted him on the shoulder. "Nah, this is my life. I'm accustomed to doing nothing else. Besides, I can't sit inside all day staring at the walls. Bea needs me. I mean... She needs help around here with the horses."

Kyle laughed and nodded. "I know. Just don't overdo it, okay? I don't want to have to take you back to the hospital from being hard headed."

Niles agreed. "I'll be careful. I promise. Thanks for caring enough to check on me."

Kyle grew quiet. "I'm thinking about heading out early in the morning. Come daybreak, in fact."

Niles furrowed his brow. "Why so early?"

Kyle shrugged. "Just seems like a good idea."

"So, you're not going to say goodbye to Bea and Abby?" Niles frowned.

Kyle lowered his head and shuffled his cowboy boot in the dirt, stirring the dust. "I don't know. It may be better for everyone, if I just leave soon."

"They'd both be real disappointed, you know."

"Yeah, I know."

"Then why do you want to run away? Run away from the place you love... This place is like home to you."

"It's complicated. You know that."

Niles laid his hands on both of Kyle's shoulders and he lifted his head. "Listen to me," he said, looking him in the eye. "Bea has been good to you these past few years. You owe her enough respect to say goodbye."

"Okay. But I'm still leaving early. I'll try to tell her I'm leaving tonight after supper is over."

"Fair enough." Niles removed his hands.

Abby looked on from the window, wondering what was going on so intense between them. She frowned. "Hmm. I hope Kyle is not in any trouble."

Niles glanced toward the house and Abby stepped back, hoping he hadn't seen her at the window, and her gut told her there was more to their conversation than either of them would later share.

Soon afterwards, there was a knock on Abby's door. It was Bea. "Can I come in?" she asked.

Abby opened the door. "Sure."

"I need to tell you something," Bea said.

"Something wrong, Grandma?"

Bea sat on the bed. "Yes. You weren't a match for Bill."

Abby was shocked. "What? I mean..." She covered her mouth in disbelief. "What is dad going to do now? Bill may die soon."

Bea bowed her head. "I don't know."

"Oh, this is bad." Abby sat beside her.

Bea shook her head. "It sure is."

"Does Niles know about any of this?"

Bea pursed her lips, wondering why Abby brought his name into this. "Niles? What does he have to do with anything?"

Abby stood and paced. "Grandma, you know he cares about you. I'm sure he'd want to know about what's going on with Bill and Mimi. Have you told him about it yet?"

She sighed. "No."

"Why not?"

"It's complicated, Abby."

Abby placed her hands on her hips and huffed. "How so? I mean..." Abby couldn't believe how Bea was acting all of a sudden. And she wondered if her behavior was caused from dealing with too much stress.

"It just is," Bea snapped, not wanting to talk any more about it.

"Okay." Abby backed off. "Any updates on Mimi's condition today?"

"No. And I don't know what I'm going to do about that dire situation either. It seems the heavens are brass right now."

Abby could see how distraught Bea is, and realized asking so many questions wouldn't help anything. "I'm sorry. I didn't mean to upset you," Abby said.

"It's okay. You're only asking because you care, and there's nothing wrong with caring." Bea reached for Abby and they hugged. "You've come such a long way. I'm proud of you and the young woman you're becoming."

Abby released the embrace. "Thanks."

Niles finished with things outside and decided to sneak over to the carriage house to see if anything of value was lying around since Bea had stopped him the last time. He had a fire safe box which housed several photos and hoped he wouldn't find it destroyed. The only photos he still had of Mary. He knew he was taking a chance by going there because if Bea found out she'd be asking questions he didn't want to answer.

He washed his face, arms and hands, changed his clothes, and decided to take a chance anyway. It was as if Mary were waiting for him to return, drawing him there like a magnet, and he couldn't fight the desire to go there any longer. He needed to see what she wanted to show him. And just being there made him feel so much better about things. He realized the idea of it seemed crazy—but he knew it was the right thing to do, whether anyone else understood it or not.

Kyle gathered his things and placed them in a bag after he put his guitar in its case. Now he needed to wait to tell Bea goodbye without bumping into Abby because he was already having a hard time dealing with certain emotions as it was. If he ran into her it would make things even worse. Not to mention, Bea may never allow him to work there again.

Lying on the bed, all sorts of thoughts reeled in

Kyle's mind. He wished Abby was eighteen as much as she did. He was pretty much a loner during the year traveling from place to place, playing one gig after another, and he knew moving from place to place wouldn't be the best lifestyle for Abby. But after being around her, he was having a hard time getting her off his mind. They had connected on a different level than he had with any girl so far, but it made him wonder if he'd ever be able to settle in one place long enough to have a wife and family. Yeah, he was still young, but being alone was the worst part of traveling. He'd witnessed other young couples with their own children. It appeared to be the joy and happiness only a family lifestyle could provide—something he knew nothing about. His biological mother had died, and so he'd been tossed from one foster home after another. On his sixteenth birthday he packed his bag and set out on a journey of discovery. It hadn't seemed fair his mother was gone, and it made him start a search for his biological father. That way, he'd at least have a connection with a family member. After a couple years, Kyle was able to get a hold of the documents where he was sent to a foster family. And that summer he stumbled upon the name of his father, Niles Davenport. So Kyle went to the ranch and applied for work as a summer helper. After being there a while, one night he asked Niles if they could talk. It was then he revealed his mother had died and he'd since discovered he was his biological father.

At first, Niles hadn't believed him. But Kyle just happened to have the same kind of birthmark as his mother Ruth Ann, a red triangular mark on his right shoulder. Niles was shocked to see it, and then agreed to listen to what Kyle had to say. Ruth Ann had once told Kyle she'd never contacted his father after the one night stand they'd had. Niles and Mary had argued and he'd walked out, later stopping to grab a few drinks to unwind, get his mind off things. Ruth Ann happened to be bartending that night and after her shift her car wouldn't start, so Niles offered to take her home. After having had one drink too many Niles was feeling vulnerable, less of man. Ruth Ann was young, beautiful, and more than happy to oblige his drunken advances. One thing led to another and Niles cheated on Mary for a measly fifteen minutes of pleasure. It was the one and only time he ever had. Since that night, he'd sworn to never take another drink. For years, he prayed for God's forgiveness and strength to forgive his own wrongdoing because he loved Mary. So when Kyle came to the ranch he was shocked to find out he'd fathered a son, and Niles knew if Mary were alive, she'd never forgive his unfaithfulness. He never told her about what happened with Ruth Ann because he figured there was no need to cause her more pain. It was one night and one stupid mistake on his part. And ever since then, God never saw fit to give him and Mary a child. Looking back, Niles figured it was a way God punished him for cheating on Mary in the first place. Something he'd since regretted a hundred times over.

Abby was curious to find out what was between Niles and Kyle, so she decided to sneak out to the barn and pay Kyle a visit. After stepping out the back door, she gazed around the yard before dashing toward the barn. In her heart she knew she needed to see Kyle once more before she left, if for nothing else but to say goodbye. Something she hated with every ounce of her being.

Lost in his thoughts, Kyle was shaken when he heard a tap on the door. He went to answer and saw Abby standing there. "What are you doing here?" he asked.

She then frowned with a pouty lip. "Aren't you glad to see me?"

"Come in here," he said, looking to see if anyone saw her standing there.

"I saw you talking with Niles earlier today. Is everything okay between you two?"

Kyle shrugged. "Yeah. Why do you ask?" he said, wondering why all of a sudden she was being so inquisitive about their conversation.

"I don't know. I guess the serious look on Niles' face had me a little worried something was wrong."

Kyle laughed. "Oh, he's always overdoing it with the horses. The doctor said to take it easy for a while, but Niles is stubborn. I guess he didn't like me reminding him to take things a little slower for a few days."

"That's sweet of you to care so much about him like that."

"Well, I've been coming to the ranch for a few years. I guess everyone here is like family to me." *If she only knew...*

Abby walked closer. "You really are the complete package, Kyle Davies." She raised her hand and ran her index finger across his bare chest.

Kyle grabbed her hand. "Don't," he said. "It's only going to make things worse."

Abby now had a twinkle in her eye. "I may not be

eighteen yet, but I do know when I love someone," she said.

Kyle grinned and stroked her silky hair. "What am I going to do with you, Abby?"

"Love me," she replied.

Kyle sighed. "If I could only make it happen, I would."

Abby laid her head against his chest as his heart thumped faster and faster. "I could stay here forever," she said, "just like this."

"I know. But we've already talked about this."

Abby ignored his words as she became lost in the moment. She wanted to stay at the ranch and be with Kyle. Be eighteen. Get married. Have babies, and live happily ever after. It was like a dream. A dream she had imagined for a long time.

"I'm leaving in the morning," Kyle said, still stroking her hair.

Abby's heart sank. "Why? I'm going to be here a little while longer."

Kyle drew in a breath. "It's time for me to get back on the road, that's all."

"Are you sure?" she asked, tears in her eyes.

Kyle closed his eyes, trying to hold on to such a tender moment between them. "Yeah, I'm sure. I'm done with things here until next summer."

"What if I don't want you to go?" she said, wrapping her arms around him.

"I have to. I have no other choice now."

Abby raised her head. "Yes, you do. We each have a choice. It's what we do with them that matters."

"I can see Ms. Bea had a positive influence on you over the summer." He kissed her forehead.

"Yes, she did. She taught me how precious life is and we shouldn't ever take anything for granted. We aren't promised tomorrow, you know."

Kyle looked in her eyes. "I'm so proud of the young woman you're becoming," he said.

Abby grew quiet, absorbing his gentle-kind words. "Thanks," she said. "Will you write to me?"

"Of course. I can't promise how much though, with me being on the move so much, but I'll try."

"Please do. I want to know you're okay and how your music career is progressing."

Kyle gave her the sweetest smile and kissed her on the cheek. "Take care of yourself," he said. "You have your whole future ahead of you. That's quite a lot to look forward to, I'd say."

Abby frowned. "You're not going to kiss me goodbye?"

"I just did," he replied.

"No. I mean on the lips. Can I at least have one more kiss?" she asked with hormones raging like a fierce waterfall.

Kyle grinned and grabbed hold of her hands. "If I ever kiss you again, I may want to hold you in my arms and never let you go."

"So. What's wrong with that?"

"Right now? Everything. Remember? You still have to finish school and go to college. I'm just a traveler moving from place to place, trying to make it in this world. Not what you need right now."

Abby stomped her foot on the floor. "Look, I know you're older than I am, but we have a real connection between us. Years ago women got married at fifteen and sixteen, sometimes even younger. It wasn't a big

deal. Besides, you're not that much older than I am."
Abby grew angry. She loved Kyle and wanted to be with
him now—not five years later.

Kyle looked in her saddened eyes. *I can't tell you
who I really am, and I can't be with you right now.* He
blinked and pulled her close again. "If we have a future
together, as I've said before, our paths will cross again.
I'm sure of it."

A tear rolled onto Abby's cheek as she feared she
may never see him again. "You promise you'll come
back here next summer?"

Kyle tilted his head and kissed the top of hers. "Yes,
I promise, Abby."

Abby raised her head and he wiped her cheek with
his thumb. She gazed in his eyes and without saying a
word, he kissed her.

It wasn't all Abby wanted, but what she needed right
then. To know she was special to someone. Accepted.
Loved.

FORTY-NINE

Niles made it to the carriage house and sifted through charred remains, hoping to find the box with photos of him and Mary. He found it lying in a corner by the kitchen door. The lid was shut, covered with soot and ashes. He held his breath, brushed off the top, and opened it. To his surprise, the photos were left untouched. He breathed a sigh of relief and placed a photo of Mary close to his heart. "I'm so sorry, Mary. I'm sorry for everything. Please forgive me," he said.

Just then, standing in the doorway, Bea looked on and walked inside. "You're sorry about what, Niles?"

Startled, he jumped. "Bea...What are you doing here? I mean..."

"This is my house, remember?" she said, wondering what was going on.

Feeling foolish, he said, "Of course. I'm sorry. I guess I'm having an off day." He shook his head and rubbed his forehead.

"What do you have there?" she asked.

Niles was holding two photos. One of Mary. The other of a woman and a little boy. "I'm not sure how to say this," he said.

"Say what?" Bea furrowed her brow as fear gripped her tight and wouldn't let go.

"Kyle is my biological son, Bea."

Bea just stared at him for a moment. "What? I don't understand. You said he was related to Mary. You and Mary never had kids. How could he be *your* son?"

Niles hung his head, feeling ashamed. "I was unfaithful once," he said, "but only once. Please believe me. I'm telling you the truth, I swear."

Bea bit her lip in disbelief. "What did you say?" She was in total shock over his confession to such a thing.

"You heard me. I'm not proud of it, but it happened. We'd had a fight and I walked out to cool off. I later had too much to drink, and one thing led to another."

"How? I mean...When?" Bea paced through the rubble after hearing his words. "Did Mary ever know about this?"

"No. I never told her. I couldn't stand to hurt her that way, especially after she got sick."

"I thought you said Kyle was your nephew."

"I know. I lied. I'm so sorry, Bea. I was worried what you would think of me if I ever told you the truth."

Bea stared at him for a few minutes. "Don't you know after all these years you can trust me regarding anything? That had to be a burden to carry around all these years?"

"I guess..." He shrugged. "I made a mistake, Bea."

Bea walked over to him. "After Mary died I tried to take her place as best I could and take care of you. I knew she never wanted you to be alone, so I promised her I'd look after you."

"And you've done a fine job of it," Niles said. "She'd be so proud of you for keeping your word."

Bea thought for a moment. "Does Kyle know he's your son?"

"Yeah, he's the one that found me when he came here for the first time a few years ago."

"Are you certain he's your son?" Bea asked, hoping for a different answer. That she could leave and return with a much different outcome.

Niles nodded. "Yes, he's mine. Mine and Ruth Ann's."

Bea felt anger beginning to brew on the inside. "Who is Ruth Ann?" she asked, feeling a little jealous.

"A woman I met that night after Mary and I argued and I had too much to drink. Her car wouldn't start and..."

"That's enough. I can read between the lines," Bea said, feeling angry and disappointed. She raised her hand to her cheek, now feeling flushed.

"I never meant to hurt either of you," Niles admitted. "If I could change the past..."

Bea drew in a breath, trying to fathom what he'd just said. "Do you have any other secrets you've been keeping from me?" she asked, both hands perched at her waist.

"No, I promise. I'm not an awful man. But I realize what I did was selfish and foolish of me."

Bea turned away from him. "Well, there's nothing we can do about the past. And Kyle does appear to be a fine young man, like his father."

"Thanks Bea. That means a lot coming from you. I was worried you'd hate me if you ever found out what happened."

Bea shut her eyes, regained her composure, and tried to put the conversation they had out her mind. But something kept gnawing at her. She knew how much Niles adored and loved Mary. Never would she have thought he would've been unfaithful. And she saw a different side of Niles Davenport, a man she didn't know if she could trust with her heart.

"I've got to get back now. You'll be at the house for supper?" she asked.

Niles nodded. "Yeah. And thank you for understanding. I know this was hard for you to hear and grasp."

Outside, Bea's emotions began to come unraveled. She'd respected and adored Niles for years, and now she worried if his one mistake would change things between them.

After Bea left, Niles fell to his knees and wept. He'd made a terrible mistake and had hurt her, Kyle, and Mary. Not to mention Ruth Ann. And he wondered if Mary was watching from heaven and frowning upon him. He still carried the guilt and condemnation, no matter how many times he'd asked for God's forgiveness. *Lord, please help me through this. I have to get past this one mistake. I need you more than ever now. I feel like I've let everyone I care about down. Please forgive me, Father.*

This was the lowest point Niles had been at since Mary's death.

Later on, Bea, Abby, and Niles were quiet over supper. Nothing much was said, which was not the norm that time of day. Abby sensed something going on between them and wondered if something had happened earlier. She was a little worried because she loved Niles and Bea. And whether they admitted it to her face or not, she knew they loved one another.

"When are we going to see Mimi?" Abby asked. "I would like to see her again before I leave."

Bea frowned. "I know. It's a hard decision I have resting upon my shoulders."

Niles stopped chewing and stared at her. "What else is going on with Mimi? I had hoped she would be doing a little better soon."

"She's on life support now. I was going to tell you but the opportunity never seemed to present itself after the fire," Bea said.

Surprised, Niles wiped his mouth and said, "Oh... I'm so sorry. We all know how much she means to you."

"She was doing better for a brief while; then took a turn for the worse. I didn't want to burden you with anything more right now."

"It's okay. I know how close you two have always been. She's like a mother to you."

Bea nodded. "Yes, she is."

Abby watched as Bea and Niles chatted about Mimi's condition. She knew being faced with having to make the right decision was ripping Bea's heart out.

Niles reached for her hand, but she moved it away. "I'm sorry," Bea said. "I'm just too emotional right now." She slid the chair back, and tried to halt her tears for a few minutes. "Please excuse me," she said and left the room.

Niles felt the sting of rejection when she pulled away, but tried to understand what she was going through, realizing Bea was not her usual self. "Certainly," he said as she turned to walk away.

Abby felt bad for Niles, but she knew this thing with Mimi was hurting Bea to the core. She'd lost William Jake, her grandson, Bill, was sick and now Mimi was lying at death's door. "She's going through a lot, so I wouldn't take it too personal," she told Niles.

He said nothing, just nodded. A lump had formed in his throat, preventing him for uttering a single word. Now he was certain the news he'd shared with Bea hadn't helped any, making him feel worse all the way around.

A few minutes later, Abby cleared the dirty dishes and set them in the sink. She knew Bea needed some space, time alone, so she decided to pitch in and take care of things. "You want to dry after I wash?" she asked, handing Niles a dish towel.

Niles grinned. "Sure. I'll be happy to help out. Bea deserves a break tonight. A lot seems to be weighing heavy on her right now." He slid the chair back and they got busy with the dirty supper dishes.

While washing dishes, many thoughts ran through Abby's mind. One being, she wanted to ask Niles if he was in love with Bea. But she didn't want to offend him in any way. "So, what do you think is wrong with grandma? I mean, other than Mimi being sick?"

Niles laid the towel on the counter and sighed. "I suppose she is dealing with a host of emotions right now. She doesn't always tell me everything, you know."

"Yeah, I guess you're right. I wasn't a match for Bill and now there's this thing with Mimi. It's too much stress for her to handle." Abby shook her head.

Niles gave her an odd look. "Bill? What do you mean? What's going on with Bill?"

Abby stopped with the dish rag in her hand and looked him in the eye. "You mean she hasn't told you about Bill yet?"

Niles furrowed his brows. "Told me what?"

"Dad's son has leukemia, and I had a test to see if I was a bone marrow match. Unfortunately, I'm not. I don't know what dad's going to do now."

"Dear Lord. There's no wonder Bea hasn't been herself these past few days. I know she has to be feeling overwhelmed by all of this."

"Yeah, a lot has been going on. Bill. Mimi. The fire. You almost dying. But she's a strong woman. I've never met anyone with as much *faith* and *hope* as she has. When I become an adult I hope I'm even half the woman she is."

"Well, even a strong woman needs a break now and again," he said, feeling worried. *And now I've burdened her with me, Kyle, and Ruth Ann,* he thought.

Abby noticed how quiet he became all of a sudden. "You all right, Niles?"

Niles smiled. "Yeah. It's just been a long day," he assured her, drying the last of the plates.

Abby put away the clean dishes and draped the wet dish rag across the faucet to dry. "Thanks for helping out," she said. "It'll be a nice surprise for grandma later."

"No problem." Niles paused and studied her for a moment. "You know Abby…"

"What?" She grinned, removing her apron.

"If I had been blessed with a daughter I would hope she was a lot like you are. You have a good heart," he said.

Abby felt her eyes well. "That's one of the nicest things anyone has ever said to me," she replied. "Thank you. I know you would've been an awesome dad."

Niles grinned, feeling humbled by her words. "I guess I'm going out to check on the animals and take one of the horses for a ride before dark. I'm sure glad Cocoa and the filly are doing well."

Abby nodded. "Me too."

Niles left to finish with a few things outside and Abby went to her room and lay across the bed. The room was much different than her room back in the city. It was quiet, peaceful. There were no loud sirens at night, no speeding cars with bass boost so loud the window panes rattled. Abby had grown accustomed to peace and quiet, and she realized going back home would take some getting used to.

Just after eleven, Abby drifted off and started mumbling in her sleep, dreaming she and Kyle were walking through the woods with two little children. He had one perched on top his shoulders and she had a baby nestled to her chest in a cloth baby carrier. There was much laughter and fun as they prepared to have a family picnic. A smile spread across her face, even if it was happening only in her dreams.

FIFTY

Marlon had ignored a call from his boss for the last time. He'd been hired to do a job, not play house with Maggie Davidson. It was her demise his boss wanted. To run her out of town, leave her with nothing. Ruin her in every possible way. However, the more time Marlon spent around her, the more he didn't want to leave. He'd made a mess out of things before, now he wanted a chance to redeem himself and make things right. They'd once loved each other until his ego got the best of him, and he thought she'd always be around. Now he couldn't believe he'd been so stupid as to agree to help with her demise. Guilt had begun to gnaw at him each day. Maggie was beautiful inside and out, and although he'd cheated before, she'd provided him a place to stay. No. He couldn't do it. He couldn't hurt her anymore, and he couldn't stand by and let anyone else. Somehow, he had to stop the plan in motion.

Beams of sunlight brightened the kitchen as Marlon ran a drink of water. Maggie had driven into town to buy feed for the animals, leaving him behind. Again, his phone buzzed in his pocket. He looked at the number and this time he answered. "Hello."

"Where have you been? I've been trying to call you," a man said.

"I guess my cell phone service is not good here," Marlon replied.

"How about the info I need? Did you get it or not?"

Marlon sighed. "No, not yet."

"What are you waiting on? I'm not paying you to sit around and do nothing."

Marlon heard anger in the man's voice. "I know. I'm sorry. I'll get on it soon, okay?"

"You'd better. I'd hate to make a trip over there to speak with you in person about this."

Marlon raised his hand. "No, you don't have to do that. I said...I'll get on it. Okay?" He drew in a breath, voice now calm.

"You have until next Friday. That's it." The man put an abrupt end to the conversation.

Marlon's phone went silent and he tapped it on the counter. "I can't let you do this to her. She's a good person, and she doesn't deserve any of this nonsense from you or anyone else."

Maggie had parked by the barn and walked in the back door of the house, overhearing his words. "What are you talking about?" she asked, feeling suspicious regarding Marlon's actions.

Marlon was caught off guard. "Umm. I mean..."

"Spill it, Marlon. What's going on?" Maggie set a bag of dog food on the floor by the table. "I know something is not right, I've known it for days. Tell me the truth or you're out of here!"

Marlon braced himself against the apron sink. "I'm sorry, Maggie. I don't know where to start with all this. Things have gotten way out of hand."

"Sorry? For what?"

"I'm not here because I needed a place to stay." He

held his breath, bracing for the worst, feeling certain she'd ask him to leave after he explained everything.

Maggie was becoming more agitated by the minute. "Then, why are you here?" she said, raising her voice.

He turned away without looking her in the eye. "I was hired by someone to come see you," he said.

"You dirty rotten scoundrel! I knew there had to be another reason. What have you done now, Marlon? And what does it have to do with me?"

"I know you're going to hate me when I tell you the truth. But first, I want you to know that I love you. I always have, even when you walked away from me in the past."

"Love...Hmm. I'm not sure you know the meaning of the word. You used me, Marlon. Then cheated on me! That was reason enough to leave you."

"I was foolish back then. You're the best thing that's ever happened to me, Maggie."

Maggie stared at him for a moment, wondering where the conversation was headed next. "Go on, I'm listening. You have five minutes to explain this."

"I knew Beau. We used to get together and drink at a bar a couple hours away. He would also play golf at one of the country clubs. I knew you two were thinking about getting married. He told me he was going to propose."

She gave him a mean look. "I don't like where this conversation is headed."

Marlon raised both hands. "Hear me out, okay? I'm trying to explain..."

Maggie felt her muscles grow tense and her jaw flinched. Anyone who talked about Beau always hit a nerve with her. "And?"

"After Beau died the way he did, Beaufort decided to contact me."

"Why?"

"He said he went through every name in Beau's contacts and tried to make sense of how he died all alone. He blames you, Maggie. He says Beau overdosed because you refused to marry him."

Maggie paced, trying to gain control of her emotions. "Oh, did he? That figures..."

She stopped and looked Marlon straight in the eye. "Well, it's all a lie. He was a repeated drug user. Plain and simple. And on bad nights he would drink also. That's what killed Beau, not me. I finally got enough of it and left." Maggie was so angry she began to cry.

"Did he ever hurt you?" Marlon asked.

"Yes, a few times. In ways I've never told anyone."

"Oh baby, I was afraid of that." Marlon felt sick to his stomach at the thought of Beau harming her in any kind of way.

"Look, this is not about me. I had nothing to do with Beau's death. And Beaufort already knows this. So, why are you really here? Get to the point."

Marlon sighed and drew in a breath. "Please don't hate me," he said like a little boy about to be punished.

"What is it? Tell me now! You're trying my patience and I don't have time to play games. Time is running out," she said, glancing at her watch. "I have animals to see after."

"Beaufort hired me to do whatever I could to help ruin your reputation and run you out of town."

"What?" Maggie was seeing red by this time and not thinking straight. On a whim she punched Marlon straight in the face, causing him to fall backwards to the floor.

Grabbing his nose he said, "Ouch! You may have broken my nose. Where'd you learn to punch like that?"

Standing over him she said, "Get up. You're a pathetic liar and a cheat like always." Maggie was ready to punch him a second time.

Blood was now covering his fingers. "Are you going to hit me again?" He cupped his other hand over his nose, and wiped his fingers on his shirt tail.

"I should've never let you stay here in the first place. How stupid can I be? Good ol' Maggie. Always nice to everyone. And look what it gets me," she said with sarcasm.

Marlon steadied himself and stood. "You're not stupid. You only choose to see the best in everyone. I'm so sorry, Maggie. I never meant to hurt you."

"Liar! Now get your crap together and get out, before I throw you out."

Marlon stayed afar with the kitchen table between them, so she couldn't reach him. "Please... let me help you," he said.

Maggie stomped her foot and turned her back to him. "Why all of a sudden do you want to help me now?" She threw her hands in the air. "Haven't you already done enough?"

"Beaufort is blaming you for something that's not your fault. You couldn't help Beau was using drugs. I want to help clear your name, get your vet's license back."

Maggie turned to face him. By now his face was a bloody mess. She reached for a paper towel and gave it to him. "Why now?"

"I told you...I love you, Maggie. And I want another chance for us to be together."

Maggie stared at him, feeling uncertain of whether or not to believe him. After all, he'd lied to her so many times. "How do I know you're telling me the truth?"

"You have to trust me now. Come. I'll show you." He wiped his face and went over to the table with a stack of law books.

"How can I trust a liar?" She folded her arms and stood beside him, waiting to see what he was going to do next.

"When you were out I decided to look through these books. There is a clause I think we can use to plead your case." He flipped the book open, and showed her the paragraph he was talking about. Then read it aloud.

Surprised she asked, "How did you find this?"

He shrugged. "I believe I stumbled upon it by accident. Or, you could call it a coincidence."

Maggie grabbed the book and studied over the words he read. "No. This is not by accident. God must've wanted you to see this."

"Well, whatever the reason. Here it is in black and white."

"Are you really serious about this, Marlon?" she asked.

"As a heart attack," he replied.

"What about Beaufort? What else will he attempt to do if he finds out you're not doing the job he's paying you to do?"

"I'm going to write a letter to the governor and share this vital information and what Beaufort did to you."

Maggie paused. "You'd be willing to go out on a limb like that for me?"

"Beaufort was the person who called me the other night when I didn't answer my phone. I knew he wanted to see if I was making progress. In fact, he called me earlier today and said he'd give me till next Friday."

"What did you say?"

"I told him I was getting right on it."

Maggie huffed. "And he actually believed you?"

"Why wouldn't he? After all, he paid me a substantial amount of money to get the job done."

"How much?" she asked.

"Ten grand."

"Wow! Just to run me out of town. He's much sicker than I thought."

Marlon nodded. "Yep. Desperate is more like it."

The mood soon began to lighten between Marlon and Maggie. "Go get your face cleaned off," she said, pointing toward the bathroom.

"So, can I stay? I will help you. I promise."

Maggie paused and thought for a minute. "Yes, but only if you're serious about me becoming free of Beaufort and getting my license back."

"Yes, I am! You didn't deserve what Beaufort did to ruin your career, and I want to help you move on, get past the awful things he and Beau did to you."

"Okay. Then let's get a plan together to take him out of office, and away from the control he has around here."

Marlon turned on the faucet and splashed cold water on his face. "Oh, this is going to be sore for a few days," he said. "I'll also have a shiner as well. I hope you have a piece of beef in the freezer."

Maggie grinned. "Well, you deserved it."

"Yeah, I guess I did." He wiped his face with a towel

and dried his hands. "We don't have long. You know I can't stall Beaufort forever. So we have to get busy now."

Inside, Maggie was uncertain about putting her trust in Marlon. He'd lied to her before, but there was something about getting back at Beaufort that gave her a needed sense of accomplishment. He'd been throwing his weight around for years, but now it was time for one of his victims to have the final say.

Later on, Maggie never felt an ounce of remorse over punching Marlon because it had been a long time coming. Something she'd never been bold enough to do years before. After their split, she'd taken a self-defense class to learn how to protect herself. And if Beaufort ever tried to lay a hand on her, she'd do the same thing to him without thinking twice about it. Maggie had been pushed around enough, and there was no way she was going to allow another man to put his hands on her. No. Beau was enough. And it stopped right there when she walked out on him.

FIFTY-ONE

Bea had another restless night, trying to deal with the stress of everything. She'd been procrastinating about taking Mimi off life support, and had asked herself and God several times about how she could do it and watch Mimi take her last breath. In her heart, she couldn't. She had prayed for Mimi several times since she'd been in the hospital, but no clear answer had seemed to come, as if the heavens were silent. *What would Mimi want her to do?* That same question played over and over in her mind. And Bea was still struggling to do the right thing, as much as the reality of it was breaking her heart.

Around eight in the morning, she threw the covers back and got dressed to go to the hospital, praying God would touch Mimi's body and restore health and wholeness. Abby was going with her for moral support, and Bea already knew she would need it to get through the inevitable. She'd need all the strength she had to pull the plug on her beloved Mimi. And with all her heart she wished William Jake were there by her side to guide her.

Abby heard Bea moving around and walked over to her room. She hesitated a moment before knocking on the door. *Here goes.*

"Come in," Bea said, brushing her hair over to one side.

"Morning," Abby said.

"Morning."

"We're still going to the hospital today, aren't we?"

Feeling overwhelmed, Bea nodded. "Yeah."

It was evident how upset Bea was and Abby had no words to comfort her. Silence was how Bea had chosen to deal with the pain she was feeling. When anything bad happened it brought back memories of when she loss William Jake and Mary. It made her come out of her cocoon, a place she'd kept herself sheltered a long time.

"I'll wait for you in the living room," Abby said, giving her some space.

"Sure. I'll be there in a few minutes," Bea said without making eye contact. After Abby left, Bea gave herself the once over in the mirror and drew in a breath. *God, give me strength to get through this ordeal. I need your mercy and grace more than ever today. Hold my hand and guide me...*

Ten minutes later, they left for the hospital. Both ladies were quiet on the way, each battling with their own thoughts of grief and loss. Abby was like Bea in so many ways, except Abby was rough around the edges from having lived in the city most of her life.

When they stopped in the parking lot, Bea reached for Abby's hand and squeezed it tight. "You ready for this?" she asked. Abby shook her head. "No."

"Me neither," Bea said, eyes teary. "Hurts my heart so much I can't even express it."

The walk inside seemed much longer than usual. Maybe it was due to the fact they were both dreading the inevitable. Standing at the elevator waiting for the door to open, Bea clasped her hands together and sighed, then stepped inside. Watching the numbers on the panel move from floor to floor, a knot formed in the pit of Bea's stomach and she felt like she might become sick right there.

Abby grabbed her hand and cradled it tight. She wasn't going to allow Bea to go through this alone. Bea needed her—and she planned to stay by her side however long it took to get through this.

The elevator came to a stop and they walked across the hall to ICU. When Bea opened the door the room was empty, no Mimi. Shocked, Bea feared the worst— Mimi had passed away and they hadn't called to inform her yet. "Oh, my. I think I need to sit for a minute," she told Abby.

Abby pulled a chair over to Bea and helped her sit. "I'll go find a nurse," Abby said. "Sit here and don't move. I'll also bring you some water back."

Bea was feeling flushed from her head to her toes. She removed an old bank envelope from her purse and fanned her face. *Oh Lord, help me not to faint.* It seemed like Abby had been gone a long time already. Glancing at her watch, Bea continued to fan her face, and tried to calm herself by inhaling and exhaling again and again and again.

A few minutes later, Abby walked in. "I have something to show you, Grandma," Abby said with a broad smile.

Bea stood. Her legs were now shaky. She reached for Abby's arm, her support system, realizing they were probably about to view Mimi's cold deceased body. *I can do this...I can do this,* she thought. Fear gripped her tight almost causing her to lose her breath. Lord knows what her blood pressure reading would be about now. They walked to the end of the hall and took a left. "Come on," Abby said, it's just a little further.

Bea gave her an odd look. "What in the world has her so happy? I can't imagine...not at a time like this," she mumbled to herself.

Abby stopped at the second room on the left and pushed the door open. Bea cupped her hand over her mouth and almost fainted. "Oh, my. You're alive!" she said.

Mimi was sitting in bed holding a glass of water in her hand. "Last time I checked I was," she admitted and laughed. "Bea, you look like you've seen a ghost. Your face is as white as a sheet."

Bea was at a loss for words. "But...I mean..."

"Yeah, I know. You all had given me up for dead. Guess the Good Lord is not ready for me yet. Don't worry. I won't go anywhere until it's my time."

Still in shock, Bea walked over to the bed and hugged Mimi. "Thank God you're alive. I'm so relieved."

"Yep. If you had pulled the plug on me the other day, I'd be six feet under now." Mimi grinned.

"Oh, I'm so glad I waited. I knew God wanted me to tarry for a reason. You are going to have a complete recovery, right?"

Mimi nodded. "I pray so. I still have some numbness and tingling in this hand, but that's about it. Doc says it's nothing some physical therapy won't take care of in a few months." Mimi coughed from her throat being sore from the vent. "I'll be on blood thinners for the remainder of my days though. This ol' ticker could quit anytime. And I have to give up my cigarettes. I reckon that alone might kill me," she joked.

Bea breathed a sigh of relief. "Don't ever scare me

like that again," she said. "I think I must've aged ten years over the past week from being under so much stress. But God heard and answered our prayers again."

Just then, the doctor walked in while making his rounds. "Oh, I see you have visitors," he said. "Just don't overdo it. You haven't been out of ICU a whole day yet." He proceeded to check Mimi's vital signs and typed some notes on his laptop. "Everything seems to be functioning like it should, but I want to keep you here for a couple more days as a precaution."

Mimi winced. "Only if you have to," she said.

The doctor nodded. "Yes. Doctor's orders."

Bea chimed in. "That's fine. Whatever you say goes."

"Mimi has come a long way in a short time. I know the Good Lord had to play a part in her recovery. Most people don't bounce back from something like this," he said. "I can't explain it otherwise. She's a living-breathing miracle."

"Thank you for all you've done to help with her treatment," Bea said.

The doctor winked at Bea. "Well, Mimi is quite an extraordinary woman. I bet she was something else back in the day." He laughed.

Bea nodded. "Oh, yes. You're right," she admitted. "And she still is...matter of fact."

Abby stood, listening to their conversation, happy to see that Mimi was doing much better.

"I'll check on her later this afternoon," the doctor said, walking toward the door to finish his rounds.

After he left, Bea grabbed Abby's hand and said, "Praise God! God is so good. He has heard and answered our prayers once again," she said. "Given us our miracle."

Abby grinned and was happy to see Bea so elated, but Abby's *faith* still needed some work. However, seeing Mimi turn away from death's door had put a glimmer of light at the end of her tunnel. Now, if God would only work out a way for her and Kyle to be together because that would take a miracle as well.

After visiting with Mimi, they left to head back to the ranch to share the good news with Niles and Kyle. But when they arrived Niles said Kyle had already left. It made Abby angry that he'd left without saying one last goodbye, and she wondered if he would still keep his promise to write.

Bea could sense something was wrong with Abby after they talked with Niles, and she'd bet Kyle Davies had something to do with it. "Are you feeling okay?" she asked, walking over to the house.

Abby shrugged. "I guess," she said. "It's been an eventful day so far." She turned her head to try and hide her disappointment.

Bea said nary word, and gave her some space, as they went their separate ways when inside the house. She knew Kyle was leaving because he'd stopped in to say goodbye late last night and get his last paycheck till next summer.

After hanging her skirt in the closet and putting on something more comfortable, Bea went in the kitchen. Mimi was doing much better, and Niles was doing much better, so that called for a celebration. She reached in a drawer for a cookbook, and soon decided to prepare a special meal. All the heartbreak she'd been feeling had somehow seemed to disappear as she began doing what she loved most—preparing a meal for those she cared about.

Abby gazed out the window, thinking of Kyle and wondered if she'd lost him forever. The events of the day had her feeling overwhelmed as runny black mascara stained her cheeks. *I really wish you would've said goodbye this morning, Kyle.* Before long, she closed her eyes and drifted off into her own *haven of hope.*

FIFTY-TWO

Jewel spent most of the day cleaning and getting ready for Abby's return home. So many things had taken place while she was away. She'd had time to think about her own life and what she wanted for the future. For years her life had existed around Abby. Abby this. Abby that. Abby. Abby. It felt good to understand she was an adult who needed a life of her own besides being a mom. Somewhere along the journey she'd lost focus on who she really is. Now it was time for her to enjoy life, live a little. And spending time with Buck Schuller had given her the opportunity to do it. No more only existing for Jewel. Now she had *hope* for the future after Abby was grown, and it had her beyond excited. Because she had worked for a long time to make ends meet hadn't meant she'd failed as a mom. When Billy walked out Jewel had no choice but to press on. He didn't love her and he didn't want to be with her or Abby. It took Jewel a long time to get over the pain, disappointment, and rejection he'd caused. Somehow these past few months had given Jewel time to think about life, find new perspective, a reason to look forward to another day. And she hoped being at the ranch with Bea had been good for Abby by giving her a different outlook on life. Regardless of how she felt about Bea, she knew Bea was a Christian woman and she never doubted for a second that she loved Abby.

After she'd finished doing things around the house, Jewel decided to make dinner for her and Buck. He was getting off work around eight o'clock that afternoon, and she wanted to do something nice for him. It was like something new had started to bloom between them. He was no longer the skinny kid with bad acne. Buck had made a good life for himself, a life which consisted of respect and loyalty because of his job. Looking back at their high school days, Jewel never thought she'd give him a chance to get to know her on a more intimate level. Since he started coming around, Jewel started to experience new things, look at herself in a new light, and she realized where she was in life was not a bad place to be. Right now she felt like she was in her prime and she hoped Abby would understand the reasons for the changes she'd made.

Later on, Buck came over for supper and they enjoyed an Italian feast of spaghetti, Cesar salad, and yeast rolls. "My, you've outdone yourself," he said, leaning back in his chair. "If I keep eating like this I'll have to buy some bigger pants." He laughed.

Jewel grinned. "I'm glad you enjoyed it. You deserve a nice meal at the end of the day. You're one of the hardest working men I know."

"You never cease to amaze me," he said with a grin. "But I'm the lucky one. Thank you for giving me a chance to get to know you while Abby was away." He reached across the table for her hand. "These past couple months have been the happiest of my life," he said, gazing into her eyes.

Jewel felt how sincere his words were. "I've enjoyed our time together also," she said, returning the gaze.

"Do you think we can continue where we left off when Abby comes home?" he asked, rubbing her fingers with his thumb.

Jewel smiled, and placed her other hand on top of his. "I don't see why we can't," she said.

Buck let go of her hand and grabbed his cell phone. "I want you to do something with me," he said.

A few minutes later, he reached for her hand again. "Come on... Let's dance."

Surprised, Jewel said, "Right here? Right now?"

"Yeah. Why not? It's just the two of us."

Jewel slid the chair back and stood. "True, I guess." She laughed. "Okay..."

Buck played one of his favorite songs from YouTube and they swayed back and forth to the music. Then Jewel laid her head on his shoulder and closed her eyes, becoming lost in the moment. The scent of his cologne took her to a comfortable place she wanted to stay. Neither of them said nary word, but their body language was exhilarating. It was like something was awakening on the inside of them both. Buck lowered his hand and placed it at the small of her back then pulled her even closer. She could feel the heat from his body next to hers—something she hadn't experienced in a long time. The way things should be. She wanted to raise her head and look into his eyes, but she was afraid of what might happen if she did. So she continued to dance.

After the song had ended, they still danced unaware of their surroundings—lost in a place where nothing else seemed to matter at the time. Then Buck abruptly stopped and let go of her.

"What's wrong?" she asked, opening her eyes.

He stepped away and turned his back to her. "What's happening here?" he asked. "I'm not the only one feeling something more am I?"

Jewel reached for his arm and got him to turn around. "No," she said. "I don't know what is happening, but I feel more alive right now than I have in years."

Buck grinned and said nary word. Jewel had given him the confirmation he was hoping for. He walked closer and looked in her eyes. She could feel his warm breath on her face. Then he ran two fingers over the contour of her cheek and kissed her. The kiss was warm and moist, yet passionate. Jewel savored the taste of his lips and wanted more, and so she kissed him back. For a few moments, their lips lingered in the passion they were both feeling. "You know, I've wanted to kiss you since we were teenagers," Buck said. "But I figured you'd never give me the opportunity."

"Well, you have it now," she said, feeling a little flustered.

Buck pulled her closer, and kissed her again and again. Like passion he had hidden over the years was now being released, ignited.

As he held her ever so close, Jewel closed her eyes and realized she was falling in love. Something she had only dreamed of happening again. But here in the living room, it was happening to her—the broken woman Billy had once hurt and rejected.

"How much time do we have before Abby returns home?" Buck then asked.

"Till the end of the week," Jewel replied.

"Then let's make the most of our time together, okay?"

Jewel nodded. "Yes, I'd like that too."

As the night went on they held each other, danced, and enjoyed being together like any other couple falling in love.

Around midnight, Buck needed to go in order to wake by five the next morning. So he walked to the door and thanked Jewel for a wonderful evening. "I hate to go but I have to," he said. "These twelve hour shifts are hard on me these days."

"It's okay. I understand."

They kissed goodnight. Afterwards, Buck acted like he wanted to say something more but didn't.

"Is everything okay?" Jewel asked.

He paused. "Yes, I need to tell you something, though."

A little worried she said, "Okay. What is it? Is something wrong?"

He grinned. "No, everything is right. Everything feels so right. I think I'm falling in love with you," he said, praying she felt the same way.

Jewel smiled as her eyes locked with his. "I know. I feel the same way," she said.

Buck grinned and held her tight for a few minutes. Then they kissed and it was hard to let her go. It was the best feeling in the world, and he was elated that she felt the same way. He'd waited a long time to fall in love and give his heart to someone special. And he realized he couldn't have picked a better woman than Jewel Conner.

FIFTY-THREE

Abby spent her last week at the ranch moping around. Things weren't the same without Kyle. But she'd learned a lesson about *forgiveness* from Bea and God. And when she returned home, she knew she'd treat Jewel much better than before. After all, she'd taken care of her since Billy left years ago. Abby hadn't had a princess fairy-tale life, but Jewel had managed to give her what she needed and a roof over her head. Being in Texas had been humbling for Abby in a way, and next summer she planned to return. The ranch and the people had really begun to grown on her.

As she walked in to eat supper Abby had a mixture of emotions, both happy and sad.

Niles came in and removed his boots then washed his hands and face at the sink like usual, while Bea fixed their plates and set them on the table. And before he had a chance to say grace, Abby chimed in. "Can I say it tonight?" she asked.

Both Bea and Niles smiled and nodded with approval. Abby bowed her head and clasped her hands together on top of the table. "Dear God, thank you for this food we are about to receive. And thank you for my family here at the ranch. In Jesus' name. Amen."

They ate with Bea and Niles feeling proud of the progress Abby had made since she'd come there.

When Niles first met her all he could think about was what a spoiled little trouble-maker she was. But since he'd gotten to know Abby, he realized she wasn't like that at all. She'd been searching for the missing pieces of her life when she arrived. Searching for a way to heal the wounds left behind from the hurt of abandonment. And he'd grown to love her like she was his own daughter.

Bea thought about the time Abby had spent there, and knew she wanted her to return again next summer. Abby reminded Bea a lot of herself when she was her age. However, Bea hadn't told her so. A grin spread across Bea's face as she remembered herself at Abby's age.

After supper, Niles offered to help with the dirty dishes. Abby looked on as she witnessed Niles volunteering to do what any husband would do to help his wife. "May I be excused?" Abby asked, figuring she'd give them some time alone.

"Of course," Bea said. "I'll check on you after we're finished with things in the kitchen."

Abby nodded and left the room as Bea washed and rinsed the dishes and handed them to Niles to dry. It was like they were a team now. Both remained quiet, but it was obvious they had something between them, by the way they worked in sync to complete a task.

When finished, Niles asked if they could just sit and talk. Bea grinned and agreed. She removed her apron and draped it across the back of a chair. "Let's go in the living room," she said.

Niles followed close behind.

Instead of sitting in William Jake's recliner, she sat on the sofa, so Niles could be there beside her. Feeling a little nervous, she brushed her palms over her thighs, waiting for him to take the lead with their conversation.

He sat and turned to face her. "I want to thank you for being so understanding about what happened at the carriage house. I was so foolish, Bea. I know how much that place meant to you. Mary and I made many memories there also. I guess..." He hung his head.

Bea reached for his hand. "It's okay. I forgive you," she said. "You're a good man Niles Davenport and I know you'd never do anything to hurt me on purpose."

He nodded. "No, I wouldn't," he said, looking at the floor. "I mean..."

Bea stared at him for a moment. "What is it? What's wrong?"

"I don't know if I should talk about this," Niles said.

"Oh, Niles, we're like family. You can tell me anything," Bea assured him.

He lifted his head, but didn't make eye contact with her. "When I went to the carriage house I was feeling lonely, depressed, and desperate to reminisce of good times when Mary and I were married. Some days I miss her so much it hurts to take my next breath."

Bea nodded as if she truly understood how he was feeling. "Go on..."

"When I set the place on fire, the smoke was quick to make me unconscious. When I later came to at the hospital, I realized I could've died if Kyle hadn't of seen the smoke and came over to check things out. I know I was knocking on death's door."

Bea listened intently, wondering what direction the conversation was headed.

Niles paused for a few minutes. "I guess I'm trying to say I know life is short. You know, we aren't promised tomorrow. When I loss Mary a part of me died, and I figured I'd never be able to love a woman again. Not the way I loved her." He sighed.

Bea's eyes welled and she reached for his hand. "I know what you mean," she said with every sincere part of her being.

"I know you've been here for me, Bea. Every day since Mary died. You never turned your back on me, and I couldn't have made it this far without you."

"Of course. You know I promised Mary I would take care of you, and I can't break a promise to my best friend." Bea smiled as a tear rolled onto her cheek.

Niles nodded as a lump formed in his throat. Feeling emotional, he blinked and swallowed hard, trying to halt tears from flowing. "Bea, I..." He paused, drew in a breath, and licked his lips. "I guess I'm trying to say this...I love you, Beatrice Bigelow. And I want to live the rest of my days with you by my side."

Tears continued to flow as Bea understood what he was saying. She wiped her face with her fingertips. "I love you too, Niles. I have for a long time," she said. "But we've both lost a lot. You loved Mary and I loved William Jake. But they are gone now. We can't bring them back, no matter how much we would like to."

"Yes, I know." He paused a moment. "And I just don't want another day to go by without telling you I love you and how much you mean to me," Niles said, palms sweaty.

Bea looked him in the eye. "So, where do we go from here after this new confession?"

Niles shifted around. "Wherever you want to go, I respect you so much. You're such a God-fearing woman,

Bea. And I know I could search the whole world over and never find another woman like you."

Bea raised her hand and ran her fingers across the outline of Niles' beard. "You're such a gentle-humble man," she said. "You have so many good qualities I can't even begin to count them all. And I feel blessed to have you in my life."

Niles' eyes danced over her face and he reached for her hand and kissed it. "No, I'm the blessed one," he said, looking in her eyes. "I love you so much." He touched her chin, raised it a little and kissed her. When their lips met, it satisfied an ache in him, like nothing else had.

Bea closed her eyes, and for the first time since William Jake died, she no longer felt alone. An empty void was filled in her heart, replaced with *hope* of a new beginning. They sat holding hands, savoring the wonder and beauty of what had happened between them.

The next morning, Niles and Bea were in the kitchen cooking breakfast together. He'd been known to cook a tasty pancake or two, and when Abby walked in she was happy to see them there working side by side. She couldn't help but notice there was something different now, like they were more comfortable with each other. The way a happy couple would be. She didn't ask questions, but continued to observe their behavior.

After Niles flipped the last pancake, he set a plate of them on the table and poured himself a hot coffee like he lived there. That was unusual because Bea had always served him everything. Abby grinned and covered her pancakes with syrup. "This smells delish, Niles. I hope it tastes as good as it smells," Abby said.

Niles pulled out a chair for Bea to sit and he poured her a hot coffee. Abby couldn't help but take notice as she stuffed some pancakes in her mouth. "Wait a minute... I mean... Are you two?"

Both Niles and Bea grinned. "Yes, Abby. We're now a couple," Bea said as Niles leaned close and gave her a quick kiss.

Abby sat her fork by her plate. "That's great! You two belong together. You're perfect for each other," she said. "By the way, these pancakes are the bomb!"

They all laughed after Abby's remark and she stuffed another bite of pancakes in her mouth.

It rained earlier that morning, but had since tapered off as a glimmer of sunlight came in through the window. Gazing out the window, Niles noticed a beautiful double-rainbow in one of the fields. "Look," he said. "Maybe that's Mary and William Jake's way of giving us their approval."

Bea smiled ear to ear. "Yeah, maybe so," she said, taking another sip of coffee.

It made Abby happy to see Bea and Niles there together. From her first day on the ranch, she'd seen the chemistry between them. So many good things had happened over the course of summer. But she only wished Kyle would've stayed a little longer, ready to take their love story to the next level.

FIFTY-FOUR

Maggie and Marlon had developed a good plan to reveal Beaufort's dirty ways. Now they only needed to see an attorney about putting their plan in motion. Beaufort had no evidence to prove Maggie was responsible for Beau's death and they intended to prove Maggie was falsely accused. It was a long shot, but they figured Beaufort hadn't paid off every attorney around those parts. With notes in hand, Maggie and Marlon left to meet with their attorney. After a few years of not being able to practice as a veterinarian, Maggie was happy to have *hope* of seeing change in her life.

"Are you ready for this?" Marlon asked as they drove off toward Dallas.

Maggie drew in a breath. "As ready as I'm ever going to be," she said. "Thanks for helping me discover a way to defeat Beaufort in his underhandedness."

Marlon smiled. "I knew when Beaufort hired me I wouldn't be able to go through with the job. When I saw you it was over. I had to do something to help out especially after I had been such a jerk to you before."

Maggie nodded. "Well, that part is true."

"I'm going to change things, Maggie. I promise. I'll do whatever it takes to make things right."

With all of her being, Maggie wanted to believe it was true, but she was having a hard time trusting

Marlon. Years before, they had met and he'd swept her off her feet with his fun personality and love of horses. She'd been a little gullible in the beginning, but his unfaithfulness ruined any chance of them being together for the long haul.

When they arrived at the attorney's office, Maggie was feeling worried the research they had done might not be enough yet.

Marlon parked and killed the engine. "This is it," he said, feeling nervous.

Maggie blew out a long breath. "Yeah, I guess so. Here goes..." They walked in and the receptionist was on the phone, so they stood by the desk, waiting for the conversation to end. A couple minutes later she said, "Hello. May I help you?"

Marlon jumped right in. "Yeah, we have an appointment right now," he said, pointing at his wrist watch.

"And what's your name?"

"Maggie Davidson."

"Okay. Have a seat and he'll be with you in a few minutes." She buzzed the attorney's office and said a few words as they walked off.

Fifteen minutes later, a tall skinny man with shaggy blonde hair walked out to the receptionist's desk. "Is my ten o'clock here?" he asked.

The receptionist smiled. "Yes, sir." Then she pointed toward Maggie and Marlon.

He walked over and introduced himself. "I'm Theodore Shaggleford but you can call me Shaggy—all my friends do." He grinned. "Please, come in my office."

Maggie was at a loss for words and furrowed her brows. "So...you're the attorney here?" His appearance had her taken aback to say the least.

He shook their hands and motioned for them to have a seat in front of the desk. "Yeah, I'm one of them. Dad is the head-honcho of this operation though. By the way, I get my nickname from my favorite cartoon show." He grinned. "I reckon you can figure that one out. I also drive a van I call the Mystery Machine."

Marlon and Maggie sat still, wondering if he was a man they could even take serious with such issues. He seemed to be quite the jokester with wearing his yellow bow tie and white leather sneakers.

He sat and leaned back in his chair. "Well, what can I do for you?" he asked.

Maggie handed him a few copies of pertinent information she'd gathered from the law books and other places. "I think this pretty much explains it," she said, hoping he'd take her complaint against Beaufort serious.

He read over the first page and flipped to the next without saying a word, then laid the papers on his desk. "Oh, I love this," he said. "I've been waiting to expose Beaufort Bedfield for the deceitful man I know he is. Dad will be elated when I tell him the news."

"Does that mean you can help me with this?" Maggie asked.

"Of course! I wouldn't miss out on this opportunity for nothing. Beaufort has caused me and dad quite a bit of grief with several cases over the years. I've been here ten years and he's been a pain in my rear end since day one."

"Do you think that is enough proof to clear her name?" Marlon asked.

Shaggy pushed a pen top back and forth with his thumb while shaking his right leg. "I believe so. An autopsy doesn't lie, and there's also enough information here to prove it was a definite overdose. I'm also surprised you stumbled upon this information. Most people never discover these two clauses on their own regarding law."

"Do I have a good chance of getting my veterinarian's license reinstated?"

Shaggy stared at the last page a few minutes and then looked straight at Maggie. "I'd say this clears your name of any wrongdoing," he said, stapling the pages together. "I'll have to send a written statement to the veterinarian board, but you have a ninety percent chance they'll drop any grievous Beaufort had filed against you."

Maggie breathed a sigh of relief. "That's the best news I've heard in years. Thank you!"

Marlon rubbed her back. "See, I told you things would work out for your good."

"As soon as I get things together, I will be visiting Beaufort Bedfield with the sheriff. What he did is against the law, period! He could spend time in jail for lying and falsely accusing you of Beau's death. We all knew he was using drugs, but Beaufort tried to hide it from everyone. I think he's still in denial because Beau was his only son, and he couldn't believe he'd do something like that on his own."

"I think he's a crazy-sick man," Marlon said.

Shaggy nodded. "Yep, he is. But this time his actions have got him in a mess of trouble. The law is the law, and even Beaufort must abide by it." Shaggy grabbed a manila envelope, slid the copies into it and wrote Maggie's name on the outside. "I'll keep these if you don't mind."

Maggie and Marlon stood. "Sure, I have extra copies back home," Maggie said. "When will I hear more from you concerning this?"

"A few days, if all goes well. I'll be in touch. Give me a number where I can reach you." He grabbed a sticky notepad from his desk drawer.

Maggie gave him her home and cell numbers.

"Great. I'll let you know as soon as I find out something more," Shaggy said.

"Sounds good," Marlon said, shaking his hand.

"Thank you for helping me," Maggie said with eyes now teary.

"You're welcome. Hang in there. Things are going to get better, I promise."

Maggie grinned, shaking his hand. "I sure hope so."

They left the office and for the first time in a few years Maggie felt like things might work out for her. "I know Beaufort will be surprised when Shaggy confronts him. I feel funny calling an attorney Shaggy. But he does look a lot like him." She laughed.

Marlon grinned. "Oh, yeah. I'd love to be a fly on the wall when he and the sheriff visit Beaufort with the news."

Right away, Shaggy gave his dad a call. "You won't believe what just happened in my office."

"Really?" his dad said.

"Maggie Davidson was in here this morning."

"You mean the Maggie that dated Beau Bedfield for a while?"

"Yeah. And you won't believe what she showed me."

"Hmm. Enlighten me, please. It's been a boring day. I'm ready for the next round of golf," he said, stopping the golf cart to listen to him.

Shaggy filled his dad in on the details of Maggie and Marlon's visit. Even after Maggie left, he was having a hard time believing the good fortune that was handed to him.

His dad laughed. "Well, it'll be satisfying to put Beaufort in his place for once. He's been a pain to deal with for years. It's about time his lies caught up with him."

"I know it took a lot of work and research to locate this kind of information, Dad."

"I'm sure it did. Make certain you help Maggie clear her name of any wrongdoing. I've taught you well."

"That's what I intend to do," Shaggy said.

"Be careful, though. Beaufort always has something else to add when he lays his cards out on the table. He never walks into the courtroom empty-handed."

Shaggy sighed. "Yeah, you're right. I've got to have my game on, for sure. What he did to Maggie was uncalled for."

"Let me know if you need any help with things."

"Thanks, Dad. I will."

His dad moved the golf cart a few feet and grabbed his putter. "I'm at the first hole on the course, so I'll catch you later. Bye."

Shaggy ended the call and studied over the papers Maggie had dropped off. It was hard to believe Beaufort could be such a devious man, especially to Maggie. The woman his son loved and wanted to marry.

FIFTY-FIVE

Right before Abby left, they brought Mimi home from the hospital. Other than having a little tingling and numbness in her hand, she was doing quite well. Listening to Mimi talk reminded Bea of what a miracle she was, and how God had been gracious and merciful by answering prayers. Now she only hoped Billy would locate a bone marrow match for Bill before it was too late. In a way she wondered if it was part of Billy's punishment because he'd walked out on Jewel and Abby when they needed him most. But she wasn't God, nor did she have all the answers. Although it hurt her heart to think her grandson, Bill, may die soon.

After Mimi was settled in at her home not far from Bea, Abby and Bea went back to the ranch to cook a few meals for Mimi to store in the fridge to reheat. It would take a while to get her strength back enough to be in the kitchen, and Bea didn't want to chance she may burn herself or the house down. No...losing the carriage house was enough. And Bea was ready to see some light at the end of her dark tunnel. Parking the truck, Bea glanced over at Abby. "I've really enjoyed you being here with me," she said. "I'm glad you came, even if it wasn't under the best of circumstances."

Abby grinned. "Thanks, Grandma. Me too. I'm glad I got the opportunity to know you."

Niles saw them and walked over to the truck. "How are you ladies doing today?" he asked.

Bea opened the truck door and wanted to kiss him, but refrained from doing so in front of a few other men. "We got Mimi settled in at home and we're going to fix some food to take over later," Bea replied. "Have you heard anything from Kyle?"

Niles frowned. "Not a word. You know how he is. Once he leaves, you might not hear from him for two or three months."

Abby furrowed her brow and wondered why Kyle would choose to keep in touch with Niles and not Bea. "Is everything okay with Kyle?" she then asked.

Niles grinned. "Oh, yes. He does this after every summer. He's really a loner type of guy, you know. Comes here to help out a couple months; then goes back on the road again to pursue his dream." Niles shrugged. "Guess he likes things that a way."

Abby felt perturbed by the answer Niles gave her and said nothing more. "Are we going inside now?"

Bea nodded. "Yeah. Go ahead. I'll be there in a few minutes." She could tell Abby was a little upset over something Niles said.

Abby opened the truck door and headed toward the house. When she walked in, she allowed the screen door to slam behind her.

"She upset about something?" Niles asked, rubbing his forehead.

Bea shook her head. "Who knows?"

Niles gave her a quick wink. "I'll see you at suppertime."

Bea smiled. "Okay. See you then. Make sure you stay hydrated out here today."

"I will." Niles tipped his hat and stepped away and Bea opened the door and walked toward the house.

Inside, Abby was sitting on the sofa. Bea could tell something was bothering her. "You okay?" she asked, stopping in front of her.

"I guess so..."

Bea took a minute and sat beside her. "Care to talk about it?"

Abby took a deep breath. "I don't know if you'd understand, Grandma."

Bea crossed her legs and leaned back. "Try me," she said. "I might not be a teenager anymore, but I am a woman."

Abby hesitated a few moments and spilled her guts. "I love a boy and..."

Shocked, Bea tried to keep quiet, but wanted to hear more in great detail. *Maybe it's a boy back home. Maybe that's why she kept getting into trouble.*

"He... He thinks I'm too young for him."

"How old is he?"

"Nineteen."

Bea smiled. "I see. Let me guess, he's ready to move on with life, but you still have to finish school and go to college yet."

Abby grew quiet and looked her in the eye. "Yeah, that's it. How'd you know? I mean..."

Bea reached for her hand. "Because I was once your age, and I fell in love with a handsome young man also."

"You did?"

"Yes."

"Did you two wind up together?"

Bea bit her bottom lip and hesitated before answering. "No, we didn't. He joined the military and moved away to California. I never saw him after that. It broke my heart. I couldn't eat a thing for days."

"Really?"

Bea nodded. "Yes."

Abby sighed. "Will I ever get over this feeling of disappointment and heartbreak?"

"In time you will. You know, they say time heals all wounds. But I'm not so sure it's true in some cases."

"Has your heart ever healed since you lost grandpa?"

Bea lowered her head and sighed. "Not exactly... I still think of him every day. Believe I always will, but being with Niles makes me happy again. Gives me back some of what I've lost. You understand?" She patted Abby on the leg.

"Yeah, I think I do. Becoming a woman is so hard. Sometimes I wish I had a rewind button where I could go back and live with mom and dad. You know, live in a happy environment. Life might've been a little easier if I had experienced that early on."

"Oh, child. You've got your whole life ahead of you. Don't rush things because you'll be my age before you know it."

Abby laughed. "I guess you're right, Grandma."

"You ready to get started in the kitchen?"

"Yeah, Niles and Mimi are counting on us."

"They sure are." Bea grinned and stood.

The ladies spent a few hours preparing supper as well as beef stew and a pot of vegetable soup for Mimi. Abby was learning a lot about cooking, and she hoped she could share some of Bea's recipes with Jewel when she returned home.

After supper, they took Mimi a couple days worth of food and Bea helped her bathe and change into clean pajamas before they left. She knew Abby would be leaving soon, but she really didn't want her to go. She'd grown fond of Abby and had enjoyed their little talks. In a way, Bea wished summer was just beginning instead of coming to an end.

Lying in bed, Abby gazed out the window that night. There were many stars visible in the clear sky, and she wondered if Kyle was somewhere gazing at the stars too. She missed him being at the barn, and she hoped they could get together again next summer. That is, if he hadn't found someone else to replace her by then. She rolled on her side and closed her eyes. Six o'clock would come early, and she didn't want to be exhausted during the flight home.

After Jewel had everything prepared for Abby's arrival, she showered and went to bed around midnight. She'd bought Abby new curtains for her windows, and a comforter set for her bed, hoping she'd like them. Lying in bed, she wondered how Abby would react to her and Buck dating. It had been a long time since Jewel had a man in the house, and she wanted everything to go as planned. That Abby would be accepting of things and they could all move on with life. And if that were not the case, Jewel would have to cool things between her and Buck for a while, so Abby could adjust to the changes.

The next morning, Abby made her bed and finished packing her toiletries. Niles was supposed to drive her to the airport. When she went in the kitchen, Bea had fixed her a plate of breakfast and a glass of orange juice. "I couldn't let you leave hungry," she told Abby, trying to hold back tears.

Abby pulled out a chair and sat across from Niles. "Thanks," she said.

Niles lifted his steaming cup of coffee and slurped a sip. "You all packed now?" he asked.

Abby nodded with a mouthful of scrambled eggs.

Bea laughed. "I'm going to miss you around here, and I want you to know you're always welcome anytime. You can even come for Christmas vacation if you'd like. We haven't had kids around in a long time. I'd love to have a reason to decorate a Christmas tree."

Niles chimed in. "Yeah, and I'll even volunteer to give you a ride in the truck from the airport," he said and grinned.

Abby grinned and finished eating her breakfast. "I love the two of you so much," she said, placing her hand on Niles' shoulder. "I will miss you both."

"Stay out of trouble young lady," Bea said.

"Don't worry, Grandma. I will." Abby set her plate in the sink, gave Bea a hug, and reached for her bags. "Let's go before I change my mind and don't want to leave."

Niles grabbed one of her bags and kissed Bea on the cheek. "I'll be back soon," he said.

Bea grinned. "You better. I'm cooking a pot of chicken and dumplings for lunch."

They were almost out the door and Niles stopped. "Oh, I wouldn't miss it," he said. After putting Abby's bags in back of the truck they got in. "You know the rules. Buckle up," he said.

Abby fastened her seat belt. "You know I never did like this old truck," she said, running her fingers over a patch of rust on the inside of the door.

Niles frowned. "And why not? This takes me anywhere I want or need to go."

She giggled. "I know. I guess it has kind of grown on me over the summer though."

Niles grinned." Yeah, the first day we met I think you hated us both."

Abby laughed. "But I can now say I have grown to love you, Niles. Being around you is contagious. You always remain the same. Helpful with a smile."

He smiled. "Does that mean you still hate this old truck?"

Abby paused. "Hmm. I might like it a little bit," she admitted, rolling her window down.

"Well, I'm glad." Niles pulled onto the highway and headed in the direction of the airport.

Abby sat, reminiscing of the things she did at the ranch. It was a time where she wouldn't change a thing except being with Kyle. Now she had to get back to reality and complete a fifteen hundred word English assignment in less than a week. But she already had an idea of what she'd write about—her summer break. The summer when she fell in love, met her grandma, and experienced ranch life for the first time. Thinking of the past couple months warmed her heart and brought a smile to her face, as the warm air of summer's end blew against her skin.

FIFTY-SIX

When Maggie received a call from Theodore Shaggleford, she almost dropped the phone. The news had her in shock. He'd accomplished what he'd promised to do—confront Beaufort for the things he'd already done to hurt her and ruin her reputation.

"He's in jail until a court hearing," Shaggy said. "And he'll be forced to write a resignation letter as well."

"Thank you. Thank you so much," Maggie said with her hand shaking.

"Oh, I almost forgot this. I talked with the veterinarian board. Your license should be reinstated within a month or two, soon as they process the correct paperwork, and run it through the system to clear your name."

Maggie grinned wide, and felt so relieved to hear those words. It was like a heavy burden had been lifted off her. Marlon knew it was good news and walked over behind her and placed his arms around her waist, waiting for her to get off the phone.

"That was Shaggy," she told him. "It's done. Beaufort is in jail for what's he done. Then he'll have a court hearing and they can decide on punishment." She grabbed Marlon's hand and spun around and back once more. "We did it. We really did it."

Marlon was grinning from ear to ear. "You did it,

Maggie. You never stopped believing you could some-how stop him from destroying someone else's career. And in the process you saved your own."

"I guess I held on to the *hope* I'd one day win."

Marlon looked into her eyes. "And you have won, Maggie."

Maggie placed both arms around his neck. "I couldn't have done it without you," she said.

"Oh, quite the contrary," he said. "I only helped a little. You were already on the right track."

A serious look covered her face. "Where do we go from here? You know, after all this…"

Marlon didn't say a word then kissed her. "I always *hoped* you'd give me another chance. I know I don't deserve it or you. But I can dream a little."

Maggie didn't pull away and kissed him back. "It's a new season, Marlon. Let's see where it takes us," she said. "If it's okay with you…"

Marlon held her tight, inhaling the sweet fragrance of her hair. "It's more than okay with me," he said, kiss-ing her again.

Maggie giggled. "I guess you'll be stuck living a hec-tic lifestyle with a veterinarian."

Marlon's eyes danced over her. "I couldn't think of any other place I'd rather be."

Niles hung around the airport and waited for Abby to board the plane before he left. She'd grown on Niles as well and he was going to miss her.

Abby placed a bag in an overhead compartment, found her seat, and fastened her seat belt on the plane. If all went well she'd be home just before dark.

After the plane took off from the runway, Abby put

her headphones over her ears and began writing notes for her English assignment. Before long she leaned her head against the window and nodded off. A few hours later, she was awakened by an important announcement. "Prepare for landing. We're ten minutes out," the stewardess said.

Abby placed her items in her carry-on bag and prepared to land on Georgia ground.

At the airport, she grabbed her bags and looked for Jewel in the crowd outside the corridor. A few feet away she saw her mom walking toward her. Abby dropped her bags and they hugged. "I'm so glad you're home," Jewel said. "Let me look at you." She grabbed hold of Abby's arms and stepped back, taking in the beauty of her daughter. "Oh, how I've missed you," she said.

Abby smiled. "Mom, you're embarrassing me," she whispered, realizing everyone was now staring at them.

Jewel just grinned and didn't care. She was happy Abby was home, a part of her heart was back with her.

Abby grabbed her bags. "It's good to be home, Mom. I've missed you too."

"Well, I'm glad you missed me," Jewel teased.

"Of course," Abby said. "I've been away all summer. I've never done anything like that before."

Outside, they loaded Abby's things in the car and headed toward home. Abby sat, gazing out the window as they traveled from the busy airport. The terrain looked nothing like the ranch in Texas. Cars were passing on both sides of them, and people were honking their horns at slow people at red lights. She smiled. "Yeah, I believe I've made it home," she mumbled.

Jewel glanced over at her. "What'd you say, honey?"

"Oh, nothing."

When Jewel parked in the yard and they got out there was a patrol car sitting in the driveway.

"Why is there a patrol car here, Mom? I hope we haven't been robbed or something." Abby felt her body grow tense.

Jewel didn't say a word as they got out and she unlocked the front door. When they walked inside a "Welcome Home, Abby," banner was spread across the span of the room. Abby was surprised when she realized who was standing in their kitchen cooking dinner. She dropped her bags on the floor along with her jaw. "Buck? Is that you?" she asked, wondering what was going on.

"Welcome home," he said. "How was your flight?"

Abby froze for a moment watching him. "Wait a minute. What's going on here?"

Jewel walked over beside Buck and placed her arm around his waist. "Honey...Buck and I are dating."

Abby raised her brows. "Really?"

Jewel and Buck nodded.

Abby grinned. "I can hardly believe it, Buck. You finally got the courage to jump her bones."

Jewel rolled her eyes. "Umm...Not exactly. But we are dating and getting to know each other," she said.

Out of nowhere Abby started clapping her hands, which was kind of odd behavior for her.

Jewel and Buck were unsure of what to think or say. "So, you're okay with it?" Jewel asked.

Abby grinned. "Of course I'm okay with it. This man has loved you for a long time, Mom. I knew it the minute he called you instead of letting me spend the night in jail."

"Okay. I'll take it you're happy for us?" Jewel said and smiled.

Abby walked over and gave them both a hug. "Yes, Mom," she whispered. "I like Buck. He's a good man. You two should've been together long before now."

Both Jewel and Buck hugged Abby and they were elated to have her approval.

"Oh, there's one last thing," Jewel said. "It's in your room."

Abby grabbed her bags and headed toward her room. When she switched on the light she couldn't believe her eyes and covered her mouth with her hand.

Jewel stepped beside her. "Do you like it?"

"Yes, I love it. It's beautiful. Thank you, Mom."

"Wasn't that the set you wanted for your birthday?"

Abby nodded, trying to hold back tears. "Yes, that's the one. I can't believe you remembered that I showed it to you before I left."

Jewel reached for her hand. "I do pay attention sometime." She grinned. "Welcome home, baby girl. I've missed you so much."

Abby reached for her mom and they hugged with a tight embrace. "I'm glad to be here," she said.

It was a bonding time between them like no other. And Jewel sensed that something had changed in a good way.

Buck witnessed the love between a mother and a daughter, and he felt like he was blessed to have them both in his life.

Abby closed her eyes and thanked God she was home. Being with Bea had changed and matured her in so many ways. She planned to move forward, not go back to the way things were before. Now she had *hope* for the future, and the opportunity to visit Bea again and see Kyle Davies. As she lay across the bed and penned the next few pages of her English assignment, Abby realized it would take more than fifteen hundred words to share all the details of her life-changing adventure. A smile covered her face as she shared about falling face-first in the hog pen and riding in Niles' rusty ol' truck. She paused a moment and gazed out the window at the night sky, wondering if Kyle was out there somewhere playing guitar. Closing her notebook she said, "Nope. I wouldn't change a thing if I could. It was the best summer of my life."

CPSIA information can be obtained
at www.ICGtesting.com
Printed in the USA
BVHW041016200619
551532BV00017B/2102/P